WHITE TRASH, RED VELVET

STORIES

WHITE TRASH, RED VELVET

S T O R I E S

DONALD SECREAST

HarperCollins*Publishers*

"White Trash, Red Velvet" and "The Necessary Arrangements" originally appeared in *The Crescent Review*, Spring 1993.

Lyrics from "Sixteen Tons" (Merle Travis) © 1947 (Renewed) by Unichappell Music Inc. and Elvis Presley Music. All rights on behalf of Elvis Presley Music administered by Unichappell Music Inc. All rights reserved. Used by permission.

HarperCollins books may be purchased for educational, business, or sales promotional use. For information, please write: Special Markets Department, HarperCollins Publishers, Inc., 10 East 53rd Street, New York, NY 10022.

FIRST EDITION

Designed by George J. McKeon

LIBRARY OF CONGRESS CATALOGING-IN-PUBLICATION DATA

Secreast, Donald, 1949–
    White trash, red velvet : stories / Donald Secreast. — 1st ed.
        p.   cm.
    ISBN 0-06-016441-7
    1. Appalachian Region, Southern—Fiction. 2. North Carolina—Fiction. I. Title.
PS3569.E287W48 1993
813'.54—dc20   92-54743

93 94 95 96 97 ❖/HC 10 9 8 7 6 5 4 3 2 1

Dedicated to Hubertien Williams

CONTENTS

WHERE THE MODERN
WORLD BEGINS

THE HOLE HE WAS DIGGING for his septic tank had become a haven for Curtis Holsclaw. The ground in Hibriten, North Carolina, was dark and loose for the first two or three inches, then sandy for another inch or two, finally giving way to the red clay that was the domain of long purplish brown earthworms and an aroma that struck Curtis's nose like a soft slap and brought out the taste of iron along the sides of his tongue. Now six feet deep in the odor of the clay, Curtis had no difficulty forgetting about the argument he'd had earlier with his wife, Adele, over the one-legged rooster.

Of course, he'd learned to appreciate holes over in Germany. That was a little more than seven years ago. "May seventh, 1945." Curtis spoke the date out loud. He'd dug his last foxhole three days and his last artillery entrenchment five days before May 7th.

Curtis thudded his pick into the clay, feeling the metal point embed in earth that was only slightly firmer than his own flesh. The sound the pick made reminded him of the punches he had thrown and received when he had tried to be a Golden Gloves boxer. He was glad that little dream had been knocked out of him at the state finals match. He'd gotten through the local and the regional bouts before he ran into a boy who knew how to box. He'd been so glad to get out of that ring that he didn't worry about how humiliated he should have felt. On his way home from the match, with his nose and lips swollen and both of his eyes black, Curtis wondered how his daddy would respond to his decision to give up boxing. If he had been a little older back then, say eighteen instead of fifteen, he would have realized that his daddy took only two activities seriously: worship and work.

Before he began shoveling the chunks of clay that he'd broken up with his pick, Curtis stepped up on the three stacked cinderblocks he used to climb out of the hole. At the sandbox under the mimosa trees sat Marleen and Phyllis, according to Adele's instructions, watching Dennis bury his toy cars in the sand. Marleen, now thirteen, was tall and slim with her mother's blue eyes. Because she stretched above the heads of all her friends, she'd already started slumping her shoulders. Curtis had warned her over and over to stand up straight—which she'd do as long as he or Adele was around, but the next time he came into the house, she'd be slumped over again. Sometimes Marleen would get exasperated and talk back to him, but Curtis couldn't get mad at her when she sassed him because she was always careful to use her Donald Duck voice. She also did good imitations of Droopy and Goofy.

About the only trait that ten-year-old Phyllis shared with her sister was her blue eyes. Phyllis was short with blond hair and never bothered to hide behind cartoon characters' voices when she wanted to be sassy. Phyllis had an edge to her that reminded Curtis of Adele's brother, Walt. Nobody in Adele's family knew where Walt got his bossy ways, since all of the Scott family virtues had been cultivated to make the men seem quiet, dull folks. Adele's father and grandfather had been moonshiners—which meant that they preferred to blend in with the forested hills where they stoked their stills.

Curtis couldn't look at his two girls without wondering what would become of them. Phyllis was sharp and stubborn enough to make something of herself—Curtis could see her working for the government or a bank someday—although she'd probably be one of those people who were in charge of putting other people in their places. Or she might just marry some man who had that kind of job.

Marleen, on the other hand, drifted along. Despite her tendency to slump, she wasn't bashful. She had more friends than Curtis could keep up with—more of them boys than he was comfortable with. It was a problem that Curtis thought Adele needed to attend to pretty soon. But Phyllis was always around to keep an eye on her sister and her friends. On more than one occasion, Phyllis had set their black chow chow, Mush, on boys who she didn't think belonged on their property. Sure, Curtis had punished Phyllis, but his heart was never in the switchings he gave the girls. Besides, even Marleen sometimes laughed at the way boys tried to escape or calm down the snarling Mush.

Both of the girls, though, doted on Dennis. And the three-year-old didn't make distinctions among his two sisters and his mother. Taking his eyes off his three children for a moment, Curtis checked one corner of the septic tank hole to make sure that he did have his quart jar down there. As he dug, he collected the largest earthworms to use as bait. Dennis was still too young to be a serious fisherman. The few times that Curtis had taken him to the local fish pond or to the river, Dennis had spent more time chasing dragonflies or throwing rocks into the water than he did watching the red-and-white float bob on the green surface of the pond. Usually in less than an hour he was ready to go home, or he'd start wandering off to see what the other fishermen were doing.

Curtis knew that would change in another year or two. Until then, he had Phyllis to fish with. For a long time, Marleen and Phyllis liked going with him, but for the last year or two, Marleen had started staying at home . . . to help take care of Dennis, she said. Even before Marleen started staying at home, Phyllis had been a better fisherman. She baited Marleen's hook for her and took the fish off when Marleen succeeded in pulling one in. Curtis figured he'd have to let Phyllis have her hand in teaching Dennis how to fish, but he reckoned he could still teach both of them a few tricks about bringing in a perch or catfish.

Curtis accepted the fact that children always loved their mamas first and most. But he knew that after what he'd seen of orphans in the German cities he'd ridden through, nobody could be as worried about his children as he could get. Now he had the communists in Korea to worry about. Boys were coming back shot up. And the government still wouldn't call it a war. Watching the girls' heads bob over Dennis's serious attempts to hide their feet with sand, Curtis felt his chest and stomach constrict in a slow concussion of affection.

He wasn't irresponsible—not in the way Adele had accused him of being this morning. That was just like her to corner him on a Saturday morning, and him with a hangover. How could she say he was irresponsible when he'd come home with twice what his paycheck was worth? Just because he hadn't let her know he was going to be out all night? She didn't understand that once in a while he had to get away from everyone he was related to. It was like taking a ripsaw apart so you could blow off all the sawdust.

She hadn't even bothered to go look at the rooster he had won in addition to all the money. Curtis let his eyes stray from his children along the dirt path out to the chicken coop. Beyond the coop, the dirt path disappeared into the woods, which curved away toward the east three miles to where Curtis's mama and daddy lived, then fanned up the rock face of Hibriten Mountain.

Even from seventy yards away, the rooster's auburn feathers shimmered like petals from some kind of Hawaiian tree. Madison Rigsby, the man who owned and operated the local radio station, WHIB, devoted three hours of Saturday afternoon airtime to a program called "Hawaii Calls." The only regret that Curtis had regarding his army service was that he had not gotten to visit Hawaii. If he'd gone into the navy like his brothers, Vernon and Daniel, he might have seen the South Pacific. He wouldn't have gotten his ears or his toes so frostbitten either. It was his own choice, though. With his two girls, he didn't have to worry about the draft. He had wanted to go. Just like he had wanted to go to the Hibriten Armory every Saturday night and get in the ring with some boy who maybe knew how to throw a punch or two but had no idea of what boxing really was. Just like he'd wanted to go to the state finals in Charlotte.

"Got that hole dug yet?" Phyllis was more insistent about having an indoor toilet than Marleen or Adele. She'd wanted to use the commode as soon as Curtis had installed it in the tiny bathroom he had built off his and Adele's bedroom.

"You'll have to hold it till I get two feet deeper." Curtis admitted to himself that it was a mistake to have built the bathroom before installing the septic tank. Phyllis had pestered him and Adele so much, sneaking into the bathroom to admire the commode and the bathtub, that he had threatened to nail the door shut until it was ready to use.

As much as he might want to, Curtis couldn't lay all the blame for his girls wanting an indoor toilet on Walt's wife, Lorraine—although she did flaunt the convenience of inside plumbing every time she opened her mouth around Adele and the girls. Walt had to indulge Lorraine. She was a grasping woman, and she had Walt wrapped around all the poles of their four-poster bed. She'd even badgered Walt into buying her a television. Of course, Walt, who had taught himself to read on his way to becoming a successful plumber, enjoyed playing with radios—now televisions. Since Walt had started working for himself he was making a sight more than Curtis made in the veneer plant. But all Walt had offered to Curtis toward building his bathroom was advice.

While Curtis refused to see the need for a television, he had had to agree with Adele when she pointed out how much cleaner and healthier they'd feel with an indoor toilet. Besides, all of the other neighbors had indoor toilets. It had become a matter of pride for Curtis that he be able to pull down the only outhouse in the neighborhood. Adele's family home down in Wilkes still had an outhouse, and his father's house still had an outhouse. His daddy had made it clear that indoor toilets were a filthy idea, maybe an idea that had infected American soldiers while they were in Europe.

Curtis had tried to tell his daddy that not much was left of anything indoors over in Europe, particularly indoor plumbing. However, what had made Curtis so agreeable with Adele when she suggested the indoor toilet was how tired he had gotten of unnecessary hardships. A man—or a woman—shouldn't have to freeze to death while trying to relieve himself. He'd been through the war, he worked hard—he'd earned an indoor toilet.

At moments like this, Curtis could see how the world was changing—it was like coming up to the top of a high hill and being able to see the horizon curve away. His septic tank was a door he was about to pass through into a world his father and his wife's father couldn't know. With the first flush of his American Standard commode, he and Adele would take a step up in respectability—in being civilized. What kept his daddy in his backward frame of mind was how the old man clung to his old habits. Although his daddy thought most of the improvements in the world were frivolous and even infernal, Curtis knew that at the base of his daddy's opinions, which seemed so stern and righteous, was a sentimentality as clumsy and outdated as the old man's outhouse.

Coming from the backside of the Brushy Mountains, Adele had her sentimental and superstitious side too, but she wanted to make her and her children's lives better. And that was what Curtis wanted too. Except he and Adele sometimes disagreed about how they should approach that improvement. Gambling had been a sore spot between him and Adele almost since the day they'd married.

Stepping back down into the hole, Curtis paused to calculate. He and Adele had gotten married when they were seventeen. He'd been working in the veneer plant for over a year, making what seemed like good money back then. He could still remember that first day of work, the day after he turned sixteen. His arms were so tired and sore by the end of his shift that he couldn't lift the lid of the drink box in Wheeling's Grocery Store. His daddy had laughed at him and paid for both their dopes. Seeing his boy exhausted by his first real job was a moment Old Man Holsclaw savored.

"Fourteen years." Curtis shook his head. "And she still can't understand why I play poker."

For Curtis, poker was more a game of hope than one of chance. If he won, he was able to share, to be generous with his family. He could buy the porcelain handles for the bathtub instead of the sharp-edged metal ones. He could afford to pay Lanny Griffin in cash for the septic tank and for using his crane truck to install it. Even when he lost, he could come home humble—more genuinely humble than any church service could make him. And Adele could feel good about putting up with him the way she did—after she got over being mad at him. He couldn't look into her blue eyes when she signaled her anger by asking him if he'd been playing poker. She always had to ask—as if he might be doing anything else until five o'clock in the morning without needing a fishing rod and a bait bucket.

Curtis wondered if maybe Adele resented how gambling allowed him to feel special. Sitting at a table, despite how much drinking was going on, holding on to a hand dealt from a fresh deck, Curtis felt like a gentleman. He'd played in basements with dirt floors, bedrooms with colicky babies drowning out the voices of the players, the backs of filling stations with stacked tires for seats, and the loading docks of furniture factories, but as soon as the game got cranked up, he could be in a Las Vegas casino or on a Mississippi riverboat for all that the surroundings mattered.

Of course, that feeling special was what got him into so much trouble over last night's game. If he hadn't been on such a winning streak, he might have realized how stupid he was to let the other men talk him into accepting Lamar Dula's one-legged rooster as part of the bet. Yes, he and Adele raised a few chickens for eggs. Both of them had been raised raising chickens. Another of Adele's brothers, Taft, who still lived in their daddy's house, had gone into chicken farming in a big way. He raised them in batches of twenty thousand, three or four batches every year for Pine Farms Poultry. Deep down, Curtis admitted to himself that he'd always had a slight fear of chickens. They were on a level not much higher than snakes or rats as far as he was concerned.

Then there was that time when he had tried raising chickens for meat. He'd talked Adele into investing in a truckload of broilers. Their coop had barely contained all of them. Taft had offered to help get the enterprise off the ground by supplying Curtis with sacks of cracked corn. It was true, Taft had warned Curtis that if the chickens were allowed to lay eggs, then the cracked corn needed to be enriched with some kind of calcium. But back then, Curtis didn't listen to what his hillbilly brother-in-law had to say. Nor was he as good about taking advice as he was now.

At first, the business looked like it might pay off. They sold not only the chickens but their eggs as well. And Curtis kept feeding them just the cracked corn. One day, Phyllis, who was probably a little older than Dennis was now, decided it was her turn to feed the chickens. What Taft had tried to explain to Curtis was that if chickens were laying regular, they could build up a calcium shortage and go a little crazy. They started craving calcium and got so they could smell it even if it was in the bones under the skin of a small blond-headed girl four or five years old. Phyllis had walked into the coop, scattering corn, and before she knew what was going on, all of the hens had gathered around her, completely ignoring the corn, going after her legs, then climbing on top of each other and going after her hands and arms.

When Curtis and Adele rushed in to pull the chickens off Phyllis, they had acted like magnets. The chickens had instantly turned their calcium-deficient eyes on the two adults, who apparently smelled more strongly of bones than the small girl. Part of what lay at the bottom of Curtis's secret fear of chickens—or was it respect—was how they could ignore pain. He had slapped, kicked, and stomped, grabbing chickens by the neck and throwing them all the way across the chicken yard only to see the pitched birds pick themselves up, get their bearings, and come flapping straight back to peck at his skeleton. Finally, he and Adele had struggled out of the coop and gotten the heavy gauge wire between them and the chickens. Then they were able to pull the more tenacious birds off and toss them back into the coop. The next day at work, Curtis had announced that people who wanted free broilers simply had to come by his house and pick up however many they needed. Now he never kept more than a dozen laying hens. And up until early this morning, he'd never kept a rooster. Not even a one-legged one.

After she had dragged Curtis around the kitchen about his poker playing, Adele had calmed herself down by leaning against the refrigerator and lighting a cigarette. Exhaling a voluptuous cloud of smoke, tinged pink by the sun just coming up, she had said, "You know we'll be eating fertilized eggs with a rooster strutting around the coop."

For a moment, Curtis couldn't tell if Adele was complaining or simply stating a fact. After all, one of Adele's favorite foods was pickled pigs' feet, so how could she complain about an egg with a little bit of chicken in it? Then he had seen the squint of her blue eyes. "Just scramble them and you won't get any complaints."

He hated to fight with Adele in the morning. Even propped up against the refrigerator with her arms crossed, she looked fetching. Her eyes could sting him, make his chest and brain feel as frostbitten as his ears and feet had, but as the day wore on, the sting softened to a prickling along his spine, then to a low hum in his abdomen.

"I wouldn't complain if you started fixing your own eggs." Adele brushed an ash off her chest.

She had him there. The few times Curtis had cooked were times he had gone hungry. The worst times in Germany had been mealtimes, when Curtis was choking down K rations or some kind of stew dipped from a ten-gallon pot and he had been struck by the memory of Adele's fried squash, mashed potatoes, green beans with onions, pinto beans with ketchup, and her breaded steak. He'd thought about her cooking at least as much as he thought about her naked. Waking up from a night of freezing his internal organs in a pup tent to the smell of gasoline and diesel fumes, cordite, and other unwashed soldiers, Curtis packed his gear, lost in his effort to recall the mornings back home when Adele would get up at five so she could have herself and breakfast ready by the time Curtis and the girls crawled out of bed. The smell of bacon and biscuits drifting into the bedroom along with the mournful songs of the Carter Family always signaled to Curtis how lucky he was to have a job, a working wife, and healthy children.

"It's a torment when you come dragging in after one of your card games." Adele moved from the refrigerator to sit down at the table across from Curtis. "Anything could happen to you at some of them places you go to."

Curtis appreciated how Adele worried about him. But it was part of her sentimental nature to have some fretful view of the places where he played cards. Once in a while a man might get mean during a card game, but most of the time the other players were men like Curtis, who, after working eight or ten hours for five or six days, were too tired to be dangerous. And most of them were so grateful to be occupied with a game instead of a job that they were careful to be jolly and polite. Other men used the gambling as a kind of social therapy. But if a man talked too much about his problems at home or at work, he could get to be a pest. Being a pest, though, was a long way from being dangerous.

As a matter of fact, Lamar Dula, the man whose house was the site of last night's poker game, more often than not became a pest. Curtis leaned on his shovel and studied the flat roof of his small house. It was pretty basic, but Adele kept it clean. Lamar's two-room shack always felt nasty. You could sit down on a chair in Lamar's house and have to peel your clothes off it when you stood up. Of course, since Lamar had it in his head to make his living by gambling, his wife had to hold down a steady job so Lamar could finance his poker games. What made Lamar such a pest was how serious he'd get about the cards. More than anything, Lamar hated to fold. He'd wheedle and whine if the betting began to get out of his range. And if his whining didn't help, he'd start dragging in whatever odds and ends he had lying around his shack.

Last night, Lamar had dragged in the one-legged rooster. Another of Lamar's enterprises was cockfights. Years ago, after going to a couple of cockfights held down in the woods below Lamar's house, Curtis realized that he didn't have the stomach for them. The bloody insanity with which the chickens fought made Curtis keep looking over his shoulder, not because he was worried about getting caught by the sheriff—since he and his deputies were frequently at the fights as spectators—but because Curtis suspected that some higher moral authority might be creeping up on the circle of sweaty men yelling obscenities at the two roosters ripping at each other. Maybe the war had burned out Curtis's capacity to be anything but ashamed of pointless ferocity at any level.

And Lamar's bird, even maimed, was nothing more nor less than ferocity with feathers. "I'd planned on selling this feller so I could put linoleum on the floor." Lamar clutched the rooster in one arm while stroking its head. All the men at the poker table could see the bird's feathers rippling. For a moment, it resembled a glass statue filled with emerald and scarlet water through which passed a progression of small, threatening waves.

Now, nobody knew any better than Curtis that he and Adele didn't need a damaged fighting rooster. But Curtis had three reasons for letting Lamar use the bird as part of his bet. First, they were, after all, playing in Lamar's house, eating his potato chips and pork rinds. Curtis knew you didn't insult a man in his own house, and by forcing Lamar to fold, Curtis would be rubbing the man's face in his bad luck. Second, all the other poker players were amused by Lamar's bet. Any other man would have offered a dog or a rooster with two legs. But there was Lamar squatting slightly over the bird, which he'd placed on the floor so Curtis could see how well it got around on only one leg. It used its leg like a pogo stick. Curtis was surprised the rooster could support its weight on that one leg because the bird stood over two feet high. Its wing span must have been three or four feet across.

"He won twenty-six fights before he lost that leg." Lamar flipped the rooster's beak and immediately the neck feathers ruffled out, making Curtis think of a small palm tree.

"Why don't you keep him for breeding?" Curtis pushed his chair back slightly. The rooster had cocked its head at the sound of his voice and taken a couple of hops in his direction.

"I'm a gambler—not a farmer." Lamar jerked the rooster's tail. Instantly, the rooster flapped into the air and spurred the back of Lamar's hand. Before the rooster had time to regain its footing, Lamar kicked it back into the air and, keeping his face well away from the bird, caught it by the leg so he could hold it upside down.

By this time, the other men were laughing, and a couple of them had assured Curtis that they had seen the bird fight. It had been something of a legend among cockfighters. If Curtis had refused to take the bet, he'd have dampened everybody's humor. You couldn't take all of a man's money and then refuse to let him joke about it.

Besides, the third reason why Curtis couldn't refuse to take the rooster—and the reason he probably couldn't explain to Adele—was that the rooster did represent a thoroughbred, of a sort. And at the age of thirty-one, Curtis knew he would never own any kind of thoroughbred. Nothing in his life was purebred. A man couldn't be born in Hibriten and not be a mongrel. Always having to do with mixed blood, mixed intentions, mixed emotions, mixed opportunities. Like that rooster. When he did have a chance to get a piece of a legend, it had a missing leg. But he wasn't any different from the other men sitting around Lamar's scratched and stained poker table, which was also Lamar's dinner table. So he had beat Lamar's three tens with a straight and brought the rooster home with him—in a burlap sack in the trunk of his '39 Chevrolet.

Not until Curtis heard Phyllis and Dennis run by his hole, yelling, "What'd you bring me, what'd you bring me?" did he realize that Adele had returned from her shopping trip with her sister-in-law, Lorraine. Adele still held to the backward Wilkes County belief that real women didn't drive automobiles, although she was very grateful for her women friends who allowed themselves to be less feminine by learning to drive. He climbed up on his cinderblocks in time to see Marleen, who'd stayed behind at the sandbox long enough to pick up Dennis's toys, strolling toward Lorraine's car, out of which Adele was pulling bags from William's Clothing Store. Bathing suits for the kids. Before helping their mother unload the groceries, Marleen and Phyllis would have to go inside and try on their bathing suits. Curtis thought he should offer his help, but as sweaty as he was, the grocery bags would be coming apart before he could get up the back porch steps. Besides, he knew he made Adele happier the closer he got to getting the septic tank finished.

Just as Curtis was getting serious once more about loosening more clay from the bottom of his septic tank hole, he heard a saw-edged *"Errr-er-errr"* followed by a panicked burst of clucking from the chicken coop. Apparently, Dennis, once he'd gotten into his new bathing suit, decided that he wanted to feed the chickens. He'd done it many times before, but the sight of the child throwing kernels of cracked corn to the hens must have driven the rooster mad. Flapping its glittering wings, the bird plowed through the surprised hens, heading straight for the small boy. In the time it took Curtis to jump up on his cinderblocks, Dennis had run half the distance from the chicken coop to the house. Already the rooster had given him three good slashes across his pale, pumping calves. That one leg continued to whip out every three or four steps trying to draw more blood.

Adele and Lorraine, who had begun unloading groceries from the car, ran to rescue Dennis. No sooner had Adele pushed herself between Dennis and the rooster than she got a spur slash just below her knee. From somewhere, Lorraine had picked up an old broom and whacked at the rooster's side. Briefly, the rooster rested, but when he saw his victim picked up and carried off, he went crazy all over again. He let out another crow—this one made Curtis's crotch hair stand on end; then he bolted for the steps that led up to the small back porch where Adele and Lorraine were inspecting Dennis's wounds.

Always quick-eyed, Adele saw the rooster fly-hopping up the stairs. Before he could get up to the third step, Adele had reached into the nearest grocery bag, grabbed a can of corn, and flung it at the cock. The can bounced off the rooster's chest and rolled over to the edge of the septic tank hole, where Curtis was struggling to get out. A small red smudge on the can, which might have been blood or clay, made Curtis realize that he was being no help at all. Another can of corn, which knocked the rooster off the steps, bought Curtis and Adele a few more seconds, however, because the rooster, after it flapped back into an upright position, paused to shred the label on the can. Then it headed up the stairs again.

By then, Adele and Lorraine both were flinging cans at the bird. Knowing what to expect now, the rooster threaded his way through them with less difficulty than a soap sliver through fingers. And Curtis saw that the women were running out of cans. So he dragged his shovel out of the hole, then thought better about it because on a bird as pumped up as that rooster, a shovel wouldn't have much more effect than a broom. Dropping the shovel, he stretched as far as he could and grabbed his pick. If this rooster had any other weakness besides his missing leg, it was its determination to get at Dennis. Intent as it was to fight its way back to Curtis's son, it completely ignored Curtis. It was already on the top stair when Curtis came up behind it, trying to make as much noise as he could. Adele had just pulled a head of cabbage out of the grocery bag. A bag of rice had broken open on the stairs and crunched under Curtis's feet. He took a moment to steady himself.

When Adele saw Curtis raise the pick, then pause to take aim, she smiled at him. She had little beads of sweat on her nose and upper lip, her bangs were glued to her forehead, but she was still fetching, crouched there with Dennis's head buried against her chest. It was a pose that Curtis had seen more than once during the war. But poor as it was, their house was no bombed-out shell with nothing but blackened walls and emptiness on the inside. Against that memory and fear, Curtis brought the pick down with all the accuracy years of digging could settle in his arms.

Even impaled to the top step by the point of the pick, the rooster flopped and strained to get to the porch. Curtis headed Adele, Lorraine, and Dennis through the screen door into the kitchen and made them sit at the table. He stood with his back to the screen door, blocking their view. He wanted to say something to cover up the thrashing going on behind him, but his mouth was too dry.

Phyllis and Marleen came into the kitchen, dressed in their new bathing suits. "What you got behind your back?" Phyllis asked, leaning to one side.

"Oh, a little bit of craziness that needed fixing." Curtis leaned against the door frame, knowing that Adele had turned her gaze toward him with a look as pure as the distillations that made her father and grandfather famous throughout the hills and hollows of Wilkes County.

In it, he felt washed free of all the old hindrances and mistakes of the past. This was how he could feel every Saturday night when he settled down to wash in a new, white bathtub. It was the way he wanted his family to feel, catching up with everybody else in 1952.

STRANGER IN
PARADISE

NOT UNTIL MARLEEN HOLSCLAW jumped the ditch in front of her house and started climbing the steep hill to her friend's house did she notice that the chain gang was working on the dirt road behind her. Now she was doubly glad that she wasn't letting her sister, Phyllis, come with her. Phyllis would try to strike up a conversation with the convicts, asking them what they had done and how long they were going to be in prison. Marleen admitted to herself that she was interested in such questions too, but she was old enough to know that a girl shouldn't be talking to convicts. She was a little nervous being on the same road where they were working, even though they were probably a quarter mile away.

Momentarily breaking into a trot, Marleen lifted her eyes to the top of the hill to gaze at her friend's house. She didn't know exactly why Celeste LeFever had chosen to be her friend two months ago. After all, Celeste lived in the biggest house in the neighborhood. Despite the fact that it was also the oldest house in the neighborhood, Celeste's daddy kept the place looking newer than any of the other houses, which had been built later. It reminded Marleen of the pictures she had seen of Monticello—except the LeFever home was slightly smaller and had a two-car garage in the basement.

As soon as Marleen felt the perspiration gathering under

her arms, she slowed down. First, she didn't want to be sweaty while she was visiting Celeste. And second, she had been told that men liked to look at a woman's rear when she was running. Marleen glanced over her shoulder. Although the prisoners were still too far away to have much of an exciting view of her rear, she put her hands in the back pockets of her rolled-up jeans and tried to take more masculine steps.

Marleen had hoped that she and Celeste could sit in the LeFevers' neatly trimmed front yard in their scalloped-backed lawn chairs, drinking lemon Cokes, and discuss the people who drove by. Marleen could feel her own opinions being shaped by the comments that Celeste made. Celeste had *Mademoiselle* delivered to her house and studied it. She and her mama would go to Charlotte or even Atlanta on shopping trips and stay gone for a week sometimes. Both of them wore hats when they made their trips. But Marleen supposed if she were being driven around in a brand-new Cadillac, she'd want to wear a hat too.

On special occasions, Marleen, Phyllis, and their mama might wear a hat to church, but traveling long distance in a hat reminded Marleen too much of a self-inflicted wound. Whenever her family went on a long trip, like to the beach, all of them wound up getting wrinkled and grumpy. Maybe if her daddy didn't always manage to get lost, the trips wouldn't be so difficult. Why, Marleen realized, by the time they went on vacation this summer, she would probably have enough road training to help her daddy drive down to the ocean.

Marleen was having her first driving lesson this evening. Her mama and daddy would come home from work. She and Phyllis would have supper ready, and as soon as her daddy finished eating, she would be on her way. Her daddy didn't know it, but Marleen had already been behind the wheels of several cars: two '40 Fords, one white, one red and souped up; one '52 Pontiac, a green-and-white two-tone; one '49 Packard, Marleen's favorite; one '53 Chevrolet with full-moon hubcaps; and a '51 Chevrolet exactly like the one that her daddy drove. However, these lessons always wound up with Marleen having to slap at the boys' hands because they seemed to feel that if Marleen's hands were occupied with their cars, then they should occupy their hands with Marleen.

As far as Marleen had been able to understand, when a boy let a girl drive his car, he thought he was giving her some piece of himself. Naturally, it was only fair for the girl to give him in return some piece of herself. That was the kind of lesson every child was supposed to learn. And Marleen had always found any form of stinginess ugly. A year or two ago, she had decided that even when she got her driver's license, she planned to let her dates let her drive their cars. Besides, if she wanted to get any driving experience, she'd have to depend on her boyfriends' cars. Her daddy used their car most of the time, and Marleen couldn't imagine a time when they'd own two cars.

Of course, Celeste LeFever didn't have to worry about having her own car to drive. She already had two Cadillacs in her family, both brand new. All she had to do was ask for a car just for her, and her daddy would bring it home that evening. But Celeste had confessed to Marleen that she didn't feel ready to start learning how to drive. Marleen suspected that Hoyt Kirby's awful wreck two days earlier had fed Celeste's natural shyness about learning to drive.

The town of Hibriten had a custom of exhibiting the more spectacular automobile wrecks in the center of the town's traffic circle. While Marleen refrained from showing the kind of eagerness that gripped her sister—who scrambled all over the wrecked car, feeling dents and twisted metal, pointing out spots of blood on windows and dashboards—she certainly didn't get as upset by the wrecks as Celeste did. As far as Marleen knew, Celeste had never actually gotten out on the traffic circle and inspected one of the wrecks firsthand. She could be reduced to tears simply by looking at a wreck from the backseat of her daddy's Cadillac as they circled the traffic island.

Marleen had heard that Hoyt's car had finally been hauled out to the traffic circle. The timing seemed appropriate because Hoyt's wife, Betty, was having visitation tonight, and because Hoyt and Betty were their neighbors, Marleen and her family had to be there. The casket had to be closed. So did the caskets of the three other boys who had been in the car with Hoyt. Those boys' families were receiving their visitors at the funeral home. Marleen thought she'd ask Celeste to come with her to the Kirby visitation, but she wasn't sure if it was such a good idea. The Kirbys were poorer than the Holsclaws. Hoyt had aspired to be a stock-car driver, so all of his spare time and spare money had gone into his two cars.

On both sides of the dirt road, honeysuckle crowded into the ditches and stretched tentatively into the road. This early in the morning, the fragrance, sweet and undulating, made Marleen look over her shoulder once more to assure herself that the convicts were still too far away to appreciate her. Apparently, they were just getting started on whatever roadwork they had to do because Marleen could see that several men were still wearing their blue denim shirts while others leaned against the prison trucks.

Wanting to give herself time to cool down, Marleen veered to the edge of the ditch where the honeysuckle was getting a pretty wide grip on the road. Pulling a pink blossom off the vine, Marleen used her fingernail to make an incision all around the bottom of the flower so she could pull the stamen free. Nectar glistened along the pale filaments, which Marleen pulled across her tongue. She stooped and gathered up two handfuls of blossoms. She thought it would be a good morning to introduce Celeste to the pleasure of licking honeysuckle. Then Marleen paused. Licking honeysuckle was something she had learned to do down at her aunt and uncle's house in Wilkes. Even if Celeste would be interested in trying it, her mother might not approve. For all anybody knew, a stray dog could have peed on these very flowers that Marleen planned on offering her best friend. She tossed them back into the ditch.

The cement walk to the LeFevers' front door was lined with perfectly trimmed box shrubs that were about waist high. Their somber, slightly raspy odor made Marleen think of insurance companies and the men, like Celeste's daddy, who sold policies to people all over the state. Mr. LeFever was a nice man, but Marleen couldn't see that he was any smarter than her daddy. He never worked on his own car. If something went wrong with the house, he always called somebody to fix it. Curtis Holsclaw, on the other hand, took large pieces of the engine out of his car and spread the parts out on flattened cardboard boxes in the backyard. He'd run electricity into the bathroom that he'd built with his own hands, and he'd tinker for hours with an oil heater that wasn't working.

Then again, Marleen had to remind herself, the LeFevers were living on a different level from the Holsclaws. Celeste probably wouldn't know what an oil heater was. They had four floor furnaces in their house. Before Curtis had agreed to take Marleen out on her first driving lesson, he had made her learn how to check the water and oil in the car and how to change a flat tire. She had lost two of her favorite fingernails learning how to change a flat. She couldn't see Celeste crouching beside one of her Cadillacs, trying to scoot the jack under the axle.

Marleen didn't think she'd ever get tired of visiting a house that had—not a doorbell—a door chime. The notes were clear and fluttery and made Marleen want to take off her clothes and dive into the sound. She had to muster every ounce of her maturity not to ring the chimes more than once. If Phyllis had been along, she would have just buried her thumb in the round button and kept it there even after Celeste had answered the door. Marleen was grateful that her sister had volunteered to baby-sit their brother, Dennis. Marleen didn't like to leave Phyllis alone too long with Dennis because Phyllis eventually got tired of the little boy's games and tried to teach him how to climb a tree or balance on the cinderblock retaining wall that ran along their driveway. Nevertheless, Marleen still needed to get her little whiff of sophistication whenever she could.

Although Fontana Barlow was supposed to be the LeFevers' maid, she didn't quite fit the role of servant that Marleen had come to expect from watching all the old movies in which the butlers and the maids moved around quietly and tried to make their masters' and mistresses' lives more elegant and organized. First of all, Fontana was much larger than anyone in the LeFever household. And while nobody doubted that she was an excellent housekeeper and cook, she made it clear that she didn't want people to be sloppy just because they had someone to pick up after them. If visitors proved to Fontana that they could stay for a few hours and not make a mess, then she eventually became friendlier. And even though Marleen had gained the maid's approval by the way she picked up after herself and on several occasions had offered to dry the dishes that Fontana was washing, the sheer size of the woman always made Marleen nervous, especially for the first few seconds when the maid would swing open the door and stand blocking the way, silent while her eyes adjusted to the bright sunshine.

"If you get up here a little earlier, you could help me do the breakfas' dishes." Fontana lumbered back a few steps and turned sideways so Marleen could come in.

Coming into the hallway, Celeste, in pedal pushers and a white sleeveless blouse, ran her fingers through her hair and stretched, as if she were still sleepy. "We don't make that big of a mess, do we, Fontana?"

"More than needs to be made." She shut the door behind Marleen. This early in the morning, she already smelled like warm bread with a faint odor of onions underneath her gardenia perfume. "All three of 'em has to have their jelly on a little saucer all by itself. And they want their toast on a little saucer all by itself." She moved herself across the room by what seemed like a force of heavy hydraulics between her two massive legs. When she had work to do, she barely had time for her complaints—much less for conversation with teenage girls.

After waiting long enough for Fontana to be out of hearing, Celeste asked, "Does she still make you nervous?"

Without thinking about what a sophisticated woman might say, Marleen replied, "Yes. But I don't know if it's because she's so big or because she's a maid."

Celeste laughed. "She's been working for us for two years,

and she still makes me nervous. I think it's because she's black and has such a different way of looking at the world. I know I'll never understand her. Some days, she seems all set to act like a maid, but other days, it's like she forgets. Dad says that more primitive people tend to be more emotional." Celeste led Marleen into the living room. Had Celeste's mama been at home, they would have gone either to Celeste's room or to the den, but when in charge of the house, Celeste liked to entertain in the living room, whose large picture window looked out across the front yard onto the dirt road.

For a few seconds, Celeste hovered over the huge hi-fi console, fine-tuning a radio station. From ten feet away, Marleen could see the long dark lashes that helped make Celeste's green eyes look so exotic. Yes, that was the word for Celeste: exotic. As far as Marleen knew, Celeste was the only girl at Blue Ridge High School who had those sea-green eyes. Sure two or three other girls had a kind of dull scuffed green that was hardly worth noticing, but Celeste's eyes were like the go signal of a traffic light. And her black hair made that green seem even more foreign. Her whole face seemed perpetually cool because of her eyes. It was a coolness that extended to the way she walked. She glided. And sometimes Marleen just wanted to lie down and take a nap in Celeste's shadow. Phyllis, on the other hand, maintained that Celeste walked as if she had too big a seam in her underwear.

Patti Page was singing "Tennessee Waltz." Carefully, Celeste closed the lid on the console. "Do you think when we get older and meet each other at a dance that you'll waltz off with my darling's heart?" Celeste was fond of asking hypothetical questions. Marleen thought it might have something to do with Celeste's interest in math.

"Well, if I do, it'll only be because I need a ride home." Marleen had tried to think about the future. She hoped it would become clearer to her once she got her driver's license. Except for baby-sitting, a girl couldn't get any decent kind of job unless she could drive. She had a few friends who were school bus drivers.

"Maybe we should go to the dances together. We could

take one of Dad's cars. Then we wouldn't have to be tied down to one particular boy all night." Celeste drifted to the picture window and pressed her nose against the pane. "Don't you dread all the complications? School is getting harder. The teachers expect more. The boys expect more."

"I guess I'm expecting more too." Marleen knew that Celeste had her moods, but she'd never seen her acting so drained before.

"Maybe if I was as athletic as you are." Celeste tilted her head back and rubbed her neck.

Marleen joined Celeste at the window. "I don't know if you should stand here posing like that. I saw a chain gang moving this way."

Celeste leaned forward to follow Marleen's gaze. "Was it a big crew?"

"Probably had about twenty convicts in it."

"Let's watch them." Celeste pulled two chairs right up to the window, then pulled the curtains together. "But we don't want them to know we're watching." She scooted her chair even closer to the window and pulled the curtain apart slightly. "How close were they?"

"Way back at the intersection." Marleen sat down in the chair beside Celeste. "It'll be awhile before they get here."

Immediately, Celeste was on her feet. "Then let's do this in style and bring some refreshments in here."

Marleen was grateful that Celeste was not the kind of person who would yell for Fontana to bring in the coffee or Coke. Aside from not wanting Fontana to think she had to wait on her, Marleen welcomed the chance to walk through Celeste's house. When Marleen thought of old furniture, she thought of the tables and beds down at her uncle and aunt's house in Wilkes. To her family, old furniture meant dark, heavy wood that reminded her of the Depression and bare light bulbs hanging down from the ceiling and the Carter Family singing some mournful song about a man whose mother was about to die.

But in the LeFever house, what few pieces of old furniture they had was what Celeste called Art Deco. To Marleen, it was elegance and New York nightclubs, feminine and exotic. Pink shell shapes and floor lamps like palm trees. Other rooms in Celeste's house, like the living room and the den, were furnished with more modern pieces—square easy chairs without arms, a huge couch shaped like an L, coffee tables with glass shelves, and in more casual corners, swooping metal chairs with canvas slings.

Once, Celeste had explained to Marleen that her mother wanted their house to feel light and fluid. She didn't want the rooms to fit together like separate little boxes. A person had to feel as if she were flowing from one moment to the next without worrying about "where" the moment was taking place. A home, Celeste said, should not confine. To combat the sense of confinement, Mrs. LeFever had knocked out a wall or two. Where support had been essential, she had changed the angle of the walls so that one room slanted off into another. While the house did definitely convey a sense of openness, Marleen wondered what it would be like trying to find one's way in the dark.

In the kitchen, which was probably the most confining room in the house because all four of its walls had been left at right angles, Fontana crooked her neck and grasped the counter against which she was leaning. "You want to drink coffee and watch the convicts work!?"

Celeste hummed "Blue Tango" while she prepared a tray. The LeFever china was pale blue and thin as Celeste's front teeth. Marleen thought of the coffee cups her mother had brought home from the factory cafeteria. They were thick, heavy affairs, turning brown on the inside. To drink from those cups, you had to hunch over the table and talk about atomic bombs. And a woman shouldn't really wear nail polish if she was holding one of those factory cups. They fit your hands better if you had been changing the tires on an old car or maybe washing dishes until your palms and fingers were wrinkled.

"I just want to know who you're trying to thrill: them convicts or yourselves?" Fontana returned to scrubbing the counter.

Marleen edged toward the door. She didn't want to be around if Celeste was going to argue with her maid. She also didn't want Fontana to think that she was too excited by Celeste's idea of entertainment. Somehow, peeking at the men from behind the curtain made her feel slightly sticky.

"I hadn't thought about it being thrilling." Celeste paused. "You have a dramatic way of looking at the world, Fontana."

When the maid refused to answer, Celeste simply finished filling the small cream pitcher and lifted the tray. "I can't see what's wrong with wanting to watch people work."

By the time Celeste got the tray settled on a coffee table and got the chairs arranged so both she and Marleen had a clear view through the crack in the curtain, Marleen had forgotten how the muscles in Fontana's neck had tightened, how she had clenched her cleaning cloth when Celeste had told her they were going to spy on the convicts. Marleen liked looking at men. And she knew that not too long into the morning all of the convicts would have taken off their shirts.

If at home, Marleen would have filled her coffee with cream and sugar, but she had learned that serious coffee drinkers used cream only to lighten the coffee flavor—not change it completely. She had skipped breakfast. Phyllis and Dennis were eating biscuits that they dipped in a mixture of Karo syrup and butter. When Marleen wasn't going to visit Celeste, she could eat more biscuits and syrup than her brother and sister combined, but she wanted to feel light and shimmering when she was around Celeste. She wanted to be the green of her eyes.

"Here comes a truck—one of those ugly prison trucks." Celeste studied the slow-moving truck. "It's spraying oil."

Marleen didn't have to peek out the curtain. The oil truck came by at least twice a month during the summer to help keep the dust under control. Phyllis liked to run along behind the truck, walking in the fresh oil so she could come home and leave black footprints all over their wooden porch. If she had seen the truck passing by, she might have followed it, teaching Dennis how to find the shallow holes where the oil was likely to collect. Marleen wondered what Celeste would say if she saw Phyllis and Dennis following along behind the truck.

"Is anybody behind the truck?" Marleen wanted to know because one of her most important jobs was to keep Dennis out of the road, despite how much she might be embarrassed by having to drag him and Phyllis back home under Celeste's sparkling gaze, their feet black up to their ankles.

Tony Bennett began singing "Stranger in Paradise." Celeste swayed to the music. "Marleen. Do you think we're leaving paradise or entering it?" Celeste's voice sounded more serious than it usually did when she asked questions inspired by the music she was listening to.

Marleen glanced around the living room with its three large Persian rugs, the chandelier, the velvet upholstery, the satin upholstery, the graceful lamps. "I think it all depends on which way we're facing."

With a pouting frown, Celeste shook her head, then looked back out the window. "That's not an answer. It's important that you give me a real answer."

"What kind of an answer can I give you?" Marleen had never heard Celeste sound so demanding. "You're the one who knows about paradise. You're the one who goes to Atlanta every month. You're the one whose closet is as big as my bedroom—which I share with a sister."

"So you think I have it pretty good?" Celeste settled back in her chair.

"Everybody likes you."

"Except Phyllis." Celeste laughed. It could easily have been the sound of her silver spoon stirring her coffee.

"Don't let that ruin your self-respect. At least she hasn't sicked the dog on you." Marleen scooted to the edge of her chair.

"What else do you want?"

Before answering, Celeste took a drink of coffee and peeked back out the window. "They're here."

Marleen stood up and parted the curtain above Celeste's head. Some of the convicts were using slings to cut the weeds and vines along the road. Following behind these men, other convicts were using shovels to clean out the ditches. None of them wore shirts. All of them had sweated enough to turn the waistbands of their pants a dark blue. They glistened in the sun. Across the LeFevers' wide yard, the sound of their digging and cutting sounded like the noise a dentist made while working on a numbed tooth. The men moved slowly and methodically, making Marleen feel as if she were watching a dream. Even the guards in their straw hats, carrying shotguns, strolled along in slow motion.

"See anybody you know?" Celeste's voice was neutral.

Marleen couldn't tell if she was teasing or trying to hurt her feelings. She had never told anyone about her uncle who had spent six months in prison when the G-men had found a still that her grandfather was operating. The government hadn't been particular about who went to jail as long as they could lock somebody up for moonshining. All six of Marleen's uncles had conferred, and Uncle Clint had been chosen to serve the time.

When Marleen didn't answer, Celeste nudged her in the stomach and asked, "See anybody you'd like to know?"

Now Marleen could tell that Celeste wasn't trying to insult her, but she could also tell that her friend wasn't teasing either. "I see about three that I might like to come by on a regular basis to trim the weeds."

"But Marleen, they're convicts." Celeste looked up at Marleen with an expression of surprise and confusion.

"But the three I'm looking at sure weren't convicted of being ugly." Marleen pretended to be studying the men who were standing beside the LeFevers' outermost box shrub.

"I'd be afraid of what they might expect." Celeste's voice sounded hazy.

"Those guys aren't exactly hardened criminals." One of Marleen's daddy's friends worked at the prison camp. "The really mean convicts aren't allowed out on the road."

"Well, how would you know that you weren't going with a convict who was just starting out, planning on working his way up to murder or robbing banks?"

Marleen sat back down and studied Celeste. "Wait a minute. You're not talking about those guys out there, are you?"

Celeste blinked three or four times as if she had something in her eye. "Maybe I'm not. Maybe I don't know who I'm talking about."

Perhaps because Marleen was the oldest of three children or because sympathy came as naturally to her as sweating, she slid from her chair and held Celeste's hand. Using Porky Pig's voice, she stammered, "D-d-don't be s-s-so d-d-d-de-pr-pr-pr-pr . . . s-s-sad, Celeste." She pulled the curtains closed with her free hand. "W-w-we don't h-h-have to look at the pr-pr-pr-pr-pr . . . convicts."

Celeste smiled and pulled herself to the edge of her chair. As she pulled the curtains apart, she said, "No, Marleen, don't help me hide from the problem."

Marleen moved back to her chair. Outside, the convicts were stooped to their work. One of them, who appeared to Marleen to be about nineteen years old, looked a little like Eddie Fisher. He raised his head for a moment from chopping weeds in the ditch and glanced at Celeste's house. Marleen could tell from the way that Celeste dropped back into her chair that she was also surprised by what seemed sure discovery of their presence. Then, without even a hint of recognition, the young convict bent back to his work.

"He looks like somebody who could go to school with us." Celeste took an unsteady sip of coffee.

"Yeah. Comb his hair. Give him a shirt. He'd fit right in." Marleen didn't know what Celeste needed to hear. "Maybe that's why he's in prison—for looking too much like a Blue Ridge High School student."

Celeste pulled her feet up under her and held her cup with both her hands. "No. Really, Marleen. He does look like all the boys at school."

"Not *all* of them." Marleen felt this was a topic on which she could set Celeste straight even if she couldn't comfort her. Something about Celeste's tone made Marleen want to take her out in the sunshine. Since she was thirteen, Marleen had been going out with boys. Of course, those first dates had been to church functions, but even then, there had been plenty of shady spots on the way home. Marleen knew that some girls didn't start dating until later, but her mama, Adele, had grown up with six brothers who always had friends coming over, so she couldn't remember when she didn't have boys flirting with her. She had married Curtis Holsclaw when she was seventeen.

Marleen had always assumed that a girl as rich as Celeste didn't stoop to dating the regular boys at Blue Ridge High. Like Marleen and most of the other girls, the boys came from furniture and textile factory families. Because the furniture factories paid a little better than the textile factories and because Marleen played first string forward, she could sit with anybody she wanted to in the lunchroom—except for two or three girls like Celeste, but Marleen didn't pretend to know anything about what went on in the rich girls' minds. She assumed such girls either dated boys who went to private schools or were so ashamed of dating the local boys that they simply made the boys swear not to talk about going out with them. Certainly, everybody wondered what went on in those girls' private lives, but Marleen had been busy enough with her own private life not to worry that much about Celeste's—until they had become friends.

"I don't mean he actually resembles all of them." Celeste rolled her eyes to the ceiling, then returned her gaze to the convict. "When I look at him, it's like I see what's *inside* all the boys at school."

"Maybe most of the boys are criminals; we girls can't hold that against them." Marleen knew better than to tell Celeste that she thought she felt some of the criminal in herself. Maybe her own criminal tendency was what vibrated so strongly when she was out with a boy. She already knew that she liked driving faster than the speed limit.

"It's not just what that boy has done." Celeste turned to face Marleen. "All the boys at school have that same kind of stoop inside them, the same kind of sweatiness. It's like they're angry and hungry and trapped all at the same time. And a girl is a door to them, a way to escape. . . ." Celeste stood up and towered over Marleen. "Tell me that's not what they need us for. Tell me what else they might want from us."

For an instant, Marleen thought she was going to have to plant her elbow in Celeste's stomach. She didn't like another girl trying to push her into a corner. But before she could raise her arm, she saw a flash of light outside. Ignoring Celeste's demand to know what boys wanted, Marleen leaned to one side to get a better view.

The flash had come from sunlight reflecting off a bucket being carried by Fontana Barlow. Without bothering to ask permission from the guards, she was out there in the road with a bucket and a dipper giving the convicts a water break.

Marleen pushed Celeste aside and went to the window to assure herself that she wasn't hallucinating. The men waded from the honeysuckle and climbed out of the ditches to gather around Fontana, leaning on their weed slings and shovels or holding them lazily across their shoulders. The light glinting off the sharpened edges and points with Fontana's bucket sparkling in the center pricked Marleen's eyes like an infant constellation, full of the future, brighter, even, than Celeste's green eyes.

ROAD SKILLS

MARLEEN WATCHED CLOSELY as her daddy ate. Nothing in the way he chewed his green beans and onions, nothing in the way he forked his mashed potatoes into his mouth, nothing in the way he pulled the meat off his pork chop from the little T-shaped bone with his teeth revealed that he was even thinking about giving Marleen her first driving lesson after supper. She wasn't above asking him if he was nervous or excited or frightened or sad, but conversation at the supper table was discouraged for the first few minutes of the meal because both Curtis and Adele were too hungry and too tired to feel up to talking with their three children.

Usually, Marleen's younger sister would keep up a steady monologue until Curtis and Adele were rested and satisfied enough to talk, but because Phyllis had been at the pool since lunch, she was as hungry and as tired as her mama and daddy. And Marleen's little brother had, before he reached the age of five, decided that he preferred listening to other people talk rather than talking himself. Marleen knew boys at school who refused to talk unless they were threatened with "corporeal punishment," and she had found them sweet. She recognized that with all the talking Phyllis and Adele could do once they got cranked up, there wasn't usually too much left to be said around their house.

However, as far as Marleen was concerned, everybody at the table should have been talking about her first driving lesson. She knew Phyllis was probably ignoring the subject because she was jealous, even though Marleen had told her that once she got her license, they could drive to the pool or the river or the skating rink anytime they felt like it. Or they could just cruise around town. Still, Marleen knew that Phyllis liked to be the center of attention, and she'd rather go against her natural talkative impulses if she thought the silence would irritate Marleen the least little bit.

"You did a good job with the pork chops." Adele licked her fingers.

"Mighty good." Curtis lifted more of the meat from the bowl. "I never knew how weak the taste of pork was until I was in the army. And they'd serve this white, broiled meat that tasted like wet dog. I never wanted to believe it was pork."

"You got to fry it hard and pepper it heavy if you want to cover up the pig taste." Marleen was just repeating what her mama had told her long ago when she was teaching her how to cook. But much of the conversation in the Holsclaw house consisted of repeating what had been said many times before.

After taking a long drink of her iced tea, Phyllis glanced at Marleen, then out the kitchen window. "Daddy, why don't you take me and Dennis to the fish pond?" As she spoke, she fastened her eyes on Marleen.

Catching the direction of Phyllis's gaze, Adele said, "Honey, you know we have to go to Betty Kirby's tonight. By the time you get the dishes washed and yourself cleaned up, it'll be time to go."

"I'm already cleaned up. I've been swimming." Phyllis appealed to her father.

"At the pool?" Curtis paused in his approach to his pork chop.

Phyllis kept forgetting that Curtis had a deep distrust of the town pool after the polio epidemic the year before. "It's clean water."

Because Curtis had gone ahead and taken a bite of his meat, Adele answered for him. "You don't know that." It was Curtis's favorite response to the unreasonable assertions always being made by his children, although Dennis hadn't shown the delight in being unreasonable that his sisters had.

For once, Marleen was relieved to hear the phrase. Whenever Curtis and Adele said, "You don't know that," they were saying they didn't want to discuss the matter. Marleen thought it was much nicer than when someone's mama or daddy simply said, "Shut up."

Switching to a thoughtful chewing motion, rolling his jaws lazily, Curtis said, "Since we're going to be up late at Betty Kirby's, I want to take a nap before we go. Them funeral visitations tie me in a knot even on the best of days."

With an elaborate yawn and stretch of her arms, Phyllis tilted sideways until her hand touched Marleen's head. "Now you're talking. Don't you think we should all take a nap, Daddy?"

Marleen pulled away from her sister's touch and leaned on the table to glare at her father. Beside her, Dennis was glancing from face to face, panic rising. Her brother was afraid he might miss the visitation, and he was excited about seeing his first casket close up. "Well, if all of you are going to be sleeping, you won't mind if Dennis and me take the car out for my driving lesson." Marleen rubbed Dennis's back.

"Ohh." Curtis sucked at one of his back teeth as if trying to calculate his oldest daughter's driving potential.

"It's five-thirty. We don't have to be at Betty's until eight o'clock." Marleen stood up and carried her plate to the sink. "We don't have time for all this foolishness." She scraped the remains of her supper into the old pot that was used as the dog's feeding bowl. Their black chow chow, Mush, would eat the pork bones first, then come back later in the evening for the vegetables. Over the three years they'd owned him, he'd developed a genuine appreciation for mashed potatoes.

Adele stood up and collected Curtis's and Dennis's plates. "You heard what your fifteen-year-old daughter said."

"How much time do you think you'll need on the road for this first lesson?" Curtis stretched and stood up. "Do I have time to sop a biscuit?" For dessert, Curtis liked to mix butter with syrup and scoop it off the saucer with bread.

Sensing Marleen's impatience, Adele replied, "Save some

of your appetite for the food at the visitation. Besides, you need to get back by seven so you can get yourself ready."

Out behind the house where Curtis kept his '51 white Chevrolet parked in the shade of a line of oaks, Marleen paced around the car, touching the warm metal every three steps. The oak trees strayed away from the forest, which lay a hundred or so yards from the back porch of the Holsclaw house. Phyllis still roamed around those woods when their parents were at work or off visiting. Up until a couple of years ago, Marleen had roamed with her. They used to spend most of the day in the woods with the Calloway kids. They carried their lunches with them and built log houses. Gerald Calloway brought cigarettes with him. And when he wasn't able to steal real cigarettes from his parents, he'd bring along little tissue papers and rabbit tobacco so they could roll their own. Phyllis was the only one of the gang who could or would smoke more than one of Gerald's rabbit tobacco cigarettes.

Leaning against the driver's side of the car, Marleen called to mind the driving outfit she planned to wear when she went to get her license: her pink angora sweater with the three pearl buttons, her black skirt, her white nylon scarf. And for pure adventure, she was going to wear a ponytail. Celeste LeFever, who knew everything about fashion, had told her that ponytails would be the rage for 1954. And before school let out, two boys had showed up with flattops. Marleen hadn't made up her mind about flattops. She'd always liked boys with curly hair, but flattops looked so clean and cool and military. And she was curious to find out how all those little stiff hairs felt to the fingertips. She'd heard that the barber, after cutting the boy's hair, had to light some kind of special stick and run the flame over the top of the boy's head to seal the ends of the hairs. That was what made them stand up. She had resolved to date the first boy with a flattop who asked her out, no matter what kind of car he had.

Curtis walked up to the car, picking his teeth. Marleen thought her daddy was a good-looking man, with his dark, fine hair and his deep brown eyes. He had a high forehead, but his hair showed no signs of thinning. His daddy, Turner Holsclaw, had the same kind of hairline, and he hadn't lost a bit of it in his sixty-some years. Given the already squarish tendency of her daddy's skull, Marleen thought he might look good with a flattop. Being in the war and working in the veneer plant helped keep Curtis slim and muscular. Marleen thought for a moment of Celeste's father. Mr. LeFever was taller than Curtis, but already Mr. LeFever looked soft and round. You never saw him out of his suit, and if he wasn't sitting in the leather seat of his Cadillac, he was sitting in the leather seat of his overstuffed easy chair in his den with the rosewood paneling.

The only fault Marleen could find with her daddy's appearance was that his front four teeth overlapped, so he was constantly having to go at them with a toothpick. Meat always gave him a hard time, pork especially. Usually, he carried five or six toothpicks in his shirt pocket—along with a stubby pencil about two inches long, which he used for marking veneer when he was at work. Very few things upset Curtis more than somebody borrowing his stubby pencil and not bringing it right back to him. The pencil and the toothpicks in his shirt pocket always made Curtis look as if he had two nipples on his left breast. But Marleen had taught herself to overlook her daddy's teeth and shirt pocket.

Marleen opened the car door and stuck one foot in. "Where we going?"

Curtis stored his toothpick in the corner of his mouth, sliding it to the side like a zipper. "Nowhere just yet." He opened the trunk and pulled out a soiled rag. "What should you do before you start out on a long trip?" He stood beside Marleen's door and held the rag in front of her face.

Marleen looked at the scrap of cloth covered with brown stains. "Make sure I've gone to the toilet and wiped?" She spoke in her Daffy Duck voice.

"Ohh ho. You can keep being smart like that and never learn to drive." Curtis tapped his fingers on the roof of the car.

"Check the oil. Check the oil." Marleen rolled out of the car, snatched the cloth from Curtis's fingers and trotted to the front of the car. Without waiting for Curtis to come around, she unlatched the hood, propped it open with the metal rod that folded up from behind the radiator, located the dipstick on the side of the engine, and pulled it out. By the time her daddy had moved beside her, she had wiped the stick off, reinserted it, and pulled it out to get her clear reading. "Just a little short of full," she said, turning to Curtis to let him see.

"And when's the best time to check the oil?" Curtis rested his foot on the front bumper and fiddled with the distributor cap.

"After the car's been turned off for an hour or so." Marleen wanted to impress her father, but she knew she had to be careful not to make him suspicious. She had taken driving lessons and automotive mechanics from every boy she dated—for the last two years. "It's best not to let the men at the service stations check your oil because it'll always read low if the engine's been running. And you don't want to overfill with oil because that'll cause too much pressure on the seals." This information was safe because Curtis always made a point to warn her about overfilling every time a service station attendant asked if he wanted the oil checked.

Curtis nodded and removed his toothpick. "What about the other fluids?"

"Check the water after the radiator's cooled down." Marleen tapped the radiator cap. "Brake fluid." She pointed at the little square container back in the corner. "But if you have to add fluid, you want to make sure you don't get any air bubbles."

Curtis smiled at Marleen. He seldom touched his children. Marleen didn't find her daddy's restraint unusual. Most of the other parents she knew, the daddys especially, didn't seem fond of touching either. She thought it might have something to do with the war.

"See if you can close the hood without losing a finger." Curtis walked around to the passenger's side of the car.

As Marleen dropped the hood in place, she said to herself in her Jackie Gleason voice, "Sammy, a little traveling music please."

She slid behind the wheel and held out her hand, palm up, in front of Curtis's chest. "Key." She tried to sound like a doctor asking for a surgical tool.

Curtis held his ring of keys over her palm. "Before you crank up, let's get you acquainted with the gears."

This was where Marleen knew she had to be careful. Officially, she was not supposed to have had any gear-shifting lessons yet. She was hoping that her daddy's clutch would feel different enough from the ones in her boyfriends' cars that she would be able to jerk enough to fool her daddy. But she didn't want to seem so stupid that he'd get frustrated and end the lesson before she actually got to drive. No matter how tired her daddy might get after ten hours at work, he could usually work up enough energy to lose his patience. "You know, I've watched you change gears all my life."

"Well, with changing gears, it's not so much what you know, but how smooth you apply what you know." Curtis turned to face Marleen and rested his right arm on the dashboard. "You know that down there on the floor is your accelerator, your brake, and your clutch."

Marleen knew which was which, but she waited until Curtis pointed before touching the pedal he indicated. However, she couldn't refrain from saying, "Right foot for gas and brake. Left foot for clutch."

"Well, you are ready to drive, ain't you." Curtis leaned back as if to get a better view of his daughter.

"I've been waiting for this for fifteen years." Marleen tapped her foot on the accelerator.

"Don't mash that pedal unless you want to get gas in the engine. If you hit it too much with the ignition turned off, you'll flood the engine."

Marleen was glad that she had made a genuine mistake. She hadn't spent much time behind the wheel of a car with the ignition turned off. Generally, when a boy turned his car's ignition off, he was finished giving driving lessons. "I'll remember that."

"And when you're going to change gears, make sure the clutch is in all the way. Otherwise, you'll scrape gears and cause a lot of wear and tear on the transmission. Just get used to pushing that left-footed pedal in all the way anytime you touch it." Curtis leaned toward his daughter. "Before you learn how to drive this car, you're going to stall it out, jump it around, and grind the gears, but don't let that throw you. You just have to get coordinated."

"I can stand it if you can." Marleen knew some boys who couldn't bear to hear their gears being scraped. A few boys who asked her out, upon learning that she wanted driving lessons, had found excuses not to show up. And Marleen admitted to herself that her gear-changing technique was far from smooth. All those different transmissions belonging to all those different guys just hadn't helped her coordination very much.

"Do you know the gears?" Curtis removed the toothpick from his mouth and crossed his arms.

Once again, Marleen didn't want to reveal how well she knew the gears, but she didn't want to seem hopelessly ignorant. After all, in Hibriten, every boy child spent part of every day pretending to change gears on his tricycle or bicycle or even while he was walking. For first, you pulled straight down on the lever. For second, you pushed the lever forward and up. For third, you pushed the lever forward while pulling straight down. You got to reverse by pulling the lever back as far as you could and then pushing up. Marleen loved going through the shifts. Her stomach gave a small quiver when she slid the lever up from first and followed the slight S-like motion to second. Second was her favorite gear because that was where the real acceleration took place. First was too slow and third was too weak. With second, you gathered up all the speed you could.

She went through the gears slowly.

"And when you go up into second, you want to make sure that you're pushing the lever forward so you don't accidentally go into reverse . . .

"Or you might need to use your rearview mirror to find your transmission." Curtis handed Marleen the keys.

She had trouble getting the car started because she didn't

pull out the little knob that was the choke. Her daddy let her sit there with the engine grinding on and on for maybe three minutes before he pointed out what she was doing wrong. Once again, Marleen was a little relieved that she had made another small mistake. Out in traffic, she didn't want to have to worry about covering up all that she did know while she was trying to keep the car on the road. Although she had gotten plenty of gear-changing experience, she had never actually driven for long stretches of time, so she knew that she would be doing a lot of weaving in the lane.

"Now before you pull out of the driveway, what do you need to always check?" Curtis kept his eyes on Marleen's eyes.

She knew that he was trying to keep from glancing at what he was talking about. "The emergency brake?"

"Well, yes. But something else." He still kept his eyes glued to hers.

"Make sure no one's behind you?"

"That's a good idea." Curtis's gaze flicked to the instrument panel. "Before you even start moving."

Marleen wasn't sure if he was trying to give her a clue or further confuse her. She thought about the little lights that flashed if something was wrong, about the speedometer. And then there was the gas gauge. "Gas! Make sure you've got gas." The other fluid. For a moment, Marleen was amazed by all of the fluids gurgling around in the white Chevrolet. The car seemed to be as much liquid as it was metal. She loved the color and smell of gasoline, the way the faintly gold and orange would sometimes quiver and reveal a rainbow, how a steel container would turn cool as it filled up with gas. Even oil had an unexpected blue tinge to it that would flash like the edge of a knife or the plumage of an exotic bird if you looked at it carefully enough. Then there was the blue-red of the brake fluid, like the blood of someone suffocating for the freedom of the road.

From the kitchen window, Phyllis yelled, "Floor it! Floor it!"

"I'll floor you if you don't shut up!" Marleen leaned out the window and shook her fist. She didn't want her sister intruding on her communion with the car. Phyllis had a talent for knowing how and when she could cause the most disturbance. She seemed to study how she could best break up a romantic mood or a serious moment.

"Watch out, watch out! You're going too fast!" Phyllis screamed, then made the noises of screeching brakes and a car crash.

"Do I have time to go into the house and quiet Phyllis down?" Marleen was pretty sure that her daddy wouldn't let her get out of the car.

"You know she's just jealous." Curtis opened his door. "Slide over here and let me drive us somewhere to practice. You might have a hard time backing past the wall in the front anyway."

For a second, Marleen felt disappointed. She had imagined herself backing smoothly straight by the white cinderblock retaining wall that separated the front yard from the driveway. Because their house was built on the slope of a hill, the front yard was at least four feet higher than the driveway. But Marleen thought the retaining wall made the house look a little more regal, even if it was small with a flat roof and asbestos siding. Then she admitted to herself that the wall was awfully close to the driveway. Besides, once she got out on the dirt road in front of their house, she wasn't sure if she could work the clutch very well on the hill. She'd been warned by several of her friends who already had their licenses that starting out on a hill was the hardest skill to master.

After Curtis had backed out of the driveway and into the dirt road, with the front of the car facing up the steep hill, he said, "You and the car have to get in rhythm together."

"Like dancing." Marleen tapped her foot. She realized that the boys who had given her previous lessons hadn't allowed her to get in rhythm with their cars.

"Yeah." Curtis dropped the gear shift from reverse to first. "See," he pointed to his feet. "I got the brake down and the clutch in. Now what I do if I'm on a hill and don't want to roll back is . . ."

"Let out the clutch until it starts to engage, then slide

your foot from the brake to the gas pedal." Marleen gritted her teeth. She'd said too much. How to start out on a hill represented advanced knowledge that she probably wasn't supposed to mention.

Curtis studied Marleen's face for a few seconds. "Have you done this somewhere already?"

"I've talked to people." Marleen hoped her daddy wouldn't go off on one of his lectures about the importance of learning how to drive from a responsible adult.

"You don't want to get the wrong start with your driving, Marleen. Don't let the fun cover up how dangerous driving can be. And you need a responsible adult to keep you reminded of what happens to people who don't learn the right way to drive. Even a boy like Hoyt Kirby, who drove better than most, gets killed when he forgets about the danger."

Sensing that her daddy realized that he was starting to lecture, Marleen thought she'd try to distract him. "I heard that Hoyt's car is on the traffic circle now." Like Phyllis, Curtis was fascinated by the wrecks when they were displayed in the middle of the grassy plot of ground at the main intersection outside of town.

Curtis rubbed his face and paused to scratch his upper lip. Then he tilted his head as if he wanted to fall asleep right there behind the wheel. "How can you tell when the clutch has started to engage? And don't pretend you don't know. I can tell by the way you scooted to the edge of your seat that your feet are itching to pump these pedals."

Marleen could see that he was both pleased and upset that she was such an advanced student. It would be like her father to worry but, at the same time, not to want to know about her private affairs. "The sound of the motor starts getting strained." She leaned forward to better hear the engine.

As he eased up off the clutch, Curtis kept his eyes on Marleen's face. When she heard the engine's pitch drop to a deep complaining throb, she said, "It's engaged."

Curtis nodded. His face lost its disapproving droop. "See, I can take my foot off the brake, and we stay right where we are." He lifted his right foot and held it out to the side, wiggling his chunky brogan in the air. "There's this little spot where the clutch will hold the car but not stall it out." He let the clutch come up a fraction of an inch farther, and the engine began to sputter, convulsing the car. "When it starts to act like this, you either push the clutch back in a little, or you give it some gas." He dropped his foot on the accelerator and produced a short spray of gravel from the back tires. "But I don't want to catch you spinning your tires like that. It's hard on the rubber and on the transmission." He stopped again halfway up the hill. This time, he eased the clutch out and touched the accelerator softly. "Now you tell me which way is smoother."

"The second one. You looked like Fred Astaire on the second one." Marleen stretched her feet out and tried to reproduce the motions her daddy had just gone through. "Talk about rhythm." She realized that there was another fluid that had to be checked when she started to drive—her own. She had to be flowing in her motion behind the wheel. Like the oil, she was there to make sure the car moved smoothly.

They rode past the Calloway house, past the LeFever house, and at the top of the hill, Marleen tried to keep her eyes off the wide lawn of her rich friend's house by studying the Blue Ridge Mountains thirty miles in the distance. A day would come, she promised herself, when she would be able to drive along those high, curving roads without even thinking about using her brake. She could go up there for picnics at Blowing Rock and Grandfather Mountain, maybe even drive to the college in Boone and see what boys getting a college education looked like.

This early in the summer, the mountains were still a sharp green that made Marleen want to take off her shoes and wade through ice-cold water. She had been up there in those mountains on the Parkway at night. There were places along that road where you could pull off, park, and watch the distant lights of Hibriten and Morganton twinkle more clearly than the stars. Marleen felt sophisticated way up there where the air was chilly even in July and you had to press yourself into the boy's arms if you didn't want your teeth to start chattering. Even though the mountains were wild and ragged, Marleen felt as if she'd been to a big city as she and her date came down the Hibriten–Blowing Rock Road, weaving out of one sharp curve into the next with the tires giving a little wail on the sharper turns.

After a half mile of dirt road, Curtis reached the intersection where the pavement began. As if speaking to the stop sign, he mused, "Once you get your rhythm with changing the gears, we'll use this dirt road for practice. But for the first few lessons, we need a place where you can stall out and not block traffic." He rested his chin on the steering wheel, considering first the road to the left, then the road to the right. "We want a quiet place where people won't blow their horns at you if you stall the car and can't get it started right off."

"How about the elementary school parking lot?" Marleen tried to remain calm. Her daddy always burned up her time like this. But just let him be on his way to a card game— although he wasn't as bad as he used to be—and he'd resent having to slow down to open their screen door. The school was close, and Marleen had already driven around the parking lot on three dates. Of course, it had been dark, and they'd kept the headlights turned off.

Curtis nodded and pulled onto the pavement. "Have you been picking out places where you'd like to practice?"

"Well, I spent a lot of time at that school. And after a while, you start trying to find some use for the place." Marleen was much happier in high school than she had been in elementary school. It was easier to sneak through your classes in high school. And the high school actually had a smoking area behind the cafeteria. Besides, the signals that were passed between boys and girls were real in high school, not as frustrating as the notes she had passed and received in elementary school. Even the teachers seemed aware of how important relationships were. Best of all, being in high school meant that you were getting ready to finally get out of school. Now, when Marleen found herself at the elementary school for some reason, she felt a strong sense of impending freedom, even though she still had three more years of high school to go.

Her daddy was all business behind the wheel. Only if he was going to drive for several hours would Curtis allow himself the luxury of resting his elbow on the window or stretching his arm along the top of the front seat. He didn't like to talk while he drove, but he was happy to listen to what Adele or his children had to say, as long as they didn't whine for food or drinks. On their trips to the beach, he would stop occasionally and let them buy Cokes and peanuts. Marleen now preferred to eat cheese crackers or Moon Pies when they stopped, but Phyllis and Dennis still thought they were getting a big treat when they could dump their pack of peanuts into their Cokes. Then again, Marleen realized that some of the boys she had dated also thought that peanuts and Coke were a special treat.

More than peanuts and Coke, more than driving down to the beach, more than sitting in lawn chairs in front of Celeste LeFever's big house, Marleen longed for the chance to cruise the two teenage hotspots in Hibriten: the Scarlet Sow Drive-In Grill and the Dome Grill. The Scarlet Sow had been around longer, and the food there was better than at the Dome, but the owners of the Scarlet Sow were more interested in having paying customers parked in their lot. Consequently, they tried, in a mild way, to discourage too much cruising. They had speed bumps and didn't repair the pavement behind the building. And of course, to properly cruise, a person had to be able to circle the area where other people were gathered.

While the Scarlet Sow specialized in barbecue and serious eaters, the Dome served more general grill food. Its milk shakes weren't as good as what could be ordered at the Scarlet Sow either. However, the owners of the Dome had built their place directly in the middle of their lot and kept the pavement patched. The Dome was the place to go if you wanted to meet people. And it had more neon lights than the Scarlet Sow. A dome actually sat on top of the restaurant. It reminded Marleen of a space observatory, which in itself made the grill look exotic and exciting, to say nothing of the constant flow of cars around the place, everybody's face blinked red, then blue, then green by the lights that outlined the dome. Marleen wondered how many nights of the week she could sneak off to the Dome and the Scarlet Sow.

"Looks like a baseball game." Curtis pulled into the gravel parking lot of the elementary school and made a big circle.

Cars were parked all over the place. Behind the school, the baseball bleachers were crowded with people. "Little Leakers." Marleen resented this crowd. "You can tell people get really bored in the summer because they can watch baseball and get excited."

"Give me boxing any day." Curtis pulled back out onto the highway and headed toward town. "Baseball is too slow."

"Yeah. When you've got eighteen boys dressed up in uniforms, but only two or three of them are actually doing anything, you got to feel cheated." Marleen hoped that her daddy didn't plan to let her try a drive through town. Even with all her illegal practice, she knew she wasn't ready for stoplights.

"I thought we'd drive along and see if we could find a factory parking lot for you to practice in." Curtis yawned and rubbed his face. "I don't really want to go to that visitation tonight. I thought I'd try to get to bed early."

If cards or fishing equipment weren't involved, Curtis preferred to work around the house. Marleen was glad that her mama had such a well-developed sense of social obligations. They had been neighbors of Betty and Hoyt Kirby for nearly seven years, and that bound them up with whatever happened to the Kirbys—good and bad. Marleen had taken care of Betty's little boy, Larry, five months ago when Betty went to the hospital to have her baby. Marleen had missed four days of school because Betty had developed some complications during the delivery and had to have a C-section. Besides, Marleen liked being with people. She looked forward to the day when she could be finished with school and go to work maybe in a furniture factory or a cotton mill.

In a factory, you could walk around and talk to people. Curtis and Adele came home almost every day with stories about men fighting over women in the parking lots or women sitting too close to men who weren't their husbands in the cafeteria. And there were always the accidents to dread. Her daddy had been standing right beside the cutoff saw a couple of years ago when Burt Sanders ran the blade up through his ring finger. Later, they had been able to find only half of his wedding band. And Lanny Propst's father had let a drill go right through the center of his hand about three months ago.

When Curtis drove past the second empty factory parking lot without even slowing down, Marleen reached over and tugged at his short-sleeved shirt. "I thought you wanted to use one of those parking lots for my practice."

"I plan to. But since we're so close to the traffic circle, I thought we'd take at look at Hoyt Kirby's wrecked car." Curtis flicked his hand at the parking lot they were passing. "Besides, you don't want to practice where people will be driving by. Either you'll distract them, or they'll distract you."

He had a point. Marleen had already spotted three of her friends, boys, she had dated. She didn't want them watching her practice with her daddy what she had practiced with them. And all she needed was one of her loud-mouthed girlfriends driving by and yelling something that her daddy didn't need to hear. "A private place would be better."

"Besides, you need to see what a second of irresponsibility can do to you." Curtis pulled himself up straighter in the seat.

Approaching the traffic circle was like approaching a large waterfall. You could hear it before you saw it. A low roar floated on the air. During rush hour, the roar was accented by the blare of horns, and the air was misty with exhaust. Marleen rated the smell of gasoline fumes right up there with the smell of fried onion rings and grilled hamburgers. Car exhaust made her think of faraway places and perpetual motion, long stretches of highway and sleeping in the backseat of the car, getting away from home and school, cool nights with wind curling around her ears and legs.

Because it was the first day of the Hoyt Kirby wreck display, traffic around the circle was fairly heavy. Only five or six people had parked their cars at the Esso station and dodged through the circling cars to visit what was left of the automobile in the grassy middle of the circle. As Curtis merged with the other cars and began circling, Marleen crawled into the backseat and rolled down the back window on the driver's side. The '53 Ford was squashed to less than half its original length. All of the hood seemed to have disappeared and the front wheels were splayed outward, pushed back under the passenger part of the car, which curled slightly upward. Marleen noticed that all the glass in the car was shattered.

"I heard at work today that the highway patrol figures he was going a hundred and ten when he left the road and run into the side of Bumgarner's Supermarket." Like Marleen, Curtis had his head stuck out the window, studying the wreck. All of the circling spectators had their heads stuck out their car windows.

"What must that have felt like?" Marleen was remembering Hoyt's curly black hair. He always blew his horn and waved at her when he saw her. A couple of her dates had taken her to the Hickory Speedway when Hoyt was racing.

"They probably didn't feel much of anything. But you can bet smacking into a wall at a hundred and ten don't feel anything like being kissed by your mother." Curtis was shaking his head.

What Marleen wanted to know was what it felt like to go a hundred and ten miles an hour. Her daddy always followed the worst implication of what everybody said. It was his way of throwing cold water on people's excitement. Marleen thought maybe the war had made him that way. Before considering what he might think, Marleen climbed back into the front seat and said, "No, what I meant was what must it have felt like to be going a hundred and ten miles an hour."

For a moment, Curtis was silent and continued to study the wrecked car from his shifting vantage point. When he came to the next exit, he pulled out of the circle, heading out toward the country instead of toward town and the factory parking lots. "I don't want you ever trying to find out what a hundred and ten feels like."

Marleen leaned back in her seat and ran her fingers through her hair. No matter how careful she tried to be, it was never careful enough. At times like this, she wished she could be more like Phyllis and not care what anybody thought about her. "Are we going home now?"

"Does this look like the way home?" Curtis seemed to be cheering up.

Her daddy's unexpectedly bright tone prompted Marleen to sit up straighter and look out the window. This was the road they used when they went down to Wilkes to visit her mama's relatives. "Looks like we're going to Wilkes." Already Marleen knew they couldn't be going to Wilkes because those visits never made Curtis this cheerful.

"We're not. But come to think of it, after you've had a few lessons, that lonesome dirt road down below Taft and Cora's house would make a good place to practice." Curtis even began to whistle what Marleen thought was the "Orange Blossom Special."

"Well, am I going to get to practice driving?"

"I thought of the perfect place to give you your first few lessons." Curtis glanced at Marleen and smiled to let her know her lesson was going to involve more than just getting used to the clutch. "It's a quiet place. Paved. And probably no traffic. It'll be a restful place to get the rhythm of the gears."

After a few seconds of trying to remember what kind of parking lots might be found on this side of town, Marleen caught sight of a large stone arch over a road that cut off to the left. It was the Mountain View Cemetery, largest burial ground in Hibriten. The cemetery driveway looped through acres and acres of rolling hills. Just about anybody, rich or poor, who didn't belong to a church wound up in the Mountain View Cemetery. Even people who did belong to a church but wanted a grave on high ground made arrangements to be buried in Mountain View.

Easing to a stop in front of a large cement fountain, Curtis stretched his neck to search for other cars in the cemetery. "I don't see a soul." After cutting off the engine, he opened his door and stepped out of the car. "Slide on over behind the wheel."

Marleen felt her heart enlarge, throbbing in her neck.

They were parked in the shade of a huge maple tree, and the shade felt cooler than even the blue water at the Hibriten Pool. The grass must have just been cut that day. Its odor wafted between the tombstones, carrying sunlight and ripeness. The asphalt of the cemetery was darker than the pavement out on the highway and looked more like a stretch of black short-pile carpet than like a road. Marleen rubbed her feet slowly back and forth on the floorboard, her arches itching to feel the pressure of the pedals.

Curtis got in on the passenger's side, inserting a fresh toothpick into the corner of his mouth. "Crank 'er up."

"Want me to check the oil again?" Marleen leaned over the wheel and grasped the key.

"Now how do you think it'd read with the engine just turned off?" Curtis cocked his head accusingly.

"Low." Marleen reached out to pull the choke.

"What're you doing?" Curtis removed his toothpick and gave a short laugh.

"Don't I need to choke it when I crank up?" Marleen wasn't worrying now about appearing to know more than she should.

"No. No. If the car's been running, you don't need to choke it. Not this car anyway. Just turn the key and see what happens . . ." Curtis's voice trailed off as if his attention were focused somewhere else now.

Marleen glanced at her daddy, hoping to catch what he was looking at. She saw that his gaze was on the floor. Using Sylvester the Cat's voice, she said, "Suffering succotash, the clutch has to be in when I crank the car."

Curtis nodded with relief. Poking the air in front of him with his toothpick, he added, "Or you could have the gearshift in neutral. But you're more likely to forget you're in neutral and roll into somebody. As far as I'm concerned, neutral is just the space you pass through when you're going from first to second or from third to first."

Two or three of Marleen's dates had used neutral when they were at the drive-in movie. They had to leave their cars running in the winter at the drive-in, and they didn't want to sit there with the clutch pressed in through a double feature and the cartoon. Marleen refrained from passing this information along to her father. She understood that putting the car in neutral meant giving up a certain amount of contact with the car, a certain amount of control. Her daddy didn't like to lose control. That was one of the reasons he didn't like to go down to Wilkes as much as the rest of his family. He found it hard to control what went on down in Wilkes. But Marleen was excited by the place.

Marleen eased out the clutch, listening for the engine to change its pitch. It had to be smooth. Her daddy admired smooth motion. He did well at his job because he was able to match the flow of the grain in one piece of veneer to the flow of another. And he was always fussing about "wasted motion." In his mind, Curtis equated efficiency with smoothness. And Marleen had been around him long enough to know that as far as her daddy was concerned, smoothness equaled intelligence.

From a couple of her bootleg driving lessons, Marleen had learned that student drivers wanted to give the car more gas than was needed, so she hesitated when she heard—and felt—the clutch engage. Already, her daddy was suspicious of how much she knew, but she was certain that she could give the car just the right amount of gas—at the risk of making her daddy more suspicious.

"Don't tease the transmission like that, Marleen." Curtis patted the dashboard. "Keep in mind that the sooner you let the clutch all the way out, the better it is for the transmission. If you sit there and hold it halfway out like that, you're going to burn out the clutch plate."

Marleen jerked her leg up and tromped on the accelerator. The engine roared, startling Marleen into lifting her foot off the gas. The car leaped, succumbed to a metallic shudder, and stalled. "I can do it smoother," she insisted.

"Turn off the ignition and start over." Curtis seemed relieved. "And try to let your feet move about the same speed. One coming up and the other going down. But smooth." As he talked, Curtis checked his watch, then began inspecting the cemetery.

On her second try, Marleen was able to shorten the distance the car jumped, and she also discovered that she could press the accelerator without racing the engine. However, as soon as she began easing forward, she felt her father staring at her. "Tell me which way to go. Tell me which way to go." She was creeping up on a five-way branch in the road. Two branches seemed to circle the bases of the hills in the cemetery. Two more climbed along the sides of the hills, and one headed straight up the hill in front of Marleen.

For longer than seemed necessary to Marleen, Curtis studied the five roads. Twice, he even raised himself out of the seat and stuck his head out the window. "I want you to take that road to the right that goes halfway up the hill." For a few seconds, Curtis was silent while Marleen made the turn. "Build up your speed enough to change to second . . . about fifteen miles an hour."

As she pressed on the gas, Marleen grasped the gearshift, her palm pointing outward. She felt the engine straining against the first gear, a faint whine rose from under the hood. She pushed in the clutch as she took her foot off the accelerator and slid the shift up through the S shape into second. She pressed back on the gas only slightly harder than she needed to, but she let the clutch out with barely a lurch. Then she realized she had made a mistake.

"Nice job." Curtis tilted his head and leaned back to study his daughter.

"P-p-p-probably just luck." Marleen knew Porky Pig was her father's favorite cartoon character.

"Looked more like practice to me." Curtis leaned his head out the car window once more. They were approaching a three-road fork. "Slow down. I want to figure out which way I want you to go."

"We're not going to get lost in here, are we?" Marleen eased up off the gas until the car began sputtering.

"You need to speed up or push in the clutch or it's going

to die on you." Curtis jerked his head back inside the car and snapped his attention back to Marleen.

When Marleen pushed down on the accelerator, the car shuddered more violently. She was going too slow to be in second gear, so she pushed in the clutch and stepped on the brake. Once the engine smoothed out, Marleen—with her palm now facing inward—slid the gearshift from second to first.

In a voice too calm to let Marleen feel comfortable, Curtis said, "Take the right fork."

Wondering what she had done wrong, Marleen neglected to let the car jerk as she let out the clutch.

"That was real nice." Curtis studied the fabric ceiling liner over his head for a moment. "Go on and get up to second gear." He watched Marleen closely as she glided up to second, allowing the engine to roar for a split second while the clutch was in. "What was also nice was how you knew to come all the way stopped before shifting down to first. Most learners don't know that you can't downshift to first while the car is still moving—even with the clutch in. How did you get so smart?"

Using Droopy's voice, Marleen replied, "I guess I was born to shift."

"I reckon I don't have a lot of control over what you was *born* to do, but you'd better *learn* to be careful." Curtis propped his elbow on the window and rested his jaw on his fist. After a second of silence during which Marleen could almost hear her daddy's jaw muscles tightening, Curtis straightened up and pointed to a freshly dug grave about fifty yards from the road. "Ol' Hoyt was *born* to drive, but he never learned to be careful, and right over there is where they'll be parking him tomorrow. Pull over to the curb."

Marleen bumped against the curb, forgot about depressing the clutch, and stalled the engine after a series of convulsions felt as if they were going to leave the car frame twisted like an apple peel. "Whoa, hoss!" Marleen pushed her hair from her eyes and turned off the ignition.

"I'll be right back." Curtis climbed out of the car and walked toward the new grave.

Marleen got out of the car and started to follow her daddy, but a breeze moved against her sweaty back. She pulled her sticky blouse from against her skin and decided to stand where she was and let the air dry her clothes. She had seen graves before. The funeral home had thrown a green canvas tarp over the pile of dirt beside the grave. Tomorrow, they'd have one of their tents set up for the graveside ceremony, and the pile of dirt would be further hidden from view by one side of the tent. But she knew the dirt would be there, just as she knew the grave was there. Her daddy didn't fool her.

Pointing at the rectangular hole, he shouted to her: "This is where you wind up when you lose control."

With the breeze on her back and the warm roof of the car under her arms, Marleen could see only a thin brown line barely disturbing the green hump of the grassy ground. Fifty yards was a long way off to try and make her see a grave. "You don't know that," she said in her own voice, shaking her head slowly, warmed by the car between her and the hole where her daddy stood.

THE MAGNETISM
OF WOE

MARLEEN WALKED WITH HER MAMA and daddy along the narrow dirt road that led to Betty Kirby's small house. Given the solemnity of the occasion, they should have driven the short distance to the widow's house, but Adele had pointed out to Curtis and her children that the scruffy yard in front of Betty's house would be crowded enough without the bulk of their Chevrolet pushed in among the cars of the other visitors who would be there to comfort Betty. Her dead husband, although one of the wildest boys in town—or because of it—had always been well liked. His success as a stock-car racer had promised to make him a statewide celebrity. But then, he had wrecked driving up Highway 421 three nights earlier, four miles from home.

Marleen had liked Hoyt Kirby because he had black curly hair, thick biceps with a vein running along the top of each muscle, and eyes that were light blue to the point of grayness. She liked him because nobody in Caldwell or Wilkes or Burke or Watauga County could keep up with him. She'd heard the boys at school talk about Hoyt's races—on the dirt tracks and on the quarter mile of straight, flat highway out at the water treatment plant. It was common knowledge in town that the police, the sheriff, and the highway patrol had given up trying to catch Hoyt Kirby when he decided to drive fast.

You could tell by looking at Hoyt that he was built for

speed. Marleen always thought he was built like a slim Buster Crabbe, but Hoyt had a better sense of humor than Flash Gordon or Tarzan. Despite all his talent as a driver, he never acted like he was better than anybody else. More than once when he spotted Marleen walking home from school or standing around by the road in front of her house, Hoyt would stop and speak to her or offer her a ride somewhere. Of course, she had her orders from her mama and daddy never to ride with Hoyt. Usually, she didn't need to take a ride, but the couple of times she had crawled in beside Hoyt, nothing had happened. He talked to her about transmissions or the wrecks he'd seen at the track the week before, but he'd never gone faster than the speed limit when he was carrying Marleen. She didn't think she'd ever understand why her mama and daddy wanted to worry as much as they did.

Remembering Hoyt's arms and the swell of his chest under his T-shirt, Marleen felt a brief chill in the June air. Hoyt and Betty had been their neighbors for seven years. But Marleen didn't know Betty all that well. Like Marleen's mama, Betty had been raised in the Brushy Mountains of Wilkes County, but she wasn't at all like Adele Holsclaw. For one thing, Betty had always struck Marleen as being a little backward. A lot of women were quiet when their husbands were around, but all the times that Marleen had gone out to the Kirby house with her mama, even when Hoyt wasn't at home, Betty had been quiet and hard to talk to. As much as Adele liked to talk, even she once complained that Betty just didn't seem to know how to act around people.

And when Betty wasn't pregnant, she seemed about to be pregnant. Out of the seven years Betty and Hoyt had been married, Betty had given him five children. Marleen smoothed the bodice of her own summer dress and wondered if she'd ever have breasts—not necessarily breasts like her mother or Betty Kirby, but just enough to distinguish her chest from her boyfriends'. Betty made Marleen uncomfortable because Betty's breasts were large, and then she had this small waist—maybe even as small as Marleen's, but Betty was twenty-three. And she had those big round hips that made her waist look even smaller. Her clothes always seemed too tight for her. For a long time, Marleen had thought that Betty was too big for Hoyt. Too big and too slow.

Betty just kind of drifted from one place to another, usually with one of her younger kids riding on her hip. More than once, Adele had warned Marleen and Phyllis that she expected them to be better housekeepers than Betty Kirby, whose three-room house always smelled of spoiled milk, soiled diapers, unwashed bodies, and piled-up dishes. If Betty had been holding down a factory job, Adele might not have been so critical, but Hoyt refused to let Betty work. People said he was too jealous to trust her in a factory.

Marleen didn't think there was much in Betty to be jealous of—unless it was her breasts and hips. Betty had never looked healthy to Marleen. She was too pale. Often, she had dark circles under her eyes, and her hair wanted to be frizzy. Marleen didn't think that Betty had ever gotten her hair cut. Her mouth made her look like she was always pouting, and Betty wore the brightest red lipstick that could be bought in Hibriten. Marleen had never seen Betty when she didn't have lipstick on her oversized lips. The red just didn't go with her cow-brown eyes.

When Betty did talk, every word was dragged out as if she were just waking up or falling asleep. Marleen decided it was a good thing that Betty didn't like to talk much. A person would probably miss a couple of meals if she had to sit around and wait for Betty to drawl through one piece of neighborhood gossip. But if her speech was slow, her body was even slower. Betty didn't seem to be comfortable in an upright position. When she sat down, she always found some way to prop herself up. Gravity just seemed to be too strong for her. On those rare occasions when Marleen had seen Betty walk, she had been struck by how much Hoyt's wife resembled a sackful of highly lubricated cantaloupes shimmying along the sidewalk.

The sudden appearance of a long black automobile coming around the curve that hid the Kirby house from view caused every member of the Holsclaw family to jump to the edge of the road and line up, with their backs pricked by the encroaching blackberry bushes. As the hearse eased by Marleen and her family, the driver raised his hand from the steering wheel and jerked his palm to one side several times as if he were winding a spring in his wrist. The three other men in the hearse merely nodded and smiled.

Once the hearse was by, Curtis stepped back into the road, brushing away the dust as it settled on his blue suit jacket. "We just about got there too early."

"We could've helped them carry the casket in!" Phyllis's voice was barbed with disappointment.

"Are you strong enough?" Dennis wasn't sure if he liked the idea of his sister having such close contact with a casket.

"Well, I'm not half as strong as my sister," Phyllis said as she lifted Marleen's arm and pretended to smell.

Marleen jerked her arm down and swung her fist in an exaggerated arc that almost reached Phyllis's jaw. "You're cruising for a bruising, little sister."

Phyllis tilted her head back, jitterbugged in front of Marleen and said, "Ha!" Then she slid over to Dennis, who was still watching the hearse ease along the rutted tracks, and put her arm around his shoulder. "Did you ever stop to think," she sang, "that when a hearse went by, you would be the next to die?"

Phyllis placed her hand on the top of Dennis's skull and tilted his head so he could look directly into her face. "They'll wrap you up in a big white sheet and let you down about forty feet. The worms crawl in, the worms crawl out, the worms play pinochle on your snout . . ."

"Phyllis, you leave Dennis alone." Adele pulled Phyllis away from him. "I'll play 'The Star-Spangled Banner' on your tail if you give your brother nightmares." Adele pushed Phyllis up beside Curtis. "Walk with your daddy. And Curtis, don't let her go poking around Betty's house when we get there." Adele took Dennis by the hand, even though the evening light was still strong enough to show the deeper potholes in the road, and the boy made his way along the washboard road easier than anyone else. "Marleen, keep your sister away from Betty. The last thing that poor woman needs is some little skunk of a girl asking her how much the casket cost and whether or not Hoyt was drinking the night he died."

"Does she get to keep the wrecked car?" Dennis was fond of going to junkyards with his daddy and hoped that Betty might begin one right there in his neighborhood.

Before Adele could respond, Phyllis turned and asked, "Will Betty keep all of Hoyt's trophies?"

"That's nobody's business but Betty's." Curtis jerked Phyllis around.

"Marleen, you got to keep both of these children from talking to Betty." Adele squeezed Marleen's hand.

"Mama, wouldn't it be easier just to leave them at home? They'll run me ragged if I try to keep up with both of them." Marleen never understood why her mama and daddy insisted on making such visits harder than they needed to be. "Or if we could just leave Phyllis at home, Dennis would behave."

"You don't have to follow them around," Curtis replied. "Just fix yourself close to Betty, and when you see Phyllis or Dennis about to open their mouth, put something in it . . . a shoe or a fist or a rug. I'll crumple you up a couple of paper cups when we get there, and you can keep them handy."

"I don't want to talk to Betty anyway." Phyllis raised her nose in the air. "I'd as soon talk to a cow."

"That's not a bad idea," Curtis said.

"If she can find a cow that'll listen to her." Marleen thought Phyllis got away with too much.

"I don't want you ruining this visitation for the rest of us, Phyllis." Adele spoke in a flatly menacing voice. "I can't think of anybody there who'll need to hear your questions, so just try to keep quiet."

"Maybe I'll just stay outside and let the mosquitoes eat me." Phyllis paused to scoop one off her arm, then rub it between her palms.

"As rickety as Hoyt let his screen doors get, you probably won't have to go outside to feed the bugs." Curtis scratched his neck, then pulled out a handkerchief and wiped his face. He wasn't used to wearing a suit in June. But he firmly believed death was one occasion that he had to dress up for, even if it meant sweating for three or four hours. Somebody at the visitation was sure to be toting a washtub of ice and beer in the trunk of his car.

"It'll sure be cooler outside than inside." Adele knew that she and the other women would have to congregate in the small, stuffy rooms that she hoped Betty's mother and mother-in-law had cleaned that morning.

Marleen fanned her face with her hand with little relief. She hoped the funeral home men had provided cardboard fans for the visitors. Usually, the pictures from Bible stories depressed her a little. The sky was always a heavy blue and made her feel as if she'd eaten too much chocolate. But if she could keep her face from sweating away, she'd try to feel grateful for whatever picture might be on the fan.

Or maybe, Marleen realized, it was the funeral home advertisement on the side of the fan opposite the Bible picture that depressed her. Whether the fans came from the Soots-Lanier Funeral Home or the Clarence Hightower Funeral Home, the lettering was either Old English style, which made Marleen think of monks and pilgrims, or it was a script that made Marleen think of old ladies making lace and reading Edgar Allan Poe. She remembered all the other grim funerals and visitations she'd gone to where everyone had a funeral home fan. If you kept the picture angled so you could see it, then everyone else had to stare at your funeral home advertisement. But if you tried to be considerate and show the rest of the room your Bible picture, then you had to contemplate the funeral home advertisement.

The Kirby house was little more than a shack with a shaky front porch that ran the full length of the house, a rectangle of three small rooms laid end to end. The outside was sided with grainy tar paper colored a brick red, a few of the thick sheets hanging askew because Hoyt spent all of his time either driving or working on cars. At one end of the house, Hoyt had taken the time to build a pit and a rack under a shed so he could work on the underside of his cars without having to lie on his back. At the other end of his house, Hoyt had built another shed which sheltered a pile of automotive parts.

Hoyt's oldest child, Larry, was the envy of all the neighborhood children because he had free access to any of the car parts that Hoyt didn't keep locked in the back of a wheel-less panel truck resting on cinderblocks behind the house.

As early as they were, Marleen counted fifteen cars already nudged up to one another in Betty's yard. Three or four men with their arms crossed leaned against one of the cars, listening to another man talk about a ride he once took with Hoyt up the twisting road to Boone. "The fog was so thick, I had to get out and walk on the shoulder of the road so Hoyt could see where to steer." The man laughed and shook his head at his feet.

"That was the slowest Hoyt ever drove, I bet," another man said.

Marleen's daddy spoke to each man, calling them by name. She wondered why Curtis didn't run for some kind of public office. He seemed to know everybody, and so did her mama. Both of them liked to get out and be around other people—but not the same kind of people. Actually, her daddy enjoyed this kind of get-together more than her mama did. He liked to talk to strangers or people he only half knew. Adele preferred to visit with her family and people she knew from work. Marleen knew that for the next three or four hours they stayed at Betty's house, her mama probably wouldn't sit down. Even if the place had been cleaned up, Adele wouldn't want to commit her backside to any of Betty's furniture. Curtis, on the other hand, could make himself comfortable anywhere. Marleen thought maybe the war had made her daddy so careless about plopping down in the mangiest-looking chairs or on a couch that was stained and smelly. But he wouldn't think about sitting tonight. He'd go in the house, maybe pat Betty on the shoulder, then go back outside to lean against the cars with the other men.

As they made their way up to the porch, squeezing between the men leaning on the rails up the steps, Marleen caught a whiff of whiskey breath. It was a sweet, dusky odor, very much like sundown after a warm, hazy day. Such a smell also carried with it a vague threat. You could never tell what a man with that kind of breath might decide to do, but Marleen liked the idea that somebody, later in the evening, might fall off the porch or maybe threaten to punch somebody. Of course, at a visitation, all of the drinking would be done in the shadows. Flagrant guzzling was considered more disrespectful than rolling down the steps of the porch or yelling about how much better off dead people were.

The porch, which had a natural sag when empty, creaked with the weight of visitors, all of whom were smoking to discourage the mosquitoes. The cigarette smoke was so thick that it looked as if someone had tacked up a gauze screen. Marleen took deep breaths. She loved the smell of cigarettes and how thoughtful people looked when they were smoking. She had practiced in front of the mirror, knitting up her brows when she inhaled. All the serious smokers who she knew seemed just about to solve a profound problem when they inhaled.

On one of their trips out in the woods with the Calloway kids from across the road, Marleen had let Phyllis and Dennis talk her into letting Dennis try to smoke. That was last summer, and they weren't supposed to be in the woods at all. Because of the polio epidemic, they'd been ordered to stay around the house. Every morning, they'd been given that order. Around eleven o'clock, when Marleen was listening to "Queen for a Day," Phyllis had come into the kitchen with three of the Calloways and begun begging her to go with them to the fort they'd built in the woods. Holly Calloway, who was Phyllis's age, was carrying one of her mother's old purses—a sure sign that they had snagged some cigarettes from somewhere.

Once they had gotten to the fort and watched Gerald Calloway, a cigarette behind his ear and a wooden match clenched between his teeth, climb to the top of an oak tree to watch for trespassers, Dennis and Phyllis had started in on Marleen to let Dennis try his first cigarette. Although Marleen had pretended to scoff at Phyllis's argument that it would be a shame if Dennis caught polio and died before he had tasted a cigarette, she had secretly agreed with Phyllis. After all, the polio was hitting close. The Welch sisters had both caught it. One had died after only a couple of weeks. The other, who had been in Marleen's home economics class, was paralyzed from the waist down and lived in an iron lung. For a week or so after Marleen had heard about the Welch sisters, she had walked around watching herself breathe. Her daddy had gone up to the hospital in Asheville with Mr. Welch to see his daughter— Carla was her name. He'd told his family at supper that evening about the sounds made by all those iron lungs in the iron lung ward. "In some ways, it was worse than anything I saw in the war," he concluded, finishing off his iced tea.

So Marleen allowed Dennis to light up. Under the pressure of Phyllis's encouragement, Dennis took big puffs, swallowing more of the smoke than he was inhaling. Like Phyllis and the Calloway kids, Marleen had laughed when Dennis had his coughing fit, but then he had turned more red and green than she'd ever seen him. No sooner had they pulled him up and walked him out of his coughing fit than he started throwing up.

From his perch up in the oak, Gerald yelled, "Don't let him do that in the fort!"

They took Dennis down to the creek that snaked its way through the woods, and Marleen rubbed cold water on his face, arms, and feet. Phyllis and Gerald brought him a crawdad to play with, but Dennis didn't like the way it kept trying to pinch his fingers, so he tossed the creature back into the creek. Marleen had been so relieved that he was over his sick spell that she let him ride the Tarzan vine that Gerald had discovered that spring. When ridden by an expert like Gerald, the vine could carry someone from one lip of the small ravine, across the creek, almost to the opposite lip. For nearly two hours, Dennis rode the vine and climbed the sides of the ravine.

When the three of them got home, Marleen could tell that Dennis was more exhausted than he'd ever been, but he still wanted to play while Marleen and Phyllis started getting supper ready. Before they could get the green beans strung, Adele had walked in—nearly two hours early. She'd just changed out of her cafeteria uniform when Dennis came in, complaining of being dizzy and sick to his stomach. Marleen and Phyllis had exchanged guilty looks, but Adele had been too busy feeling Dennis's forehead to notice her daughters.

The doctor had been called; Curtis was called. Marleen had never seen her mama so frightened. At first, she thought she should tell her about the cigarettes, but then she thought if Dennis really was getting polio, then the cigarette didn't matter much. Of course, Phyllis was all for keeping quiet about the cigarette. And when the doctor announced that Dennis was just suffering from a mild form of heat exhaustion, both Adele and Curtis were so relieved that Marleen couldn't bring herself to tell them about the cigarette. She didn't want to unsettle their relief by stirring up their anger. Marleen did take the responsibility for letting Dennis play too hard in the heat, but she still felt guilty. Since last summer, though, the guilt had simmered down to a little nagging occasionally in one corner of her stomach.

Her guilt was always stronger in places like Betty Kirby's crowded, smoky porch. And just being around Betty Kirby made Marleen feel guilty. She wasn't quite sure why. Tonight, maybe it was because Betty's husband was dead, packed in his casket right there in the living room. Through the smoke, through the rusty screen door with the little tufts of cotton blocking some of the larger holes in the screen, through the numb air in the shack, Marleen could see the casket, seeming to float on top of a heavy skirt of black velvet, against the wall opposite the door. At either end of the casket stood black wrought-iron flower holders stuffed with lilies whose cool whiteness seemed about to ignite the dense smells of special-occasion perfume and Vitalis.

Marleen looked over her shoulder, back to where the men were leaning against cars, talking about the rides they'd had with Hoyt. Marleen tried to imagine how it felt to drive faster than the posted speeds, with the windows rolled down and a cigarette burning close to her lips. If she had taken more rides with Hoyt, she might have eventually found herself doing an illegal quarter mile with him.

She had seen Hoyt that morning before he got killed. He was coming out of his driveway, the engine of his Ford throbbing as if the car had swallowed several bass drums. As usual, he had asked her if she needed a ride, and she had said no. Why, she might have been riding with him that night. Marleen glanced around the people on the porch to see if anyone was staring at her. She and her family had joined an informal line that slanted its way through the front door and circled off to the left of the living room, out of sight.

"Now, Marleen, I meant what I said a few minutes ago." Adele checked her lipstick in a compact mirror. "After you say your regrets to Betty, you park yourself close by and keep an eye on Phyllis and Dennis."

"What's holding that casket up?" Phyllis was asking the question to anybody on the porch within hearing range. She knew her mama and daddy would just tell her to keep quiet.

"I bet it's a table under that black tablecloth." Dennis was leaning to one side, trying to catch a glimpse of wood or metal under the velvet skirt.

"It's an expandable cart," one man said to Phyllis, holding his fists out in front of him and moving them together, then apart to the full extension of his arms as if he were playing an accordian. "It's made out of steel. Squeezes up to about three, four feet wide, but still takes two men to carry it."

"I'd like to see that." Phyllis leaned over like Dennis, trying to find a space in the velvet skirt.

Adele gave Phyllis a shake and straightened her back up. "Act like you've got some sense, honey." She kept her hands on Phyllis's shoulders and aimed a smile of appeal in Marleen's direction.

One of Hoyt's aunts came to the door, looking like she might be counting how many people were still waiting to get in. She held her watch up close to her eyes, shook it, held it up to first one ear, then the other. "Nobody's watch is working in here," she announced to the crowd on the porch. Several arms went up and went through the same motions that the aunt's arm had just gone through. From different parts of the porch, voices echoed, "Mine's stopped too."

Curtis and Adele held their watches up to their ears. "Mine's all right," Curtis said, loosening the band so he could wipe away the sweat around his wrist.

"Could be they just forgot to wind them." Adele held her watch up to Curtis's ear so he could hear it ticking.

By this time, they had eased their way to the front door. Marleen felt the warmer air pressing against her face. Inside, she saw a few funeral home fans waving slowly. Hoyt's aunt remained standing by the front door. As wrinkled as her dark blue dress looked, Marleen supposed that the woman had been preparing for the visitation all day. Easing by the aunt, Marleen noticed that two of Hoyt's brothers were standing at the foot of the casket, munching on celery sticks stuffed with pimento cheese. Marleen was surprised that Betty would be serving that kind of food, since most people saved the stuffed celery for wedding and baby showers.

Hoyt's brothers were not as famous as Hoyt and always seemed to resent their brother's success. They drove souped-up cars, but they didn't drive as well as Hoyt. In fact, it was Hoyt who helped his brothers get their cars sounding throaty and mean. But when they tried to drive fast, the law always managed to catch them. Even with their backs partially turned to her, Marleen could tell that the brothers were dissatisfied with something. When one of the brothers wasn't rubbing the casket or fingering the silver ornaments on the side, the other one was testing the steadiness of the stand supporting the casket or he was exploring the fine line that showed where the casket would open if it had been opened.

At the opposite end of the room, sitting on a scarlet love seat beneath a picture of a cottage illuminated by a large crescent moon, Betty Hoyt leaned against her elbow and listened to the words of condolence being shed by each visitor who stood over her, stroking her plump hand. Beside her sat Odeena Kirby, Hoyt's mother.

On the wall behind Betty and Odeena—and looking very much out of place in the house of mourning—was Hoyt's collection of racing trophies. Marleen wondered how the fragile walls of the shack supported the gaudy weight of trophies shaped like cars, checkered flags, and car tires with little wings sticking out of the hubs. Marleen remembered how disappointed she had been three or four years ago when Hoyt had told her that the trophies weren't really gold, and she had learned from Gerald Calloway that Hoyt often traded his second- and third-place trophies for cartons of cigarettes.

Beside Betty stood Larry. As soon as a visitor dropped Betty's hand, Larry stretched out his hand to be shaken. Unlike his mother, who simply let her hand be held while she vaguely studied the face expressing sympathy for her loss, Larry would gaze intently into each visitor's face and hold on to the sympathetic hand with both of his. Marleen had seen that double-handed shake before at church. Preacher Dillard always grabbed you with both of his hands, one squeezing your palm and the other squeezing your wrist. Marleen could imagine Preacher Dillard coming over earlier in the day just to give Larry handshaking lessons.

On the couch beside Betty, Odeena swayed slightly as she fanned herself and shook hands. The front of her dress glistened, at first making Marleen think that the woman had mistakenly bought a black evening dress with sequins for this occasion. Then Marleen realized that the woman was crying so much, refusing to use a handkerchief, that she was getting her dress wet. Sloppy sorrow—that's what they'd call it at school— but Marleen knew that all the women in the neighborhood, especially women like Odeena and Betty, and even her own mother, gave in to grief the way they probably once gave in to love, like standing under a falling piano with their arms spread out.

Somehow, Phyllis had gotten detached from Curtis's grip and had drifted back beside Marleen. In a slightly softened voice, Phyllis was singing "Come on-a My House." It was Phyllis's favorite song, and had been for three years. Whenever she wanted to cause trouble, she sang that song because she thought it was sexy and shocking. Marleen could tell by Phyllis's glance that she was planning on easing her way back to where the casket was displayed. Trying to appear loving, Marleen slipped her arm around Phyllis's neck and pulled her

back into line, bumping Adele as she did. Without even looking back, Adele pulled Phyllis in front of her and locked her
arms over Phyllis's shoulders. This restraining embrace meant
that Phyllis would be dragged from group to group until the
visit was over, a way of controlling Phyllis that was probably
harder on Adele than on her daughter.

"Thank you, sugar. Thank you, sugar," was all that
Odeena Kirby said when Marleen finally got to shake her
hand. It was moist from all the other hands it had held, and all
Marleen could feel were tendons and knuckles against her
palm. Odeena's face was wet from her eyes down. The sight of
the water collecting along the older woman's jaw made Marleen's neck itch.

Fighting the urge to wipe her hand on her skirt when
Odeena released her grip, Marleen wasn't ready to take
Betty's hand, but the widow, without taking her eyes from
Marleen's face, somehow got her fingers wrapped around
Marleen's hand and pulled her closer. Marleen was more
unsettled by this hand than she was by the mother-in-law's
hand. Holding Betty's hand was like holding on to a large,
slightly moist mushroom. When Betty took hold of Marleen's
wrist with her other hand, Marleen noticed that Betty's fingernail polish was as red as her lipstick.

"I'm glad you come," Betty said, pulling Marleen into a
stoop. "And I know Hoyt would be glad."

Before she could answer, Marleen heard Phyllis, who had
been whispering to Larry, start laughing. For a moment, the
din of conversation sagged just enough to let Adele know that
her daughter had been heard. She clamped her hand over
Phyllis's mouth and headed off for the darkest part of the
house she could find.

"That's okay, Adele, let her laugh." Betty spoke too slowly
to have any effect on Adele, who only smiled back at her and
pulled Phyllis across the room.

"Don't encourage Phyllis," Marleen said. "I'm supposed
to stand guard close to you so she won't get on your nerves."

"Why, I don't know if I've got nerves that can be got on."
Betty turned to Larry and said, "Go get Marleen a chair and

put it here beside me." She watched the boy disappear into the crowd, then turned back to Marleen. "You was one of Hoyt's favorites."

"Oh, I think he liked everybody." Marleen glanced to her side, wondering how much longer Betty was going to make her hold up the line.

"No. He was friendly to about everybody, but he didn't like a whole lot of people." Betty continued to hold Marleen's hand.

Marleen noticed that two people in the line right behind her had stood looking down on Betty for a few seconds, but when they realized that Betty was talking on and on to Marleen, they drifted off without expressing their sympathy. "Look, Betty. There's a lot of other people who want to talk to you." Marleen glanced over her shoulder, expecting to see her mama wading through the crowd, coming to pull her away from Betty the way she had pulled Phyllis away from Larry.

"I'll get around to them by and by." Betty didn't actually smile, but her drawl contained a faint vibration that made Marleen dip her head and study the widow more closely.

Beside her, Marleen heard someone say something to Odeena about the closed casket. As if a nerve had been pinched, Odeena flared up and replied, "Nobody asked me about keeping the casket closed."

Betty let go of Marleen's hands long enough to grasp Odeena's elbow. "Now, Odeena, you heard what Mr. Soots said about Hoyt's condition. We don't want people seeing him all misfigured."

Although Odeena let Betty hold her elbow, she continued to hold the hand of her most recent sympathizer. "Maybe you and Mr. Soots don't want to see Hoyt one last time, but I do. And I know his two brothers do."

Betty leaned back on the love seat and occupied herself for a few seconds with fluffing up the ruffled collar on her dress. Marleen realized that the dress wasn't solid black but had faint waves of dark purple woven in the fabric. Once Betty felt more adjusted, she turned back to her mother-in-

law and said, "Mr. Soots is the expert. And he said we was better off not seeing Hoyt." She put her arm around Odeena's
shoulder. "Mr. Soots said he just finally had to give up on fixing Hoyt. And everybody says you got to be pretty bad for
Mr. Soots to give up on you."

"I don't want to see him because he's pretty but because
he's my son." Odeena refused to look at Betty. Instead she
appealed to the woman whose hand she held on to.

Larry plowed through the visitors, dragging what looked
like an old kitchen chair he'd found outside somewhere. It
was rusty and the vinyl seat was ripped, cotton stuffing rising
from it like small explosions.

"Lordy, baby," Betty almost sat straight up. "Is that the
best chair you could find?"

"All the good chairs got people on 'em." Larry pushed the
chair in beside the couch.

Fishing behind her, Betty found a red satin pillow in the
shape of a heart. "Put this on the seat."

Marleen was glad to move out of the flow of sympathiz-
ers. And sitting beside Betty gave her a good view of the room
full of visitors. If she knew her daddy, he had dragged Dennis
outside to sit on the bumper of a car while he drank beer with
the other men. Adele had probably forced Phyllis into the
kitchen to help her keep the food trays neatly arranged.
Working in the factory cafeteria, Adele was better than anyone in the neighborhood about knowing how to arrange cold
cuts and cut-up vegetables. For the most part, people were
just clumped together talking about their jobs and their families.

During a lull in the hand shaking, Betty leaned closer to
Marleen and said, "Don't that casket look clean?"

It was a silver-blue coffin. The corners were rounded, and
the top edges were beveled all around. To Marleen, it looked
like a jet. And it did look cleaner than anything or anybody in
the muggy room. "Did you pick it out?" Marleen hoped that
she wasn't going to start sounding like Phyllis. But she didn't
quite know what to make of Betty. This was the longest conversation she'd ever had with the woman.

Before answering, Betty glanced at her mother-in-law, then leaned closer to Marleen. She had her long hair in a bun on top of her head, and Marleen was able to see how small the widow's ears were. "To tell the truth, I couldn't find a casket that I thought Hoyt would like, one with dual exhaust and a V-8 motor, so I went ahead and got one that made me feel good." She spoke carefully, as if she knew Marleen wasn't used to hearing her talk.

"It looks like a piece of sky." Marleen caught a whiff of Betty's perfume, and she was almost certain it was coming from behind her ear.

"That's what I thought." Betty nodded her head a little closer toward Marleen. "Fresh and clean, like in the morning when you just get up and look out the window toward the mountains and don't have to answer to anybody for a few minutes, before you have to settle down and look around at what's to be done."

"It must make you awfully sad, though." For a moment, Marleen wondered if she would feel so awkward if Betty instead of Hoyt had been killed. Sitting beside him, listening to him talk while he gunned his engine was like running her finger along the blade of her daddy's knife—that blade he sharpened on the belt sander at work.

Without answering, Betty leaned away from Marleen, picked up one of the funeral home fans that she had stuck between her thigh and the arm of the love seat, and waved the cardboard slowly under her chin. She had the funeral home advertisement side facing Marleen. Death, Where is thy sting? Courtesy of Soots-Lanier Funeral Home. Although Marleen couldn't feel the air being stirred up by Betty's fan, she could see the stray hairs along Betty's temple quivering.

On the other side of the room, Adele had appeared, a bleached feed sack tied around her waist. In one hand, she carried a gut of bologna about ten inches long. Her other hand she shook, then held her wrist up to her ear. Marleen couldn't hear what her mama was asking the man who stood beside her, but in a moment, the man looked down at his watch, studied it briefly, then shook his wrist. When Adele realized that the man's watch was also stopped, she turned to the men who were standing around the foot of the casket. Marleen saw at the same time her mother saw that those men were too absorbed in watching Hoyt's brothers inspecting the bolts on the casket lid to give her the time. Adele turned and disappeared into the kitchen.

Imperceptibly, Betty had leaned back within confiding range of Marleen's ear. "It's going to be a lot different with Hoyt gone."

"Well, if the place gets too empty for you, come over to our house." Marleen saw that Phyllis had somehow escaped from her mama and was moving through the crowd with Larry, giving everybody the two-handed handshake.

"With the five kids, I don't expect emptiness to be the problem." Betty twisted around, her breasts straining the fabric of her dress, in order to look Marleen in the face. "There's a kind of man . . . "

Before she could finish, one of Hoyt's brothers eased up to Betty and tapped her knee. "Can I have the key to Hoyt's storage truck?" He was stooped and skinny. As he made his request, he kept two fingers on Betty's knee and his other hand hooked in his back pocket.

"Them tools belong to Larry now." Betty still talked slowly, but she sat up straight as she talked.

"I just want to *use* a socket wrench. I don't aim to pilfer from my dead brother's tool chest." The brother turned to Odeena. "Mama, tell Betty that she can trust me for a few minutes with one of Hoyt's socket wrenches." He took his mama's hand and pulled her up. "You can come with me and watch for Betty."

Betty leaned back and stared at the ceiling for a few seconds. Marleen thought maybe she had fallen asleep, so completely exhausted was her attitude.

Moving her eyes only slightly from the ceiling, Betty said, "The keys is on the nail just inside the kitchen."

As he led his mama away, the brother looked back at Betty and said, "We'll get that wrench right back in that truck."

Watching the two heading for the door, Betty waved her

fan lazily in their direction. "I don't care what you do with it."

"He's not going to work on his car now, is he?" If Phyllis weren't wandering around loose, Marleen could escape to the kitchen.

Betty reached out and clutched Marleen's arm. "Come up here on the couch before one of Hoyt's aunts sees this empty seat." She pulled Marleen to her feet and guided her around to the couch.

"Then you think he's going to really steal the wrench?" Marleen picked up the fan that Odeena had left in her seat. The picture showed the angel sitting at the mouth of the tomb with the stone rolled from the entrance. The other side of the fan said, He is not here but is risen. Courtesy of Soots-Lanier Funeral Home.

"Let me tell you about Hoyt Kirby and his brothers—and his mama for that matter." Betty squirmed around on the couch, getting more settled in. Then she leaned closer to Marleen, still fanning herself, and said, "They want everything their own way."

"We're all like that, ain't we?" Marleen knew she liked for people to act the way she wanted them to.

"Not like the Kirbys." Betty patted Marleen's arm. "Look at that casket again. I'm Hoyt's wife, and I wanted it to be closed. I had a brother get burned to death. I saw him. But Hoyt's brother has gone out to get a socket wrench, thinking he's going to open that casket one last time. And his mama is right beside him."

"I can tell my daddy . . . " Marleen actually pulled herself toward the edge of the couch, but Betty pulled her back.

"No. I want them to do it. I've thought about it, and I want everybody who's curious to see." Betty smiled.

While Marleen was trying to figure out how to get off the couch, Hoyt's brother and mother came back into the house, the brother carrying a wooden toolbox. Followed by his mother, he headed directly for the casket without even glancing at Betty.

"I'm going outside." Betty stood up and watched the people at the casket.

By the time the news reached the kitchen and Adele came hurrying out, untying her apron, Betty had guided Marleen up to the door. Adele caught up with them while she was still folding the apron. "Betty, I'm going to have to get my family out of here before they get that casket open." She looked around the room. "I don't see Phyllis anywhere."

"Adele, I'm going outside until they get their fill." Betty slipped her arm through Marleen's. "I think I saw Phyllis go outside with Larry. Why don't you round up your husband and boy while me and Marleen look for Phyllis."

After inspecting the room once more, Adele remembered she had the apron in her hands. When she started to return to the kitchen, Betty took it from her and tossed it behind a chair. "I'll pick it up tomorrow."

When they got into the yard, Adele drifted toward the parked cars where she suspected Curtis would be drinking beer and lining up a poker game. Betty suggested that she and Marleen circle around to the side of the house where Larry and Phyllis might have gone to look at auto parts. After the heavy air of the living room, the night air felt frail and treacherous, and her feet didn't want to go where she wanted them to. But Betty kept pulling her along.

Trying to appear casual while she waited for Betty to loosen her grip on her arm, Marleen pretended to search the shadows under the shed for Phyllis and Larry. "I don't think they're here."

Pulling Marleen into the deeper darkness under the shed, Betty replied, "Well, we can wait on them a little bit. Larry would sleep out here if I'd let him."

"I bet he misses his daddy." Marleen was briefly numbed by the smell of old motor oil and grease, which made her tongue feel dry and grainy. Drifting through the dark air at a higher altitude was the smell of gasoline. As her eyes adjusted to the shadow under the shed, Marleen caught glimpses of glittering steel from the corners of her eyes. Her hand brushed against an oil drum whose sides were unexpectedly cool. This was the place where Hoyt cleaned his automotive parts. More of his presence rested here than in the casket.

Betty let go of Marleen's arm, and from the rustling of her dress, Marleen could tell that the widow had hopped up on a table. Betty's voice came from an unexpected altitude, but she seemed to be leaning close to Marleen's ear. "Do the mosquitoes get you bad?"

Seeing a chance to get away from Betty, Marleen slapped her arm loudly. "They eat me up. I ought to get back inside."

"You don't want to go back in there with the casket about to be opened." Betty grew very still.

Since Betty had mentioned it, Marleen did notice that the mosquitoes seemed to be paying a lot of attention to her. "Maybe if I get back moving around and try to find Phyllis, I can keep the bugs off me."

"No. Don't do that. Give them a chance to get satisfied." Betty's voice grew softer, more preoccupied. "They don't take that much, really."

"I don't even like the idea of one landing on me." Marleen rubbed her ear to block a high-pitched buzz.

"They're more delicate than butterflies," Betty replied. "They look like letters from some foreign alphabet that somebody wrote with a real sharp pen." She spoke as if she were sitting extremely still. "And they can talk, you know."

Marleen took a step away from Betty, then turned so she could keep her in full view. The yard between the shed and where the cars were parked was full of holes and clumps of grass. She knew she could outrun Betty, but she wasn't sure if she could cross the yard without falling on her face. "What do they say, Betty?"

"They tell the future." Betty settled softly in the dark. "I knew a long time ago that Hoyt was going to get killed."

Marleen found herself moving back toward Betty. "That's awful."

"Yes, it was. There wasn't anything I could do. Hoyt didn't like me to talk to him about what I knew. He had this need to fill me up, Marleen. Like it was his only job in this world to keep me full of babies. That was what love was for him, and he didn't want me intruding on his plans with who I

was. I was something he just wanted to fill up with his self."
Betty's voice had begun to swell.

"You don't have to worry about that now." Marleen realized that Betty wasn't simply talking about herself. The
widow's voice had reached a crest and was curving over Marleen's head. She wanted to get away from the shed before that
wave broke, but she felt as if her feet had become part of the
dark ground where she stood.

"Oh, I do, Marleen," Betty insisted. "And so do you.
That's why I wanted you to come out here with me." Her
dark form shifted slightly on the table. "You and me draw
men like Hoyt. I told you he liked you, and I meant it. There's
men out there who'll want to fill you up . . ."

As Betty talked, Marleen was aware of a low roar growing
inside the house. Two figures banged through the screen
door, jumped off the end of the porch, and came running to
the shed. Marleen recognized Phyllis's round blond head in
the light that spilled from the kitchen window. Marleen
darted from the shed and caught her sister around the waist.
"Did they get the casket open?" she asked, stepping in front
of Phyllis.

The roar rose in volume, spreading out now to reveal a
fluttering, soprano scream. For a second, Marleen, Phyllis,
and Larry froze, staring at the people pouring out of the back
door, trying to pour out of the front door but blocked by the
curious on the porch who crowded toward the front door,
pulled in by the shouts. Other visitors inside the shack fumbled with the flimsy window screens and tumbled out in a
gush of legs, arms, and heads—no longer separate bodies but
a stream of sweaty Sunday clothes wrapped around waving
appendages.

Burrowing through the uproar from the house, a small
sound came from Betty's dark form. Marleen thought maybe
the widow was laughing. It was a noise edged with the thread
of a small screw and buzzed against Marleen's ear, insistent.

Marleen grabbed Phyllis's hand. In it, she felt a dull chunk
of metal, which Phyllis let slide into her sister's fingers. Sur-

prisingly heavy for its size, but too hard for lead, the magnet tingled in Marleen's grasp.

"Don't tell where this come from." Phyllis kept her eyes on the house. "Or you'll get me and Larry in a lot of trouble. The last man whose watch we stopped caught us, but then the casket popped open."

The roar from the house, folding in on itself, now hung from the woman's scream as it was joined by several others, as if Hoyt had joined the party and was touching individual mourners on the shoulder.

A sob came from Betty's dark form. At least, Marleen wanted it to be a sob. It was a noise of moisture being sucked in, though, rather than being heaved out.

Darting toward the dirt road, Phyllis yelled, "Run!"

And glancing at the shadow sitting under the shed, Marleen did run, staying close to her sister, feeling the weight of the magnet settling in her abdomen.

LOST AT SEA

EVEN IN THE QUARTER-MOON July night, Adele
had no difficulty following Curtis along the path that ran
through the ragged field between their house and Curtis's
brother's house. Between the scrub black pines, the broomstraw, and the briers, the pink dust of the path glittered, seeming to throw back even the pointed light from the stars, even
the angry glow of Curtis's cigarette.

Of course, Curtis wasn't the one who was angry. Adele
knew that her husband could hardly wait to sit down at Lula
and Daniel's kitchen table and help them lay out their plans
for this summer's beach trip. Daniel was Curtis's closest
brother, but he still had a selfish streak in him that irritated
Adele. But all the men in Curtis's family were a little self-
centered. Adele had to admit that even her own brothers
could be a little inconsiderate . . . except for Dennis, who had
been killed in the navy, lost at sea. She had forgotten all of his
bad points long ago. Not all that long ago, she reminded herself. He had disappeared into the ocean in 1944—just about
thirteen years ago.

Darkness and warm weather always made Adele think of
Dennis. She had named her own son after her brother. She
wondered if that hadn't been a crazy notion. As if responding
to his uncle's name, little Dennis had yearly grown more and
more like a man he had never met: quiet, moody, dreamy, but
smart and stubborn. Then again, all three of Adele's children
were stubborn, her two older girls more than her son.

The glow of her husband's cigarette suddenly swooped from his mouth down to his side. "Now look there," Curtis said.

Adele could hear him aiming his raspy voice toward Lula's kitchen window, the only square of illumination attached to the uncertain form of the house fifty yards in front of them. Adele didn't have to glance back at their own house to know that as soon as they had gotten off the back porch and across their dirt driveway Phyllis had probably turned on all the lights in their house—which would be five, not counting the porch lights.

"One light is all that needs to be on." Curtis continued to walk, but Adele could tell from the way his voice sounded slightly strained that he had twisted his head back in her direction, probably counting the lights shining in their own flat-topped house.

"I think you're talking to the wrong person about burning lights." Adele smiled to herself. Curtis wasn't as bad as he used to be, but maybe once a month he'd manage to lose enough money playing poker to pay a light bill for a house three times as big as the one they lived in.

"I hoped you'd pass it on to the young 'uns." Curtis put the cigarette back to his lips.

"Advice always means more when it comes from their daddy." When she said this to Curtis, Adele wasn't actually thinking about the number of light bulbs sucking electricity in their house. She was thinking about her oldest daughter, Marleen. Maybe because she was tall and played basketball at school, wearing short pants and jumping around, Marleen had a fairly regular supply of boys stopping by the house. But Adele hadn't started worrying until the last few weeks, when Marleen began dating Gaither Drum, who was twenty-two and already working as an upholsterer for Blue Ridge Furniture. Marleen was about to turn eighteen and was more independent than Adele wanted to admit.

"Well, some subjects just don't get absorbed by young 'uns." Curtis resumed his walk, exhaling a plume of smoke that looped lazily over his head and splashed against Adele's face. She inhaled deeply.

As much as she wanted a cigarette, she didn't want to smoke around Lula. She had to keep on her guard around her sister-in-law. Lula and Daniel had been married for about six months now. From what Adele could see, more than anybody she'd ever known, Lula wanted to be more than what she was. Adele had told Curtis, several times, that if she ever caught Lula talking down to her, she was going to lower her sister-in-law's opinion of herself—even if she had to start by knocking her butt on the floor. Lula was raised in town, her mama and daddy working in Hibriten Fibers, factory workers just like most everybody else, but Lula always had to make some remark about Adele growing up in Wilkes County, as if Adele had run barefoot through the woods of the Brushy Mountains. Of course, Adele had spent a lot of her summers running barefoot through those woods, but her daddy had owned five hundred acres of land and a general store at one time—not to mention the three moonshine stills that eventually caused him to lose the store.

But the main reason Adele didn't want to enjoy a cigarette in Lula's company was so she could pay full attention to her own crazy notions. If she smoked, she got relaxed. If she got too relaxed, she might let her family craziness do a naked dance in front of Lula. Adele couldn't think about Lula without shaking her head. Lula with the copper hair and the splotchy freckles and the voice that had a slushy rattle to it, like a dollar's worth of pennies being shaken in a quart jar of water. It fell just short of being a whine and for that reason made Lula seem always full of her own noise and primed for correcting whoever she was talking to.

What really made Adele mistrust her sister-in-law was how normal she seemed. Lula wanted the world to be correct and wiped down. In the right place, Adele admitted, normal was fine. But it simply didn't belong in the Holsclaw family. At least it didn't belong to Curtis's branch of the Holsclaw family. But maybe his brother, Daniel, did deserve a wife like

Lula. After all, Daniel was getting some control of his life. And having control was part of what being normal meant.

Curtis and Adele had stepped over the small ditch that separated the field from Daniel's backyard. The grass was already damp, and Adele could feel her feet getting wet in just the short time it took her to reach Daniel's basement door, which Curtis was pulling open. The scent of creosote swept out of the basement and made Adele's feet feel even wetter. More often than not, Daniel smelled like the creosoted phone poles he stored in his basement. After all, he spent six or seven hours a day hugged up to them. Adele could tolerate the smell, although if she had to breathe it straight in for too long, she could feel oily patches forming in the lower part of her brain. The smell reminded her of the men who worked in the finishing room at the furniture factory where she worked as a baker and server in the cafeteria.

Adele could hear Curtis fumbling for the light switch at the bottom of the basement stairs. "You'd think they'd leave the light in the basement on for us."

"It'll be on soon enough." Curtis continued to fumble. His bobbing cigarette told Adele that despite the tolerance in his voice, Curtis was getting irritated because the switch didn't seem to be anywhere close to where it usually was.

"You ever worry about grabbing hold of a big old hairy spider when you're feeling around for that switch?" Adele wanted Curtis to be more honest about how irritated he was.

"As long as Dan keeps them poles down here, the smell will keep away all the spiders . . . and the snakes too." Curtis found the switch. A yellow bug light bloomed at the top of the stairs.

It was just like Lula to have a bug light at the top of her basement stairs. Adele had bug lights on her front and back porches, but if she had a basement, she wouldn't have thought about putting a bug light there. "If them poles keep their basement so free from bugs, why does Lula burn that yellow light?"

Curtis swiveled around to face Adele. "Don't start in on her." He tried to drop his voice to a whisper, but the years he'd worked in the factory, having to yell all day long to be heard by the men around him, had limited the flexibility of his voice. When he tried to whisper, he just sounded raspier.

To Adele, her husband's voice came like a patch of wide-bladed grass. Whenever he whispered, the thickness of the grass stayed the same, but its color changed from green to brown. She patted Curtis on the back. If Lula had been just a little more grateful for the advice that Adele offered her when she had visited the newlyweds the first few times, Adele would have liked Lula more. But Lula always responded to advice by correcting whoever gave it to her. And usually she was right. She had told Adele once that she could learn more from reading magazines than she could from talking to her neighbors. Adele knew that Lula hadn't meant to hurt her feelings—but she had hurt them.

Adele had met people like Lula back during the war, when she worked at the big hotel up in the tourist town of Windy Gap. But all of them had come down from up north or up from Florida. Usually, they came to Windy Gap in the summer to get away from the heat, but the hotel had stayed open all winter in 1943 because people who had the money wanted to get away from the coast. They felt safer up in the mountains. While all of them acted nervous—but relieved—not that many treated the hotel workers with much consideration. Or when they were considerate, they were trying to work you into a corner . . . Adele gave Curtis a push so she would stop thinking about the Windy Gap Hotel and Resort. It reminded her of how crazy she was even when she was separated from her husband's family.

"Company's on the stairs." Lula's voice vibrated through the door.

Where Adele had grown up, "company" referred to people who weren't related to the people they visited. Knowing that Lula thought of her as company made Adele feel awkward, and she resented Lula for keeping her at a distance. However, Adele knew that Curtis would tell her to stop being so sensitive about a word. People who were raised in town used "company" to refer to relatives—and that was that.

Adele wanted to explain to Curtis that in Lula's mouth, "company" sounded like a step down from "relative." But Curtis would just argue that she was being unreasonable.

Lula opened the door. She carried a box of vanilla wafers. "Is the dew out yet?"

"In buckets." Curtis raised one of his brogans for Lula's inspection.

"You might want to slip them off so you don't slide on the linoleum." Lula remained in the doorway.

"You mean you don't mind if your company goes barefoot in your house?" Adele knew that the linoleum would be slick, and she didn't like to sit around with damp shoes. Nevertheless, she suspected Lula of treating her like a hillbilly.

"I'm barefoot." Lula shifted a little to one side when she saw that Adele had begun to remove her shoes. "I don't know what it is about Daniel, but he refuses to take off his shoes, even if it means tracking mud into the house. I wonder if it's because he fought the Japanese during the war."

As he leaned against the wall and slid a shoe off his long, narrow foot, Curtis shook his head. "Daniel and me and all of us was raised to keep our shoes on. Our daddy thought walking around the house barefoot was as bad as walking around without your pants on. All your clothes was equal."

"Even when the weather is as hot as this?" Lula's voice straddled being a question and being pure agreement.

"Old Mr. Holsclaw would tell you that if you pay too much attention to the weather, you're in danger of not paying enough attention to more important matters." Adele slapped the soles of her shoes together—more to call attention to them than to knock off any loose dirt. She didn't want to leave them on the basement stairs. No telling what might crawl into them once the bug light was turned off. Adele didn't fully share Curtis's belief that the smell of creosote repelled spiders.

"Just leave your shoes on the top step." Lula moved toward the kitchen.

As Adele eased by Curtis, who was having a little trouble getting his socks adjusted, she whispered, "Don't let me forget to shake out my shoes before I put them back on."

"I hope we never live in a house that has a basement or you'll never have any peace." Curtis squeezed the toe of his sock. "I'm wet."

Adele stooped down, and using her fingernails, pulled Curtis's sock up. She didn't think to say anything sarcastic because she knew Curtis's fingertips had been damaged by German frostbite. His toes and his ears were also marked by small bluish red explosions that resembled mimosa blossoms. The only color of socks he could wear was white because the dye from other colors irritated his frostbite. Before the war, Curtis had always liked burgundy socks—regardless of what color his pants might have been.

Although Daniel had been in the navy—in the Pacific—he had come back with foot problems, too. Some kind of fungus. Given a choice, Adele thought she preferred being married to a man with frostbitten feet. Fungus could be passed along to others. If Dennis hadn't been lost at sea, he'd probably have come back with a fungus, too. But Dennis would have pulled off his shoes and aired his feet out until the fungus dried up. Of all her brothers who went off to the war, and came home, Adele thought that Dennis was the one who had wanted to come home the most.

She'd found out about Dennis being lost while she still worked at the Windy Gap Hotel and Resort. The housekeeping supervisor, Gill Mathis, had told her that losing one brother out of seven wasn't so bad. Then he had told her to follow him up to the hotel's attic. She'd been too upset to wonder what he might need with her help up in the attic. Adele didn't want to think about Gill Mathis or about being lost at sea.

She didn't really want to think about going to the ocean, but Curtis, Phyllis, and little Dennis wanted to go. Of course, Daniel and Lula wanted to go, too. That meant Curtis and Daniel would spend their days fishing either from a pier or from a boat. Lula would probably cook herself on the beach, while Adele would have to watch Phyllis and Dennis to make sure they didn't wind up lost at sea.

This was the first summer that Marleen didn't want to

make the trip. Adele didn't know if she was relieved or irritated. Usually Marleen was awfully good to help keep a watch on the two younger children, but for the last couple of years, since she'd gone boy crazy, Marleen couldn't always be depended on. And she'd gotten even worse since she started driving a car. Adele wasn't sure if it was the driving or the boys that made Marleen seem so wild. Maybe one led to the other. Or Adele was just as willing to admit that maybe her oldest daughter seemed so wild because she came from the Holsclaws and the Scotts.

Once Adele was off the basement stairs and facing toward Lula's kitchen, a darkened bedroom and a darkened living room between her and the dome-shaped ceiling light of the kitchen, the odor of creosote began to give way to that of coffee. Sometimes when they visited Lula, she forgot to offer them coffee. Lula, Adele suspected, didn't like to give herself any more work than necessary. And if you fixed coffee for people, you had cups and saucers to wash. Besides, fixing coffee for her relatives probably made Lula feel too related to them. But Daniel must have made Lula realize that planning the trip to the beach was important business.

Making her way slowly toward the kitchen—somewhere between the bedroom and the living room was a small table where the telephone sat, which always managed to sneak up against Adele's knee—she fought the impulse to switch on the lights in each room. From the kitchen came the sound of vanilla wafers being poured into a bowl. On other visits, Lula had simply passed around the box. And Adele could see how that made sense. But what she wanted was for Lula to be nicer—even if it meant making less sense. Adele didn't trust people who made sense all of the time.

Already sitting at the table, Daniel had two maps in front of him. "Did Curtis get lost?" Daniel leaned to the side so he could see around Adele. "Lula, why didn't you turn the lights on?"

"I figured they knew the way. They made it all the way across the field without any lights." Lula smiled as she spoke.

It might have been the kind of smile a person used when

she had pulled something over on you. Or it might have been the kind of smile that showed how self-centered she was. Adele studied Lula's face. All she wanted was the slightest clue that her sister-in-law knew how uncomfortable she was making their visits.

On the other hand, Adele wanted to guard against her own craziness. She remembered how, for a brief second, she had felt quite excited by the impact of the slop jar against Gill Mathis's head. That had to show she was crazy. She had followed him up to the hotel's attic. In one of the dusty storerooms, he had shown her where the hotel kept all its old slop jars. At first, the hundreds of white porcelain chamber pots looked like a field of giant skulls. In one corner of the room was a couch, which was conspicuously less dusty than the rest of the contents of the room.

Before Adele could get over her amazement at the expanse of slop jars, Gill Mathis was pushing up against her, feeling her breasts and moving her toward the couch. Used to being roughed around by her brothers—all of them stronger and meaner than Gill Mathis—Adele had felt angry more than fearful. Falling back on the lessons she'd learned as a child, she turned her attention to finding a way to make the odds more even. In a roomful of slop jars, the obvious choice of a weapon was one of the five-pound pots. So intent was Gill on trying to untie Adele's apron, he didn't even notice when she leaned over to grab the handle of one of the slop jars or when she turned slightly around and slung her arm sideways to slam the pot against his ear and jaw.

Gill Mathis had twirled around a couple of times, once up on his toes, then once with his knees starting to buckle. He'd slumped over one arm of the couch. Adele didn't feel the need to check him for damage. She could see that he was still breathing. "You can take that as my notice," she said and left the hotel, still carrying the slop jar. They had used that pot up until five years ago, when Curtis had built them an indoor toilet. Now Adele used it for her geraniums.

On some nights, especially when Adele was worrying about how her children would grow up, the thought of what she might have done to Gill Mathis made her stomach turn cold. If she had been afraid of him as well as angry, she might have swung that pot even harder. He might have been killed or turned into a vegetable. She'd have been sent off or maybe locked up in the insane asylum.

To clear her head, Adele went over to where Lula was pouring out the coffee and took a deep breath of air. Tonight she'd drink her coffee black, even though she liked milk in it when she was having vanilla wafers. Black coffee kept her alert to what was going on around her. The memory of Gill Mathis always made her want a cigarette, but it was going to be a long wait because Daniel and Curtis could never agree on the best route to the beach. They'd always start out by disagreeing about which beach to go to. Curtis favored Carolina Beach because he didn't like driving the South Carolina roads to Myrtle Beach, which was Daniel's first choice. Daniel preferred Myrtle Beach because he argued that South Carolina beaches felt more tropical to him than North Carolina beaches. Because Curtis was the older brother, they always wound up going to Carolina Beach, but Adele thought this year might be different. Now, for the first time, Daniel had someone on his side. Lula would surely want to go to Myrtle Beach just to help Daniel finally have his way.

For her part, Adele would prefer to stay at home. The ocean was too hot. The people were too rude. She had to keep an eye on Dennis and Phyllis to make sure they didn't drown or let the sand in their bathing suits give them rashes. But all the time they played close to the ocean, Adele felt as if she were holding her breath. She had been in the water and knew how it pulled you away from the land. She had felt the sand speeding from under her feet. And if you fell down, trying to crawl out of the back rush, the beach felt as if it were sinking right out from under you, so if you weren't pulled out into the dark water, you'd simply disappear into a sandy hole like one of those little sand crabs.

She didn't like the way the waves boomed either. Sometimes they were as loud as cannons. Curtis had told her that they sounded like artillery. Sometimes the waves exploded. Adele had been knocked down enough by the water to know how roughly her brother must have died. Then disappeared. Oh, she knew people could disappear in the mountains, but at least they had a chance to walk out. That was all Adele asked for was a chance to get out of a place on her own power. Being crazy wasn't hopeless as long as you could feel the ground. It wasn't so bad as long as your family could come and pull you out, the way Curtis and Daniel had pulled their daddy out of Norfolk. There was another town too close to the ocean as far as Adele was concerned. She would bet a month's paycheck that Daniel hadn't told Lula about his daddy running off to Norfolk back in 1940. But on the other hand, Adele couldn't imagine a woman being married to a Holsclaw and not suspecting a few hollow branches on the family tree.

Lula poured Adele a cup of coffee. You had to go to Lula to get your coffee. She wouldn't wait on her company. On her way to her place at the table, Adele paused to study the maps, leaning over Daniel's shoulder. She knew that Lula was a little jealous of her, even if she did come from Wilkes County. Lula was about as hugable as a hatchet. Adele still wondered what Daniel found attractive about his sharp-shouldered wife. Maybe he hoped to tone down the Holsclaw blood with Lula's miserly tendencies.

"Got the roads marked for Carolina Beach yet?" Curtis eased into the kitchen, uncomfortable in his sock feet. Because of his frostbite, he had to wear the ends of his socks pulled well beyond the tips of his toes. With his skinny ankles and his socks pointed out, he looked like an elf.

"Well, we've got a couple of possibilities to start with." Daniel leaned back in his chair and studied his maps from a distance, and he continued to study them until Curtis had received his coffee from Lula and sat down at the table.

"Wait." Curtis pulled his chair closer to the table. "Don't you want to tell me about how much nicer the beaches are at Myrtle?"

"No." Daniel smoothed a corner of one of his maps. "This will be Lula's first trip to the ocean, and she wants to stay as close to home as she can on her first visit."

"I thought for sure Daniel would tell you how Myrtle Beach is really closer than Carolina Beach." Curtis pulled one of the maps toward himself. "See, the coastline curves in at South Carolina . . ."

"It's not the distance." Lula spoke in Curtis's direction, but her gaze was over his head.

Lula drooped slightly at the shoulders. Adele suspected it was a pose she had picked up from some of the magazines that she was always reading. Nevertheless, Adele wondered if Lula's insistence on staying in North Carolina might indicate that her sister-in-law was not as normal as she wanted to appear.

"I've just heard that people in South Carolina are more likely to rob you, especially if you got out-of-state license plates on your car." Lula poured a cup of coffee for herself and smiled at everyone. "You know a state that lets its people sell fireworks is more rowdy than a state that don't."

Adele couldn't help but nod. She had to agree, as disappointed as she was to realize that Lula had her sane reasons for staying out of South Carolina. Although Adele was supposed to come from one of the rougher parts of North Carolina, she had been amazed by the way the people in South Carolina touted their fireworks: the huge cinderblock buildings painted red, white, and blue with gigantic fake skyrockets planted on the roof or hanging from poles beside the road. And the owners always had some kind of snake or lizard collection for the children. The land itself looked whipped— whether you were driving through the swamps, which were all saw grass and stunted black pines, or you were driving through the cotton fields, which were skeletal and dry-looking even in the summer.

Once they had decided on which beach they were driving to, Daniel and Curtis always had to argue about when they were going to make the drive. Curtis preferred driving at night. Daniel maintained driving during the day was safer. Again, because Curtis was the older brother—and had three children—Daniel usually wound up agreeing to leave at Curtis's favorite time: midnight. Except for making the trip with the children asleep, Adele thought she would have preferred making the trip during the day. She always worried about what would happen if the car broke down at two o'clock some morning. Curtis assured her that between him and Daniel, no mechanical problems could keep them off the road for very long. Long ago, Adele had learned how to pack their vacation clothes around the clumps of replacement parts that Curtis always carried with him.

"You'll be glad to know that Lula wants us to leave in the middle of the night." Daniel frowned theatrically. Adele thought he looked like Robert Mitchum—except Daniel's face was longer and narrower.

"You should have married her a long time ago." Curtis propped his elbows on the table and glanced back and forth at Daniel and Lula.

"Our car gets so hot even with the windows rolled down." Lula spoke now to Adele. "Besides, I figure I can sleep most of the way."

Adele wondered if Lula would sleep in the front seat or the back. She had a theory that you could tell a person's craziness by how she slept. She wasn't sure if the theory was true for men. But she had watched her daughters sleep, and she was worried. Phyllis was restless. Even as an infant, Phyllis had traveled all around her crib each night. She wouldn't wake up, but she would roll, crawl, and twist as if she were drowning. Not until Phyllis was three did Adele discover what pattern she followed. One night, Adele was watching her fumble across her bed. Through the window, Adele noticed the moon edging across the sky. Phyllis was tracking the moon in her sleep. When she realized what her daughter was doing, Adele had to lean against the door frame. For the following week, Adele had watched Phyllis. And each night, the child had crawled across her bed as if pulled along by the moon. As she had gotten older, Phyllis had slept more peacefully, but Adele suspected that somewhere inside, her daughter still swiveled along behind the moon.

Marleen was just the opposite of Phyllis. But what could be the opposite of one kind of craziness if not another kind of craziness? After all, Marleen didn't just sleep—she died. She could sleep anywhere, in the lumpiest bed, on the straightest chair, on the hardest couch. She slept as if she were starved for it—or as if it were starved for her. She didn't move. She didn't make a sound. For as long as Adele could remember, she had been checking Marleen's breathing while she slept. And she still did.

While Phyllis wanted to make an orbit in her sleep, Marleen seemed to be trying to sink into the bed. Although Marleen was tall and slim, as soon as she fell fully asleep, she seemed to gain a couple hundred pounds. About two weeks ago, Adele had tried to move Marleen from the couch where she was taking a nap. It was as if her daughter had become part of the couch. Not only had Adele not been able to pick her up, she hadn't even been able to separate her from the fabric.

But Adele couldn't picture Lula in any sleeping position but some sane one, like the women stretched out in mattress advertisements. Even in a car, Lula probably slept with control. She wouldn't let her head flop around or her mouth hang open. She'd probably keep her arms folded over her chest and both feet flat on the floor. Adele recalled how she and her girls always woke up with their hair swirled all over their faces, plastered here and there to their skulls with patches of sweat. She could imagine Lula waiting for her and Phyllis to comb out the snarls in their hair every time they stopped at a gas station. Lula's tight auburn curls probably wouldn't even get limp on the trip down.

"Now, Curtis, since I'm being so cooperative on this trip, I want you to agree not to go exploring if we happen to drive past some little side road that makes you think you've discovered a shortcut." Daniel straightened his tall frame in defiance.

Curtis finished off his coffee and held his cup a few inches off the table, as if he were too hurt to let the mug touch his brother's table. "Well, Daniel. You know if you don't get lost, you ain't been anywhere."

"I'm not interested in being anywhere. I just want to get to the beach and back." Lula sipped her coffee. "What if you got so lost somebody had to come looking for you?"

"If I ever got that lost, I'd just go back the way I come." Curtis settled his cup on the table and pulled it backward.

Adele and Daniel simultaneously choked on their coffee. "When did you ever backtrack?" Adele wiped coffee off her chin.

"Yeah, when?" Daniel dribbled coffee from his cup, his hands were shaking so hard. He took the dish towel that Lula handed to him. "Lula, my brother would rather disappear into a Georgia trailer park than back up and follow the road he came in on."

"Ain't you ever heard that getting there is half the fun?" Curtis reached over and picked up a vanilla wafer. He preferred to drink his coffee first because when he tried dunking vanilla wafers, he wound up with chunks of the cookie floating around in his coffee.

"We've heard it, but we don't believe it." Adele dipped a vanilla wafer into her coffee.

"Is he really that bad about getting off the main roads?" Lula shook Daniel's wrist.

As he dipped his wafer into his coffee, Daniel replied thoughtfully, "The only time my brother wanted to stay on the main road was the trip we made from Norfolk when we had Daddy trussed up in the straitjacket."

From the way Lula's forehead went jagged, Adele knew that she was hearing of the old man's craziness for the first time. From the way Daniel forgot to pull his vanilla wafer out of his coffee, Adele knew that he regretted what he'd let slip out. The big Holsclaw secret.

"When did your daddy wear a straitjacket?" Lula turned to face her husband.

"It wasn't like a doctor put it on him." Daniel pushed his coffee away. "Curtis thought it'd be easier to get him back home if he was . . . what'd you call it, Curtis?"

"Restrained." Curtis picked up another vanilla wafer. He glanced around the kitchen.

Adele could see that Curtis was uncomfortable for his brother. The Holsclaws believed that family interrogations should be carried on in private. She just hoped that Curtis wouldn't try to make a joke out of Lula's alarm. Sometimes Curtis had enough sense to keep quiet. But other times, he pretended not to see what the problem was. She worried about him at poker games just because he didn't always pick up on how people were really feeling. More than losing his paycheck, Adele feared that one day Curtis might try to joke with some poker buddy at the wrong time and wind up getting shot.

"Before it gets too late, why don't you and Daniel go get that ocean fishing equipment you said you'd need." Adele stood up and stared as obviously as she could at the coffeepot. She knew if she wanted to distract Lula for a moment, all she had to do was challenge her authority in her own kitchen.

Everybody stood up at once. Lula rose, frowning and leaning toward the stove. She threw a warning glance toward Adele but then settled her gaze heavily on Daniel. Her look was lost on her husband, though, because Daniel was digging in his pocket, searching for his car keys. Curtis had turned slightly sideways at the table so he could pull his billfold from his hip pocket. This was the summer when he planned to replace all of his old ocean line, sinkers, hooks—and he had declared two nights earlier that he needed one more deep-sea rod and reel. That would give him five. He had found a secondhand rod and reel at Mack Roberts's bait and tackle shop. Adele knew that Curtis would keep Daniel out of the house for at least three hours haggling with Mack about what the used rod and reel was really worth.

Neither Daniel nor Curtis kissed his wife in front of other people. Adele could tell that Lula was still mildly irritated by the Holsclaw modesty, but tonight Lula was more irritated by the Holsclaw secrecy. Adele watched her sister-in-law closely as she wiped off the table and rinsed out the men's coffee cups. Lula cleaned with jagged sweeps of her arm. Her elbows pumped sharply. She clicked her tongue several times, but she didn't speak.

Adele had been raised by a mother and a father who didn't allow their children to make odd noises inside the house. Mumbling, sighing, whining, clicking, and shuffling were likely to be rewarded with a slap on the most protruding body part. Although Adele seldom raised her hand against her own children, she really wanted to knock some sense into—or was it out of—her sister-in-law. Instead, she took a drink of her coffee and pushed her chair a few inches from the table.

"You and Daniel got it good."

Lula looked up from wiping the table for a third time, her mouth crooked as a mountain rail fence.

"I wish me and Curtis could have started out as fresh as you and Daniel have." Adele wondered just how afraid of craziness Lula was. To a person not born into it, craziness might be worse than being lost at sea.

Lula dropped down in her chair and scooted close to Adele. "What was that business about old man Holsclaw wearing a straitjacket?" Her voice was flat, withdrawn, as if this was not her first time being surprised by her husband's family.

For a second, Adele bristled. She figured that her own family history had taken some explaining by Daniel. But Lula was so far below her usual level of self-satisfaction that Adele was a little concerned for her. "Well, that's what I mean about you and Daniel getting to start fresh." Adele leaned closer to her sister-in-law.

"We'd been living with Old Man Holsclaw and Teense for about five years. I thought we was about ready to move out on our own, but then it started looking like we was going to get into the war, so we just lived from one day to the next."

"Was Old Man Holsclaw still preaching then?" Lula was the kind of person who wanted to trust lay preachers but couldn't bring herself to.

"No. He'd cooled down from his preaching and was doing more carpentry. But somehow, he heard about all the money a man could earn working up in Norfolk."

"I guess because of the war." Lula straightened up and took some interest in her coffee.

"I guess so." Adele picked up another vanilla wafer. "I never could figure out if our government knew it was going to get involved all along or if Norfolk was making ships for them people overseas. Anyway, Old Man Holsclaw left one night, promising up one side and down another that he would send money back to Teense and me. You know, back then, Curtis and Daniel both worked at the furniture factory."

"One good thing that come out of the war was Daniel getting educated in telephones." Lula held the dishcloth against her cheek.

That summer when Old Man Holsclaw had left for Norfolk had been so hot that Adele and Teense had sat on the porch stringing green beans and soaking their feet in dishpans full of water. "The money come pretty regular for a month or two, but then weeks would go by and we wouldn't so much as hear a word. Finally, Teense got a letter from some woman Old Man Holsclaw was renting a room from. She told Teense she'd better send somebody up to get her husband."

"Had he gone up there and gone wild?" Lula leaned forward, her head level with her coffee cup.

"Maybe he'd been a preacher for so long that he couldn't help but come unraveled. From what Curtis told me, women were like lint up there on the docks, just settled everywhere and anywhere there was a flat place. And Old Man Holsclaw just snapped. He'd work all day and hound dog all night."

"No wonder he just sits around now." Lula nodded. "Burned himself down to the nub."

"Curtis and Daniel borrowed a car and drove up to Norfolk." Adele thought it was time to flush through the story. "Old Man Holsclaw refused to come back home, told his two youngest sons that he'd throw them down the stairs before he'd leave Norfolk with them. And Curtis believed him."

"Crazy as a bedbug by then, talking to his boys like that." Lula crossed her arms and shook her head.

"While Daniel kept an eye on their daddy, Curtis went walking around town, trying to figure out what to do. He happened to walk by a medical supply store and saw an old straitjacket hanging in the window. He bought it and a bottle of whiskey. Then he talked a woman into taking the whiskey up to Old Man Holsclaw's room. When she got him drunk enough to go limp, Curtis and Daniel came in and saddled him with the straitjacket. They kept pouring the whiskey into him all the way home, just so he wouldn't tear up the inside of that borrowed car."

Lula's mouth was now straight. Her eyes were slightly squinted. She took several even breaths. "How long ago was that?"

"The summer of 1940." Adele stroked the lip of her cup. She felt her own hardness. Four years after that summer, her brother had disappeared. She had seen a craziness in Gill Mathis's eyes that must have been the same kind of craziness that glued her father-in-law to the docks at Norfolk.

"Thank heavens we don't live in Norfolk." Lula stood up. "Do you think men are as likely to go crazy at Carolina Beach as at Norfolk?"

Briefly, Adele thought about all the young girls in bathing suits. Whatever Curtis and Daniel looked for in women, it couldn't be seriously found on the beach. Oh, they would look, but they wanted something out in deeper water. Adele knew you couldn't get lost at sea while sitting on the beach. "No. Sunburn is a bigger threat than insanity at Carolina Beach."

"That's a relief to hear." Lula paused between the sink and the table, considering. "I want to show you something I bought for the beach. I wanted to wait until we got there, but if you're like me, you'll be able to enjoy the drive down more knowing what I bought." Lula disappeared in the direction of the bedroom.

Adele felt angry. Nothing seemed to sink into Lula. Maybe that was the secret to her being so normal. She could feel threatened for a few minutes by the Holsclaw insanity, but explain what it really meant, and Lula was ready to run off and parade around in a new bathing suit or two. Adele wondered if she had time to slip out of the kitchen, put on her shoes, and get down the basement stairs before Lula returned. But she could already hear her coming back toward the kitchen.

Instead of a new bathing suit, Lula was wearing a bright orange life jacket and carrying six more, three draped over each arm. "I know you know how dangerous the ocean can be, so I bought one for all of us." Lula did a clumsy turn, showing Adele how the white straps crossed in the back. "I know the orange don't go with my hair, but the man at the store said it's easier for the Coast Guard to see you if you wear orange."

Too full to speak from the tide of appreciation rising in her, Adele stood up and moved closer to Lula. She took one of the life jackets from her sister-in-law's arm and slipped it around her neck. The bright fabric was cool and coarse. Adele stroked the front of her vest. "How long will it float?"

"Till somebody finds you." Lula spoke with certainty and cinched Adele's strap.

WHITE TRASH, RED VELVET

ON A BUSY DAY, Gaither Drum could carry twelve tacks at a time in his mouth. He kept five lined up between his lips, their heads pointed outward, ready for the magnetized tip of his tack hammer to swing up and tug each tack from his mouth. Meanwhile, seven more tacks waited just behind his teeth, carefully kept in line by Gaither's trained tongue, which delicately fluttered across the blue-tinted points aimed at his throat. As soon as the last tack on his lip slid onto the circular end of his hammer, Gaither slipped his tongue under the tacks resting against his upper teeth, dropped his jaw slightly, and deposited the second line of tacks on his lower lip. He kept his extra two tacks on the tip of his tongue, to use in case he needed to replace any of the ten tacks he'd just hammered into the couch or chair that he was upholstering. If none of the ten tacks he'd just nailed needed replacing, then Gaither used his two spares to smooth out any uneven spacing he might have left between previously placed tacks. Once a tack went into his mouth, it had to be put into a piece of furniture. This was a law of upholstery that helped Gaither concentrate.

When Gaither wasn't in a hurry, he preferred to carry only five tacks at a time in his mouth. He didn't like having tacks rest against the back of his teeth. Upholsterers who habitually carried tacks against their teeth eventually developed "tack teeth," receding gums accompanied by rampant decay of the front upper and lower teeth. Although Gaither's red hair was still fairly thick, he knew his hairline was getting higher year by year. He thought his hair loss was especially unfair because no one in the whole furniture factory took more pains with his appearance than Gaither.

Working as an upholsterer for six years, Gaither had developed strong hands and sinewy arms. He was proud of the way his biceps bunched up when he bent his arms, and how the vein running along the top of each muscle emphasized the hardness—not only of his arms but of his whole body, because when covering a piece of furniture with fabric, a man had to pull with his back, his stomach, and his legs. His arms and hands were just the places where the rest of him was attached to the material being tightened over the padded frame.

Aside from the cutoff saw operators, who worked way over on the far side of the factory in the rough end, trimming down the long raw planks that came in from the lumberyard, upholsterers were the only people who got to work on a platform. Gaither's platform was about four feet wide and twelve feet long, raised three feet off the factory's concrete floor. At either end of his platform sloped a ramp. Up one ramp, Gaither's apprentice, Cecil Younce, pushed the frame of the couch or the chair to which he had just tied and tacked the padding. With Cecil watching—and sometimes lending a hand—Gaither covered the furniture, always starting at the same end in the same corner, firming up the arms and face of the furniture, then moving toward the back, always tugging and tightening until his callused fingers tingled and his fingernails took on the same bluish tint of the tacks he transferred from his lips to the tack hammer, then with one almost choplike stroke drove into the fabric and the frame of the furniture.

When Gaither had finished and the piece he had covered stood in front of him—by the time he had finished, Gaither had hopped off the platform and been working on the floor so he could tighten and tack down the lowest parts of the upholstery without stooping over so far—a couple of men had come in from the shipping department. For a few minutes, while Gaither inspected his work, Cecil and the two men would simply stare at what Gaither had accomplished. The piece seemed as tight and vital as the muscles in Gaither's arms. Once Gaither gave his approval—a slap on the chair's cushion and sweep of his arm directed toward the shipping department—the men would slide the piece down the ramp and either carry or cart it off to be crated.

Gaither's was the highest paying job in the factory, and as far as he could tell, he was one of the best upholsterers in the whole town—which probably meant the whole state because Hibriten was known as the Furniture Capital of the South. He had dropped out of school at sixteen. After a summer of doing odd jobs around the upholstery department of Blue Ridge Furniture, he had decided that school couldn't offer him what the factory could. Now he was twenty-two and already made more than the teachers who had tried to talk him out of quitting school.

If he had wanted, Gaither was certain he could open up his own upholstery business, but aside from the regular paycheck and the benefits given to him by Blue Ridge Furniture, what the factory gave him that even his own business couldn't was prestige. He knew a few independent upholsterers. And they were slaves. A man could tell his foreman to go to hell if he felt like it, but a man couldn't say that to a customer. Besides, Gaither preferred getting praise from a big company for how well he covered new furniture than ignorant gratitude from some little old man or dried-up woman who dragged in some mouse-infested, mangy old family heirloom for him to refurbish.

Then, too, there was the pleasure of having other factory workers recognize him as one of the best. Sometimes Gaither even felt a little embarrassed by how often Cecil came to him for advice—and Cecil was twenty-seven, five years older than Gaither. As Gaither recalled how much Cecil had changed in the one year since he had been transferred to the upholstery department from the machine room, he had to break his concentration on wrapping the arm of an oversized couch and study his apprentice.

Unlike Gaither, Cecil was short with bristly black hair. For the first few weeks, Cecil had worn the same clothes in the upholstery department that he had worn in the machine room. After Gaither had tolerated Cecil's smudged, sometimes wrinkled work pants, his occasionally tattered and always limp shirts, some with stains from either grease or intense sweat, Gaither had explained to Cecil that they were the aristocrats of the factory. More than anybody else there, they had to be something to look up to. Besides, Cecil was a veteran of the Korean War and needed to take more trouble with his appearance.

Gaither had been careful not to suggest too strongly that Cecil start wearing nicer work clothes. Gaither certainly didn't expect his assistant to come in, as he did, wearing a lightly starched, freshly ironed shirt. Gaither preferred solid, intense colors, like turquoise, deep green, and burgundy because they went best with his red hair. It went without saying that even in the winter Gaither wore short sleeves in order to keep his arms free and on display. He had learned a few years earlier that if he rolled up his shirt sleeves twice, people were able to see his muscle veins just at the point where they most dramatically defined themselves from the flesh around them. Depending on his mood, Gaither wore either tan slacks or dark blue ones. Blue jeans, at least ones tight enough to make him look sexy, didn't allow him to bend as easily as he needed to. But he always made sure his pants creases were sharp. Long ago, Gaither had sworn that he would never wear shoes with laces. His penny loafers were always polished, and he wore dimes in the slots instead of pennies.

Because Cecil was Gaither's apprentice, Gaither did not join in on the joking the other upholsterers enjoyed behind Cecil's back, despite how much Gaither wanted to see Cecil shape up and stop acting so humble. It was rumored that Cecil had been a prisoner of war. Gaither had missed his chance to go to Korea but thought the least he could do was help educate a veteran. Besides, the jokes had died down once Cecil started wearing shirts that had all their buttons and pants that didn't have pockets missing or threads from the cuffs dragging the floor. Perhaps the first direct advice Cecil had asked from Gaither—not related to upholstering—was where Gaither bought his shoes. Gaither had almost hugged his apprentice for wanting to get out of the scuffed, warped brogans that had carried him through long hours of running a lathe sander. Those thick-soled clunky shoes were maybe necessary in a room filled with steel machines and stacks of unstable couch arms and legs, but in the upholstery department, Gaither argued, a man had to think about how his feet looked as well as how they felt. If a man couldn't dress himself neatly, how could he ever learn to cover a couch neatly? Nobody could argue with Gaither's logic on this point.

Slowly, Cecil had absorbed Gaither's advice, and lessons. Being an upholsterer, Gaither felt, was more than a job—it was a way of dealing with the world. He admitted to himself, as he jumped off his platform and began tugging the plaid wool fabric over the curved ridge of the couch's back, that he now found *himself* in a difficult position in terms of dealing with the world. And not his clothes, not his new '57 Chevrolet, not his respect on the job, and not how he was improving his apprentice's life could help him solve his problem.

Junior McLaughlin had threatened Gaither's girlfriend, Marleen Holsclaw.

Actually, Marleen wasn't Gaither's girlfriend. She had made it clear that she didn't want to get serious—not while she was still in high school. Gaither had pointed out to her that being a senior, she was practically out of high school. While she had allowed him to run his hand up her thigh—on the inside—she had not let him take off any clothes, not hers or his. But when they kissed and rubbed against each other, she had given herself up to such heavy breathing and sincere moans that Gaither had, on more than one occasion, when he couldn't take the pressure any longer, jumped out of his car and walked on his hands to get the blood drained out of his crotch and back in circulation to his brain.

Marleen drove a school bus. Several times, after they got back from a movie, Gaither and Marleen had climbed aboard her dark vehicle and wrestled around on the frustratingly narrow and short seats. They could have made out on the floor, Marleen kept her bus so clean, but she said the rubber flooring might leave marks on her that would be detected, and reported, by her younger sister, Phyllis. Marleen's concern, especially for the condition of her bus, further inflamed Gaither's desire. When it came to cars, Marleen drove and thought like a man. Never before had Gaither met a woman who brought together a tall womanly body and a firm grasp of automotive mechanics. She had been excited by his '57 Chevrolet, not just because it was a red Bel Air Convertible Sport Sedan but also because it was a Super Turbo-Fire V-8, 283 cubic inches with 220 horsepower. Marleen had approved when he told her he had paid extra for the dealer-installed four-speed transmission. Working after hours, Gaither had spent a month and a half reupholstering the seats in his Chevrolet, replacing the flat-stitched vinyl covering with roll-pleated Russian leather. But Gaither insisted on calling it simply red leather because he didn't want anybody calling him a communist. Marleen had hinted that one night they would have to drive up into the mountains, get on the Blue Ridge Parkway, take off their clothes, and cruise up to the Virginia Line. She'd always wanted to ride naked on leather upholstery in the mountains.

Gaither raised up from his work to stretch his back and toss five more tacks into his mouth. In the middle of an oversized couch was not the place to think about Marleen naked. Besides, he knew she wasn't serious. Oh, she was serious about wanting to do it, but she needed a reason, some special occasion, for doing it. But as long as she had to be on her guard against the likes of Junior McLaughlin, she wasn't going to be in the mood for much of anything.

Five days earlier, as Marleen was carrying her last load of kids home from school, she noticed in her rearview mirror that a bigger boy, Ray McLaughlin, was punching a smaller boy in the face. As soon as she could, Marleen pulled off onto the shoulder of the road and jerked Ray McLaughlin off the other boy. She had warned Ray at least three times a week for the whole year not to bully the other kids, but Ray, like all of the thick-skulled McLaughlins, preferred to pursue his own pleasures regardless of requests made by teachers and bus drivers. When Ray had stubbornly refused to apologize to the boy whose nose he had bloodied and when he told Marleen that he didn't care for riding on her stinking bus, she had dragged him up the aisle, tossed him out the door, and told him if her bus was so stinky, he would probably be happier walking home. Actually, she was only a quarter of a mile from his stop anyway, but she thought the extra time it took Ray to get home would give him a chance to feel guilty or humiliated—anything as long as he realized he had been doing wrong.

Instead of learning his lesson, Ray had walked in the opposite direction of his house and made his way to the auto graveyard where his older brother, Junior, sometimes worked and always hung out. Ray knew he was likely to get more sympathy from Junior than he was from his mama and daddy because Junior understood that a McLaughlin boy's life was too complicated to worry about the rights of weaker children. It took all of Ray's energy simply to keep up with getting what he wanted. As Ray had hoped, his older brother had bulged his eyes and spit out his cud of tobacco when he heard that some girl had thrown his little brother off the bus.

Although not a serious criminal, Junior McLaughlin was shiftless enough and stubborn enough to be considered dangerous by the local law. When word got around to Marleen's parents that Junior McLaughlin thought she needed to learn a few manners and he planned to teach her some free of charge, they called the sheriff, who assigned a deputy to follow Marleen on her bus route. Aside from Ray, the only other people to enjoy the suspense were the other children on Marleen's bus. For five days, when she was followed by the deputy, the children hummed the theme song for "Highway Patrol." Of course, Ray stayed out of school, and although the sheriff had given Junior an hour-long warning about his threat, Marleen had not been in any mood to go out on dates, much less make out down by the river or at the Pine Ridge Drive-In.

She had told Gaither that she didn't feel safe outside her house. This confession, made two nights ago, had stung Gaither's pride.

The other boys that Gaither knew Marleen dated were still in high school and afraid of a character like Junior McLaughlin. Marleen's daddy, Curtis, was tough enough, but he wasn't the type who would drive over to the auto graveyard and try to pick a fight with Junior. From what Marleen had told Gaither about her uncles who lived down in Wilkes, they might be crazy enough to go looking for Junior, but she didn't want them getting into trouble over nothing more than a threat. Besides, a few of them still had the reputation of being moonshiners and might have more to fear from the law than Junior did.

As Gaither saw the matter, he was the only person Marleen could count on, not simply for protection but for relief. But if he was going to fight Junior, he wanted it to be in a public place where a lot of people could see it happen, where Junior wouldn't be able to pull a knife or gun on him. It had to be a place where Junior knew that the beating was meant to be a kind of public announcement. The crowd had to contain a few people who would be sure to tell Marleen what Gaither had done for her. Better yet, it had to be a crowd in which Marleen might be standing with a couple of her friends. The places where she was most likely to be with a bunch of friends were the Hibriten skating rink, the Scarlet Sow Drive-In Grill, or the Dome Grill. But the problem, Gaither realized, was getting Marleen out of her house, then finding Junior in one of those public places.

Gaither shook his head. He didn't like having to schedule his life around the migratory habits of white trash like Junior McLaughlin. If he simply wanted to pick a fight with Junior, Gaither knew he could go to the auto cemetery, but that place wasn't public enough. Besides, Junior might be able to get one of the other derelicts who worked around that place to side with him. A place like that always had a gun or two on the premises. And Gaither didn't want to get shot. Come to think of it, he didn't much want to get hurt, but he figured he could take Junior. In a fair fight. Gaither thought of himself as a good, fast puncher. All he asked of Junior was to come out with a couple of wild swings, just give him a chance to crack his windpipe or get his nose bleeding.

When the whistle blew for the nine o'clock break, Gaither told Cecil to go on to the canteen without him. But before he could get completely settled on the couch he would finish upholstering before lunch, Cecil returned carrying two cups of coffee. With his elbows fanned out and his eyes on the cups of coffee, Cecil glided up the ramp to where Gaither sat, handed the coffee to him stiffly, and sat down beside him.

"Not like you to stay on your platform during break." Cecil sat on the edge of the couch and leaned forward as he sipped his coffee, cautious about spilling on the fabric, cautious about being caught on a piece of furniture still on the production line.

For a moment, Gaither studied his apprentice's knotted posture. In a man like Cecil, caution turned to awkwardness. His humbleness turned to awkwardness. Gaither didn't know how long it would take him to smooth out this side of Cecil. Or even if he could smooth the man out. "Got a lot on my mind, Cecil."

"That's the time when I most want to be with loud people." Cecil glanced at Gaither across his shoulder.

Gaither smiled, took a drink of coffee, then tilted his head back, letting it rest on the taut curve of the couch. Somehow, Cecil had learned that Gaither liked four packs of sugar and extra cream in his coffee. Then again, Cecil was always springing little surprises that made Gaither a little nervous—but not enough to complain. After all, why shouldn't his apprentice park slantwise in a parking place so Gaither would always be assured of a parking place close to the upholstery department. Nobody knew exactly what time Cecil arrived— just that he got there before everybody else.

Far above where he sat, Gaither could see the orange steel beams, laced with power cables, exhaust ducts, and hydraulic lines. "It's a loudmouth I'm trying to deal with."

"Junior McLaughlin?" Cecil slid closer to the edge of the couch as if he were getting ready to stand up.

"You hear what he did?" Gaither was not surprised by Cecil's knowledge. Everyone in the factory took an interest in everyone else's business, especially the important people's business, and while Junior's threat didn't quite make the newspapers, it certainly stimulated much discussion through-out the factory. Several people who worked in the factory had children who rode Marleen's bus. In a sense, Gaither felt that the people who worked around him were also expecting him to make a move. Unlike Cecil, who probably didn't mean much to the other workers, Gaither knew people were watch-ing him.

"Threatened your girlfriend." Cecil's voice dropped, like vending machine coffee going cold.

Gaither exhaled deeply and pulled himself into a crouch on the edge of the couch, a more elegant version of Cecil's. "Oh, I know I'm going to have to whip ol' Junior. But I got to be careful where I do it."

Cecil nodded. "Well, nobody deserves a beating more than Junior McLaughlin, but I don't know how much good it would do him."

"You know him?" Gaither twisted his torso to get a better look at Cecil. Now that he thought about it, Cecil did have some of the traits of people like the McLaughlins. That was why his apprentice was having so much trouble adapting to the upholstery department. Usually, the white trash worked outside in the lumberyard. Some of them drifted inside of the factory and worked in the rough end. Rarely, one of the shabby fellows squeezed his way into the machine room, but as far as Gaither could remember, nobody who didn't belong there had been brought into the upholstery department.

"Used to live right beside his family. And I'll tell you, if Junior's daddy couldn't beat good manners into that boy, nobody else will." Cecil slid off the couch and hunkered down, gazing up into Gaither's face. "I'm not saying you can't beat the boy. He's not half the man you are. No. I'm saying you can beat him, maybe do him some hurt, but he'll just be meaner after that. Maybe decide to really try and hurt your girlfriend. Maybe find out what kind of car you drive and take a icepick to it some night. See, where Junior thinks he's special is in his meanness, his craziness. He learned a long time ago that lots of people in this town are stronger than he is. Hell, your girlfriend is probably stronger than Junior McLaughlin, but he don't operate on that system. I guess he's cultivated his meanness because he did get beat up so much. All that's left in that boy is contempt. It runs through him as black and deep as coal in a West Virginia mine."

For a moment, Gaither studied Cecil's face. For the year that they had been working together, Cecil had brought two cans of Beanee Weanees for his lunch. He had eaten so much Beanee Weanees that his body gave off a soft, sweet odor of beans and weanies. Usually, Gaither didn't like to talk to Cecil so close up. But today, Gaither didn't pull back. Instead, he leaned slightly closer to Cecil, folding his arms across his knees. "So you say I ought to take him to supper at the Hibriten Fish Camp?"

"No, no. I'm just saying you'd waste your time to fight him. You want to give him a surprise. You want to let him know you're crazier than he is. That's the only thing he respects. You got to make him afraid of what you can do if he pushes you too far, but it's got to show him what he don't want to see, take him where he don't want to go."

This advice settled over Gaither like the grainy fumes from the finishing room. Fishing a comb from his hip pocket, Gaither stood up and thoughtfully groomed the wings of hair on the sides of his head. "I can make that boy see stars and send him to the hospital." Gaither spoke as if the upholstery department was filled with people. He tried to make his voice sound as convincing as Billy Graham's.

"Everybody knows you could." Cecil stood up slowly, keeping his face turned away from Gaither's. "But that won't control him. For Junior, a beating just screws him that much deeper into his own meanness. I'm telling you. A man who operates on contempt will despise you whether you back down from him or knock him on his butt. If you knock him on his butt, he'll despise you for not knocking him on his back. If you knock him on his back, he'll despise you for not loosening his teeth. If you loosen his teeth, he'll despise you for not breaking his jaw."

"Well, look, Cecil. I've not spent much time around the insane asylum." Soon the whistle would blow and Gaither looked forward to getting back to work, getting back to his own plans and away from having to listen to Cecil's advice. But when Gaither turned his attention back to Cecil, the man was stepping off the platform, talking, but not looking at Gaither.

"What we want to do is make Junior think he's helpless. That's how you get a man to do what you want. A crazy man don't understand a beating, but he does understand helpless . . ." Cecil's remarks dissolved under the flat sizzle of the buzzer announcing the end of the break.

For the rest of the morning, Gaither could tell that his apprentice was thrashing through a thick undergrowth of ideas, but Gaither didn't feel the need, as he usually did, to tell Cecil to keep his mind on the job. To tell the truth, he was slightly irritated that his apprentice didn't think he was mean enough to deal with Junior McLaughlin. Just because he liked to dress nice didn't indicate that he lacked meanness. Besides, Gaither asked himself, what did Cecil Younce know about meanness? He had been to Korea. But nobody knew what he had done over there. Just that rumor of being a prisoner. He wouldn't talk about it. To a lot of people in the factory, being in the war but refusing to talk about it was worse than not having been at all.

Gaither had just missed getting to go. He'd almost enlisted when he was seventeen, but then he got offered the chance to be an upholsterer. Of course, Junior hadn't gone to the war either. He was probably too crazy for military service. No. Cecil, in all likelihood, didn't do enough in Korea to talk about during lunch when the men pushed back from their emptied paper bags and their sticky bowls of vendomatic chili and tried to smoke enough and rest enough to finish out the last three or four hours of work, hoping that something said in the conversation would amuse them enough to forget how tired they were and would be tomorrow morning.

As he drove in the last few tacks on the couch, Gaither wondered if maybe Cecil didn't think he was mean enough because he hadn't moved out on his own—and him twenty-two. Maybe he was too fond of the way his mama waited on him. She was the one who kept his pants pressed and his shirts ironed and just stiff enough to always feel new and sexy. Gaither had buddies who had gone out and rented themselves a place in some cinderblock string of apartments and wound up smelling like the dishes they never washed and having to pay some stranger to clean their nicer clothes. Gaither didn't see any advantage to that kind of life. Only reason a man would want his own place would be to take a woman there, and if it looked and smelled like a landfill, not likely such a place would put the woman in the right mood. No, a man who looked nice, smelled nice, and drove a nice car, even if he did live at home with his mama and daddy, was more likely to get what he wanted from a woman.

As far as living at home went, the general consensus held that Junior McLaughlin, when he did leave the auto cemetery, usually spent his private time with his mama and daddy. That might be, Gaither realized, the place where he'd have to go if he wanted to jack Junior's jaw. Then again, all the wrong people would be there to see Junior get whipped.

While Gaither inspected his work, he kept letting his eyes stray from the pleats along the front leg panel of the couch to where Cecil stood waiting beside the two men from the shipping department. One of the shipping room men, Trent Woodard, leaned against a steel post with his arms crossed and one foot tapping out a slow rhythm, as if he was thinking of a Nat King Cole song. The other shipping room man, Darrell Beard, had one hand in his pocket and carried a strip of cardboard in the other. Occasionally he would scratch his knee with the cardboard, or he would rub it thoughtfully along his thigh. Both men blended in with the work going on around them. Even when *they* weren't moving, the motion of the factory seemed to echo through their bodies. They were at home here. Despite how dissatisfied they might get with their work, they belonged.

Then there stood Cecil. He hadn't learned how to stand at ease. In the machine room, a man always had something to do with himself. If he wasn't running the machine, he was adjusting it, cleaning it, or trying to repair it. Take the machine away from a man like Cecil, though, and he turned clumsy. Cecil waited beside the two other men. Where they were casual, Cecil stood with his knees locked and his arms attached to his sides as if he had nothing to do with them. Once in a while, one of his fingers would twitch, but Gaither couldn't fit the motion to any kind of song.

Who was Cecil, Gaither asked himself as the two men slid the couch down the ramp onto the flat cart with its metal wheels while Cecil ambled back to the easy chair he had been working on, who was Cecil to explain to him what meanness was? To question how well ol' Junior might respond to a few punches to the head? Take away his job at the factory and he'd be white trash just like Junior. Take away his year with Gaither, learning how to dress, and he'd look pretty much like Junior.

Yet, slouchy as he could be, Cecil did get results. He'd convinced the bosses, despite his grimy clothes and greasy hair, to move him to the upholstery department. And Gaither had to admit, the man was surprisingly skillful in attaching the pads to the furniture springs. With other apprentices, Gaither had spent half of his time showing them where a pad would eventually slide off the spring and create a "sore spot" on the furniture, where the spring would either poke through the fabric or punch a hole in the spine of the first person to lean back too hard. Maybe Cecil was a little slow, but once Gaither showed him the tricks, he always remembered. On a good day, Gaither was tempted to admit that Cecil might be smart, but it wasn't the kind of smart he wanted to drive around in his convertible.

During lunch, Cecil had lagged behind in the upholstery

department. What with people asking Gaither questions about his new car or what he planned to do about Junior McLaughlin, he soon forgot about his apprentice. Toward the end of lunch, Gaither got so irritated with Porter Lambert, who said Chevrolet was not the first company to come up with a V-8 engine able to give one horsepower per cubic inch but that the 1956 V-8 Chrysler 300-B had made one six months before Chevrolet had, that he ignored how Cecil was sweating over the culled frame of a love seat that they had been meaning to take to the boiler room for almost a month now.

"That Porter Lambert drives a '55 Dodge and thinks he knows about cars." Without noticing that Cecil had added a few extra crossbars to the inside frame of the love seat, Gaither helped him pull the piece out of the way. "I can't see any '56 Chrysler putting out more power than a '57 Chevrolet. Power output don't work backwards like that."

Cecil smiled, showing large irregular teeth. "Only people I know who drive Chryslers is schoolteachers and unsuccessful undertakers."

Gaither nodded and choked slightly on his laugh. "I don't know anybody who drives a Chrysler. As soon as a man climbs in one of them machines, I forget who he is."

"That's the kindest way to treat 'em, I suppose." Cecil took two quick steps toward Gaither, almost rubbing elbows with him. "You got any plans for tonight?"

Quickly, Gaither tried to come up with some plan. He didn't want to get started running around with Cecil—despite how much help the man needed. "I usually got plans. A man with a '57 Chevrolet convertible's always got plans."

Instead of faltering in his presumption, Cecil circled around until he was standing in front of Gaither, blocking him from the ramp up to his platform. "I've spent all morning figuring out how you can get to Junior. I guess I've spent other mornings thinking about the likes of Junior McLaughlin. But this idea come to me. I even went out to the lumberyard and asked one of Junior's cousins where we'd be likely to see him. This happens to be one of the nights he might be out running around."

"So I won't have to go over on his side of town to get him. . . ." Gaither's hand automatically went down to his pocket to check his car keys.

Cecil took a step back, ascending the ramp, making him taller than Gaither, and glanced down at his shoes, then back at Gaither. "I've got to go with you."

"I appreciate you wanting to help, but this is between me and Junior." Gaither remained standing still despite how much he disliked anybody who deliberately stood in front of him. However, stronger than his irritation was his disappointment with Cecil. Wanting to gang up on Junior: that was just the kind of white trash plan a man like Junior would come up with. "I don't need no help aligning that boy's front end."

Jerking his hands up to just below his chest and giving an awkward wave of his hands, palms out, Cecil said, "I think you do need help." He raised his hands higher, uncertainly, touching his left index finger with his right. "First, I can help you get Junior in your car . . ."

"What makes you think I want that turd in my car?" Gaither leaned a little forward and glared at Cecil.

Cecil raised a second finger on his left hand and held it between him and Gaither as he pointed to it with his right index finger. "And with me along, you won't have any trouble getting him to come to the factory with us."

"I don't need to bring that little shit . . ." But then Gaither glanced around the upholstery department. The place did have a persuasive power. It had convinced him to drop out of school. Unlike the other departments, which were cluttered but almost cozy with machinery and pieces of incomplete furniture, Gaither's department was full of open space. All of the work from the other parts of the factory funneled into the upholstery section in a single line in which the raw frames were first fitted with the springs, then the springs covered with the padding. In his whole life, Junior had probably never seen such pure efficiency, such industrial-strength concentration. All of the production energy of Hibriten came together on its way up the ramp toward Gaither's platform. Even white trash like Junior McLaughlin would have to see how Gaither was connected to this power, represented this power in its most skilled form.

Almost as if he had been waiting for this recognition to pass across Gaither's face, Cecil pointed at him with three fingers wiggling. "And it's going to take more than one man to carry him when we've got him helpless."

This unexpected aggressiveness coming from the usually slumped shoulders of his apprentice made Gaither falter. It also made him suspicious. More than ever, he saw a similarity between Cecil and Junior. Gaither stretched his hand toward Cecil's chest, as if he intended to push him back, but just before his fingers touched his chest, Gaither stiffened his palm, cautioning Cecil but not actually making contact.

"What'd Junior do to you that makes you want to get at him?" Gaither figured if Junior could be so crazy, then Cecil could just as easily be a lunatic.

"I don't work like that." Cecil's face bent around a large, goofy grin. "Korea taught me a man does his best work when he's not worked up." He scratched his ear. "Just think of my offer as a way to pay you back for teaching me upholstery. And if you don't trust that, just think of my offer as a bribe. Let me help you with Junior, and you can let me spend more time up on the platform, planting tacks."

That evening, after supper, Gaither went to pick up Cecil at his house, a small place with a patchy yard surrounded by pine trees. When Gaither drove up, Cecil was working on a room he was adding to the side of his house. A large woman with a bandana tied around her dark hair held the end of a two-by-four that Cecil was sawing. Seeing the two people hard at work, sweating, and completely absorbed in their piece of wood made Gaither wish he had waited until later to have lowered his car's top. The convertible was designed to be seen in motion or at least parked in a place where everybody else was having a good time. Parked in a rutted driveway in front of an asbestos-sided house where a man and his wife were wrestling with a new room under the prickly gaze of a pine forest, Gaither felt as if his car was too large, too shiny, too pretty.

All he could do was blow his horn. Immediately, the woman disappeared inside the house. Cecil waved. In a moment, the woman reappeared and handed Cecil two objects. One, Gaither could tell, was a shirt. Then, after Cecil had peeled off the shirt he was wearing and began rubbing his body with the other object his wife had handed him, Gaither realized that she had brought him a washrag. "Hope she brought you some deodorant too," Gaither said as he watched Cecil clean his torso and underarms. He knew you couldn't wash sweat off with a washrag.

He wondered if maybe Cecil's wife wasn't one of them women who wanted her man to smell like a five-year-old leather watchband. Still, he could feel a dull hum down in his crotch from the way the woman stood holding the shirt for Cecil, her eyes following the circles the washrag made over Cecil's chest and abdomen. If the woman hadn't resembled Cecil so much in shape and size, Gaither might have felt more excitement. He wondered how it would feel to wash off in front of Marleen, who was tall and slim and who liked to smell his Old Spice.

Brushing sawdust from his pants with one hand and trying to button his shirt with the other, Cecil approached the convertible. Because Gaither had not gotten out of his car, he had signaled that the nature of his visit was business, not social. Consequently, he didn't have to go through the ceremony of being introduced to Cecil's wife. He was afraid if he was too friendly then Cecil might want to bring her along as well. Nevertheless, Gaither knew how sensitive men like Cecil could be about their wives or girlfriends. So as Cecil slid into the passenger's seat, Gaither honked his horn again and waved at Cecil's wife as she picked up the saw and leaned over the piece of wood Cecil had been working on. She stood up and waved the saw in the air. Cecil threw up his hand, fingers splayed, and jerked his arm once.

Throwing the car in reverse and bumping down to the paved road, Gaither briefly twisted around to ask, "Does your wife know what you're up to tonight?"

"As long as I'm not losing my money in a poker game, she don't worry much about me." Cecil watched his wife working until the pine trees cut off his view.

"I never cared much for poker myself." Gaither thought if the men who went to the games weren't so sloppy, he might have enjoyed playing more.

"It's a waste of time and money. About the only time it's worthwhile is when you're in the army stuck in some foreign country waiting to get your head blowed off . . . or worse." Cecil stopped abruptly. He rose up in the seat to let the wind ruffle the back of his hair for a few seconds. Then he slid back down and rubbed his eyes with the back of his hand. "Nobody has less business playing poker than a working man, but nobody needs to gamble more."

"I'd rather spend my time with a good-looking woman." Gaither backed onto the paved road, shifted into first, dropped the clutch, and stomped the accelerator just enough to squeal his tires for about ten feet, white rubber-scented smoke rising along both sides of his car. Usually, he hated to burn his tread like this, but he wanted to show Cecil what he was riding in, and he was pretty certain that Cecil's wife would hear him as she sawed her two-by-four.

Over the squealing tires, Cecil yelled, "Did you bring the liquor?"

Letting his hand drop lazily, his thumb motioning toward the floor, Gaither yelled back, "Under your seat."

Gaither was grateful that the wind made too much noise for talking when his Chevrolet clipped along at forty-five or fifty miles an hour. He knew why Cecil was wanting to talk about gambling. That was part of his plan, how they were going to get Junior to come to the factory with them. It was Junior's love for gambling that kept him working. Had he been smart enough to earn his gambling money from crime, Junior would have become a criminal. One of Junior's dreams was to gamble for big stakes. If somebody would offer him a big enough game, Junior would follow him anywhere—at least according to Cecil he would.

Soon the road got wider; the pine trees gave way to maple and oak. On the right, down in a small hollow, Gaither could see the blue water of Hibriten Pool glimmering between the trees. Up a short hill, and they hit the official city limits of Hibriten. At the top of the hill stood the Scarlet Sow, first possible spot where they might run into Junior McLaughlin. Gaither slowed down. On such a mild evening, the Scarlet Sow was packed. He hated the cracked asphalt that the Scarlet Sow owner cultivated in order to keep the traffic moving slowly around his place.

"Look for a '49 Pontiac." Cecil was leaning across the door, his elbows hanging over the side. "It'll be painted half red and half gray primer."

As Gaither scanned the faces behind windshields and bodies tilted against fenders, he wondered just how many times he had actually seen Junior McLaughlin. Back when he drove the '46 Chevy his father had dug up for him, he had gone by the auto graveyard looking for parts. At least two times a year for six years. But you didn't get to know a man like Junior by just talking to him or by walking behind him around the muddy field between rows of junked cars looking for a fuel pump. You came away from those encounters with less knowledge about the man than if you had been reading a wanted poster on him. At least, if you read the wanted poster, you'd know what kind of crimes he had committed. With Junior, you couldn't tell if he actually had committed a crime or if he was simply waiting for the chance to commit one.

"Don't think he's here." Cecil slumped back inside the car.

"Maybe we started too early." Gaither eased out of the parking lot and into the main road, headed south, toward the Dome Grill. "If I was Junior, I'd wait till dark to come out and see the world." As he spoke, Gaither took his eyes from the road to glance at the Welch house. He'd always thought it was a sign of good luck if, as he drove past the house, he could see

Carla Welch through the large front windows, lying in her iron lung. He thought she must enjoy seeing a man like him driving by in a red convertible. Gaither wasn't surprised to see that Cecil was also staring at the Welch house. "You ever seen an iron lung up close?"

"Nope. But I saw a man get bit by a cobra and suffocate to death." Cecil turned to face Gaither. "You ever seen a iron lung up close?"

Pulling his attention back to the road, Gaither shook his head. "Where we just come is as close as I care to get."

"We all got them kind of feelings." Cecil turned in his seat so he could lean closer to Gaither. "See, I bet you don't even know why that iron lung back there makes you nervous. It's not nothing but a big vacuum pump connected to a big tank. And there ain't no germs to settle on you from that crippled girl."

The urgency in Cecil's voice troubled Gaither. He also didn't like the fact that Cecil had one knee digging into his leather upholstery. Two men riding in a convertible were supposed to stay on their own ends of the bench seat. And certainly, the man who was the passenger didn't crouch over toward the man who was driving. Yet, despite his instinct to tell Cecil how to sit, Gaither felt he needed to hear as clearly as possible what Cecil was telling him about iron lungs because he had never been clear about why the sight of that pale girl's head sticking out of that large white tank had always filled him with a desire to look and look and look while at the same time pressing down, down on his gas pedal.

"See, a man who knowed how you felt about iron lungs could use that against you. It's like them people who touch you where you don't want to be touched." Cecil was now staring at the road, talking as if too much wind was going down his throat.

Not liking the sound of Cecil's voice, Gaither kept his eyes on the road. Twilight was falling, and the combination of what Cecil was saying and the failing light made Gaither feel as if he might be letting his apprentice complicate what should have been a fairly simple problem. A real man would simply go up to Junior, tell him to leave Marleen alone, then jack his jaw.

After all, he had only Cecil's word that Junior wouldn't be persuaded by a beating. Something about making a *plan* to put Junior in his place struck Gaither as cowardly. "You know, Cecil, if we do happen to find Junior tonight, it might be simpler if I just do some roadwork with Junior's face; then I can get you back home to your wife sooner." The lights of the Dome loomed in front of them.

"You'll just be wasting your time, I told you." Cecil's voice narrowed and hardened against Gaither's resistance like the point of a chisel bouncing across a sheet of steel. "Then we'll have this to do all over again. As soon as Junior sees that you want to be honest with him, even if you're fixing to put skid marks across his nose, he'll spit on you. What I'm proposing you try with my help is to take him down from behind. Lead him along. Make him think he has the chance to get something from you, then take all of that away from him, and while you're doing that, let him know that you can take away a lot more than that. The only way to make him do what you want is to show him that at any time, you can pull the ground right out from under his feet."

"I just ain't used to all of this sneaking around." Gaither saw that the parking lot around the Dome was also full.

The Dome was a few years newer than the Scarlet Sow. However, it was built along the same functional lines, a low rectangular building with two large picture windows in three sides of the building. Where the Scarlet Sow had a small neon pig carrying a plate of barbecue on top of the building, the Dome had a huge phallic tower on its top. The tower was outlined in alternating neon of green, red, yellow, and blue. The neon ran from the top of the dome down its sides, spread out along the flat roof of the restaurant, then draped off the sides of the building to outline the windows and doors. Gaither always felt as if he were closer to Hollywood when he ate at the Dome. But like everybody else, Gaither agreed that if you wanted the best barbecue, you had to go to the Scarlet Sow.

"You got to start out by meeting Junior where he lives. A sneak don't respect anything except somebody who can out-sneak him." Cecil sat up straighter in his seat, leaned across the door, and said over his shoulder to Gaither: "Just keep thinking about that girl in the iron lung. Her disease scares us. The way it eat up her nervous system. Nobody likes that—the idea of something eating away at him and him not able to do anything to stop it. But what scares us most about that Welch girl is how she could suffocate. We're all afraid of suf-focating. What a lot of people don't like to think about is all the different ways we can suffocate." Cecil leaned toward Gaither even closer.

"A man who operates totally on contempt the way Junior does is easy to tilt. The first little tilt we give him is toward poker. Junior likes poker because he sees it as a chance to humiliate you. And we want him to think he can do that. Then we tilt him toward despising what you do." Cecil stared silently at Gaither for several seconds with his round brown eyes.

"All a man like Junior enjoys is tearing apart. Once we get him to the point where he thinks he can humiliate you, tear apart what you do, *and* take away your car, then we got him."

Gaither shook his head. "I still can't see Junior coming with us to the factory. Not willingly."

"He'll come to defy you and me. He'll come *because* he knows he don't belong." Cecil raised up a little out of the seat to better inspect the cars parked in the lights of the Dome.

Trying to think about more practical matters, Gaither cleared his throat and asked, "Are you sure you got enough material to cover that love seat?"

"I checked it before I left from work this evening. You'll have plenty to do the job." Cecil's voice had dropped back down to the raspy texture that reminded Gaither of burlap.

Plenty of people recognized Gaither and his '57 Chevro-let. For the first few moments as he circled the building, Gaither had to keep giving people he knew his index-finger wave. You'd have thought he was pulling a float in a parade. But then, on the back side of the Dome, sitting in a dark corner, Gaither caught sight of the half-painted '49 Pontiac.

Because the back side of the restaurant was not the most favored place to park and because few people thought they could enjoy their food in full view of Junior McLaughlin, the Pontiac had open parking spaces on both sides. Gaither maneuvered his car into the space on the left of the Pontiac. This was Cecil's idea. He had convinced Gaither that he could find out from Junior just how much he knew about Marleen's boyfriends. The less Junior knew about Gaither's relationship with his intended victim, the easier it would be to get him to go back with them to the factory.

"He's by himself," Gaither observed as he pulled up, evening out the space between his car and Junior's. He wanted to make sure that Junior wouldn't dent the Chevrolet if he opened his car door.

Cecil turned his head away from his window and spoke toward the ashtray on the dashboard between him and Gaither. "Shit. Junior run out of buddies about ten years ago. Most people come to a place like this to meet other people. Junior just comes to eat and look. You could feel sorry for him if you didn't know he'd despise you for it."

As he turned off his engine, Gaither took a long look at the man in the car beside him. Junior's hair was thick and spiky like Cecil's, but Junior had given up trying to keep his under control. It hung over his ears and his forehead. Gaither thought that Junior's skin grew right out of his skull rather than simply over it because his complexion was dull and heavy, pitted and pocked like an old bone. Even from the streaked neon light coming off the dome on top of the restaurant, Gaither could see the sullen brown eyes that forever kept watch over Junior's idea of his own dignity. The man couldn't sit in his car and eat a barbecue pork sandwich without appearing to need somebody to apologize to him. And for Junior, the only acceptable form of apology occurred when he could make somebody sorry.

From the top of his heavy forehead, to the bottom of his undershot thick jaw, Junior looked threatening. He had the face of a man who would eat his own work boots if he knew it would irritate someone he didn't like. But attached to his rough head, Junior had a body that was generally acknowledged as "wormy" by those who ran into him. As much as Junior would have liked to push through the world head-on, he simply never had the stamina nor the strength for it. What he lacked in muscle tone, he made up for in viciousness. He wasn't even really cunning except in his ability to recognize negligence in other people or in his willingness to wait for a moment of negligence.

What Gaither realized as he studied his adversary was that a man who didn't mind riding around in an old car with only half a paint job surely didn't have a mind that he would ever understand. He admitted to himself that a man who couldn't be humiliated by the looks of that '49 Pontiac was probably beyond anything he could do to him. From the way Junior had his foot resting on his dashboard as he chewed his sandwich and swigged his Pepsi, Gaither slowly recognized that there sat a man who prided himself on being low. The lower you took him, the prouder he would be.

"Let's start being buddies." Gaither reached over and flipped the back of his knuckles against Cecil's shoulder.

Cecil nodded and propped his elbow on the window ledge of his door. "That you, Junior?" His voice rose up and folded over on itself, becoming a greeting and a challenge.

Chewing, Junior lowered his sandwich and turned to face the man who had spoken to him. His eyebrows pulled together. He sat up in his seat and regarded first Cecil, then the red Chevrolet in which he sat. Briefly, his eyes swerved to take in Gaither, but not recognizing him, Junior turned his full attention to Cecil.

"How's it hangin', Cecil?" Junior took another bite of his sandwich.

"Long and true." Cecil kept his eyes on Junior, slightly inclining his head. It gave him a shifty look. And although Gaither had never seen such a look on Cecil before, it didn't seem out of place on him.

Junior draped one hand over his steering wheel and slumped down, turning slightly more toward Cecil as he drooped. "You still married?"

"Oh, I wouldn't never think about being a single man again." Cecil paused to watch a car drive by. A teenage girl drove. Three girls, all about the same age, crowded in the front seat while at least six girls occupied the backseat.

More intensely than Cecil's, Junior's gaze followed the carload of girls as it eased along the parking lot and pulled out into the flow of traffic headed toward Hibriten. "Guess they didn't see who they was looking for." Junior's voice was edged with scorn. Then he looked at Cecil and leaned his head slightly out of his window. "Bet one of them girls could make you think about being single."

"Junior, you're talking like a man who needs to get married." Cecil chuckled and scratched his cheek. All the way on the other side of the car, Gaither could hear Cecil's fingernails scratching against his beard stubble.

"No. When I'm ready to get married, I'll ask you to come over and dig the hole for my corpse." Junior interrupted his thought to hunch over and take another bite of his barbecue.

A curb hop came out of the building and asked Gaither and Cecil what they wanted to order. After watching Junior eat, Gaither realized that he wanted a barbecue. One minute, the breeze, which kept shifting directions, carried the smell of grilled meat and french fries over the asphalt and splashed the aroma over Gaither's front windshield. The next minute, the odor of food twisted away and was replaced by the odor of raw lumber, most of it pine, some of it cedar, which was stacked in hacks twenty-five feet high in the lumberyard a hundred yards up the road. At other times, the smell of lumber gave way to a smell of gasoline and heavy lubrication. Infrequently, another odor drifted across the parking lot, the smell of spring-ripe fields full of broomstraw, weeds, and young grass.

"When you going to finish painting your car?" Cecil sat up as if he had just noticed the mottled surface of the Pontiac.

"I am finished painting it." Junior continued to eat.

* * *

"Your brother got throwed off the bus anymore?" Cecil kept his voice casual. The curb hop had just brought out their order: Gaither's sandwich and onion rings, Cecil's lemon Coke. Cecil squeezed the juice out of the lemon slice floating around in his drink and stirred it with his finger.

"I told him not to ride that damn bus anymore, not until I can adjust that Holsclaw girl's irregular notion about who she can tell to walk home."

Gaither felt he needed to say something, but his mouth was full of barbecue. He kept his eyes off Junior and tried to concentrate on keeping his hammer hand steady. Tonight, he had to do the tightest upholstery job he'd ever done. He was going to show Junior just how hard a tack could be driven.

With his cup of lemon Coke, Cecil pointed toward Gaither. "Do you know my buddy Gaither?" His voice had the effect on Gaither of a door opening suddenly right in front of his face.

Gaither leaned forward so Junior could get a clear look at him. This was a tense moment because Cecil had told Gaither at work that he didn't want Junior putting up too much resistance. If he knew Gaither and if he knew he was trying to be Marleen's boyfriend, he would be a lot harder to lure to the upholstery department. "You used to help me find used car parts."

Junior studied Gaither's face, but it didn't belong to any of his familiar enemies. "I helped everybody in this whole county look for used car parts."

Gaither saw Junior's gaze drop, then take in the length of his red Chevrolet.

"You didn't get any used parts for that car at my place." Junior's heavy brows bumped into each other in the middle of his forehead. "We've not started getting wrecked '57s yet."

"Well, I just bought this one about four months ago." Gaither glanced at Cecil because Junior had begun to scrutinize Gaither's face more narrowly.

"And he's a little bit short of this month's payment, so we was driving around, looking for somebody who might be interested in doing a little gambling." Cecil took a long drink of his Coke, signaling to Junior that he could think about the invitation.

"And he thinks he might win a car payment off of me?" Junior laughed, a high-pitched hoot wavering on top of a deep, straining gargle. He leaned farther out his car window, still chewing on a mouthful of barbecue. "Hey, Gaither. What if I wind up taking *your* money?"

"The finance company don't care whether I'm a little short or a lot short of their payment." Gaither rested his elbow on his red dashboard. "I thought I might at least have some fun trying to get caught up with what they expect me to give them."

"We can get drunk, too." Cecil reached under the seat and held up a paper bag containing a bottle.

"I just don't know about playing poker with a man who can't make his car payments." Junior scratched his arm slowly, one corner of his mouth pulling up in calculation and pleasure. "What kind of work you do that you can't meet a car payment?"

"I'm an upholsterer." Gaither kept his voice level. Cecil had warned him about how Junior might respond to this kind of occupation.

"Upholsterer." Junior tilted his head back as he said the word. When his gaze came back down to meet Gaither's, he added, "I thought women did all that kind of work. Matching the seams so all the flowers face in the same direction."

"There's a little more to it than that." Cecil rattled the paper bag as he stooped over to conceal the fifth under his seat.

"Hey, what flavor's that bottle?" Junior tossed his sandwich wrapper and his empty drink cup out his window.

Retrieving the bottle from underneath the seat, Cecil unscrewed the lid, breaking the seal. He waved the bottle under his nose. "You oughta come over here and see."

The warped hinges of the Pontiac's door croaked when Junior swung his door open. Had Gaither not taken pains to get enough distance between his car and Junior's, the bony piece of white trash scrambling into his backseat without waiting for Cecil to open his door would have dented the side of Gaither's Chevrolet without a second thought.

"Watch your shoes on the upholstery." Gaither tried to keep from yelling at Junior.

"Why?" Junior asked, dragging one worn-down shoe heel across the red leather. "In a few days, this buggy might be sitting in the repossessed corner of the finance company's parking lot."

Cecil handed the bottle to Junior, who immediately took a long draw out of it. "Whooooeee," he said, jerking the bottle from his mouth as if it had tried to swallow his tongue. "Boy, that knocks the snot loose." He lowered the bottle between his thighs and sucked in a deep breath of air. "Better than pecan pie."

While Gaither watched Junior sprawl out in his backseat, his arms locked over the top of the seat, Cecil turned to face Junior. "Take a couple more swigs, then get out. Me and Gaither got to find somebody to gamble with us."

"Don't get bossy." Junior took another swig, keeping his eye on Cecil. When he stopped to catch his breath, Junior began stroking the seat. "Custom job. You do the upholstery on the seats?" Junior was now looking at Gaither's face in the mirror.

Although Gaither was reluctant to give Junior any sort of information about himself and his car, he could see Cecil giving him a slight nod. "Yep. They can save that vinyl shit for their Corvette seats."

"Seats, my ass." Junior leaned forward, hooking his elbows over the front seat and stretching his head between Gaither and Cecil. "The whole damn car's made out of plastic . . . fiberglass. Take the motor out of it, pull out the chassis, and it'd float like a boat." Junior dug his fingers into the leather pleats of the front seat. "I just don't see how it'd be worth a man's time to stretch cloth or leather over furniture. I'd think it'd be like playing with paper dolls or something."

"You ever tried it?" Gaither leaned away from Junior. He knew he was being baited, but he also knew that Junior was sincere in his confusion.

"Why would I want to?" Junior swiveled his head to rest his reddening eyes on Gaither.

"Hey, Gaither, maybe if you make it worth Junior's time to give upholstering a try, you could teach him how hard it really is and win some car payment money at the same time." Cecil gave Gaither's shoulder a friendly slap.

"What you mean?" Junior pulled his elbows off the seat and braced them on his knees so he could sit up a little straighter.

"Yeah, what're you talking about?" Gaither glanced at Junior to see if he was even slightly interested in Cecil's proposal.

"Instead of playing cards, why don't we drive over to the factory and let you and Junior kind of have a race. The man who can do the fastest and best job of upholstering is the winner." Cecil looked first at Gaither, then at Junior. "What d'you think?"

Before answering, Junior pulled his billfold out of his back pocket and counted his money. "I've got a hundred and twenty-five dollars on me. How much is a man who can't make his car payment carrying?"

Gaither bit his lip like a man who didn't want to have to confront the bad news in his billfold.

"Oh, come on, Junior." Cecil rapped his knuckles on Junior's knee. "If you can't trust a man who drives a new red convertible, who can you trust?"

For a second, Junior held his breath, then leaned back with his hands behind his head. He hooted softly to himself and dropped his hands to stroke the leather again. "How about if Gator put his upholstered seats up against my hundred and twenty-five dollars?"

"What do you want with my seats?" Gaither thought that Junior would ask for the car as collateral. The fact that he wanted the seats struck Gaither as somehow more greedy, more slimy than if he had asked for the whole car.

"If I win the bet, I can take the seats right then and there. But the car ain't really yours to bet or mine to win. I'd ruther leave the car for you and the finance company to fight over." Junior leaned over and smelled the leather. He looked up, surprised. "Do I smell perfume? No telling what beautiful butts have rested on this leather."

"But these seats won't fit in your Pontiac." Cecil sounded genuinely indignant.

"Even if they won't, I can probably get three hundred for them at the auto cemetery." Junior licked his finger, then rubbed it against the leather. He rocked his shoulders to the squeaking of the leather. "If you hadn't spent so much money on your upholstery, you could have used it to make your car payment."

"I don't want to bet my seats." Gaither didn't have to be much of an actor to make his voice quaver.

"It's not even a bet, Gaither." Cecil spread his hands out in a gesture of expanding reassurance. "Junior don't know nothing about upholstering."

Once again, Junior's face was thrust between Cecil and Gaither. "Sure, Gator. I'm likely to rupture myself when I have to lift the cloth off the floor. You're looking at a man who don't know how to deal with any of the dangers of covering furniture. Besides, if the finance company comes and gets your car, you're going to lose your seats anyway."

For a moment, Gaither doubted Cecil's plan because his apprentice seemed too eager, too much like Junior, in his attempt to get him to take on the bet. The two of them even looked alike: Junior with his brown eyes squinting in mockery, Cecil with his eyes squinting . . . but Gaither couldn't tell why Cecil was squinting. Maybe Cecil really wasn't trying to overcome his white trash roots. Maybe Cecil was really buddies with Junior and they were just trying to get Gaither's red leather seats. Gaither tried to imagine his upholstery bolted down in Junior's Pontiac. He thought of the whiskey and Cokes spilled on the leather, the grit and oil from old car parts tossed in the back, the tobacco slobber congealing in the pleats.

Then Gaither thought about tomorrow evening when he could go to Marleen's house and tell her about how he took care of Junior McLaughlin. She'd have to accept the fact that he was the only man who could take proper care of her. If she could just understand that she didn't have to be afraid of anything or anybody with him as her steady boyfriend, Marleen wouldn't have to hold back anymore. Gaither thought of Marleen in her black bathing suit, those long legs . . .

Interrupting Gaither's vision, Junior draped himself farther over the front seat. "But why the hell do I want to spend my time showing you how to do your job?! I don't need to work up a sweat when I can get your seats in a game or two of cards."

"Yeah, that'd be more fun for all of us." Slipping a piece of ice into his mouth, Cecil glanced at Gaither. He blinked his eyes very slowly, then turned to face Junior. "Besides, Gaither is the best upholsterer in town. You'd be foolish to try taking him at his own job."

"If it's a job, it's a sissified, constipated kind of job." Junior raised his head and hooted. "I can see ol' Gator fussing around a little chair with his tail up in the air. I suppose you boys drink tea during your break." Junior hooted himself into a coughing fit.

Grateful that the darkness prevented Junior—and Cecil—from seeing the red spreading along his jawbone, Gaither didn't have to fabricate the scorn in his voice. "How about if we bet that I can put the fabric on better than you can tear it off?"

"What do you mean?" Junior straightened up enough to prop his elbow on the seat back and rest his cheek in the palm of his hand.

"We'll let Cecil time us." Gaither leaned back against his door. "We've got a little old love seat back at the factory. I'll upholster it. If you can tear off all the fabric quicker than I put it on, you get my car seats."

For a moment, Junior studied Gaither's face. Then he glanced at Cecil. His jaw slid from side to side several times as he studied the neon lights atop the Dome. "Well, I've been taking cars apart for close to ten years. What's a little bit of cloth to me?"

Gaither cranked his car, pumping the accelerator to let the world know his body heat was rising. "I'll put my seats in your Pontiac myself if you can rip better than I can tack."

"I don't know." Junior settled into the backseat again. "It might save me some trouble if you just drive over to the junkyard afterwards and leave them there. I can guarantee you that some buck from Barlowtown will be plopping down three hundred dollars for them by the end of next week."

Gaither knew that Junior was trying to rattle him even more, but he had seen inside some of the nicer cars in Barlowtown and those boys took better care of their cars than Junior and his kind did.

Because Gaither had gone to school with the security guard at the factory gate and because upholsterers were the most important workers at the factory, the three men had no trouble getting in. In Hibriten, the factories represented a forbidden, if not sacred, territory. They also had the reputation for being dangerous. A vandal who might be adventurous enough to climb over one of the twelve-foot-high Cyclone fences stretched around the factory was more likely to be injured in the factory than to do damage to it. Besides, a large portion of the male population in town knew that they would wind up in the factory soon enough.

This forbidding aspect of the factory, Cecil had explained earlier in the afternoon to Gaither, was exactly what they needed to get Junior further off balance. As much as he might snarl, Junior held an abiding distaste for the factory: it represented confinement, responsibility, hard work, discipline, authority—all the discomforts that drove white trash like Junior to the margins of Hibriten society. Nevertheless, Junior would be the last person to treat the factory with any respect.

Pulling up to one of the large loading bays—one of eight at this corner of the building—Gaither realized that the factory was an imposing sight. This particular loading bay dwarfed Gaither's Chevrolet. On the other side of the building, where the boxcars were loaded, the doors were about twice as wide. But as large as the doors were, the brick building loomed over them as if they were nothing more than faded bathroom tiles.

At this particular angle, standing at the corner of the building, looking up at the dark bricks that stretched up and with their own massive darkness blocked out the softer blackness of the spring night with its nebulous haze and spangle of stars, Gaither felt the sensation, for a second, that the wall was actually tipping over and would squash him, Cecil, and Junior—along with his convertible. They'd be so mashed together that no one would be able to tell master upholsterer from apprentice, white trash from Bel Air Sport Sedan. Gaither had to take a shaky step backward and run his hands along the sides of his hair to clear his head of the vision. When he stepped back, he bumped into Junior, who, though he broke his gaze from the top of the building, still left his jaw hanging slackly.

"It's something close up, ain't it." Cecil crunched on the gravel, moving closer to Junior and Gaither.

"My pecker is something close up." Junior walked over to a side of the building out of the range of the utility lights and began pissing.

"We got toilets on the inside." Gaither kept his attention on his ring of keys, sorting through them to find the one to unlock the employee entrance. He also checked to see if he had the key to the upholstery department's panel truck, which was used to deliver special pieces to the showrooms around town. He and Cecil would need the truck later.

"I think indoor toilets are nasty." Junior rolled his head around. "And factory toilets just got to be about the nastiest. I suppose the toilets at the drive-in movie are the exact nastiest." Junior bounced his torso a couple of times after he finished and then joined Gaither.

Inside, the factory was still but not silent. The dim security lights hummed. Bleeder valves on the compressed air lines gave off frequent but irregular hisses as air pressure was relieved. Gaither was tempted to take a detour through the machine room just to expose Junior to the hulking drills, saws, and planers. In the shadows, those tools looked more like instruments of torture, like devices that space monsters might use to extract vital fluids from human victims. But following Cecil's advice, Gaither went directly into the upholstery department.

From his position at the switchbox, Gaither had a sweeping view of the place where he worked. Its emptiness struck him as the lights began flickering on. Somehow, the dimensions of the room, bouncing between darkness and light, were amplified and hinted at hidden distances that weren't visible in full light. Gaither raised his hand to his forehead and took another look at Junior, who was standing close to Cecil. Gaither wondered if the emptiness was snatching at the corners of Junior's stomach the way it was at his.

Cecil led Junior to the work station where stood the padded frame of an ornate love seat. Although heavily padded on the right and left sides, this love seat had a conspicuous section missing right in the center. Gaither had helped Cecil that afternoon further modify the insides of the love seat by constructing a chair within the couch's frame. They had built two small armrests and a small seat in the middle back section. Their carpentry was rough but very stout.

"If I was you, Junior," Cecil suggested roughly, "I'd see if Gaither would let me sit *inside* this little couch." He lowered his voice and leaned casually toward Junior's ear. "If you get the back *pushed* off this thing, all of the other tacks'll just come shooting out of the frame."

"Are you helping him take my car seats away from me?" Gaither had to remind himself that his resentment was about Marleen—not car seats. But the resentment was in his voice, and he knew Junior detected it.

However, Junior couldn't respond at that moment because he was taking another deep draw from the bottle in the brown paper bag.

"Let's just set a time limit to begin with. See how much upholstering you can do in fifteen minutes, Gaither. That way we can get down to some serious drinking sooner." Cecil jerked the bottle out of Junior's hand as if he were planning on taking a drink.

Junior wiped his mouth with the knuckle of his thumb. "Suits me. I can get them new seats in my car sooner."

Gaither picked up his favorite tack hammer and a box of tacks from the toolbox and joined the two other men. As he walked toward them, he shook the can of tacks. "Junior, why don't you just give me the hundred and twenty-five dollars right now and you won't have to work up a sweat."

"What kind of sissy hammer is this?" Junior held the slim hammer up and studied it closely. Then he rested his index finger and thumb along the thinnest part of the hammer, measuring about an inch between his two fingers. "Know what that looks like?" He nodded his head toward the small space pinched between his two fingers.

"What's it look like?" Cecil moved beside Junior so he could more closely study the part of the handle Junior indicated.

"An upholsterer's dick." Junior hooted and pulled his shoulders together as if his rib cage was going to collapse. For what seemed to Gaither an overly long amount of time, Junior continued to laugh at his own joke. When he had recovered from the effects of his wit, Junior tossed the tack hammer into a pile of padding beside Gaither's platform and said, "Get yourself a real hammer."

Cecil pulled a large swatch of red velvet upholstery material from the supply closet. He and Gaither had agreed to use the red velvet because it happened to be the highest quality material they had and was not likely to tear, no matter what kind of struggle it confined.

Strutting to the love seat, Junior paused, as if studying the frame. Then he twirled himself around and flopped into the makeshift seat. "Cecil says I ought to start my part of the bet from inside the upholstery. I got to go along with him there." Junior rested his arms on the wooden slats beside him and twiddled his fingers in Gaither's direction. "Besides, I can get a better view of a genuine upholsterer at work."

"You can watch me piss." Gaither picked up his tack hammer and slapped his palm with it. "Get your ass out of that couch."

Junior studied Gaither's face. Then he smiled, his lips sneaking back toward his ears. "Now, Gator, don't try to take advantage. Cecil just wants you to be fair." Junior slid deeper into the wooden seat. "If you want a chance at my money, you got to let me start from where I sit—right here. It's not like I'm asking you for a crowbar or even one of them little kiss-my-ass hammers." He inspected the love seat, not budging from where he sat. Staring Gaither in the eye, Junior said, "Get ready to watch your clock, Cecil."

Cecil pulled the red velvet up to Junior's feet and spread it out the width of the couch. "I think you ought to do as Junior says, Gaither. You do want to be fair."

"Get over here," Junior said to Gaither. "And get that little hammer of yours busy."

For the first time in his upholstery career, Gaither didn't count the number of tacks he tossed in his mouth—at least half of the contents of his can. And he didn't bother getting them lined up. Gathering up the red velvet in his left hand, Gaither could feel the blue steel pricks of the tacks in the roof of his mouth, his tongue, his cheeks. His eyes threatened to water, but he bent to his work, beginning in the lower corner of the couch because that was his usual beginning point and because he didn't want to alarm Junior, not this soon. Moving quicker than he ever had, Gaither tacked the first third of the material, somehow moving one tack at a time out between his lips, using his tongue to shove and position each tack, the frequent prick filling his eyes and ears with electrical flashes until slowly, the taste of blood began to blend with the taste of tacks. But by this time, he had reached the middle of the couch where Junior was sitting. He couldn't remember when his rhythm had ever been this fast or smooth, one tack, one swing, one tack, one swing.

Without looking at Junior, Gaither dropped down and began tacking material to the rough armrest. Junior continued to watch with contemptuous interest and didn't seem to realize how he was being bound until Gaither had pulled the material taut across his abdomen then tacked the velvet firmly to the other armrest. Gaither could also feel saliva oozing out of the corner of his mouth.

"What the hell're you doing?" Junior tried to raise an arm but could move only three or four inches.

Gaither, assured that the tacks would indeed hold Junior down, now looked up at him. He didn't expect to find all the color draining out of Junior's face; even his brown eyes looked more like wet paper sacks than like a rat's.

"Cecil, get over here!" Junior yelled. "This fucker's gone crazy! He's bleeding from the mouth!"

Gaither continued to work, although a drop of red had fallen from his chin and landed in the bend of his elbow. Cecil leaned over from the front of the couch and studied Gaither's face from an upside-down position.

"What have you done?" Cecil was careful to stay out of Gaither's way.

In response, Gaither parted his lips slightly and exhaled through the tacks, through the blood, and through his mouth. A red froth bubbled from his lips. Back in his throat, he began humming "Party Doll," making sure that the froth continued to pour out of his mouth. He worked fifteen more minutes, finishing the last third of the love seat's back. He admitted that he had done neater jobs—but none quicker. When he finished, he straightened up and spat the remaining tacks onto the floor in front of Junior. But he didn't wipe his mouth. Gaither could feel the blood drying on his chin and along his neck. But the taste stayed fresh in his mouth.

Only Junior's neck protruded from the upholstery. In his concern to constrict Junior's arms and legs, Gaither had left several loose inches around Junior's neck.

Seeing that Gaither was finished with his part, Cecil picked up his own hammer. "Can I tighten up that part around his neck?" Cecil took a few tacks from the can.

Gaither nodded, not sure if he wanted to move his tongue.

Cecil took a tack from his lips with the hammer and tapped it tight.

For the first time since he'd seen Gaither's bleeding mouth, Junior noticed that he was now part of the couch's upholstery. "Wait, Cecil. This is between me and Gator."

"No, Junior, not really." Cecil drove in another tack.

"Well, I know it's my turn to get out." Junior twisted against the velvet.

"Nope." Cecil drove in another tack, not looking at Junior.

"Damn you!" Junior tried twisting again, but mostly his head just thrashed.

Cecil drove in another tack, this one barely an inch from Junior's neck. Then he turned to Gaither. "Can you drive in the last couple? Junior's not cooperating like he should."

Exhaling again, this time a single large red bubble yawning from his mouth, Gaither came over, picked up a tack from the palm of Cecil's hand, and with one motion, dropped his hammer's tip flush beside Junior's neck. Casually, Gaither performed the same operation on the other side of Junior's neck.

Cecil leaned over and inspected the tacks. "Quality workmanship."

"He nicked me. He nicked me with that last tack." Junior's voice was uneven and fading.

"Tight as the fit is around your neck, I don't think you have to worry about bleeding to death." Cecil stroked the material around Junior's neck. "Must be hard to breathe now. And I'd be surprised if you could even swallow."

Junior closed his eyes, struggling to swallow.

"It's what we called in Korea the slow choke. They probably got it from the Chinese." Cecil pulled up a stool and sat down in front of Junior. "See, you can still breathe—almost enough. And you can still swallow—almost enough. But Junior, that brain of yours is going to start picking up on the fact that it's not getting as much as it's used to. Now depending on how much control you have, you could last for days—just about to suffocate. It's about the worst way there is to go because the more control you got, the longer it takes. And Junior, I know you're a strong boy. Oh, not necessarily in that wormy body of yours but in your head." Cecil tapped Junior's head.

Junior tried to throw his body sideways but all he could do was vibrate. He turned red in the face and began coughing.

"Move around too much, and you'll choke yourself a lot quicker." From his back pocket, Cecil produced a flat-head screw driver whose edge had been filed down, then nicked in the middle. This was what Hibriten upholsterers used to remove tacks. "And you know, long before you actually go unconscious, you empty your bladder and bowels all over yourself. Then you have to sit around in that mess. And the people who find you won't feel the least bit sorry for you because you stink so." Cecil twirled the screw driver in his fingers. "It's one kind of hell, I'll tell you."

Junior tried to speak, but his throat only went chug-chug-chug.

"Your voice box is starting to swell. You probably done that when you thrashed around." Cecil glanced over his shoulder at Gaither. "Now me and Gaither are treating this way because of how much we respect you." Cecil rested his elbows on his knees and leaned closer to Junior's face. "You've crossed some lines you shouldn't have, Junior. Listen to me, now. You've crossed some lines you shouldn't have when you threatened that Holsclaw girl. She's Gaither's girl-friend." Cecil patted Junior's cheek to get him to open his eyes. "She's Gaither's girlfriend, and we want you to leave her alone." Another pat to the cheek, a little harder this time. "But before we *ask* you to leave her alone, we have to take another ride."

Because Gaither and Cecil had loaded so many pieces of furniture into the upholstery department's panel truck, they didn't have to speak to each other. They slid the love seat to a more remote loading dock where, earlier that evening, Gaither had parked the truck. Then Gaither drove across town and up the dirt road to the Pine Mountain County Landfill in complete silence. During the twenty minutes it took them to make the trip, Gaither had kept his window rolled down and gulped the soft night air, trying to soothe the stinging left in his mouth by the tacks. He didn't want to talk because he felt slightly ill—not because of the pain in his mouth but because of the wetness he had seen in Junior's eyes as they had loaded him into the truck. He didn't know if he was feeling disgust or sympathy for Junior.

The landfill was a huge excavation filled almost full of garbage. During the milder winter nights, boys would come out there to shoot rats, usually using shotguns with flashlights taped to the barrels. Once the weather turned warm, however, the hunting stopped because the snakes came out to hunt the rats.

Gaither backed the truck up to the very edge of the dump site. Then he and Cecil went to the back and pulled the love seat containing Junior to the end of the trailer. Junior's hair and face were soaked; his breath was ragged and underscored with a panting groan. Cecil and Gaither turned the couch around so Junior was facing the landfill. Both men squatted down on either side of Junior.

"Snakes or no snakes, this is a quiet place." Cecil leaned over and rested his arm beside Junior's ear. "Listen, Junior. All you can hear is that little sound like the leaves rustling." Cecil paused. "But there ain't no wind." Cecil held his breath. "If you've been up here enough times, 'specially in the winter when there ain't no leaves, you'll have heard that sound a bunch." Cecil moved a little closer to Junior. "That's the rats gnawing, Junior. And they gnaw even when they ain't hungry because they got to keep their teeth worn down." He patted Junior's cheek again. "People's kind of a special treat for them, you know. We've got skin for when they're hungry and bone for when they're not."

Gaither could hear Junior's breathing catch.

"We could leave you out here, Junior. Roll you and this fine piece of furniture right down there with the rest of the trash, and I'd say by morning, a big part of you would already be on its way toward the shit end of a rat's ass." Cecil edged the love seat closer to the end of the trailer. "Your ears are probably ringing right now. And you might have some trouble keeping your vision clear. But I want you to hear me real good, Junior. Me and Gaither ain't playing with you. We ain't going to *ask* you to leave Marleen Holsclaw alone. If any trouble comes to her, we're going to get you again, and what we've done tonight will seem like a trip to Myrtle Beach in a refrigerated beer truck."

Without another word, Cecil and Gaither began pulling tacks out of the couch. Gaither thought the gnawing sound behind him grew louder as he worked, and the pain in his mouth was soon overshadowed by chilly undulations around his shoulders. He couldn't see himself driving with his top down for a long time. When he tried to think about how grateful Marleen would be, he couldn't get her face clearly into focus because although the first tacks they had loosened had been the ones next to Junior's throat, he was still breathing as if some large, misshapen flywheel was thumping around inside his chest. As soon as they got down to peeling the red velvet from across the arm rests, Gaither could smell the tang of fear in Junior's wet clothes.

Cecil and Gaither pulled Junior out of the couch and lowered him to the ground by his arms.

"By the time you walk back to your car, you'll be dried off." Cecil squatted down to be face-to-face with Junior. "Watch where you step around here. You can bet the ground is crawling tonight."

Holding his hands slightly in front of him, Junior stumbled wordlessly down the road and was soon out of sight—at least out of Gaither's sight. He observed that Cecil seemed to be following Junior's departure long after all sight and sound of him had disappeared.

After Gaither had stood his apprentice's stiff, attentive pose for as long as he could, he asked, "What'd that boy ever do to you to make you hate him so much? I wanted to hurt him, but it never entered my mind that we'd do to him what we did." Gaither realized that he was exhausted, as if he had been hanging from a high limb all day long, using every part of his body to keep from falling.

Cecil leaned against the side of the trailer and tilted his head to one side. "Now you see, that's why you needed my help to deal with Junior. He's grown up hating and being hated. If you're going to torture somebody, you've got to love him. That's the only way you can know what scares him, what really hurts him. I knowed I could get to Junior because me and him are a lot alike. If it hadn't been for the army and Korea, I probably would have been just like Junior."

"When you was talking to him, you didn't sound like yourself." Gaither wanted to leave, but Cecil didn't seem finished yet; he was staring up at the sky as though he was thinking about taking a nap. Gaither thought he might as well ask him the question that a lot of people in the factory had wondered about. Even if Cecil didn't answer it, at least it might shock him out of his dreamy pose. "Where'd you get all this torturing know-how? Did they torture you over there in Korea?"

Shaking his head, Cecil laughed. "No. I got to torture them. And I was good at it too, because I could interrogate and sympathize at the same time. I could have made a career out of it, but I wanted to come back home and get married." Cecil leaned over and slid the love seat away from the end of the trailer. "We ought to go back and upholster this piece proper. Tell your girlfriend how you rescued her, give her a love seat, and she'll follow you anywhere." He leaned out of the truck. "You ever noticed that the brightest stars are always over the trash dumps?"

Gaither pushed the love seat even farther back inside the trailer. He told himself he had done his part as a boyfriend, but he needed a few more seconds before he could trust the ground that seemed so vague under the puncturing light of the stars throbbing in unison with the pain in his mouth.

"I tell you," Cecil continued. "I learned a lesson tonight. I knew ol' Junior was ours as soon as you started blowing that blood." Cecil jumped to the ground, then turned to look up at Gaither. When he spoke, his voice had lost much of its tautness. "That girl of yours got herself a lover man who knows how to set the mood."

IF YOU SEE
ME COMING

BY LUNCHTIME, Phyllis was so bored with staying at home that she decided to risk walking to the Dixie Diner for a cheeseburger. If anybody asked her why she wasn't at school, she could say that she was eating lunch before going to the dentist. She happened to have a couple of cavities that never hurt her, and while she kept them secret from her mama and daddy, she never hesitated to show them to any teacher who might get too curious about her frequent absences.

One day, she knew her bad teeth would start hurting. She had already decided that she was going to have all her teeth pulled once they started causing trouble. Dentures appealed to Phyllis like some piece of exotic jewelry. Because most other teenage girls didn't even like to talk about false teeth, Phyllis was convinced that they helped establish a girl's maturity. Phyllis promised herself that she would take much better care of her false teeth than she did of her real ones.

As she crossed the front yard, she turned to admire her house. They had moved from their white wooden single-story house to the brick two-story house almost two years ago, but Phyllis knew she would always call it their new house. She loved looking at it from the outside, but living there with her parents and her younger brother made her feel a little suffocated. Since her older sister, Marleen, had gotten knocked up, given up the baby, then run off and married the boy who got her pregnant in the first place, Phyllis's mama and daddy had been riding her every minute.

Where Marleen had been allowed to go out anytime she pleased, Phyllis could date only on the weekends—and her Sunday dates had to take her to church. And even on Friday nights, she had to be home by eleven. She had been able to stay out later than that back when she was fourteen. But once Marleen got into trouble, their mama and daddy started treating Phyllis as if she had been the unwed mother. Even though Phyllis never had a chance to see the baby—Marleen had turned it over to the social worker while she was still in the hospital—she couldn't let herself call it a bastard. She liked babies. And Marleen had cried off and on for three weeks after she came back home from Aunt Cora's house down in Wilkes. If anybody was a bastard, Phyllis thought, it was the baby's daddy, now Marleen's husband, Gaither Drum.

Jumping the ditch and enjoying the slick feel of the pavement under her loafers, Phyllis glanced once more at her new house. It was March. Daffodils were pushing up beside the road. The air moved gently against Phyllis's face, making her think about the river and stretching out on a blanket, waiting for boys in motorboats to come up and ask her and Marleen if they wanted to go for rides. But no, she had to correct that thought. Marleen was married, and Gaither was jealous. He could be mean about it, too. After what he did to that McLaughlin boy who threatened Marleen, everybody should have realized that Gaither was a maniac. But at the time, he was protecting Marleen. Phyllis had to admit that she probably appreciated Gaither's solution to Marleen's problem more than anyone.

At one point, Gaither had even offered to teach Phyllis how to drive—in his red '57 Chevrolet. Of course, Curtis and Adele had immediately pulled the plug on that idea. They might have to accept Gaither as their son-in-law, but they didn't have to trust him with their other daughter. And Phyllis knew that they didn't trust her either. If good ol' Marleen could succumb to Gaither's manly attractions, then little Phyllis had to be equally stupid.

Phyllis pulled up a dandelion puffball and struck it against her hand. If anybody was stupid, it was her mama and daddy for not being able to see the difference between her and Marleen. First of all, she wasn't crazy about cars the way Marleen was. No boy could get her in the backseat just because he had roll-pleated leather seats. Phyllis admitted to herself that she did like Gaither's Chevrolet because it was a convertible. You felt freer in a convertible.

But she could feel just as free riding around in Vernon Propst's '53 Ford. Her mama and daddy liked Vernon because he had refused to teach her how to drive. Vernon knew that Curtis and Adele didn't want Phyllis learning how to drive too soon. Even when Phyllis had threatened to stop dating him because of his regard for her parents' wishes, he had kept coming around to visit with Curtis and Adele. Phyllis had introduced him to one or two of the boys who came to take her out, but she could tell that the boys were intimidated by Vernon and her parents. She always wound up going out with Vernon after a week of denying him. More than anybody she went out with, Vernon was trusted by Adele and Curtis.

Phyllis had to laugh at that trust. They had no idea that Vernon had already asked her to marry him three different times. And he was serious.

For as far back as she could remember, Phyllis had never cared much for school. Since the first time that Vernon had proposed to her, she hadn't been able to take even her P.E. class seriously. Going to school was like undergoing surgery as far as Phyllis was concerned. Social studies cut out this part of your mind. Algebra cut out that part of your mind. English cut out another part. And all the time, your body was numb, obviously in the way. Last year, her civics teacher had suggested that Phyllis try some of the secretarial courses. Of all the secretaries Phyllis had seen, not one looked any different from a waitress. At least a waitress got to talk to a bunch of different people. And she got tips. If she knew what she was doing. Then again, Phyllis thought waitresses were pretty stupid, too.

Vernon had told her that if she married him, she wouldn't have to work.

At the bridge that crossed over the new four-lane highway, Phyllis slowed her pace. She liked to pause in the middle, where she could look down at the grass median or stare into the faces of people driving east, toward Hickory. Fifteen miles west, the Blue Ridge Mountains resisted spring and gave off a cooler breeze, which ruffled Phyllis's blond hair. The new highway followed a valley that twisted its way almost all the way to Windy Gap, where there was a town park with a Ferris wheel that never failed to flutter Phyllis's stomach because, on the way down, the seats swung out over Windy Gap Gorge and, for a few seconds, the sky seemed to split the world in two.

Phyllis turned her back to the wind, leaned against the grainy concrete of the bridge rail, and rubbed her arms. Now would be a good time for a cigarette, but they were harder to come by since Marleen had left home. From her parents' viewpoint, cigarettes, like boys and cars, had the power of getting a girl in trouble. Easily enough, Phyllis could buy a pack of cigarettes at the diner, but then she'd have to go to the trouble of hiding it from Adele, and Phyllis didn't like to sneak around like that. Marleen had been the sneak, only Curtis and Adele hadn't realized it until too late.

A hundred yards away, at Hibriten Elementary School, Phyllis could see lines of children waiting to enter the cafeteria. She knew as soon as she got off the bridge and out of the wind blowing from the mountains, she'd be able to smell the cafeteria food. Whether they were serving clotted spaghetti, hot dogs, or meat loaf, the aroma from the squat cafeteria with its walls half windows and half bricks was always dominated by the smell of stale milk. It was a smell unique to school cafeterias, Phyllis was certain, because when she visited the factory cafeteria where her mother worked what she smelled was coffee and raw lumber.

As Phyllis leaned against the rail, wondering if working in the factory cafeteria was as boring as it looked, she noticed a battered Studebaker approaching the bridge. The car belonged to Fontana Barlow, the black woman who cleaned house for the LeFevers. Phyllis was extremely grateful to her father for moving out of the little white house that sat at the bottom of the hill that belonged to the LeFever house. Their new brick house wasn't quite as large as the LeFevers' house, and it didn't have the four white columns on the front porch, but it did have a garage in the basement.

Celeste LeFever, who had been Marleen's friend one summer, had gone to college—up there in the mountains. Phyllis looked over her shoulder at the aristocratic blue peaks. You didn't have to be smart to go to college. You just had to be good in school and have a daddy who drove a Cadillac. Limp celery. That was what Celeste made Phyllis think of. Went to college because she couldn't do anything else. That was what was nice about being rich. You could just wait around until you made up your mind, even if you had to wait until you were thirty. Celeste probably went to college so she wouldn't have to marry any of the local boys.

The Studebaker stopped in front of Phyllis. Fontana Barlow leaned her bulky torso across the seat and asked, "You ain't figurin' on jumpin', is you?"

Phyllis leaned forward and rested her arms on Fontana's half-rolled-down window. "No, more like who I'd like to throw off in the middle of quitting-time traffic."

"That's good." Fontana laughed. "That's healthy." Her voice was deep and rolled like the mountains at Phyllis's back. "You need a ride somewheres?"

Phyllis had always felt a bond with Fontana, even though she hadn't spoken to the black woman more than a dozen times since she'd met her in the LeFevers' kitchen. Being the middle child in the Holsclaw family, especially when your older sister had gotten knocked up and your younger brother could do no wrong, made Phyllis feel like a nigger herself: nobody took her seriously except when they worried about what kind of trouble she might cause. Fontana seemed to respect what Phyllis had to put up with, even before Marleen had gotten into trouble. To make up for the way Celeste and Marleen ignored Phyllis, Fontana always gave her a larger glass of Coke than she gave the older girls. Or she would make Phyllis's sandwiches thicker.

"I was going to the Dixie Diner." Phyllis already had her hand on the door handle. "Been to the dentist and I want to get the taste out of my mouth."

"I never tasted a dennist." Fontana shifted into first and gave Phyllis a wide smile that showed a mixture of gaps and brown teeth.

The few times that Phyllis had seen Fontana at the LeFever house, Fontana had never laughed or displayed her teeth. Phyllis could believe that the big woman had just murdered Mr. and Mrs. LeFever and was now running off with their jewelry and money. "Why are you in such a good mood?"

"You heard of people gettin' touched by the moon?" Fontana drove slowly, but she kept the wheel absolutely still. "Well, when spring gets close, I get sunstruck—not sunstroke—but sunstruck. I come out of my house or a house where I'm working and the sun touches me, kind of sucks out the blues and the worry."

"You coming from the LeFevers'?" Phyllis wished that she could be satisfied as easily as Fontana.

"Yep. Got their big ol' house clean. It's easier to do since Miz Celeste went off to school. When she was home, I could spend most of the day pickin' up after her, puttin' her records back in they jacket." Fontana shook her head vigorously.

Phyllis had long been fascinated by how Fontana let her hair grow bushy. Most of the black women that Phyllis saw in town either had short, short haircuts or tried to make their hair straight. As Fontana's head waved back and forth, Phyllis noticed a straight, silver line glinting down inside the black woman's hair. When another wag brought her head closer to Phyllis's face, she leaned as if to adjust the cuff of her jeans. Almost touching Fontana's hair with her nose, Phyllis saw the silver sharpness and dull blue rectangle of a single-edged razor resting carefully against Fontana's scalp. Phyllis slid sideways until her hip hit the door.

"So you off now?" Phyllis decided to keep her eyes on Fontana's hands.

"Lawd, no." Fontana shook her whole body. Although her massive breasts and stomach amplified the motion, the quivering stopped abruptly at her shoulders. "Only off I know is goin' from one job to another."

Phyllis had never suspected that Fontana might belong to somebody besides the LeFevers. "You work for somebody else?"

"Three days a week I work for Miz LeFever. Then the other two days I work for Miz Welch. On weekends, you look for me up at that Windy Gap Hotel. When I'm not in the laundry room, I'll be making beds. I have to wear a green uniform up there, and had to buy me a pair of nurse shoes. Look at this big woman here driving this car." Fontana half turned toward Phyllis and put her hand flat on her bosom. "What you think I look like in a green uniform? Nobody knows. Nobody seen anything like me in a green uniform. One old mountain goat who runs the boiler said I looked like night coming out of a rhododendron patch. Lawd knows what that means."

Not wanting to get drawn into a discussion of Fontana's size, Phyllis half nodded and half shook her head. "But do you just work half a day for the LeFevers? Or are you taking a break to go eat lunch?"

"I got to go to Miz Welch's house today 'cause they need a special cleaning. They took Miz Carla to the doctor up in Asheville to see if she's ready to come all the way out of her iron lung."

Phyllis knew Carla Welch because her daddy was the accountant for the factory where Curtis worked. But everybody in Hibriten knew the Welch family because Carla and her sister, Linda, had both come down with polio during the epidemic in 1953. Linda had died. Carla had come close; paralyzed from the neck down, she was confined to an iron lung, but so she wouldn't feel so isolated, her father had built a bay window onto the living room and turned that part of the house into Carla's bedroom. Anytime a person drove to town, he had to pass the Welchs' house and could see Carla through that bay window, lying in her iron lung.

The Dixie Diner was a narrow building that resembled a double-long mobile home. At lunchtime, its gravel parking lot was filled with cars. Usually, Phyllis didn't pay attention to the crowd. She always knew a few people who were eating and could invite herself to sit with them. However, she wanted to be more careful about facing the Dixie Diner crowd today.

"You never get fed in that place." Fontana studied the steady stream of people coming out and going in through the double screen door of the diner. "Best let me take you on down to school."

Phyllis jerked her attention from the diner. "No. No." She touched her tongue to one of her bad teeth and put her hand on Fontana's shoulder. "The dentist told me to stay home because I'll probably hurt a lot when the numbing wears off where he worked on my tooth."

Fontana nodded. Her eyelids dropped half closed as she regarded Phyllis. "It'd be mighty hard doin' the books with a pain in yo' mouth."

"Even without a pain in my mouth, I have trouble." Phyllis shared this fact with Fontana because she didn't like lying to the black woman. After all, she was one person who didn't try to lord it over Phyllis. Still, Phyllis knew she had to be careful. People could really trip you up when they tried to make you do what they thought was right.

Checking the traffic, Fontana said, "Some people's meant for school and some ain't. I never was. 'Bout everybody I know's not meant for school. Look at all the trouble them people causing in Little Rock."

"Yeah, fightin' to go to school." Phyllis wondered if she should get out of the car and pretend to walk back home. The diner was more crowded than she had expected it to be. It wasn't much farther to walk up to the Scarlet Sow barbecue, but if some of her friends had sneaked off from school to eat at the Scarlet Sow, somebody might accidentally mention to a teacher that Phyllis Holsclaw was eating lunch at a public place when she was supposed to be sick. All of Phyllis's friends talked too much. That was what happened when people were immature.

"Well, if yo' teeth wasn't about to hurt, I'd offer to take you along with me. Maybe you doin' a little housecleanin' could keep your mind off your mouth. I got to run back to Miz LeFever's when I finish at Miz Welch's." Fontana shifted into low gear. "Or I'll be glad to run you back to yo' house right now."

"I *could* help you clean!" On a couple occasions, Phyllis, having gotten bored with Celeste and Marleen, had wandered into those parts of the house where Fontana was working. Phyllis had impressed Fontana with her eye for order and strong hands.

Besides, Phyllis had always wondered what the Welch house was like on the inside. And she liked the idea of being inside a family's home without their knowing about it. A burglar had to feel the same kind of thrill. Noticing how closely Fontana was watching her excitement, Phyllis added: "That kind of work *will* help me keep my mind off the pain." She returned Fontana's stare. "That's why I was out walking around to begin with."

Checking the traffic once more, Fontana pulled into the road. "I can fix us a sandwich at the Welchs'."

"Think you'll get in trouble having me in their house?" Phyllis didn't want Fontana to think she wasn't aware of the favor the black woman was doing for her.

"I know you won't break anything. And I sho know you won't steal anything. Me and you might not have much, but we don't need to take what other people got—we know that's not what we need." Fontana dropped her smile for a few seconds. "Just don't want nobody pushing us."

"Did they take Carla's iron lung up to Asheville with them?" Phyllis didn't like the heavy tone in Fontana's voice. But she had always wanted to get a closer look at the machine.

"No. You don't tote the iron lung around in a reg'lar car. They comes for it with a hospital truck."

Phyllis felt a tremor of relief. Unlike her sister and a lot of her other friends, Phyllis had a curiosity about how the world worked. Two summers in a row, Phyllis had spied on the boys in their dressing room at the Hibriten Pool. The men's and the women's dressing rooms were two large square roofless rooms separated by the concession room. By climbing up the shelves where girls stored their clothes in wire baskets, Phyllis could crawl along the top of the wall, over the roof of the concession room, and arrive at the wall of the men's dressing room. A chicken wire cover had been stretched over the mens' open roof because the boys kept making the trip over to the women's dressing room. Nobody had thought that a girl would want to make the crawl.

Although she was still a virgin, Phyllis figured she had seen enough naked men during those two summers not to be surprised on her wedding night. Vernon had promised Curtis and Adele that he and Phyllis would wait until after they were married, but Phyllis knew that Vernon often left her on her porch and had to drive home with "blue balls." She liked the idea of causing that kind of pain with her attractiveness. Men seemed to ask for it, were so open to it.

Of course, Phyllis was curious about rabies, too. Every summer, she volunteered to go with her daddy to the rabies vaccination clinic, which was held at the elementary school. She was the only one who could control Mush, their black chow chow, around other dogs. And while they stood in line, she could always hear rabies stories. Two or three times every summer, the local radio station carried rabies alerts. People who spotted stray dogs staggering down the road or a neighbor's dog foaming at the mouth could call the radio station and warn people. Despite being out of school in the summer and having the chance to ride in motorboats at the river, Phyllis dreaded summer because that was when dogs went mad, and you cut your feet on broken glass, and wild animals escaped from carnivals. And you had to worry about sunstroke and polio. On one hand, it was exciting, but on the other hand, if you didn't want to get sick, injured, or attacked, you had to stay inside too much in the summer. Phyllis knew she was braver than most of her friends, but what her friends didn't realize was that she was a lot braver than they realized because she saw a lot more danger than they did.

Just maybe a husband could be of some help in dealing

with all the other dangers a girl had to face. Then again, he could also be part of the danger.

"Anybody in your family get polio?" Phyllis felt her stomach tighten as they topped the hill and came within sight of the Welch house.

"Thank God, no." Fontana sighed. "People say we's too mean up on our end of town to get polio."

"It's a germ causes it—not how mean or good you are." Phyllis wondered if Fontana knew about germs.

Without seeming to take her attention from the road, Fontana asked, "What you think decides the germ who he'll infect?"

"What do you mean?" Phyllis had been ready to explain about germs, but not about their decision-making process.

"Say a germ comes to town. Now he can visit these folks—like Miz Welch—or he can visit your folks. Or if he's got time, he can travel on up the road and visit some niggers in Barlowtown." Fontana glanced at Phyllis and raised one eyebrow. "What helps them germs make up they mind?"

"That's not how it works." Phyllis waved her hands in the air.

"You ain't so sure as you make like." Fontana laughed. "I say germs got druthers just like you and me. Who else you know that come down with polio?"

"Well, Carla." Phyllis tilted her head back and concentrated on the stained headliner. "The Starnes sisters. Travis Bryant. Ray Mathis. Patsy Connelly. Eddie Lambert. That Story girl . . ."

"Now just of them you named, who be the meanest?" Fontana slowed the car and still avoided looking at Phyllis. The Welchs' driveway was cement, but steep and narrow.

Phyllis waited until Fontana had negotiated the turn. "I wouldn't say any of them is mean."

"I wouldn't suppose you could." Fontana changed to a lower gear, one that matched the growl in her voice.

Phyllis chewed on her lip a moment. The paralyzed people she had seen had been what most people would call sweet. She had always assumed that, being helpless, polio victims had to be sweet. As close as she had come to polio was when they thought that her brother, Dennis, had caught it. Although he turned out to be just overheated, Phyllis admitted that he was the least mean of the three Holsclaw kids. Marleen was the next-to-the-least mean. Sneaky and loose weren't the same thing as mean. Maybe Fontana was right.

". . . I 'bout laughed till I cried when the city trucks come round cuttin' down all the mimosa trees cause somebody got the idea the polio come from mimosa blossoms . . ."

The day after Dennis had his heatstroke, their daddy had cut down their five mimosa trees. "So you think it's safer to be mean?" Phyllis strained to see the iron lung through the bay window, but the sun glared too brightly on the glass.

"Seems so in this life." Fontana eased the car to a stop behind the Welch house.

It was a gray house with white trim. Phyllis could see into the kitchen as she climbed out of the Studebaker. The cabinets in the kitchen had glass windows, and all of the plates and cups and glasses were stacked neatly. The arrangement reminded Phyllis of the LeFever kitchen. You'd never think from looking at the back of the house that the front of the house contained an iron lung. Phyllis had half-expected to see a huge generator fenced off in the backyard or a Quonset hut filled with medical supplies. There was a small garage, the same gray as the house, but the rest of the yard could have been attached to anybody's house, anybody's life.

While Phyllis waited for Fontana to open the Welchs' back door, she slid her hands into the back pockets of her jeans and soaked up the scenery available from the top of the hill. Over the roof of the house, Phyllis could see the top third of Hibriten Mountain. The air was so clear that she could make out the huge wire-and-wood frame that the civic-minded Hibritens had erected years ago, as far back as Phyllis could remember, which during the Christmas season was lit up to reveal a gigantic star. Then, during Easter season, by a different configuration of lights, a gigantic cross watched over the town. As Fontana swung open the door, Phyllis realized that from Carla's iron lung in the front room, the view of

Hibriten Mountain had to be overpowering—especially with her lying on her back and having to see all of it sideways.

Before Phyllis could cross the tiny glassed-in porch, Fontana was already in the kitchen, digging in a closet filled with cleaning equipment. "Let me do the vacuumin' befo' we eat."

Catching sight of some gray rags hanging from a rack over Fontana's head, Phyllis realized that since they had climbed out of the car, she had begun to feel awkward. On one hand, she knew Fontana was a maid. But on the other hand, Phyllis couldn't pretend that she was somebody like Celeste LeFever who felt perfectly natural parked on her ass while a simmering black woman cleaned up after her. Lazy as she was in school, Phyllis could clean better than anybody in her house. "You mind if I dust?"

Fontana, grasping a round brush attachment, straightened up slowly, then leaned against the door frame, balanced on her knuckles. "You do as good a job as you used to do for the LeFevers."

"I'll do even better." Phyllis took a bottle of Old English furniture polish from the shelf. She liked the scarlet color of the polish, and the smell brought to mind two of Phyllis's favorite songs: "Come on-a My House," which was slightly sexy, and "Mockin' Bird Hill," which was slightly oily—but nice as far as Phyllis was concerned.

She thought it was odd that furniture polish would make her think of those old songs, but she had to admit that cleaning house didn't have much to do with rock and roll. In a way, the smell of the furniture polish reminded Phyllis of Vernon. Because he worked in the spray booth at Blue Ridge Furniture, he always carried around a faint odor of varnish. He certainly wasn't any Gaither Drum. Working as an upholsterer, Gaither was part of the furniture factory aristocracy. He didn't work around any machinery. Even the conveyor belt stopped right outside his workroom. The boys who tacked the padding over the springs carried the furniture in to Gaither. So he could afford to wear his Old Spice aftershave, his Vitalis, and chew his Juicy Fruit gum. To smell him, you couldn't tell that Gaither worked any kind of job.

"All you have to do's the dinin' room, the back bedroom, the den, and the livin' room." Fontana handed Phyllis four or five of the gray rags.

"Is the livin' room where the iron lung is?" Phyllis gave each rag a shake and tried to sound casual.

"Yeah, but we don't have to clean it. Miz Welsh keeps that job for herself. And that suits me with gratitude." Fontana picked up the canister vacuum and lumbered into the dining room.

Phyllis followed, unscrewing the lid from the polish. She poured the red liquid on a rag and took a deep breath. Perhaps two rooms away was a machine she had seen only from the highway. She wasn't sure if it was silver or white. She'd seen ones like it on television, but she'd never been sure of the color.

The furniture in the dining room was heavier than what Phyllis had expected. The Welchs were rich enough to buy new furniture. She thought only her parents and her friends' parents used the thick tables and chairs that they had probably picked up back before the war. Of course, before Adele moved to the new brick house, she didn't have a dining room table. They hadn't had a dining room until they moved out of the little flat-topped house that sat in the shadow of the LeFever house. Certainly, the LeFevers had all that light, curved, graceful modern furniture that you saw in movies, but Phyllis didn't count Celeste as anything but a rich girl who didn't know what to do with herself.

What really irritated Phyllis about Celeste was the fact that she didn't have to decide what to do with herself.

She stooped over the table and began polishing, breathing deeply. The scarlet polish was slightly thicker than water, like spit or sweat with body oil mixed in. Yes, Vernon was like the furniture polish. It almost smelled good, almost sweet, almost tangy—like an orange. But underneath was a serious odor. The odor of work, of responsibility. And that was Vernon, too. Adele had told Phyllis more than once that she wouldn't find a more responsible man than Vernon. Phyllis didn't think her mother was pushing her to marry Vernon. He had sworn up and down that her mama and daddy didn't know he was proposing to her.

No. Adele liked Vernon so much because she disliked Gaither so much. Where Gaither was flashy with his red hair swooped back into a perfectly shaped ducktail, Vernon wore a flattop—clean and honest. Where Gaither wore his shirt collar turned up, even at work—and wore only rolled-up short-sleeved shirts to show off his muscles as much as he could—Vernon wore a white T-shirt at work and work shirts, like her daddy's, when he wasn't spraying furniture. Gaither moved like Elvis Presley where Vernon moved like everybody in Hibriten.

Although Fontana seemed fully occupied with her vacuuming, Phyllis knew that she was evaluating how well she was polishing the table. She worked slowly, not only because she felt she was being watched but because she liked the way the sheen emerged from the wood. It might not be so bad, she thought, working in a furniture factory. Except you had to be there the same number of hours every day. And it was harder to cut days at work than days at school she'd heard. In fact, Marleen had told her that even if you had a real reason for missing work, they'd give you a hard time if you got sick more than once or twice a year. Phyllis believed her sister. Their mama and daddy crawled to work no matter how sick they were. Phyllis admitted to herself that to anybody with half a brain and only one eye, factory work was more confining than school.

Marleen had gotten through, but she had a social streak to her. She liked being at school, even when she didn't do any of her homework, because she liked being around people. As Phyllis began polishing the legs of the table, she shook her head. Marleen was doing pretty good with her night job at Hibriten Fibers because she liked the people she worked with. It didn't seem to bother her that she was wedged between the hours on the time clock. She couldn't go talk to somebody just anytime she pleased. She had to arrange her conversations around broken machinery, slow bobbin boys, and official breaks. Still, Marleen was simple-minded enough not to realize how her soul belonged fifty minutes to the hour to Hibriten Fibers.

"Some people say a man is made out of mud," Phyllis began singing.

"But a po' man's made out of muscle and blood." Fontana gave her head a twist and drowned out the vacuum cleaner.

Phyllis plopped onto her butt and leaned away from the table. "Muscle and blood . . ."

"Skin and bone . . ."

Fontana swooped over to where Phyllis sat and dipped her head next to Phyllis's to harmonize on the next line.

"A mind that's weak and a back that's strong," they sang together.

By the time they had finished the song, Fontana had finished the dining room carpet and Phyllis had moved from the table to the china hutch. As she unplugged the vacuum cleaner, Fontana wiped her face with her forearm. "They's mo' difference between rich and poor than black and white."

"They just live better's all." Phyllis worked carefully around the glass of the hutch. She didn't like to leave oil smears. While the Welchs' furniture wasn't too different from what Phyllis was used to, she had to admit that Mrs. Welch had much nicer china than Adele did. And more of it. Bone-colored plates and saucers with blue clover trim. All of it matched.

Fontana chuckled like molten lava as she picked up the vacuum cleaner. "The rich man thinks we's all niggers." She gave the machine a shake, catching Phyllis's eye. "You and yo' kind well as me and mine. You jus' got a little more maneuverin' room."

"You seem to get along with them." Phyllis kept polishing.

"I don't know no rich people." Fontana cocked her head as if confused.

"What do you call the LeFevers . . . and the Welchs?" Phyllis turned to face Fontana.

The black woman tossed her head back, and her laugh popped open like a large umbrella. "Lawd, honey. I don't call *them* rich."

"What do you call them?" Phyllis thought of the LeFevers' two Cadillacs and their contemporary furniture, the magazines lying all over the place. She was with Marleen in Celeste's room that day when Celeste had started to toss out all of her 78s because she had replaced every single one of them with 45s. Phyllis thought of the matching china in the hutch she was polishing, of the carpet on the floor, of how the house smelled like Lysol and roses instead of bacon and heating oil.

"Oh, they's comfortable enough. More comfortable than a lot of us. But I sees they socks, they underwear. I sees Miz LeFever sweatin' over they bills. And Mister LeFever some days don't even get home till way late at night. He works for his Cadillacs. They not somethin' he just give hisself. And Mister and Miz Welch still payin' for they girls' polio. You think a Cadillac's expensive? Come on in here and let me show you expensive." Fontana, still carrying the vacuum cleaner, disappeared through the doorway.

Still carrying the bottle of polish and her rags, Phyllis chased after her. Fontana had to lift the vacuum cleaner in front of her as she passed through the narrow hallway that led by two bedrooms and a den. Then the hall opened out into the living room. Once again, Phyllis was not impressed by the furniture. Maybe the Welchs' two couches were a little newer than the Holsclaws'. Maybe their two stuffed chairs looked a little more comfortable than the ones Phyllis sat in when she watched television, but she could tell Mrs. Welch shopped at the same places Adele did.

Perhaps what made the furniture in the living room look newer and cleaner was how much light came through the bay windows, even more than came through the picture window in Celeste LeFever's living room. In the brilliant sunlight, the iron lung stood, like a race car on stilts. For a second, Phyllis remembered that wreck in France a few years before, in which eighty race car drivers were killed. She was glad the tank was white. Even its four little wheels had white hub caps. For some reason, Phyllis hadn't expected the metal tank to look so big.

At the foot of the iron lung were four rectangular windows, two on each side, at the top and the bottom. At the head end were two more rectangular windows on the upper sides. Below these rectangular windows were two round windows. What Phyllis had not expected to see was a large glass dome at the end of the tank where Carla's head would stick out of the machine.

"I didn't know they kept Carla's head in that bowl." Phyllis moved closer to the tank.

"Most of the time, they don't." Fontana stepped beside Phyllis. She pointed to the latches that connected the dome to the tank. "This an Emerson iron lung. Before this one come along, you had to tend to the sick person through these windows." Fontana tapped one of the round windows. "Awful hard to wash the girl or turn her so she keep from gettin' bedsores. See, all you could do was open the whole tank up and hope they didn't suffocate too much while you washed and changed 'em. Or you stuck a tube down they nose. It was a mess no matter what way you choose." Fontana tapped the glass dome. "But with this, you can feed 'em air while they out of the tank gettin' a bath, or jus' being touched. Miz Carla tell me she get lonesome in her tank after a while. And her paralyzed all the way down."

"Do they ever let you work it?" Phyllis stooped over to study the latches on the dome. Farther down, where a wide white metal band secured the head hatch to the rest of the tank, was a second row of larger latches.

"Not much to work it." Fontana took Phyllis's arm and pulled her to the middle of the iron lung. Underneath it was a second, smaller tank, stainless steel, topped with a control panel containing three gauges, two toggle switches, one green, one red, and three adjustment dials. From the bottom of the tank, a curved handle extended upward.

"Them dials set the pressure and the time and the fullness," Fontana said, flicking a finger at the gauges. "Nobody touch them switches but the doctor or Mister and Miz Welch." Fontana paused. "It'd be like messin' with Miz Carla's insides."

Phyllis pretended to gag. "I wouldn't want to do that."

With a slight squint in Phyllis's direction, Fontana continued. "That green turn on the machine. Jus' flip it up." She flipped the air above the switch. "I been around a lot of sickness. You know, my man come back from the wo' with a leg gone and a steel plate in his fo'head. My mama got a bad hip. I got a boy with ..." Fontana exhaled powerfully and strummed her lips with her finger—an expression Phyllis had seen Marleen use to communicate the unspeakable and that she had borrowed from the cartoons she was so good at mimicking.

"What about your boy?" Phyllis started to lean against the iron lung but then thought better of it. Still, she wanted to touch it with some part of her body, so she rested her hand against the bottom of the white tank, as if she was trying to soothe a nervous horse.

"He got nothin' to do with how this iron lung operates." Fontana pointed to the red switch. "That red for cuttin' off all the power underneath, in case they be some kind of fire."

Phyllis nodded. The iron lung was like a lot of machines, even like the machines she had seen in the furniture factory. Green for starting up and red for emergency stops. But looking through one of the rectangular windows at the narrow bed inside the tank, Phyllis realized that instead of wood, you put a human being inside this machine. And it breathed for the person. Unlike the factory machines, which would just as soon rip off a finger or cut off a hand, the iron lung was there to keep somebody alive. Even if the person couldn't keep alive herself.

"That must be nice, not even having to worry about breathing for yourself." Phyllis knew that she was supposed to be thankful for her good health, but sometimes she thought it would suffocate her.

Instead of looking shocked, Fontana laughed. "Too much life lodged between yo' ribs?"

"I go to school, and I got teachers standing on me. I get home, I got Mama and Daddy standing on me." Phyllis realized she wasn't making it clear to Fontana how everybody seemed to be squeezing her. It was like being trapped in a car crash, the steering wheel rammed against her chest. "And I've got a guy who keeps pushing me to marry him."

"You old enough to marry?" Fontana crossed her arms over her chest and, cocking her head, inspected Phyllis more closely.

"Sixteen." Phyllis tried to shape the word into a blade.

"But Jerry Lee Lewis married his cousin, and she's just thirteen." Phyllis stepped back and fingered one of the larger latches. "I've been thinking maybe that's some kind of sign."

"What you know about signs?" Fontana sounded more curious than challenging.

"Little Richard thought the *Sputnik* was a sign from God that he should give up rock and roll." Phyllis hoped Fontana would appreciate her bringing Little Richard into the discussion.

"I don't think it's the music in the man that's Little Richard's problem, but the man that's in the music." For a second, Fontana seemed to be humming "The Girl Can't Help It."

"Home's a dead end. But all I've got outside it is Vernon." Phyllis turned from Fontana to prop her elbows on the iron lung and rest her chin on her knuckles while she stared at Hibriten Mountain.

"Vernon's yo' man?" Fontana moved closer to Phyllis and leaned one elbow on the tank, studying Phyllis's profile.

"He tells me he is." Phyllis felt her body getting bottom heavy with frustration. "I know why he wants to get married." She turned to Fontana. "And I don't mind what he expects of me. I'm ready to give him what he wants."

"If he like mos' men, he only half know what he expect but wholly expect what he want." Fontana followed Phyllis's gaze out the window. "That what pull us women to 'em, I suspect. Even Miz Carla talk about gettin' married. Flat on her back all these years, and she still got an eye for the boys. I heard her doctor say ain't nothin' wrong with her 'cept her muscles don't work. When I clean her, I give her a little gooch on her side, and she laugh. Know what I'm sayin'? She can't move but she can feel."

Phyllis had always assumed that paralysis meant numbness. The people she had seen in wheelchairs or in iron lungs never seemed to be thinking about what they might be feeling. All of their attention seemed centered in their heads. Otherwise, she had once wondered, how could they stand to live with themselves? Here she was, with all of her parts working, and she was reaching the point where she couldn't stand to feel or be felt. She resented her parents' fear that she would turn out to be as wild as her sister—"wild" meaning that Marleen had felt too much for men and dived right into that feeling. She resented Vernon for wanting her to have those same feelings that had gotten her sister into trouble but at the same time to hold those feelings in control until he and her mama and daddy gave her permission to let them pour out and wash her into marriage.

She felt paralyzed herself. Maybe that's what polio was. Maybe it wasn't a germ after all but some kind of destructive feeling that slithered into a person's spine and sliced off the nerves. She remembered the lessons she'd been taught about polio after that summer of the epidemic. She remembered standing in line at the elementary school with Marleen and Dennis and a million other kids, waiting to get her shot of gamma globulin which turned out to be useless after Dr. Salk came along and explained what was really going on. Too bad Dr. Salk didn't turn his attention to emotional diseases. Come up with a vaccine for confusion. Or if only somebody would come up with an iron lung for people who were being squashed by their families.

Stepping back a couple of steps, Phyllis studied the white tank thoughtfully. "Let me try the iron lung, Fontana."

Fontana chuckled, dropped one arm to her side, and turned to face Phyllis. "You think this thing a party dress of some kind?" She shook her head. "Why'd anybody healthy as you want to climb in such a thing? I'd as soon climb in a casket."

"No, no, no. It's not the same thing." Phyllis slumped in front of the big woman but bounced back up and patted her arms while pleading with her. "Maybe I can think better in that iron lung. Maybe I can see how lucky I am to be healthy and that'll make me feel more satisfied. Maybe I'm having so much trouble making up my mind because I'm not getting enough oxygen to my brain. Maybe I had a touch of polio back in 1953 and didn't even know it."

"And maybe you just tryin' to get yo' way. What that sick girl goin' say if she know some wild woman been tryin' on her iron lung?" Fontana asked her question in denial but not necessarily flat refusal, and Phyllis perceived the black woman's guarded curiosity, her complicity.

"You said yourself that she's got feelings like other girls." Phyllis moved sideways, inserting herself between the tank and Fontana. She thought being close to the tank might help Fontana see that she wasn't asking such a big favor. And she also wanted the light coming from behind her. With the glare, Fontana wouldn't be able to inspect Phyllis's face too closely. Phyllis didn't think she was trying to lie to Fontana, not exactly, but she certainly didn't want the black woman to see how much she resented being called "wild."

"I think Carla would like knowing another girl had been interested enough in her to want to feel what she feels in her iron lung. Maybe she wouldn't feel so lonely knowing she wasn't the only person to be in that place." Phyllis turned to the tank and contemplated it for a moment. Then she turned back to Fontana. "Besides, didn't you tell me that Carla is about to shed that thing?"

"That's right." Fontana shrugged. "She's up to Asheville gettin' fitted for a cureass."

"What's wrong with her ass?" Phyllis wondered if Fontana was trying to change the subject on her.

"It sound like somethin' to do with ass, but it really for her lung. This man come down from the hospital and show us all this thing called a cureass. It look like a metal vest that fit over Miz Carla's chest so she can breathe but get out of her tank."

Phyllis studied the black woman's face closely. Fontana had planted one large fist on her hip and was rubbing her chin with the other. "I'm not so different from Carla. Like you said, I just have more room to maneuver, but I'm maneuvering myself dizzy." Phyllis thought she needed to tell Fontana that the two of them were also alike, that maybe she could come back from the iron lung like Lazarus from the grave and have some kind of secrets to tell her.

Before Phyllis could present her other argument, Fontana said, "Well, if gettin' in that thing will do you *and* Miz Carla so much good, I'll give you the chance." She went to the iron lung and began opening the latches that held on the glass dome. As she carefully placed the dome on the couch, she jerked her chin in the direction of Phyllis's feet. "Get them shoes off."

By the time Phyllis got her shoes off, Fontana had already unlatched the top of the tank and rolled out the bed, doubling the length of the iron lung. Fontana supported Phyllis by the elbow while she climbed up on the narrow bed.

"You jus' relax and let me open up the collar." Fontana adjusted the foam rubber circle at the top of Phyllis's head. Then without warning, she bent over, grasped Phyllis under her armpits and slid her head through the collar. In almost the same motion, she tightened the collar around Phyllis's neck.

For the first time, Phyllis noticed the mirror attached to the tank above her chin. She could see up the hallway, into the den, but the reversed image made her feel slightly dizzy, so she closed her eyes. She could smell the metal, the foam rubber, and the electric odor of the motor. But what came to her most strongly was the smell of shampoo from the pillow where her head rested. And around the edges of the shampoo drifted the odor of perfume—My Sin. Phyllis thought this could be her pillow and wondered if Carla had a friend who sneaked her the sexy perfume when her parents weren't watching.

Interrupting her communion with Carla's odors, Fontana pulled the bed section back toward the tank. "You want it latched?"

Phyllis felt her mouth go dry. "Give me the whole treatment."

"Feelin' nervous?" Fontana latched the top. "You look like you swallowed a bar of Lifebuoy." She latched the sides and laughed. "I wonder if this is how the woman feels jus' befo' the magician saws her in half." She latched the bottom.

Briefly, all Phyllis could feel was her head. The collar amplified the pulse in her neck and caused it to echo through her skull. At first, she thought the hum and hiss in her ears was just another part of her own internal sounds. Then she realized that air was forcing its way into her mouth and nose, filling her up. At that point, discovering the iron lung was operating, Phyllis became aware of her body. Not only her chest, but also her stomach and her thighs were being pulled. She tried to regulate her breathing, but she wound up filling her lungs to the point she thought her ribs would crack.

"Don't fight it, honey." Fontana leaned around the corner of the tank so Phyllis could see her in the mirror. "Let it breathe for you. Make like you dancin' and the tank is yo' man. Jus' follow how it go. Otherwise you trip up."

To Phyllis, the fluctuating pressure in the tank felt like water. She tried to think of herself as floating, sometimes her body rising out of the water, sometimes sinking. And she had to let the water push the air in and out of her lungs. "I should be wearing a bathing suit." Her voice sounded slightly quavery, the tone it had when the water was too cold.

"You got the idea now." Fontana stood up. "Want me to stay here with you?"

"Does somebody always stay with Carla?" Phyllis turned her head slowly to look at Fontana. But she kept her body perfectly still.

"No. She got this room to herself a lot of the time."

"Then I want it to myself for a little while." Phyllis felt a slight chill around her abdomen. "Is my shirttail out?"

Fontana looked through one of the rectangular windows. "No. You's as neat as can be. I'm gonna go finish with the vacuum, then."

"Give me a few minutes and I'll finish the dusting."

Already, Phyllis looked forward to returning to the boring world of dust and the smell of furniture polish.

"Jus' yell when you want me if I don't get back before then." Fontana disappeared into the hallway in the direction of the bedrooms.

Phyllis had always thought the iron lung somehow squeezed a person's body and made it suck in the air, then blow it out. She soon realized that what she felt was a total absence of squeezing. Certainly, she felt her lungs and her stomach moving. And she could feel the air pouring down her throat. All this movement, though, seemed to come about without pressure. The iron lung was taking pressure off of her! The air was coming in because her lungs were free from pressure. Even the air was looking for freedom, Phyllis realized.

As she was turning this idea over in her mind, wondering what to do with it, wondering if such knowledge could be used against her parents, Phyllis noticed that her skin was beginning to tingle. Although still throbbing in her ears, her pulse had begun to echo in her arms, her chest, stomach, crotch, legs. Her blood was trying to get out! She felt as if she were blushing all over her body. A warmth enveloped her. It was the warmth of sunbathing, summer light on her skin right after she'd come out of the water and was just starting to lose the chill. Phyllis wondered if Carla had sunbathed. She was a little older than Marleen, but like Celeste, Carla and her sister had not mixed with the children of Hibriten's factory workers. However, the tingling was spreading deeper now and prevented Phyllis from feeling her usual resentment.

In fact, Phyllis found herself wishing that she could bring Vernon with her inside the iron lung. Of course, she wasn't sure if a man would get the same sensations. But any human being, she reasoned, would have to feel the same smoothing out of the deeper nerves, the ones that ran along beside the thicker veins and arteries—the ones that ran into the wild, dark places, where you always found trouble but you never had to worry about suffocating if you just learned how to breathe with it, knowing you couldn't breathe in the regular shallow, dull way you did on a normal day, but the way you did dancing to forbidden music or swimming in dangerous water. And all of this tingled right there between her and the air, threatening to dissolve the iron lung.

From the other room, above the sound of the tank and vacuum cleaner, Fontana had returned to Tennessee Ernie Ford's song: "If you see me comin' better step aside . . ."

Uncertain if she could persuade Fontana to climb inside the iron lung, Phyllis thought she'd let her finish singing before she screamed to return to the world she now knew how to escape.

SOUL FOOD 1958

ALTHOUGH IT WAS MID-APRIL, the wood stove in Turner Holsclaw's living room was kept stoked by the long line of relatives passing through to Turner and Teense's bedroom, where Teense lay dying. By some quirk of location or construction, the house stayed cool even in July and August when everyone else in the county was sleeping with three or four fans blowing all night long.

Turner had built his squat, four-room house at the end of a dirt road, right at the point where the road became a path leading off into a crescent of thick woods about three miles long and three miles wide at its broadest section. The house stood at the edge of this forest with a small garden and a tangle of blackberry bushes to act as a buffer against the forest. Although surrounded by trees on all sides, the house wasn't in the shade enough to explain the coolness of the rooms.

Dennis Holsclaw, who'd been brought to visit his dying grandmother, sat at the supper table across the small room from the stove. With his eyes closed, Dennis was able to think of the stove as a black dragon squatting in the middle of the room with its tail sticking in the chimney. It blew its hot breath on him, trying to melt the side of his face. Waiting for death had to be uncomfortable because, as his parents had told him, it was a serious matter.

Of course, Dennis had always found his grandfather's house uncomfortable. There was no television. The toilet was outside. Someone was constantly reminding him to watch out for snakes. And while he had seen only three snakes in nine years of being brought to visit Teense and Turner at least twice a week, he'd stumbled across more wasps, hornets, and yellow jackets than he could count. Before Teense had been brought home from the state hospital—even before she had been carried off to the state hospital—the tumor in her head had caused her to hear things around the house.

Shifting in his chair as quietly as he could, Dennis felt sorry for his grandmother having to sit or sleep in these rooms and hear footsteps out on the back porch or the heavy breathing in one of the rooms on the other side of the dark hallway. Besides, no one had explained to him how they knew the noises were caused by her tumor. Although Teense had five grown sons, false teeth, and a silky black mustache, Dennis had noticed that because she was such a small woman, everyone—even her own sons—treated her like a child. He had heard Turner threaten to slap her once when she kept insisting that he go check the spare bedroom across the hall. That was before she'd started going blind.

First, she'd heard things that scared her; then she'd started having her headaches; then she'd gotten so she couldn't see. Now, she was going to die. It was like a sermon that Dennis had heard many times at Midtown Baptist Church. As a matter of fact, for the last few days, sitting in this room had reminded Dennis a great deal of sitting in the pew at church. Dennis shifted in his chair so he could keep his eyes on the stove. It sat defiantly on its asbestos-sheathed-in-tin mat, like a cast-iron dwarf waiting for a wrestling opponent.

By squinting his eyes and slightly jiggling his head, Dennis could make the stove do a little waddle step. Maybe it had been the stove moving around that Teense had heard. On one "Inner Sanctum" episode, a woman had been killed by the clothes in her closet because she was so vain. Vanity was a sin. Dennis's Sunday school teacher, Mrs. Lambert, was always surprising him with a new sin. Dennis wanted to hate the stove, but he knew hatred was a sin. Hatred could get you sent to hell. But as Preacher Dillard had pointed out, a person had to sometimes cover a lot of suffering ground before getting to hell—or heaven for that matter. But more people went to hell than to heaven. That was a fact.

Dennis was quick to remind himself that God always gave you a warning if you were bound for hell. Chastisement, Preacher Dillard called it. Of course, you shouldn't confuse chastisement with tribulation. You were chastised by God to let you know you were sinning. You were tribulated by the devil to discourage you from doing what was right. This evening, when Dennis's mother found out that Teense was much worse than she had been that morning, she had hustled him and his father out of the house without fixing them supper. Because Dennis couldn't think of anything he had done wrong that day, he assumed he was suffering tribulation. Coming to see Teense was right. She'd come around earlier in the day long enough to ask specifically to see Dennis. But his mother had told him to wait out here because she didn't want him to see her unconscious.

The stove grumbled and ashes rattled into the ashpan. The breeze outside his grandfather's house squeaked the chimney cover around as the stove settled back down to its nasal consumption of wood. It was the sound of Dennis's father sleeping. Cautiously, Dennis let his eyes drift to the mica windows of the stove. From inside, the fire looked out and licked against the hazy film. Once, Dennis had found a fish. Its eye—the other had been eaten by ants, which jittered like nervous bits of licorice—was dull as the window of that stove. All dried up, the fish's skin was tight like wax paper.

Dennis closed his eyes again. They felt hot. His mouth was hot. This felt like sickness. And sickness could be chastisement or tribulation. As far as Dennis had been able to decide, the two worst diseases were polio and cancer. Polio wasn't as bad as it used to be, but it had scared him more than even The Blob. He vaguely remembered that summer in 1953 when he had been playing outside and suddenly felt like he was going to throw up, but before he could get really sick to his stomach, the world had closed in around him, dark and stretchy, as if he'd been folded up in an inner tube. When he had woken up, he was lying on the couch in the living room. His sisters, Marleen and Phyllis, were holding his hands, and on his forehead he had a washrag wrapped around crushed ice cubes. His mama had run across the dirt road in front of the house to the Calloways so she could use their phone to call the doctor.

That had been five years ago, so Dennis didn't remember much. After his mama called the doctor, she called the factory where Dennis's daddy worked. He had gotten home right after the doctor had taken Dennis's temperature and squeezed his abdomen. Although Dennis hadn't known what an epidemic was at the time, he had noticed that Phyllis and Marleen were made to stay at home almost every day during that summer, and there had been no picnics or trips to the river. Even his daddy stayed at home more and hardly ever went fishing.

Dennis also remembered watching his father chop down all five of the mimosa trees that shaded his sandbox. From somewhere, the theory had drifted down to people with children that the epidemic was caused by mimosa blossoms. Throughout Hibriten and all the surrounding towns, the trees with their pink blossoms that looked like high-altitude fireworks were cut down, and parents took their children to county health clinics or elementary schools to stand in long lines so the children could be given shots of gamma globulin.

Dennis's daddy had been especially worried about his son because two weeks earlier, Curtis had gone up to Asheville with a friend of his from work to visit the man's two daughters, both of whom had come down with polio and were in iron lungs. Before the summer of '53 was over, one of the girls had died and the other was so shriveled up by the disease that she had to come home in her iron lung. A year or so ago, Preacher Dillard had announced to his congregation that "Praise God, a miracle had occurred, and the Welch girl had recovered enough to be taken out of her iron lung—for short periods of time."

As it had turned out, Dennis had blacked out because of a minor heatstroke. But he remembered that, for a while, he could ask for anything he wanted and almost always get it. Phyllis had whispered in his ear to ask for a television. But his daddy balked at that request. However, not too long after the summer was over, his daddy and Uncle Daniel had come struggling in with a big box. Television had helped him forget about polio for a long time.

But then his third-grade teacher, Mrs. Chesterfield, had announced to his class that for the next few weeks during the rest period following their afternoon recess, she was going to read a new book to them, which should have special interest because it was by a man all of them should know: Mr. Welch. It was the same man whose two daughters had caught polio. Of course all of the children knew him because his daughter had become a landmark, no less significant than the huge cross of lights that burned on top of Hibriten Mountain during the Easter season and the huge star of lights that burned there during the Christmas season.

If the book itself had not been filled with the horrors of twisted bodies and thunderstorms that knocked out the power in the iron lung ward of the hospital, Mrs. Chesterfield's personality would have still embedded the book in that part of Dennis's brain where he stored *The Creature from the Black Lagoon*, *Invaders from Mars*, *The Blob*, *The Crawling Eye*, and *Invasion of the Body Snatchers*. Mrs. Chesterfield was a large woman with a bulldog face. She had a serious case of psoriasis and spent a few minutes out of each hour standing in front of her desk rubbing large patches of dry skin from her hands and wrists.

She represented a special source of anxiety for Dennis because Phyllis had also been in Mrs. Chesterfield's class and hadn't gotten along with the woman. In fact, Mrs. Chesterfield had given Phyllis such a hard paddling—Mrs. Chesterfield used a paddle with holes bored in the business end—that Phyllis had developed blisters that got infected. For nearly two weeks, Phyllis had to stand in the back of the room while her wounds healed.

Dennis thought that the book wouldn't have been so scary if Mrs. Chesterfield hadn't pulled down the shades before she started reading. Without a window to glance out of and reassure himself that the world was actually full of sunshine and free from the polio of 1953, Dennis felt sucked into the book, even though he had learned in the second grade that Jonas Salk had come up with a cure for the disease. The gravel in Mrs. Chesterfield's voice scraped away any confidence that Dennis might have had in Jonas Salk's work.

But as bad as polio was, hell was worse. Preacher Dillard had said that over and over again. In fact, compared to the suffering in hell, any disease in this life would be considered a blessing if it helped the person turn his life around. That was the whole point of chastisement. Of course, Teense couldn't turn her life around. Even if it wasn't almost over, she couldn't get any better than she already was. Dennis propped his forehead on the palms of his hands, a position that helped him think more clearly. He still had three or four of the sock monkeys that Teense had made for him. On special occasions, she also gave him a silver dollar or two, but he never got to keep them.

Everyone said Teense was good—even Preacher Dillard. She certainly didn't have to worry about hell. Since she'd come back from the hospital, all she talked about was heaven. She had lost weight and had to have somebody around to sit her up and feed her. Dennis thought that he'd like to see her one more time in her tiny kitchen, getting ready to bake corn bread. She always fried a handful of cornmeal in her iron skillet before pouring in the batter. The living room seemed to brighten up as long as the corn bread was baking.

Dennis could imagine Teense as she lay in her bed. Her hair would be in a tight bun. Most of it was still black. She had a pint or two of Cherokee blood in her. But not enough for her ever to talk much about it. Her mouth would be caved-in looking because she kept her teeth in a frosted pink jar. Four glass angels held the jar up. If you looked hard enough, you could see the teeth smiling through the angels' wings. Because she dipped snuff, the teeth were stained brown. But she hadn't used her teeth since she'd come home.

The older and the sicker that Teense became, Dennis had

noticed, the more she resembled Grandpa Turner. Turner always sat close to the head of the bed. His chair had crouched in the darkness of that bedroom for so long that it was no more than a shadow to Dennis. Having given up color, shape, and size, it was now just a dark thing that somehow held Grandpa Turner's slumped figure as he sat, ignoring the relatives who stared at Teense's face, methodically picking his crinkled face. As many times as Dennis had watched his grandfather, he'd never been able to see what the old man was picking at. Before Phyllis and Marleen had gotten married and left home, he had watched them mash pimples, but they had either used a mirror or gotten the other sister to do the mashing. Grandpa Turner just stroked his face a few seconds, then seemed to pinch a piece of skin without getting anything out of it.

Turner was like a cough as far as Dennis could tell. He was the kind of cough you get when dust gets in your nose and throat. The old man's eyes were gray, smoky but clear. He didn't wear glasses, but he did use a magnifying glass when he read. Back before Teense's tumor had taken so much out of them both, Turner had been more talkative, but he'd always been friendlier to Phyllis and Marleen than he had been to Dennis. They acted as if they'd never been afraid of the old man. Dennis had always been confused by his grandfather's preference for his sisters. Neither one of them had taken church seriously. And Phyllis had actually dropped out of school so she could get married. Phyllis, though, back before she left home, had avoided the visits to Teense and Turner's. Marleen, who always seemed to enjoy the visits, hadn't been by since the first day that Teense came home because she was too tired after working the graveyard shift at Hibriten Fibers. Besides, Grandpa Turner was upset about how Marleen was turning out.

No one ever wanted to disturb Turner because he had a temper. Long ago, according to Dennis's daddy, Grandpa Turner had been a preacher. It was okay for a preacher to have a temper. During a good sermon, Preacher Dillard got worked up as if he had a temper. He turned red in the face and shouted, jerked off his coat and tie, sweated, and waved his arms. But Grandpa Turner would sometimes fly off the handle if you let the screen door squeak too much or if you walked through the house one too many times. Actually, he'd quieted down since Teense's tumor. He didn't pay attention to anyone. Preacher Dillard had never said that Grandpa Turner was good. Grandpa Turner didn't look as if he cared where he went when he died.

The worst place in the living room was over the mantel above the fireplace. Curtis and Daniel had bricked up the fireplace when they installed the stove for Teense and Turner. To celebrate the new stove, Marleen had told Dennis, their father had given his parents a huge picture of an old ship out on the ocean. The ship's sails were billowed out and the waves were high and rugged. A few weeks ago, one of Dennis's older cousins, Loan Holsclaw, had told him that if he watched the ship long enough, he might see it start to move. If the ship did start to move, then that meant that he was going to go crazy. As much as Dennis disliked Loan, he was inclined to believe what he said because on one of the "Inner Sanctum" episodes, Dennis thought he'd seen a similar situation.

As uncomfortable as Loan made Dennis, he preferred to think about his cousin rather than about that picture of the ship. Despite how nice Loan's mother, Nelly, was, Loan had to be about the meanest person Dennis knew. One day, Dennis hoped, he would be taller than Loan because Loan wasn't much taller than Phyllis—who was small for a woman. Dennis had no doubt that Loan was kept short because of his sinful life. In fact, his life was so sinful that Dennis had no clear notion of what Loan did in his almost nightly wandering. Loan's loose ways were partly explained to Dennis by his mama and daddy as the result of his working at the Tate-Johnson Funeral Home. Perhaps not being tall enough to become a mortician, Loan worked mainly as an ambulance and hearse driver. If Dennis had been on better terms with his cousin, he might have been something of a celebrity among his friends—being related to an ambulance driver—but Dennis's piety always seemed to irritate his cousin.

As far back as he could remember, Phyllis and Marleen

had protected him against Loan, who was maybe a year older than Marleen. However, Marleen was maybe a couple of feet taller than Loan. And she had been a basketball player. Before a game, when she was chasing around the house in her Blue Ridge Hornets green-and-white uniform, Dennis had thought she was more powerful than the Lone Ranger and Captain Midnight. Once, he had seen her knock down a girl who was trying to take the ball away from her. Marleen also enjoyed that elevated status of being a school bus driver. More than once, Dennis had seen her throw hulking high school boys off her bus if they got too loud or rough.

The room felt even colder when Dennis realized that Marleen might soon have her own baby and would probably be coming around less often than she already did. On the other hand, people like Loan always seemed to be around, just waiting to bring tribulation into someone's life—or did Loan bring chastisement? No. Dennis was convinced that Loan was an instrument of the devil. He liked that phrase. Preacher Dillard had warned about hanging around with instruments of the devil. Several times, Dennis had seen his cousin wailing along the road in the red ambulance with his face bathed in the flashing red lights. At those times, Loan had certainly resembled a devil in a souped-up Cadillac.

Because Loan would probably be coming by to pick up Nelly, Dennis knew he would, most likely, have to face Loan before the night was over. As if responding to his dread, his Aunt Nelly slipped through the door to Teense's bedroom. She kept her prominent nose close to the edge of the door so she wouldn't have to open it any wider than she had to. Taking one last look into the sickroom, she gently closed the door and faced Dennis. Unlike Dennis's mother, Nelly had lost her shape. Her faded yellow hair clung close to her skull like some giant sinewy hand.

"Has Loan come yet?" Her eyes searched beyond Dennis and into the small kitchen, which had once been part of the back porch.

"No." Dennis knew that his answer made Nelly more nervous than she already was.

"I told him to be here. I told him to be here." Nelly squeezed the back of her neck as she leaned against the table and looked out the window.

Uncle Daniel came out of Teense's bedroom in much the same way Nelly did. He didn't bother to close the door. "Are you going to be sick, Aunt Nell?" His voice was water running through a long hose, filling a green plastic pool. Most of his voice came through his nose, but because it was wide and resonant, everything he said sounded as if he were reporting the latest and most important news.

"I told Loan to be here. He knows good and well this is supposed to be Teense's last night."

"Well, look. I'll go out to the house and call—see if I can get in touch with him. You go on back in with Mama."

Nelly crept back through the door, keeping her nose as close to the edge as she did when she came out. Dennis couldn't tell if it was the way Daniel talked that made people like Nelly obey him so quietly or if Nelly was just too run over by the likes of Loan to have any kind of backbone left. Loan seemed to enjoy making people uncomfortable. Dennis hoped that he never needed to be carried in an ambulance. He could imagine being in a car wreck and getting a broken neck and having to listen to Loan criticize him for not being a careful driver.

"You getting along okay, sport?" Daniel searched his pockets for his car keys.

"I guess . . ." Dennis yawned.

"As sleepy as you are, you ought to let me take you out to the house. You can sleep with your cousin Carl—help him baby-sit his little brother."

"I'm supposed to be here when Teense wakes up. She asked to see me." Dennis felt more hungry than sleepy.

"You might have a long wait." Daniel spun his keys meditatively on his finger.

"That's okay." Dennis tried to sit up straighter in the wooden chair.

"Well, if she asked for you special, I guess you want to do what you can to satisfy her. I'll see you later."

Empty of Nelly's and Daniel's company, the room felt even smaller than before. Grandpa Turner had only grudgingly allowed electricity to be brought into the house. He still preferred kerosene lamps to electric lights, so he went to no unnecessary trouble when he brought the wires into the room where Dennis sat. One naked bulb gave off a feverish, discolored light that failed to find the corners of the room. As daylight faded, the room darkened into roundness. Sitting in this room at night was like sitting in the bottom of a well.

Just as Dennis was getting ready to join the people standing around his granny's bed, despite his father's order to stay out of the room until he was called for, he heard the kitchen door open. He could tell it was yanked open because the spring on the screen emitted a startled twang, then seemed to swallow the echo of its hum. All of Teense's respectful visitors had tried to sneak through the kitchen door without alarming that spring. Whoever was now coming through the door clearly wasn't worried about disturbing a dying woman. It was also a person who was used to opening heavy, well-lubricated doors. Even before Dennis saw his bony cousin saunter into the living room, the dread that expanded inside his stomach let him know that Loan had finally arrived.

"You mean she ain't dead yet?" Loan wasn't really talking to Dennis.

Nevertheless, Dennis replied, "No."

"What are you waitin' out here for, preacher?" Loan leaned against the wall. "Teense would want you to be in there by her bed."

"Daddy told me to stay out here." Dennis didn't like the way Loan called him preacher. Loan was fond of using good words to mean bad things.

"You know, you're just about to let the fire go out, preacher." Loan picked up a poker from behind the stove and stirred the coals. "'Course, your job as preacher is to keep things from burning instead of making 'em burn. Right?"

"I don't know."

"Well, I don't mind keeping the stove light burning." While closing the stove door, Loan held on to the wire bulb of the handle too long. He jerked his hand down to his side, slapped his thigh, and rocked his shoulders. "Damn stove." Even when he wasn't trying, Loan made Dennis nervous.

"Uncle Daniel went looking for you." Dennis thought a change of subject might interrupt Loan's cussing.

"He didn't find me." Loan, noticing the worry in Dennis's face, added, "Damn him."

"Where was you at?" Dennis tried to sound friendly.

"Doin' my job." Loan stretched his hands above his head and arched his back until several bones popped. "I had to answer a ambulance call up in Barlowtown."

Dennis nodded. The news from Barlowtown always seemed to be violent and exotic because Barlowtown was the black section of Hibriten. Once or twice, Dennis had gone with his father to Barlowtown when Curtis needed to visit one of the men he worked with. During the day, the place seemed quiet enough. But from what Dennis heard from people like Loan, as soon as it got dark, Barlowtown turned into hostile territory, and if you didn't have Tarzan to carry you through, it was best to stay away.

"I've not seen that much blood since them four boys got squashed in Hoyt Kirby's car wreck four years ago." Loan sat down in the chair at the other end of the table and leaned back, sprawling his legs. "I could have come over here directly from the hospital, but I had to go back to the funeral home and wash the blood off me. I'll probably have to throw away the clothes I was wearin'."

Having learned that Loan enjoyed talking about his work, Dennis welcomed the chance to let his cousin unfold his adventure. "Was it another car wreck?"

"No. If it had been a wreck, I'd never gotten here." Loan scanned the room lazily and smiled with one corner of his mouth. "What we had tonight was a felonious assault."

Dennis nodded. He had watched enough "Dragnet" to guess that somebody had been in a fight.

"Shit." Loan straightened up and looked directly into Dennis's eyes. "I bet you know the woman who did the assaulting. She used to be a maid for the LeFevers."

Celeste LeFever had been Marleen's best friend, and Dennis had sometimes walked up the hill when Marleen went to visit Celeste. He remembered their black maid, Fontana Barlow.

". . . a big woman," Loan was saying. "Right close to three hundred pounds."

"I thought she disappeared." Dennis had heard that she was in a jungle somewhere, looking for gold.

"Well, preacher, she was out of town for a while. But today she got back to town. The first thing she did before she even got settled in was to let all of Barlowtown know that she was going after the man who had done her wrong. Little ol' wormy Winston Ferguson." Loan laughed. He shook his head, then rested his elbow on the table. "Winston Ferguson is so skinny that he has to squat to fart." Pausing long enough to pluck a cigarette out of the pack in his shirt pocket, Loan scratched his face with the match before lighting it. After two long draws, Loan took the cigarette from his mouth and pretended to offer it to Dennis. "Not started yet?" Loan asked when Dennis didn't reach for the cigarette. "I know preachers who smoke."

"I'm not a preacher." Dennis felt betrayed by the tone of pleading that colored his voice.

"That's not what Teense has been sayin' all these years." Loan studied his cigarette as if it were the first one he had seen. "A fine grandson you are, callin' your granny a liar on her deathbed."

"Did Winston Ferguson die?" Dennis braced himself. Either Loan would jump down his throat for trying to change the subject or he would welcome the chance to get back to a subject that interested him more than exploring his cousin's guilt.

To let Dennis know that he knew what the boy was up to, Loan narrowed his eyes and gave him that lopsided smile. Then he yawned to let Dennis know that he was bored with him, no matter what they talked about. "He should've died as much as he bled. See, Fontana—like a lot of them black women up in Barlowtown—carries a razor blade down inside that tumbleweed hairstyle of hers. Well, once she tracked Winston down, she cornered him in the grocery store and slapped him so hard his teeth rattled. Of course, Winston couldn't do anything against a woman like Fontana, so he just held his jaw and told her that he'd tell the police if she didn't leave him alone. But Fontana just smacked him again. By then, a crowd had gathered, and even a little worm like Winston don't like to get smacked in front of an audience, so he told her by damn he was going to the police right then. This time, when Fontana rared back to smack Winston, she caught her razor blade in between her two fingers, and sliced Winston from his left ear all the way down to his mouth." Loan, holding the cigarette in his two fingers, sketched the line of Fontana's blow down his own jaw with his little finger. "Hooo. Talk about a man who'll be able to grin from ear to ear. He'll know not to fuck with Fontana Barlow in the future." Loan saw Dennis squirm under the impact of his last statement.

"Did I say somethin' to upset you, preacher?" Loan pulled himself up in his chair. "Your sisters wouldn't be disturbed by what I said." Loan studied his cigarette again. "Did Phyllis have to get married . . . like Marleen?"

"They wanted to get married." Dennis could tell from the way that Loan was looking at him from the corner of his eyes that he shouldn't be talking about his sisters. Loan wanted him to say something dirty about Marleen and Phyllis.

"Ha!" Loan hunched over his exclamation and glanced at the door to the sickroom. "Maybe they wanted something else."

"I'm hungry." Dennis now hoped that changing the subject would make Loan angry, better to have his cousin fuming about him than about his sisters.

Slowly, Loan put his cigarette to his lips. While he took a deep draw, he scratched his chest and regarded Dennis with a scowl. Sensing the possibility of another game, Loan said from the corner of his mouth, "Go see what you can find in the cupboard."

Dennis rose limply from the chair and went to the corner

where the triangular cupboard stood stretching to the ceiling.

"Quaker Oats is all I see." Dennis remembered that since Teense had come home from the hospital, relatives had brought food to Turner for every meal.

"Then Quaker Oats is all you'll eat." Loan mimicked Dennis.

"Is it okay to eat them raw?" Dennis tilted the cylindrical container and heard a dry shifting inside.

"Well, I ain't gonna cook the damn things for you." Loan pulled himself up indignantly and menacingly.

"I—I didn't mean that," Dennis stammered. "It won't hurt me to eat them like this, will it?"

"I'm gonna hurt you if you ask me any more questions."

Deliberately avoiding his cousin's gaze, Dennis started to put the oats back on the shelf.

"You said you was hungry."

"I know."

"Preachers ain't liars. If you don't eat, you'll be a liar."

Lifting off the lid, Dennis looked at the brown flakes.

"Don't stand there in the corner like some kinda damn orphan. Eat at the table."

Dennis sat down at the table and stuck his hand into the cardboard cylinder. They were very dry—like little flakes of brown dust. But he felt Loan's eyes watching, so he put a handful into his mouth. There was the almost tasteless sweetness of oats, and the dryness seemed to draw all the moisture from the very top of his head. As he fought an impulse to gag, the door to his grandmother's room opened and his father snapped, "Get in here, Dennis." Choking and trying to swallow, Dennis obeyed his father.

When Teense had begun losing her sight, she had also insisted that no electricity be used in her bedroom. She complained that the smell of it made her sick. Two kerosene lamps lit the room, holding their flames like shivering butterflies. One sat at the head of the bed on a small table. Its light barely touched Turner's head. All Dennis could clearly make out about his grandfather was his hair. It rose from the darkness of his collar like a thread of smoke from a chimney. Drowsily, it floated up, following the contour of the old man's head, and swirled around the crown of his head. The tip of his nose was illuminated by the yellow light. Briefly, Dennis thought of a three-quarter moon that he had once seen floating below a shelf of clouds.

A hand he recognized as his daddy's led him by the shoulder to the side of Teense's bed.

"Your granny wants to talk to you, Dennis," he heard his mama say.

The room was silent, heavy with the smell of relatives of various ages. Teense spoke so quietly, she almost didn't disturb the silence: "Dennis?"

With his mouth full of what felt like paste, Dennis gargled, "What, Granny?"

"Dennis?"

"What, Granny?" Dennis tried to speak louder, but all he got was another gargle.

"Dennis?"

"What, Granny?" The oats seemed to grow into a larger wad.

"Get closer so she can hear you," his daddy ordered, "and stop making that noise."

Dennis bent down by the bed and touched his grandmother's arm.

"Dennis?"

Remembering his father's warning, Dennis swallowed— trying to force down the doughlike mess in his mouth. Half went down, but the other half paused and then entered his windpipe as he started to answer. He buried his head in his grandmother's blankets as he was shaken with a spasm of coughing.

"Stop crying, Dennis, you'll upset Teense." Curtis's whisper was harsh.

Dennis wished that he was crying. The oats floated down into his chest like snowflakes with razor blade edges, and he coughed until tears did burn his eyes.

"Oh, sweet Dennis," murmured his grandmother. She tried to put her hand on his head but succeeded only in scratching his ear with her thumbnail. Dennis's father laid the old woman's hand on top of Dennis's shaking head.

"Don't cry, angel," she whispered. "Your Granny's just fine." Teense opened her eyes for the first time in three days. "I'm on my way to Glory."

Dennis saw her turn her head slightly, taking in the whole room with that motion. Then she closed her eyes again. No one spoke for a few seconds.

"Is she dead?" Nelly's voice quivered.

Behind his back, Dennis heard his father reply, "Loan can tell better than anybody."

CAUTION CAR

PHYLLIS WAS IN NO MOOD for company—not even a visit from her sister. How long had it been since she'd seen her sister? Two Christmases ago. Marleen and Walter had come down, delivering a mobile home then as now, and spent three days. Walter couldn't spare more than three days off the road. On a good trip, depending on what he was carrying in his tractor trailer, Walter had once told Phyllis and her husband, Vernon, that he could make four or five hundred dollars a day.

Of course, one of the reasons Phyllis was in no mood for company was because she despised her brother-in-law: Walter Triplett. One of Vernon's friends, who also drove a truck, assured Phyllis that Walter had been telling the truth. A man willing to stay out on the road and drive himself to death stretching too many miles out between too many pills could make a lot of money.

What Phyllis wanted to know, though, was where all of Walter's big money went. He'd go out on the road for three or four months at a time and leave Marleen a hundred dollars. Out of that piddling amount and what she earned driving a school bus and being a motel clerk at night, Marleen had to make house payments, buy groceries, pay bills, and occasionally lend her three children money. Like Phyllis's own, Marleen's kids were more or less making their own way.

Phyllis wandered to the spare bedroom to make sure that she had left extra towels for Walter. Large and hairy, he required about three regular-sized towels to get completely dried off. Even when he was bathing regularly, Walter gave off a sweet musky odor barely balanced against a stale undercurrent that Phyllis associated with very old canvas sneakers. Back when Marleen had first started dating Walter, she had told Phyllis that she found his odor primitive and provocative. Phyllis had wondered what men's cologne label Marleen had been reading to be talking like she did. But that was the way her older sister had always been. Romantic. Too fond of sex. Men always found that combination attractive at first.

On her last visit, Marleen had brought photographs of the furniture that Walter had let her go into debt for. It was all imitation Spanish Colonial. Even from the photographs, Phyllis could tell that Walter had probably found the ornate chairs and tables in a trailer that nobody wanted. When Marleen and Walter had gone out later in the afternoon to look at the ocean, Phyllis took the photographs down to Vernon's shop, where he restored and finished the extravagant and exotic furniture of the Lakeworth, Palm Beach, and Miami wealthy. As Phyllis had suspected, Vernon concluded that what Marleen had bought was probably pressed plastic glued to chip-core frames, not even the quality of good old veneer. But the furniture would feel heavy because when you poured sawdust and glue into a mold and squeezed it, the result always weighed more than a solid piece of wood cut along the same pattern.

And that was exactly the kind of mistake Marleen was likely to make—to confuse heaviness with quality.

The tall wooden chairs with their fake velvet upholstery and dark stain depressed Phyllis. It reminded her too much of Marleen's life. Phyllis paused when she came out of the hallway and into her living room. One of Vernon's most popular finishes made wood look like marble. He could make blue, green, pink, gold, and red marble—and Phyllis had samples of all his work throughout her house. She'd even had Vernon stain her bamboo seats and couch to look like they were made out of marble. It was a style that had caught on even among the Miami snobs. The various shades and textures of marble made her living room feel cool and sleek. In strategic places, Phyllis had broken up the marble furnishings with glass tables of various sizes. A house full of glass and marble furniture never felt crowded. Of course, she had made herself wait until her three kids were more or less on their own before she bought all of the glass that she thought she needed.

Standing in front of the living room's picture window, Phyllis hoped that Marleen and Walter wouldn't arrive before her son, Dale, had a chance to come by and get the wild boar out of the pool.

Dale was her middle child. Ray was her oldest. Frieda, who was all the way out in California now, was Phyllis's baby. All three of them, Phyllis suspected, liked Marleen better than they liked her. They suffered from the same sloppy sentimental notions that made their aunt fumble through life. And that kind of fumbling eventually pulled everybody down.

If Phyllis needed proof of how everybody else's messy lives encroached on hers, all she had to do was go out to the backyard and look at her pool. Next to glass and marbled wood, Phyllis loved tile—especially the turquoise tile that lined her pool. Now, good-hearted as Dale was, he had a hard time concentrating on one job. He was supposed to be working for his daddy. Ray had decided against going into the family business, preferring to work for the Lakeworth water department. Frieda could probably have learned to finish wood better than her two brothers, but instead she had run off to California to be with her boyfriend and pick vegetables.

Dale was also supposed to be working as an animal handler at the Lakeworth Zoo. Phyllis had never seen anybody better with animals than Dale. One of the reasons he had finally left home was because Phyllis would not allow him to raise pit bulls in the backyard. If he had concentrated on the business end of pit bulls, Dale could have made a living as a breeder, but he didn't raise his dogs with the idea of selling them or even fighting them.

Reluctantly turning toward the kitchen and the view it offered her of the pool, Phyllis admitted that compared to Dale's passion for wild boar hunting even Frieda's lust for her boyfriend seemed a poorly pieced-together imitation of passion, just plastic and glue and sawdust. And out there, as Phyllis paused at the sliding glass doors that led to her patio, the large white umbrella painfully bright in the afternoon glare, the bleached concrete glittering in relentless harmony with the sun, even the turquoise tiles had lost their promise of cool relief. Too many hot days had passed since the pool was last filled with chlorinated water, trembling with its own coolness.

From this angle, she couldn't see the boar. Three days ago, she had tried to help Dale out by letting *him* clean the pool instead of calling in the usual team that serviced the other neighborhood pools. Despite all of his supposed jobs and abilities, Dale stayed short of cash. He had to buy special food for his dogs. On pig hunts, the dogs might run solid for two or three days straight.

Of course, Dale and his buddies who followed the dogs also had to run solid for the same two or three days. Phyllis understood the attraction. Hunting wild boars in the Florida swamps was pure chase. The boys carried knives but no guns, no bows, not even sharpened sticks. In Florida, it was open season on boars all year long if you didn't use weapons. And pit bulls weren't considered weapons.

Special high-protein, high-energy food for the dogs was fine. Phyllis preferred for Dale to spend his money on feeding his dogs than on feeding the kind of women that Ray was running around with. What Phyllis didn't approve of was the money Dale spent on the energy food for himself and his hunting buddies. They drank a lot of beer just before they let the dogs loose. They'd spend all morning grilling steaks and hamburgers, guzzling beer, and teasing the dogs. Then they'd let the dogs off their chains and splash out into the swamp. Once in the marsh, after a pig, all the boys had time to eat was drugs.

Of course, as Dale argued, some of the chemicals might have saved his life. He had been bitten by every kind of snake in Florida—sometimes bringing home the snake that bit him to be stuffed and hung on the wall of the cinderblock house he shared with four other boys—but he never left the swamp until they had caught their pig.

If Phyllis had wondered about the state of Dale's mind while he was on the hunt, she now had four-legged proof right outside that her middle son wasn't fully rational when he was running after his dogs.

While at the Greater Dade County Antique Restorers' Convention with Vernon, Phyllis had constantly assured herself that Dale would have no trouble finishing the simple job she had awarded him. Drain the pool, disinfect the tile, clean the drains, replace the filters, refill the pool. Well, he had gotten as far as draining the pool. But then, he heard the call of the wild.

Barely had Dale begun to use the large brush broom to apply the tile disinfectant when a couple of his hunting buddies dropped by with what they considered the business deal of their lives. They'd run into a man from Iowa who told them he'd be willing to pay two hundred dollars for a wild boar. He had this idea of taking it back home with him to set loose in one of his fields so he and his friends could hunt it.

Phyllis could imagine that Dale thought he was hearing his dreams come true: getting to hunt pigs and be paid for it. That's really all he wanted out of life.

So the boys had taken Dale's dogs out, cornered a pig, but instead of letting the dogs kill it as they usually did, Dale pulled out one of the tranquilizer pistols he had borrowed from the zoo and put the boar to sleep.

Dale had also borrowed one of the medium-sized transport cages from the zoo—one used to restrain tigers and lions. By the time they got to the tourist trailer park where the Iowa man had parked his Airstream, the boar was awake and trying to break out of the cage. After only a few minutes of watching the boar, foam rolling down its chin, dripping off the tusks as it pounded the bars with its bristly broad shoulders and slashed at the space between the bars with its snout, the Iowa man decided he didn't want to carry the pig back with him after all. Then he had given the boys twenty dollars for letting him see the pig.

Concerned for the damage the pig was doing to the zoo's cage, Dale had first thought about taking the pig back to where he lived and using his dogs' kennel for a cage. Of course, the boar's first job would be to start rooting its way out under the heavy gauge chicken wire. No, Dale realized what he needed was a cage with a concrete floor—or some kind of floor as hard as concrete. Then he remembered the tiles of his mama's pool.

To prepare herself for the sight of her pool and its occupant, Phyllis stopped at the refrigerator and took out a beer. At least ten times over the last twenty-four hours, she had asked Dale why he didn't just take the boar back to the swamp and let it go.

"Catching a boar ain't the same as catching a fish you don't want to keep," Dale had explained as he sat on the edge of the pool at the deep end, watching the boar trot back and forth, just waiting for something to get in or out of its way. "You can't just toss 'em back. They either got to get away on their own or die."

On one level, Phyllis could see how what he was saying was just part of that silly romantic jumble that Dale had probably inherited from his Aunt Marleen. At least Dale was consistent in his jumbled beliefs. Pig hunting wasn't something he played at. Phyllis knew that. Still, she wanted that thing out of her pool. At least twice each day, the boar would try to bash its way out. It'd charge over to the shallow end of the pool.

Luckily, the man who had built the pool had been a serious swimmer who had no use for a real deep end and a real shallow end. Instead of dropping from two feet to ten feet like most of the other pools in the neighborhood, Phyllis's pool dropped from four feet to seven feet. Had the shallow end been two feet, the pig would have been long gone. Phyllis suspected it might have been able to clear three feet, but the four feet of tiled wall frustrated the pig just enough to attack that end.

Phyllis loved the simplicity of her pool's straightforward rectangular design. A pool with too many curves in its sides struck her as tedious—not to mention harder to keep clean. She was also glad her pool didn't have any steps in the shallow end. The neighborhood kids had quickly learned that if they tried to sneak a swim in her pool, they'd have a hard time getting out. And the ladder at the deep end was safely out of the boar's reach.

Each time Phyllis saw the exposed concrete where the boar had succeeded in tearing off the tiles, her stomach went limp and watery. She took a long drink of her Busch to bring back some of her abdominal elasticity. Dale had promised that if he couldn't find someone to take the pig off his hands, he'd tranquilize the boar and get it out of the pool.

But not five minutes after Dale had left, Marleen had called from a truckstop up in Jupiter to tell Phyllis that she and Walter were delivering a mobile home down below Pompano Beach and would stop at her house on their way back. That had been five hours ago. Surely they'd had enough time to be finished with the delivery and heading north again.

Phyllis saw a flicker of tusk and shoulder in the middle of her pool. The pig was getting restless. She calculated it would probably be another thirty or fifty minutes before the boar got restless enough to attack the pool again. It would charge over and over, short angry runs, grinding its head and tusks into her tiles until it exhausted or injured itself enough to return to the deep end, where it would fall into a deep sleep. The attacks might not have been so bad if the neighbors hadn't started complaining about the way the pig squealed when it struck the wall.

Marleen would get a good laugh out of the pig. Phyllis couldn't hold that against her sister. Maybe she needed the laugh more than she needed an afternoon sitting beside a pool filled with water. This might be the occasion, Phyllis decided, when she could tell Walter it was time for him to take Marleen on as his driving partner. Long ago, Marleen had begged Phyllis not to mention to Walter how much she wanted to join him on the road. But she couldn't because of the kids. Now that they were making their own way, Gerald in the navy, Thomas a carpenter, and Anette a waitress, Phyllis thought Marleen needed a nudge to get back to work on her dream. Even if she did offend Walter, presuming to tell him how to treat his wife, Phyllis couldn't see Marleen being any worse off than she was, stuck at home while her husband trucked all over the country. Besides, Phyllis thought everybody needed to be offended once in a while—a philosophy that made Vernon very nervous when she was at the shop with his customers.

As far back as Phyllis could remember, Marleen had been out on the road maybe twice since Walter had started driving his long routes. As close as she ever got to actually taking part in the trips was driving the caution car when Walter delivered a mobile home. Such trips were rare. Walter delivered motor homes only when he thought he needed a vacation from his usual routes out to California and up to Canada. He saw delivering mobile homes as a way to finance his wife's need for a vacation.

From the driveway came a hiss that cut the cool air in Phyllis's living room and kitchen like a blade of dry ice, and before she could fully recover from the shock, a diesel horn clamped the trembling air between its dual-toned bellow, crushing all respose out of the house like one of Dale's buddies who could flatten a beer can with his teeth. Phyllis couldn't bring herself to see how the horn had affected the boar.

Walter had pulled his truck up into the driveway as close to the house as he could get, and still the truck's huge rear tires blocked the sidewalk. Except for its heavy chrome trim, the truck was a deep purple. Gleaming. Brand-new. On the passenger's door was painted a monster with one eye, a horn rising out of the middle of its shaggy head and a person's leg hanging out of its wide mouth. Its lower body resembled an ape's. In one hand, the monster carried a club. In its other hand, it held a sign: PURPLE PEOPLE EATER. Phyllis remembered the song. It had come out in 1958. Sheb Wooley had done it. That was the same year that "Witch Doctor" had come out, but David Seville was no Sheb Wooley, even if he had invented the Chip Monks. That year, when all those silly songs were coming out, Phyllis had married Vernon. And barely over one pregnancy out of wedlock, just after giving the baby away, Marleen had married Gaither Drum.

"What do you think of our new truck?" Marleen yelled at Phyllis from the curb, where she was climbing out of the red caution car with its two yellow dome lights attached to the roof.

Even from across the space of her yard, Phyllis could tell that Marleen was worn out. Although slimmer than Phyllis and their mother, Marleen had always drooped when she was tired or ill. Today, she was visibly sagging, her face, her shoulders, her hips. In the past, Phyllis had always been surprised by how long drives seemed to revitalize Marleen. But here she was, crawling out of her car as if she had been driving with weights tied to her arms and legs.

"You look like you've been the one pulling the mobile home instead of that man in the purple truck." Phyllis walked over to where Marleen was struggling with two suitcases.

Marleen cast a glance toward the truck, where Walter was standing on the wide chrome front bumper using his fingernail to scrape a flattened bug off the chest of his Mack truck hood ornament—a chrome bulldog standing on its hind legs. "Some wives weren't made to follow behind their husband's oversized loads. Warning lights or no warning lights." Marleen handed Phyllis a suitcase and hugged her with her free arm.

With her arm around Marleen's waist, Phyllis walked toward her house. "The trucking business must be going awfully good." She noticed that Marleen kept her eyes on Walter all the way across the yard.

From what Phyllis observed of her sister, Marleen seemed to have gotten goofier as she got older. It was how she dealt with her disappointments—in love, in marriage, in work, in sex. She never got exactly what she wanted. Never. When she finally got Gaither Drum to marry her, he turned out to be more upholsterer than husband. The only fulfillment Marleen got out of that marriage was a daughter and a red velvet love seat that stayed at their mama's house. More than once, Marleen had offered to let Phyllis have the love seat because their mama's house was slowly filling up with her collection of salt and pepper shakers, many of them provided by the ever-traveling Walter, others by friends and relatives who returned from vacations and business trips. Chairs, couches, and coffee tables were slowly being replaced by shelves of shakers.

Secretly, Phyllis had two reasons for not wanting the love seat. First of all, she thought upholstered furniture was nasty. It absorbed body odors, and if it absorbed odors, it was absorbing other invisible excretions as well. She used cushions in her bamboo furniture, but they were small, hypoallergenic, and washable at least twice a week. Phyllis's second reason was one she didn't like to admit, but she thought there was a possibility that the love seat was bad luck. Since that first day when Gaither Drum brought it to their house, Marleen had been led around by her nose—first by Gaither, now by Walter.

Still keeping her eyes on Walter, Marleen paused at the front door. "You ought to see that tractor when it's hooked up to the trailer—the trailer's purple, too—you'd think the sun was setting over the desert."

"Ol' Walter seems awfully fond of it." Phyllis was surprised by how smoothly her brother-in-law had produced a rag and an aerosol can and began cleaning the truck's chrome radiator grill.

"Oh, he's a man full of fondnesses." Marleen pushed beside Phyllis and went into the house.

In the guest bedroom, Phyllis started to help Marleen unpack, but her sister said, "Never mind about unloading, we have to head back tomorrow."

Phyllis leaned against a closet door and crossed her arms. "This sounds like them trips me and you and Dennis used to make with Mama and Daddy to the beach. You know, when we'd get down there at the crack of dawn, play on the beach all day and get ourselves sunburned to the bone and be so miserable the only thing that'd make us feel better was just to pile in the car and drive straight back home."

Marleen sat down on the bed, cradling her elbows. "I'd welcome the chance to get sunburned like that again."

Sitting down beside Marleen, Phyllis said, "I don't see why you bothered stopping at all."

"Oh, business is underneath it all." Marleen smiled. "Walter wants to buy a pit bull from Dale."

"Dale don't like selling his dogs." Phyllis couldn't help but wonder how much Walter would be willing to pay. She regretted she hadn't tried to get an estimate on replacing those pool tiles.

"I've told him that, but Walter thinks him being family will make a difference." Marleen slid the suitcase out of the way and motioned for Phyllis to sit beside her.

For a moment, Phyllis remembered a brief time in her life—just a few months or maybe a few weeks, maybe a few days before Marleen got into trouble with Gaither and just when she was getting serious about Vernon—when for a few nights, she and Marleen had actually talked to each other about how much they wanted to get older and get away from home.

Once Phyllis got settled, one leg on, one leg off the bed, her position mirroring Marleen's, Marleen slid closer to her and, dropping her voice, asked, "Could Dale maybe lend Walter a dog?"

"I think Dale would be less likely to lend one than sell one." Phyllis didn't expect Marleen's disappointed frown.

"How about if I was to tell Dale that the dog was really for me?" Marleen leaned closer to Phyllis, her voice getting softer.

Phyllis couldn't help but lower her voice too. "You know Dale'd do anything for you." Phyllis knew that Marleen was aware of just how rough Dale could get. And from the way Marleen allowed her smile to work its way back upon her face, Phyllis knew that Marleen was counting on her nephew's devotion and wildness. "Just what do you want with one of his pit bulls?"

Before answering, Marleen rose from the bed and went to the window, pulled back the curtain, and leaned against the glass. Satisfied that Walter was still cleaning his chrome, Marleen sat back down beside Phyllis.

"Two weeks ago, Walter came back from one of his four-month trips. As usual, he had brought back a load of dirty laundry, mostly his jockey shorts—but a few shirts and a couple pairs of pants. In one of his pockets, I found a sales receipt from a furniture store in Spokane, Washington. At first, I thought it was a receipt for something he had delivered, but then I realized that this piece of paper was not like the bills the trucking companies use. This was the kind of receipt that you or me would get if we bought some furniture." Marleen's voice had started to go dry, but when Phyllis offered to get up from the bed to get her a drink, Marleen stopped her.

"Let me get this out. Then we'll drink." Marleen squeezed her sister's arm. "It was a big bill. Itemized." She tilted her head back and closed her eyes. "Two recliners. Dining room table and chairs. A couch. A kitchenette set. A rocking chair. Four easy chairs. Queen-sized bed, mattress, box springs. Right at five thousand dollars. A lot more than the furniture I'm still paying for. And the receipt had an address for the delivery . . . and a phone number . . . for a place right there in Spokane. It just didn't seem right, Phyllis. So I called the number, and a woman answered. I guess working at the motel has made me sneaky, but I tried to sound like one of them dispatchers at the truck terminal and told the woman that we needed Walter Triplett for an emergency long-distance delivery and could she tell me when he would be back from the East Coast. Phyllis, the woman didn't hesitate a second before she told me she thought Walter would be back in about a month and a half. Which is when he's supposed to be back out there." Marleen balled up her fists and pressed them against her thighs. "Phyllis, he's got another house and another woman out there."

As they sat at the table eating supper, Phyllis tried to reconcile her sister's appearance with her plan to get even with Walter. Marleen had inherited her dark hair and slimness from their father. Phyllis, short and blond, resembled their mother's side of the family. Up until they hit middle age, Phyllis had mildly resented Marleen's tall body. But after three children, four counting the child she gave away, Mar-

leen had grown bottom heavy. Of course, that maternal shape
wasn't obvious sitting at the supper table. Stocky to begin
with, Phyllis's body hadn't been much altered by her children.
She told everyone that her kids had been harder on her mind
than on her body.

Ray and Dale sat across from her, dwarfing their aunt,
who sat between them. Since they had become teenagers, Ray
and Dale had gotten larger than any relatives that Phyllis or
Vernon could recall. Although Ray was two years older than
Dale, he was slightly smaller than his younger brother. When
they had company, Ray and Dale always showed up for the
free food, and Ray, always more social than Dale, tried to
reveal the most embarrassing secrets about Dale's swamp-
centered life.

At the beginning of the meal, Walter—refreshed by a
long shower and a short nap—had asked Dale to sell him a pit
bull. Seeing a chance to torture his brother and perhaps help
him make some money, Ray was trying to get Dale to tell one
of his latest pig-hunting stories, while carefully steering clear
of the subject of the pig out in the pool, which Dale had tran-
quilized during Walter's nap. Phyllis did not want her
brother-in-law wandering around the edge of her pool making comments about the kind of trophies her sons brought
home to their mother.

"You can't get a tougher dog," Ray was saying. "Tell Walter about that dog of yours that got gored." Ray punched his
brother's shoulder.

"That was Lady." Dale forked another bouquet of salad
into his mouth.

"Which makes a better guard dog? The males or the
females?" Walter paused with his glass of iced tea halfway to
his mouth.

"All depends on what kind of guarding you want done."
Dale chewed slowly. "The males are stronger usually, but the
females are smarter." Still chewing, Dale slowly spread his
large arms out on the table, tapping the glass top with the
tines of his fork. "A German shepherd or even a Doberman
would make you a better guard dog. Most pits don't have the

patience for that kind of work. The dogs I raise would rather bite than bark. And if you want a guard dog, you want one that'll make a lot of noise."

Walter nodded vigorously. "I don't want a noisy dog. And I don't want something as big as a shepherd. I want a dog that can ride with me in my truck and still look like he means business."

"You mean on them long trips you take?" Dale sat up straight and scratched his neck.

"Well, if I can take it, I don't see why a pit bull couldn't take it—if they're as tough as you say." Walter shifted his own considerable weight in his chair so he could look more directly at Dale.

"Go on and tell him about Lady." Ray elbowed Dale's ribs.

Directing his story more toward Marleen than Walter, Dale spoke in a monotone and toyed with a sliced tomato in his salad bowl. "Last year about this time, we was out running a pig. The dogs had just sniffed out this boar. He'd started out like he was going to try and get away, but after about a hundred yards, he turned back on the dogs. Before we caught up with the pack, he'd opened up Lady with one of his tusks. Caught her right at the top of her chest and slit her all the way back down to her hind legs." Dale picked up the tomato and mashed it between his fingers, dribbling juice and slimy seeds onto his plate. "The pig had taken off again with the other dogs right behind him. I thought Lady was already dead, but I didn't want to leave her slit open like she was—open to the flies. I found part of an old barbed-wire fence and broke off pieces of it to use for clamping Lady's hide back together."

"Then he went off after the pig." Ray was always the first to get Dale to tell his hunting stories, but he was also first to get impatient with how slowly Dale talked. "And didn't come back to where he'd left Lady until three days later."

"We just happened to track back right to where we'd started from, and there was Lady, but she was still warm and not stiff at all." Dale picked up a few pieces of lettuce with his fingers, his voice becoming more animated. "I took her to the vet; he sewed her up. And she had a litter of six puppies about four months ago."

Holding his iced tea in his hand level with his jaw, Walter propped his elbows on the table. "Now that's the kind of dog I want. But I don't want no puppy."

"Don't you want to go to the trouble of making sure your dog is going to be loyal?" Phyllis was becoming less and less shocked by Marleen's desire to have Walter attacked by one of Dale's pit bulls.

As they had fixed supper, Marleen confessed that her only thought, since finding out about Walter's second house—and life—in Spokane, was to have one of Dale's dogs drag him around by his unfaithful organ for about forty-five minutes. She would have felt even better if she could have borrowed enough dogs to drag Walter's truck around the neighborhood a few times, but she would be satisfied just to see the driver mauled.

"Do you have to raise them from pups for them to like you?" Walter leaned back in his chair and drained his glass.

"No." Dale shook his head slowly, rolling his eyes toward the upper right corner of his skull, as if probing there for a more profound answer. "But you do have to be likable."

"How likable?" Marleen was crouched over her plate as if she were trying to memorize every bite she took.

"That's something the dogs have to decide." Dale crouched over his plate to be on the same visual level with his aunt.

"I'd qualify, I think." Walter swayed forward, almost with a slight bow of confidence. "I've got friends all across this country."

"Careful, Walter," Phyllis warned. "You might be too likable."

"It's not caused me any trouble so far."

"Well, maybe being likable is like speeding," Marleen said, pushing her plate away, smiling first at Dale, then at Ray before she faced Walter. "Maybe you can push your rig seventy-five miles an hour driving through Arizona. Maybe you can even ease up to eighty or eighty-five, but maybe at eighty-six or eighty-seven miles an hour, some patrolman will decide you're going just a little too fast, or maybe you'll find that edge where you ain't in control anymore."

"Naw." Walter laughed. "With the Purple People Eater, I doubt if I'll ever let myself lose control. Success only makes me more careful."

"I hear being careful is a sign of old age." Marleen rose from her chair and began clearing the table.

Handing his plate to her, Walter replied, "You heard wrong. Being careful is how you reach old age."

"Well, I'm reaching old age, but I was hoping for a more interesting prize." Phyllis stood up to help her sister.

"My philosophy is 'It's not how old you get, but how you get old.'" Dale moved around the table, picking up the stray forks and glasses left by Marleen and Phyllis. Once in the kitchen, he herded his mother into the corner farthest from the dining room table and whispered, "I don't want to give Walter one of my dogs. I don't care how likable he is." He grabbed Marleen by her wrist and pulled her over beside Phyllis. "I'll give you a dog. I'll even name one after you, Marleen, but I don't want one of my dogs riding around with Walter. Don't ask me to give him one." He moved closer to the two sisters. "I'd give them all to you. But let them stay where they belong. Not one of my dogs would be happy riding around in a purple truck."

Not until Vernon, Walter, Dale, and Ray had left—first to look at Dale's dogs, then to visit some of the Lakeworth bars—did Marleen reveal how disappointed she was that she wouldn't have the pleasure of seeing Walter castrated by one of her nephew's pit bulls. "But I can't ask Dale to give up one of his dogs. And they do shoot dogs that attack people—even a person like Walter—don't they?"

"Or they'd gas it." Phyllis didn't want to think about how much Dale would suffer, knowing one of his dogs was being gassed. He'd rather be gassed himself. He probably felt more for his dogs than they felt for themselves. She realized that

Vernon had the same attachment to his finishing business—the tools, the supplies, the building. Maybe because they couldn't get pregnant, men got attached to their tools or their toys in a way that had always struck Phyllis as foolish. The darkness in her backyard was soft and enticing, the kind of night that would persuade her to go out to her pool and take a swim in the nude. But where that green-blue water would have shimmered, caressed by the underwater pool lights, all Phyllis could see tonight was the darker cavity where the pool dropped out of the reach of her house lights and the street-lamps. It was the velvety purple black of an old bruise.

And somewhere in a corner at the deep end would be an even darker shape, asleep now in whatever position it had assumed before the tranquilizer knocked it out. According to Dale, the pig would probably sleep until morning because he had used a strong drug.

Phyllis handed a plate to Marleen for her to dry. "Does Walter's truck have one of them little sleeping compartments behind the seats?"

"The Purple People Eater is a *de*luxe model, sis. He's got almost a full-sized single bed behind his seats. Leather wall liner that matches the seat upholstery. You'd think a man with a truck like that wouldn't need two houses." Marleen dried the plate several times, front and back.

"Would you say he loves that truck as much as his balls?" Phyllis stirred the water in the sink and gave her sister a side-ways stare.

Without hesitating, Marleen tilted her head sideways and replied, "More. If he'd given me a chance to drive it, I'd probably cared more for the truck than his balls. And we could have been happy."

"Does that mean you wouldn't be interested in using Walter's truck to punish him?" Phyllis couldn't imagine Marleen being greedy enough to hope that she might be able to get possession of the Purple People Eater in a divorce settlement.

"No. I'd be willing to sacrifice Walter's truck if it'd make him see the error of his ways." Marleen could tell that her sis-

ter was not simply daydreaming. "I'd hope it would be something I could help bring about. Are you thinking about
putting sugar in his fuel tank?"

"No. Nothing that technological." Phyllis walked over to
the sliding glass doors that led out to her patio. She flipped
the switch that turned on the pool lights. "Come out here
with me."

With their toes hanging over the pool's edge, Phyllis
pointed to the unconscious boar. "This one comes out of the
tranquilizer kind of slow. Walter would know he had something in the truck with him a few seconds before the pig
started trying to find a way out. But I'll be honest with you,
Marleen, I don't know what the pig would do if it found its
way up to where Walter was driving."

Marleen stooped down to more closely examine the pig.
"How heavy is it?"

Phyllis walked over to the ladder and climbed down to
within a few feet of the pig. "Dale says this one's a medium-
sized boar. About fifty-five or sixty pounds." The pig snored
audibly. Still, Phyllis felt short of breath as soon as she realized that she was going to drop from the ladder to the floor of
the pool. "Hand me that brush broom up there," she said to
Marleen.

With the brush end of the broom, Phyllis gently nudged
the pig's front feet. Its snoring continued without any change
of rhythm. Stepping a little closer, she nudged harder, thumping the pig's chest as well as its legs. Still it slept. Glancing
back at the ladder, Phyllis took another step closer to the pig
and this time pushed the broom against the pig's moist snout.
The snoring continued. Laying the broom down within easy
reach, Phyllis circled to the pig's back legs and gave one of
them an easy tug. No response. Phyllis tugged the leg with
both hands, taking note of the sharp hooflike toes. Even its
fur was sharp, but Phyllis knew she was imagining the stinging sensation in the side of her hand that was touching the
bristles.

"See if you can find some gloves up there in that utility
shed." Phyllis gave a sincere pull, using both hands, and was

surprised that the pig moved so easily. Of course, the tiles were slick.

"I found two pairs." Phyllis hadn't expected Marleen to bring the gloves down to her. "There was this piece of canvas in the shed, too." Marleen slid a heavy piece of fabric up against the pig.

"It's a piece of tent the boys used to have." Phyllis put on her gloves.

"Let's wrap the pig up in it. If it wakes up, we'll have a better chance of getting out of its way." Marleen moved to one end of the boar.

They were able to slide the wrapped pig up to the shallow end of the pool. With both sisters lifting, they had no problem getting it out of the pool. But Marleen had to sit down on the pool edge and rest. She was breathing heavily but beginning to laugh.

"This feller'll fit right up at the end of the sleeping compartment. Even if Walter opens the curtains back there, he won't notice his surprise."

"It could be dangerous." Phyllis tried to imagine I-95 early in the morning. Maybe Walter would have time to pull off the highway. Or maybe the pig would come blowing out of the sleeping compartment like a cannonball with tusks.

Marleen patted the pig's flat slumbering skull. "I'll be right behind him, driving the caution car. I'll let people know if something dangerous starts happening." She took off her glove to feel the boar's hide, and as she stroked it, she looked up at Phyllis, a few of the lines in her face smoothing out. "You want to ride with me?"

Even before Phyllis said yes, she and Marleen both knew she had to.

TWILIGHT TIME

AFTER PASSING BY COUNTLESS CLINICS inside the main building of the sprawling hospital, Dennis Holsclaw found himself outside once again, this time on a plank sidewalk that followed with angular fidelity the high board fence hiding the foundation work that would eventually provide enough space to nearly double the size of what Dennis thought was a hospital already large beyond human comfort.

Disoriented by the size of the Chapel Hill Hospital, Dennis found his nerves being further frayed by the sounds of construction work. From the other side of the fence came the voices of men yelling instructions and corrections to instructions, voices somehow raised above the sounds of busy but secret diesel engines, electric saws and drills, hammering, and riveting. Dennis wondered how many of these abrasive sounds reached his sister Marleen, who had been hospitalized now for three weeks, getting her first series of radiation treatments.

She was being given a two-week vacation. Then she had to come back for another series. The man Marleen was now living with, Jessie Parham, couldn't get off early from his job at the Wilmington Nuclear Power Station—which meant he couldn't come and pick Marleen up until Saturday morning. Since it had been Dennis's weekend to drive down to Chapel Hill and visit his sister, he had offered to drive her to Wilmington. His boss at the music store in Hibriten had even given him Monday off so he could make a long weekend out of his trip.

Although no stranger to the five hospitals around Hibriten and its neighboring towns of Hickory and Morganton because of his being a member of the Mountain View Baptist Church Visitation Committee, Dennis had an acutely fastidious nature that would not let him be comfortable in any institution connected to disease. Left to his own fears, Dennis would never have volunteered for the Visitation Committee. He knew such good works would worry him, but during a Training Union class one Sunday night, one of the members of the class had started talking about a book she had just finished reading, *St. Francis of Assisi*, by a writer with a Greek name. She claimed that the book offered wonderful insights into understanding what God wants each person to do.

Dennis had always wanted to know what God wanted him to do. He was so mediocre at most everything he tried, he figured he couldn't be satisfying God. Unfortunately, the primary guideline that *St. Francis* had offered him was that what he wanted to do least was probably what God wanted him to do the most. It was an idea just masochistic enough to strike Dennis as absolutely true. The next day, he had joined the Visitation Committee. Religious conviction, Dennis realized, came upon him like undulant fever. He could go for weeks without feeling too righteous, then some bit of news about a relative struck down with a variation of some biblical misfortune would cause Dennis enough anxiety to burn away his doubts about Billy Graham, the Reverend Hugh Tucker, and *St. Francis*. However, whether Dennis was riding a crest or a trough of religious conviction, he discreetly refrained from sitting on the furniture when he was visiting church members in the hospital. His squeamishness went unnoticed because the Visitation Committee always had enough people to fill up all the available furniture in a room, with two or three visitors left over.

Perhaps it was his brush with polio—or what everybody thought was polio—back when he was four years old that made him so conscious of germs. Or maybe it was his third-grade teacher, Mrs. Chesterfield—with the swollen glands and psoriasis, who forced her class to sit in a darkened classroom after recess each afternoon for three weeks while she read to them a book written by a local man, Roy Welch, about the polio epidemic of 1953 and about how both of his daughters had come down with the disease. Still, more than twenty years later, Dennis could close his eyes and see Mrs. Chesterfield reading in the dim room, her head tilted down until her jowls made a nest for her chin on her chest. And as she read, she rubbed her hands, back and forth, building up on her desk a small pile of white scales that she would casually brush away just before closing the book at the end of that day's reading.

Dennis took a deep breath and surveyed the parklike grounds through which he was walking. He knew he washed his hands too often. But a big part of his job at the music store was repairing musical instruments. He was a mediocre clarinet player, had a less than mediocre ear for chords and intervals (the main reason he had gone into music merchandising instead of performance or teaching), but he *was* slightly better than average when it came to unsticking trumpet valves, unjamming trombone slides, removing stuck mouthpieces from brass instruments, straightening woodwind keys, and replacing the cork on clarinet joints. As he worked, he had to keep his mind tightly shut against a vision of all the slow rivers of spit that had passed through each instrument he handled.

For reasons Dennis didn't attempt to understand, Marleen was staying in a "facility" for radiation therapy patients: Group T. This was the message on the signs that Dennis had been following for close to fifteen minutes. The "facility," as far as Dennis could tell, coming around the last corner of the fence, was a series of small brick cottages connected by short, glassed-in breezeways. Each cottage, Marleen had told him over the phone when she was giving him directions, housed four patients. It was like being in a motel, a motel with nurses, Marleen had explained.

These cottages looked a lot more sophisticated than any of the motels that Dennis had seen. Chapel Hill ivy grew up the sides of the building. The oak trees were tall and elegant, as if all of them were there on eternal scholarships. Having graduated from a small mountain college, Dennis felt threatened by the whole landscape of Chapel Hill. Even if he wasn't here to pick up a sister with tumors in her abdomen, he'd still have felt guilty and vulnerable wandering around the university grounds. The place made him acutely aware of how weak his grasp was on a large and rapidly spinning planet.

Then he had a spasm of sympathy—his only genuine assurance that he might actually be religious instead of merely superstitious—for Marleen. She was in this place trying to have her life saved, daily on display for roving bands of interns, and had never been in a school larger than Blue Ridge High. Certainly, she had worked at that motel out beside the Charlotte Airport, but it didn't have the ivy or the oaks. However, that was the place where Marleen had met Jessie Parham, the man, Marleen was convinced, who would finally fulfill all of her desires, after two marriages—one that lasted two years and the other twenty-two.

Passing through a heavy outer door, Dennis found himself in a small vestibule, slightly larger than an elevator car, facing another door, this one equipped with a peephole. Beside the door was a call box with four buttons and a name beside each button. Dennis pushed the one beside Marleen's name. A dense fog moved from his chest to his throat.

In response, Marleen's voice, doing a Bugs Bunny imitation, burst out of the speaker. "Eehhhhh, what's up, Doc?"

Since he had gotten old enough to know that Marleen tended toward promiscuity, Dennis had trouble talking to her. He assumed it was a symptom of her promiscuous mind that she constantly bounced from one level of conversation to another. But Dennis was determined that he wasn't going to let any uncomfortable silences come between him and Marleen on the drive to the coast. Assuring himself that no one else could overhear him, Dennis pushed the button again and said in what he hoped sounded like Elmer Fudd's voice: "Be vewy vewy quiet. I'm looking for the wabbit who wants the wide to Wimmington."

"Look no furder." Marleen buzzed the door open.

The inside of the cottage was divided into two large rooms joined by double swinging doors. Each room contained two beds, but they were separated by a small hallway formed by movable partitions made of a material that drifted between cardboard and plastic. Marleen's partition was pushed all the way open and so was the partition for the bed area across from hers.

To Dennis's relief, she didn't look as ravaged as his mother had led him to expect. Certainly, Marleen had lost weight, but now she looked more like the sister he had known back when she drove the school bus and played basketball. She had lost all of her middle age spread. Her slimness allowed Dennis, for a moment, to overlook how she stooped slightly. Instead of the gangly movements of a woman who'd never quite accepted how tall she was, each step, each torque of Marleen's body, seemed calculated. But rather than making her look like an invalid, her caution gave her an air of elegance that intensified the starched blue linen of her eyes. She smiled at Dennis and lifted her suitcase from her bed.

"I'm going to have to teach you how to drive faster." Marleen met Dennis at the foot of the bed and hugged him.

Dennis didn't know how much he should hug her back. He had always been unclear about hugs, though, long before his sister started having radiation treatments. To compensate for what might not have been enough pressure, Dennis patted Marleen's back. "What's the rush? We're only driving to Wilmington."

Marleen grabbed Dennis by his elbows and pushed him back arm's length to frown in his face. "I want you to get your mind out of that gear right quick, right now. You and me are going to get to Wilmington tails down and ears back."

When she frowned, Dennis could see that the skin along her jaw and under her eyes was slack while the skin on her forehead and cheeks was tight, almost glassy. Dennis flipped her nose, a method she had once used to calm him down when he was one of her chores around the house. "Look, you're going to have two weeks with that man. Surely, you can spare enough time to see a movie before we start down to the beach."

Reaching into his pocket, Marleen fished out Dennis's keys. "Find a movie you can sit through for two weeks. I'll leave your car on C level of the parking deck when I get back."

Dennis walked over and picked up Marleen's suitcase. It was the aquamarine of a Ford Thunderbird that Marleen had once longed for. That was how she had managed to survive, Dennis realized. She was able to be satisfied with a vinyl suitcase as long as it was the color of a car she could never have. "Somewhere, you've got to let me go through a Hardee's or McDonald's drive-through."

Shaking her head, Marleen glided to the nightstand on the other side of her bed and lifted a white paper bag. "I got some plastic-wrapped sandwiches from the hospital cafeteria. I know how much you like plastic-wrapped sandwiches."

"It's a four-hour drive. I just might have to stop to use the bathroom." Dennis moved toward the hallway.

With a bigger smile and still shaking her head, Marleen stooped down and rose up slowly, lifting with her fingertips dramatically arched a stainless-steel bedpan. "You're going to be traveling with all the comforts of the hospital."

Even though Dennis had pushed Marleen all the way through the huge hospital in a wheelchair, by the time they had walked across the skywalk to the parking deck and found Dennis's car, Marleen was visibly tired. And when she did get settled in the car, she still kept her slight stoop, as if she were reluctant to completely straighten her back. And in the yellow October light, Dennis noticed that Marleen's skin looked dry; her lips looked as if they were about to crack. When Dennis asked her if she wanted to get a Pepsi on their way out of town, she had opened up her purse and pulled out a large thermos and a stack of midget paper cups, clearly stolen from her "facility's" bathroom. When Marleen saw Dennis eyeing her cups, she held them up right in front of his nose and said, "Don't think I'm not paying for these things. By the time I get my three series of treatments, I'll probably have paid enough to carry away one of their operating rooms in complete good conscience."

As soon as they were outside of Chapel Hill, heading south on Highway 501, Dennis pulled a miniature wooden crate out from behind Marleen's seat. The crate held five cassette tapes that Dennis had recorded specially for the long drive to Wilmington. Although the October evening was overcast, with the smell of burning leaves sifting through his partially opened window, Dennis realized that the music he had spent a good part of the week recording would fit right in with the way a cloudy Friday evening should feel. He was sorry he hadn't arranged the songs with particular themes in mind, but he didn't think he knew more than one theme that Marleen might respond to. Nevertheless, given the hazy sky and patches of smoke drifting across the road, Dennis wished he had started the collection out with the Platters doing "Smoke Gets in Your Eyes." Instead, what started playing was Roy Brown singing "I Almost Lost My Mind." It was an old song, 1950, but Dennis knew it was one that Marleen used to sing even before she got her driver's license.

Her mouth dropped open, pulling her eyes wider. She stared at the tape player for several seconds, then looked at Dennis. "Where in the world did you get that song?"

Dennis felt compelled to tell Marleen a long version of how he got all of the songs. He wanted to let her know that he thought about her a big part of each day. On the other hand, he didn't want her to think that he was obsessively worried about her. Clearly what was needed was a professional tone.

"This fella came into the store about a month ago with his son to buy a box of clarinet reeds. The kid is about fourteen, and he wants a whole box of number two reeds." Dennis noticed that Marleen's left eyebrow had curved upward, a sign that she was puzzled. "Reeds are given numbers. A low number like two means the reed is soft. That means it's easy to make the reed vibrate. A kid with a number two reed doesn't have to work as hard to get the sound out. But while it's easy to play, a soft reed will always make a fuzzy tone. A beginner needs a soft reed until he gets his lip and lungs built up. But that fourteen-year-old kid had been playing for three years. So I told the boy's daddy that his son ought to be using number three or number four reeds if he ever wanted to sound like he was playing a real clarinet and not some plastic toy."

Though still facing Dennis, Marleen had closed her eyes and was nodding her head in time to the music.

Dennis stopped talking until the song ended. He had hoped that Marleen would let the music take her mind off the hospital. But as absorbed as she seemed to be, her mind wasn't just off the hospital but off the eighties, the seventies, and the sixties. Dennis had left a couple of minutes between each song just so they could chat or allow the effects of each song to soak in. He'd always resented how recording companies crammed songs together as if they really were nothing more than one-dimensional electronic signals that didn't need the time to inflate and unwrinkle in the listener's mind. The people on the radio were just as bad.

After a few seconds of silence from the tape player, Marleen leaned back in her seat, still keeping her spine slightly curved. When a few more seconds had passed, Marleen glanced again at Dennis. "Did you record just that one song?"

"No. I just left a lot of space between the music, so you can roll each one around in your head. And if you don't want to do that, you can try to figure out what song is coming up next." Dennis slowed down for a battered station wagon that had its right turn signal blinking for no apparent reason.

Marleen leaned forward and studied the station wagon. "Be careful. That guy looks drunk."

As soon as she spoke, the car swerved to the right, throwing up dust and gravel from the shoulder. Dennis floored his accelerator and pulled around the drunk before he could weave to the other side of the road. Marleen clutched the dash with both hands. Not too many years ago, she would have yelled at Dennis for getting too close to a reckless driver. Now she simply clenched her teeth.

By way of apology, Dennis said, "There's no telling how far down this road we would have had to follow that guy." He checked his rearview mirror and saw that the station wagon was still swerving slightly but staying more or less in the proper lane.

"That's okay." Marleen eased her grip on the dash. "What I've been going through just makes me take my life a lot more serious."

The Dominoes began singing "Sixty Minute Man." Marleen settled back, but not all the way back.

Feeling his own spine beginning to tighten up, Dennis asked, "Marleen, are you in pain? You can't seem to get comfortable in your seat."

Marleen sighed. "The radiation makes me feel like I've got these dead, dried-up twigs in my guts. I'm afraid if I let myself stretch out too far, the twigs will break and I'll come in half." Slowly, she rolled her shirt up and rolled down the elastic waist of her pants.

Dennis glanced once to see what she was doing, but when he saw his sister's exposed abdomen, he quickly turned his attention back to the road.

Tapping her right side, just below her navel, Marleen said, "See how they've tattooed me." In an irregular line across her abdomen were four yellowish orange circles slightly larger than half dollars with small cross marks drawn exactly in the center of each one. "They want to be as *pre*cise as possible with the dosage." Marleen adjusted her clothes, tapping her foot to the Dominoes. "So where'd you say you got these songs?" Marleen dug around in her purse and pulled out a pack of chewing gum.

Even before she had gone into the hospital for her hysterectomy, only to be told that she was full of tumors, Marleen had been trying to give up smoking. Jessie wanted her to take long walks, paddle canoes, and explore abandoned mineral mines with him, but he knew she wouldn't enjoy that kind of activity if she wasn't in shape.

Okay, Dennis admitted to himself. Jessie was a good influence. But just about anybody would have been an improvement over Walter Triplett. What Dennis didn't like about Jessie was his self-importance. He was a glorified mechanic whose main job was to repair radioactive machinery. Jobs, Jessie pointed out proudly, that were too hot for the college boy engineers. Dennis could tell that Jessie was amused by the idea of a man who made his living by gluing on the felt pads that dropped off the tone-hole covers of saxophones. Of course, out of deference to Marleen, Jessie never came right out and said that he thought Dennis needed to go out and find a real machine to repair.

"After I explained to this fella about his kid's reeds, we started talking, and it turned out that he collected old records . . ."

"Don't call them old." Marleen shifted in her seat, keeping her hand over her abdomen. "That's the same as calling me old."

"It turned out that he collected *classic* rock and roll, so he let me borrow some of his records, just so I could tape them for you." Dennis wondered if Marleen could fall asleep in her half-leaning position. "And some of those babies were 78s and heavy as one of Mama's stoneware serving platters."

"You are so thoughtful." Marleen reached over and patted Dennis's arm. "You ought to be married."

Marleen had told him that before. "I can't afford to get married." Dennis tried to recall what Marleen's two marriages had been like. He had been too young to remember much about her first husband, Gaither Drum. He could pull up the memory of a tall, slim boy with red hair brushed back on the sides. Like Marleen, Gaither had worn his shirt collars turned up and talked mostly about cars, particularly about his red '57 Chevrolet convertible. Back then, people like Gaither and Marleen had chewed their gum in short, irregular snaps. Insolent, Dennis could remember one teacher calling such gum chewing. And Walter, husband number two, had also been insolent in his truck driver sort of way.

Always worried about pleasing the people around him, as he had been taught in Sunday school, Dennis had never practiced insolent sneers even privately in the bathroom mirror. But part of his reverence for Marleen evolved from how well she had moved among her insolent and wise-cracking crowd, insolent herself but never cruel or insulting. It was an art—an aesthetic of attitude that Dennis associated with bobby sox, ponytails, tight angora sweaters, loud cars, and promiscuity.

"If I had it to do all over again, I'd sure start out not getting married but just living with the man." Marleen rolled down her window a few inches and tossed out her gum. Then she put a new stick in her mouth. She inhaled sharply when "Blue Tango" began to play. Resting her hand on her chest, she said, "Drive faster. That song fills me up like a Scarlet Sow banana split." Marleen pulled one leg up under her, a pose which, in the mellowing light, made her look like a teenager. "Really, you could live with a girl, Dennis, and not get into any trouble. God wouldn't mind that as much as he would you getting into a bad marriage someday."

"I couldn't get away with something like that in Hibriten." Dennis turned to emphasize his point with a prolonged stare. Certainly, Dennis didn't believe in sin the way he once did, but he did believe in how much the people in Hibriten loved to gossip, especially about people who ran stores and people who were regular churchgoers.

"Maybe you need to get away from Hibriten." Marleen pulled a jar of Nivea cream from her purse and rubbed the cream on her hands, cheeks, and neck. "Want some?" She offered the jar to Dennis.

"I like Hibriten, Marleen. I'm comfortable there." Dennis stuck a finger in the Nivea and smelled it. Then he dabbed the cream in the middle of his forehead. "Soon, I'll have enough money saved to buy into the franchise, and I can spend all my time at the Rexall sandwich counter talking with the other store owners."

"Ebb Tide" began playing. "Frank Chacksfield and His

Orchestra," Marleen said, turning up the radio. "Ain't you afraid you're missing something, staying in the same town where you were born, single? And you with a college education. As smart as you are, you could find a job in some far-off place where the girls wear grass skirts and split you coconuts for breakfast."

"Would they go ahead and scrape the meat off the shell for me? That's the job I hate most." Dennis detected a serious undertone in his sister's voice, a very rare coloring for Marleen's conversation with him. In his entire life, he had probably heard Marleen get serious with him six or seven times. On each occasion, she had been talking about her marriages going bad. Seeing that Marleen had dropped the conversation to listen to the music, Dennis reached over and turned up the volume a little.

For twenty miles, Marleen listened to the music: "Steam Heat," "Three Coins in the Fountain," "Sh-Boom," "Rock Around the Clock." She sat perfectly still, periodically chewing on her lower lip. Dennis thought maybe the radiation therapy was making her act so withdrawn and troubled. But he was reluctant to ask her about the treatments. Actually, he was reluctant to speak to her at all. He wondered if perhaps Jessie wasn't convincing her that working in a music store was no job for a real man.

When the opening bars of "Tutti-Frutti" came on, Dennis thought his spirits would pick up. But then Marleen very deliberately reached over and turned down the volume until Dennis could barely hear Little Richard's voice.

Her own voice was so soft that Dennis wished she had a button on her that could increase her volume. "I need for you to answer me a few questions, Dennis."

"Talk louder." Dennis slowed down, expecting Marleen to perk up and get imperative with him. "I can't hear you over the road noise."

After adjusting herself so she was tilted closer to Dennis, and not noticing their loss of speed, Marleen said, "I've had a lot of time to think since I've started these treatments. And I've talked to some of the nurses. One of them has a cousin who majored in music. And Dennis, I just want to know why *you* majored in music." Marleen bit her lower lip again and smoothed the fabric on the back of her seat. "Are you not married because you majored in music?"

Dennis frowned at his sister. He resented her asking him a question that had begun torturing him even before he got out of college. He didn't know how to explain to her that the music department was the only place on campus where he felt safe. Once he had accepted the fact that he didn't have the talent to be taken seriously as a performance music major, he had found a comfortable place in the classrooms and hallways of the Spencer Music Building. He had his comfortable place in the concert band—even the university orchestra, more for his clear clean tone than for his technical virtuosity.

He really didn't have to compete for the first chair or solo positions, so he didn't have to deal with the artistic jealousy that soured the relationships of the gifted majors. And when he sat through his business classes, he was happy with his C's and occasional B's because all he wanted was a rudimentary knowledge of accounting and finance. And when those business courses put too much pressure on him, Dennis could find an empty practice room and spit out his anxiety on a few chromatic scales.

Could Marleen understand, Dennis wondered, how music was a womb for him, a fetal position. All the way through high school and college, music had been his Disneyland, his Oz, his erotic dream. Yes, music was erotic. Denied certain basic sexual exploration because of his fundamentalist religion, Dennis had discovered the dizzy moments when, caught up in a Wagnerian passage or even a Sousa trio, his breathless gaze had come to rest on the band's voluptuous oboe player or one of the smoldering flute players, and he felt a harmony deep inside his internal organs . . .

"Are you a queer?" Marleen heaved the question as if it were a harpoon.

In response, Dennis lost so much speed that Marleen reached over with her foot and pressed down on the top of his numbed accelerator foot. "I don't mind if you are," she assured him, patting his shoulder but still keeping her foot on top of his. "But I've spent a big part of my life wondering about you."

Dennis laughed, tapping his right foot to make the car jerk in rhythm with his laughter, which seemed to modulate toward a hysterical cackle. Wanting to give Marleen a shock similar to the one she'd just given him, he replied, "If I've not gotten married, a lot of the blame belongs on you." He held his breath so he'd be sure to hear Marleen's response.

Marleen almost pulled herself out of her seat. "What do you mean!?" Her voice was dense as freshly poured cement.

Dennis exploded into a cackle. "Oh come on, sis, you know you've had the same feelings." Dennis tried to make his voice oily and suggestive. He remembered how Gaither Drum used to sound when he was trying to be romantic.

"Watch what you're saying, boy." Marleen's voice lost its seriousness.

Seeing that his sister no longer felt the need to be defensive, Dennis knew she had caught on to his teasing. He had never been able to fool her, even after he got his college degree. "It wasn't really you who ruined me for marriage, but a woman like you."

"Beautiful and sexy, huh?" Marleen pulled out another stick of gum and offered one to Dennis, which he decided to take.

"There's more to her—and to you—than that." Dennis leaned back in his seat, wishing Marleen could relax. "Her name was Caverly Heath."

"Like the candy bar?"

"Like Heath Furniture Company." Dennis was sure that Marleen would remember the company because she used to pass it on her bus route. "She had these blue eyes that changed shades. Have you ever noticed how saxophones change color during a concert, depending on what they're reflecting? That was how Caverly's eyes worked. And she had thick eyebrows, a lot darker than her long brown hair. But what hooked me on Caverly was her husky voice and how, instead of saying hello when she first met you, she'd ask, 'Well?'"

Marleen frowned, concentrating, rolling her eyes upward, consulting her memory. "I remember the factory, but not the girl. Did you date her?"

"Just once." Dennis took a deep breath. "I took her to our senior prom. She wore a burgundy evening gown—something between velvet and satin. I wore a rented tuxedo."

"Did I ever see pictures of you at that prom?"

"Caverly didn't want pictures. It wasn't a happy time for her." Dennis couldn't help but feel a little ashamed, but over the years, he'd decided that shame, like a glacier, helped preserve other, less magnificent emotions that happened to get trapped in the crystallized walls of guilt.

"I had to take her in Daddy's old Malibu, you know, the one with the silver paint already peeling off the plastic trim." Dennis knew he sounded petty.

"You should have asked me to let you use Walter's Oldsmobile. We had that big old brown Delta 98."

"With the back doors that opened up backward, like a Continental's." Dennis nodded his gratitude. "But you and Walter were gone to Fayetteville that weekend. Don't worry—I wanted to track you down, but I was too nervous to try driving all over the state, looking for you."

"Mama should have called us." Marleen shook her head slowly. "I don't think she or Daddy ever understood how important cars were to you and me. Of course, I never had to worry about providing the cars when I went to proms." She paused, rubbing her shoulder. "And as far as I can remember, Phyllis never went to any proms. So Daddy probably didn't know what you were going through. Especially when you were taking out one of them Heath girls."

Dennis thought he heard Fats Domino singing "Ain't It a Shame." The saxophone settled in his stomach like a large plate of yellow smoky noodles. Mellow. Completely unlike the moments he had spent with Caverly. "I had been devoted to Caverly since the seventh grade when I was first nicked by her wit. Even way back then, she approached life with a frightening blend of irreverence and contempt. To love her was to carry around a roll of barbed wire in your abdomen." Dennis felt more comfortable making his confession when he could sound as stilted as possible. He knew Marleen was amused when he consciously tried to sound as if he had a college education.

"I can identify with that." Marleen shifted in her seat. "Why didn't you go out with her more than just that once?"

"I wasn't really her type." Dennis took a deep breath, but was careful to let the air out in small installments. He didn't want Marleen to hear how much his lungs were affected by the memory of Caverly Heath. "She went to the prom with me out of sympathy. I think she believed I asked her to the prom out of sympathy. It was charity. I was comfortable with it, but Caverly wasn't. She spent the first two years of high school going steady with Carl Cleff—that was his name. And he played a bass clarinet. He had red hair and a bony skull. Not that handsome, really, but he was the most sarcastic guy in the band."

"I always noticed that the sarcastic people were usually the smartest people." Marleen's voice sounded as if it were folding in on itself, as if she were on the verge of talking to herself.

"After Carl graduated, Caverly started going with our cousin, Erwin." Dennis knew that Marleen liked Erwin. Because he had been a football player and Marleen had been a basketball player, Erwin thought some special bond existed between him and Marleen. Years had gone by before Dennis let himself admit that he had been jealous of that connection between his cousin and his sister. "At least when Caverly was dating Erwin, it was like she was part of the family. She and I would sit together in the band section of the bleachers and yell for Erwin. She always brought a thermos jug of Russian tea, and we would sit there throwing our voices away on Erwin."

"Well, if she was going steady with Erwin, how did you wind up taking her to the prom?" If Marleen had any strong moral prejudices, they were built around her disgust with infidelity.

"Now, don't get disapproving." Dennis could tell that Marleen wasn't as upset as she usually was when she had to deal with infidelity. "Toward the end of football season our senior year, we started hearing these rumors that Erwin was sneaking around and dating Shirley Shoun—the head cheerleader." Dennis was surprised by how satisfying it was to let Marleen know that her favorite cousin was a two-timer.

"I always thought Erwin had that slippery gleam in his eye." Marleen stretched her arms in front of her, left palm pushing against the back of her right hand.

"But you always asked him to go with us to get milk shakes and banana splits."

"He was cute." Marleen yawned. "He talked cute trash."

This was the side of Marleen that had never quite made sense to Dennis. How could she recognize trash for what it was and still be attracted to it? Looking back, he could tell that Gaither had talked cute trash, Walter had talked cute trash, and Jessie talked cute trash. As far as Dennis was concerned, a woman should have been warned off by a man who couldn't talk anything but trash, but here was his sister, going through radiation treatments so she would be healthy enough to marry her third speaker of trash.

"Well, Shirley liked Erwin's trash, too." Dennis measured out each word. He had never been able to learn how to speak trash. He thought his disability had something to do with being too religious when he was a child. To talk trash successfully, a boy had to master the art of sexual innuendo, and Dennis had been too concerned for too long about morality to be good at sexuality or innuendo.

Noticing her brother's clipped speech, Marleen patted him on the shoulder. "You're too serious sometimes. I bet you get too serious whenever you get around women. Be more playful."

"Playful!" Dennis twisted his whole body sideways to glare at Marleen.

"That's what I said." Marleen nodded once and crossed her arms.

"Well, let me tell you how playful Caverly was when she found out that the rumors about Erwin and Shirley were true." Dennis wasn't sure if he wanted to share the memory with Marleen. It was too much a part of his frustrated sexual history—perhaps the very source of his history. Still, he wanted to make Marleen understand why he couldn't marry. At the same time, he couldn't make his confession sound too emotional. Marleen wasn't used to hearing either his confessions or his emotions, and she would be quick to suspect pity if he didn't make his history as formal as possible.

"It was the last football game of the season." Dennis turned his attention back to the road, trying to camouflage the vividness of the memory by concentrating on his driving. "Everybody in the band thought something was up because Caverly climbed on the band bus, carrying her flute case. She didn't play a flute at football games. She played a piccolo because its higher pitch carried better outside. Caverly didn't like to carry a horn case, so she always carried her piccolo inside her jacket. It made a small vertical propeller on her left nipple."

"And you found that irresistible." Marleen spoke in a flat voice, but she fought to keep a straight face.

Dennis ignored her. "When I asked her why she had her flute case, she said, 'It's Tampax. My pride is having its period tonight.'"

"This girl isn't what I would have imagined for you . . ."

"Yes, I know," Dennis said. "Sounds like you've been imagining boys for me."

"That's not my fault." Marleen let her voice bubble with barely controlled laughter.

"When we went out to play the national anthem, we had to crawl out of our surplus army overcoats and line up in the cold on the end zone line. There stood Caverly, shivering like the rest of us, holding her piccolo."

"So what did she have in her flute case?" Marleen knew when to ease up on her teasing.

"When we got back in the stands, Caverly stuck her piccolo in her jacket pocket and then put her flute case on her lap. Instead of her Silver King flute—which probably cost her father around eight hundred dollars back then—all she had in the case was a jumble of metal and rubber tubing. I could tell that she had been practicing putting the tubing together because she worked like a magician. What she had when she finished was a slingshot—not those innocent things that you and Daddy used to make for me out of forked tree limbs. Caverly's slingshot was a weapon. Two pieces of metal formed the prongs then joined at the bottom of the fork to form the handle. After about four inches, the two pieces of metal separated again to run along the outside and inside of Caverly's arm. Just in front of her elbow, the two pieces of tubing curved over her arm and joined to form a brace.

"The rubber tubing was that surgical material, a dried blood brown. Caverly had to screw it onto the slingshot prongs. After she got it all together, she persuaded a kid to pick up rocks for her. All this time, she didn't speak to anybody in the band. Not even to me. When the kid brought her a handful of dime-sized rocks, she didn't look at him. Her eyes were scanning the sidelines. She barely glanced at the concession stand, made out of corrugated steel, which was about thirty yards from us. But in one motion, she'd drawn the slingshot, sighted on the building, and clanged that rock into the side of that shack. A couple of people who were buying hot dogs later told me that the drinks lined up on the other side of the wall rattled for three seconds after the rock hit the wall.

"Across the field, about fifteen feet above the top of the bleachers, was a large sign advertising Sunbeam bread. Little Miss Sunbeam was holding a piece of batter-whipped Sunbeam bread in one hand and signaling okay with her other pudgy little hand. Caverly took aim and knocked a mole onto Little Miss Sunbeam's nose. Marleen, it was a straight-on shot. No hint of an arc.

"Caverly popped her fingers when the cheerleaders came

out to get us ready for the football team's arrival. I didn't yell because Caverly wasn't yelling. She'd picked up her slingshot and was studying Shirley's gyrations. A couple of cheers went by; then Shirley started leading this cheer where, as the team stampedes out onto the field, all the cheerleaders go high into the air into a kind of spread-eagle. This was exactly the cheer that Caverly was waiting for.

"For the entire minute or so that the cheer went on, building up to that spread-eagle leap, Caverly held her slingshot on Shirley. If Caverly's arm trembled the least little bit, I didn't see it. Then Shirley went up, her back to the stands, and Caverly let loose.

"The rock hit Shirley exactly in the rear, right where the pleats of her skirt stressed the fullness of her upper thighs. For a second, it was like the whole night sky moved back a couple of inches. The shot was magic, Marleen. Shirley came down in a crumple. While the other cheerleaders were helping her up, Caverly took her slingshot apart and fitted it back into her flute case. She hadn't brought the Russian tea with her that night, but we didn't need it since we didn't scream for Erwin during the game."

Marleen clapped her hands once. "Good for Caverly." The sound of her voice made Dennis think of how a bed felt in the morning, with the sheet, the blanket, and the quilt warm from his own body.

"For the rest of the year, she didn't have much to do with boys." Dennis thought of Caverly. How after that night with the slingshot, she had practiced her flute so much that she began to seem silver and hollow herself. "I asked her to the senior prom more out of curiosity . . ."

"Not a good reason for asking a girl out—especially one you really cared for." Marleen frowned.

"Well, I had other reasons, but I never expected her to accept." Dennis felt his chest get heavy. "I remember the first thing she told me when she got in the car was that she had gotten a letter from Carl. He had written to her about his latest girlfriend. All Carl had been doing for entertainment was bowling, and all his new girlfriend did was ride horses. Carl wrote to Caverly to tell her that when he and his girlfriend stood side by side their legs spelled ox."

Marleen laughed. "I can see why Caverly went with Carl."

Dennis didn't want to hear that. "That was how the whole evening felt, like an ox—especially when I had to walk her to her front door. I knew Caverly felt obligated to kiss me good night. Goodbye. Don't you hate mercy kisses? I could feel my satin lapels fizzle in the glare of her porch light. It must have been five hundred watts. And I remember that her yard was full of trees and the smell of deeply dug earth. Her father was having a pool installed in the backyard.

"At her front door, she looked at me and said, 'You're a wonderful person. I'll never forget for the way you helped me without knowing it.'"

"You should have realized what she was saying." Marleen grew serious. "Women like Caverly do need all kinds of different help."

"I was happy with what she'd said." Dennis felt the back of his neck grow suddenly tired. "But then she had to ask me if I'd ever been French-kissed. I was thrown by the question. I mean, of course I'd been French-kissed—but not by Caverly. So I said no. She stood up on her toes—she'd taken off her shoes when we got on her porch—and put her lips to mine like she was attaching jumper cables to a dead battery. Her tongue went into my mouth and hesitated, the way a nurse looks in on a sleeping patient just to make sure he's still breathing. Then it was over. The kiss. The whole evening.

"Except I didn't want to let her go. So I asked her if she still had her slingshot. And you know what she said?" Dennis turned to face Marleen as if he really wanted her to answer.

"That she had it bronzed?" Marleen shrugged her shoulders, leaning closer to Dennis.

"She said she cut it into pieces with her daddy's blowtorch when she got home from the game. She said she hated for tools to let her down. Then when I said, 'Let you down? Your shot was perfect,' she said 'No, it wasn't. I was aiming for her head.'" Dennis rubbed the back of his neck with one hand and looked at Marleen. "She was trying to kill Shirley. Over Erwin. Over love." Dennis looked out over the road. "And that's how I have wanted to be loved. That's what I've been looking for all my adult life." Dennis paused, leaning forward to exhale noisely on his knuckles. "Or maybe that's what I've just been waiting for." He paused again and looked at Marleen. "Have I wasted my life?"

Marleen studied her brother's face, her eyebrows following some internal calculations. "No," she finally replied, looking out the window. "We don't waste life. It wastes us."

And in the last light of the evening, Dennis saw her slowly, carefully lean her back against the seat, regaining an echo of her teenage pliancy, waiting for him to turn the music back up so both of them could hear it without straining.

THE NECESSARY
ARRANGEMENTS

ADELE DID NOT WANT to be part of the arrangements, but she knew that now was not the time to argue with
her husband or her son-in-law, Jessie Parham, about what
should be done with her oldest daughter's mortal remains.

Of course, Jessie had not been at the hospital when Marleen died. He was too important a worker over at the Wilmington Nuclear Power Station to wait beside his wife's bed
for the few hours the doctors had agreed she could survive. So
when the time had come, and the nurses in their paper masks
and disposable gowns came in, asking Adele and Curtis to
leave, Adele had realized that the only way she could keep
from making a scene was to get away from the hospital and
away from the two men who had agreed to send her daughter's body to the medical school up at East Carolina University.

She could tell that Curtis was surprised by her request to
be taken back to their motel. Adele herself was surprised by
how her sense of loss was obscured by an overwhelming craving for a banana split.

At other deaths of close relatives—her brothers, Dennis
and Matthew; her mother-in-law, Teense; her Aunt Dove—
she had fainted, both at the times of the deaths and at some
point in the funeral services. It had become a family tradition
to make sure that two strong family members sat beside Adele

whenever she attended funerals. In the long spaces between deaths, her brothers, her husband, and even her son joked about who would have "Adele duty" at the next funeral. But this was the first death that had brought with it sorrow and hunger for an elaborate dessert.

Growing up in the Brushy Mountains of Wilkes County, Adele had learned early to expect loss. Still, she was surprised by how the death of someone she loved could knock her on her tail so completely. She had helped slaughter pigs on her daddy's farm. She had nursed brothers, sisters, sons, daughters, and her husband through every kind of disease. She could clean up the worst messes, from spilled blood to splattered vomit, and not for a second feel sick.

As Adele stood in the hospital corridor, waiting for Curtis to pull himself together, waiting for herself to return to a stable form, to feel her lungs get solid inside her chest once more, waiting for her throat to let go of the pain it had locked around, she studied her hands.

She had a Band-Aid over her most recent injury from work. Eight hours a day, five days a week, Adele stood beside a conveyor belt and stapled the backs onto dressers and chests. Three days ago, she had shot herself with her pneumatic staple gun. Since Marleen had come back to Wilmington to die, after living a year in Massachusetts, Adele had begun shooting herself in the hand with her staple gun. In eleven months, she had shot herself fourteen times.

This last accident was the worst. The staple had gone into the web of skin that stretched between Adele's thumb and index finger. Never before had she actually stapled herself to the piece of furniture she was working on. The conveyor belt moved slowly enough that Adele had no trouble keeping up with it, but over the noise of other staplers and the machines in the other departments, Adele couldn't get anyone's attention. Finally, she was able to pick up a screwdriver off one of the workbenches she passed, and, clenching her teeth, wedge the screwdriver head between her skin and the staple. After taking a deep breath, she popped the staple out of the wood, all the way out of her skin.

Casually, she had walked back to her workstation, pulled a Band-Aid out of her purse, slapped it over the two little holes out of which oozed two drops of blood, and gone back to stapling. She had stopped taking her injuries to the plant nurse after her third accident. She liked the work that she did. It was clean, and she had people to talk to when she wanted to talk. If her foreman had found out that she was shooting herself so regularly, she would have been taken off that job.

One of the nurses came out of Marleen's room and whispered something to Curtis. As soon as the woman disappeared back into the room, Curtis came over to Adele and put his arm around her, just as awkward as usual. But his awkwardness didn't bother Adele. She knew how he had been raised. Like most men she knew, he didn't know how to behave when he was hurting. Most of the men Adele knew didn't know how to behave around women except when they had nothing to share.

She put her arm around Curtis's waist and pulled him against her. For a second, feeling both sides of her husband's rib cage, Adele wondered how much more than Curtis she weighed. What was left of Marleen couldn't have weighed more than eighty pounds. A few months before Marleen discovered that she had cancer, when she had just started going out with Jessie Parham, she had worried about putting on weight. Then she had gone in for the hysterectomy only to be told that she was full of tumors down there. The doctors just sewed her up and discussed what to do.

"The nurse says we ought to go down to the cafeteria and wait there." Curtis actually began pulling Adele toward the elevator. "They already called Jessie at work."

It was on the elevator that Adele became determined not to be part of the arrangements. Curtis had sidled closer to her and taken hold of her elbow. "Do you feel a faint coming on?"

For a few seconds, Adele searched inside her brain for signs of a blackout. Of course, in the past, they had always come without warning. One minute she was crying, and the next minute she was waking up, stretched out on a couch or on a church pew with some Baptist ladies fanning her and trying to find one of her shoes.

What she did remember was a sensation of falling. Of being so heavy that nothing could hold her up, not her legs, not her brothers' or husband's arms, not the church floor. Of being so heavy that she had to fall away from the light, away from the sound of the people around her. She had to fall from hearing and seeing, as if she had gotten too heavy for her own body.

Adele bounced slightly, barely flexing her knees. She twisted her head around. "Right now, I feel pretty solid." But more hungry than she could ever recall being.

"I still think you ought to stay with me at the hospital." Curtis stepped off the elevator and glanced up and down the hallway, trying to remember how to get to the hospital cafeteria.

"If you take me back to the motel right now, you can still get back here in time to meet Jessie." Adele wanted to go on and say something angry about the arrangements that Jessie had proposed and Curtis had accepted, but Curtis had been through enough. And she knew they wouldn't be able to change Jessie's mind. Letting her girl be cut up by a bunch of doctors-to-be. Then they would cremate her. At least Jessie had promised Adele that she could have the ashes. Still, Adele had to say something. "I know why the nurse wanted us to leave." Adele stepped off the elevator and stood behind Curtis, forcing him to turn around and look her directly in the eyes. "Don't you think I know that when a person is in Marleen's condition they have to put her in a plastic bag?" She didn't expect Curtis's face to contract the way it did. She took Curtis's arm and led him toward the cafeteria. Having once worked in a furniture factory cafeteria for close to ten years, Adele could follow the smells, despite the other odors of disinfectant, perfume, and offices, without even thinking about where her sense of direction came from.

"I guess nurses got busy mouths." Curtis usually enjoyed talking to nurses.

Adele stopped in the middle of the hallway. Curtis still resented what the other nurse, Marleen's day nurse, had told Adele that day when Marleen had finally been taken to the

hospital after spending eight months in her and Jessie's apartment, getting weaker and thinner.

Although Adele knew the day would come when Marleen
would have to go into the hospital, and she had seen enough
sickness in her life to know Marleen would die, Adele had
been certain, as they talked and waited for the ambulance to
come, that more than the cancer was causing Marleen's pain.
Then, after the ambulance left and Curtis and Jessie left, leaving Adele and the day nurse to straighten up the apartment,
the nurse—who was about Adele's age—had tried to reassure
her that Marleen wasn't as bad as she first appeared to be.
Before Adele could prepare herself for what came next, the
nurse went on to tell her that Jessie had made love to Marleen
that morning and probably caused some irritation, possibly
even some minor damage.

Adele had received that information three months ago,
and it still shocked her. Friends and family she told the story to
were all pretty much in agreement that Jessie had acted like an
animal. But that was the kind of man that Marleen had always
been attracted to. Only Adele's son, Dennis, had offered to
defend Jessie. He had pointed out to Adele that maybe *Marleen* had asked Jessie to make love to her one last time.

Yes, Adele could believe that Marleen might make such a
request. But Adele also had this picture in her mind: of Marleen's insides, her female parts as delicate as tissue paper down
there, and Jessie on top of her and knowing what he was
doing to her. No, Adele always had to come back to her belief
that Jessie could have reassured Marleen in some less damag-
ing way.

"Why are we going to the cafeteria?" Adele asked the
question as if she were just waking up, as if she were asking
what day it was. Wednesday, she reminded herself, although
it felt like a Sunday. She and Curtis seldom missed work
the way they had during the last couple of months. Marleen
had been given three months to live, but she had gone for
eleven.

Then again, nobody knew better than Adele how strong
her oldest daughter had been. She had survived two sorry

husbands, raised three children mostly by herself, and held down two jobs for the last five years of her marriage to Walter Triplett. At least, Jessie Parham had let Marleen rest. He had given her a year of marriage as Marleen had always thought it should be. Too bad, Adele said to herself, that he had taken her to Massachusetts during that year. Adele had always wanted to see Marleen happy instead of so restless and frustrated.

"Do you really want to go back to the motel?" Curtis was digging in his jacket pocket, looking for his Tums. His voice sounded watery.

At first, Adele thought she might be getting ready to faint, but then she realized that her husband was fighting to keep his voice clear.

"I don't know how long me and Jessie will be tied up at the hospital." Curtis coughed, plumbing his sense of loss by how raw his lungs felt.

"I've got to start calling people." Adele turned back in the direction from which they had come. She didn't want to break down in front of the hospital crowd. Once she got back to their room at the Sea Oats Motel, facing the telephone and all the sad voices of her relatives, she could break down. But she might have to have that banana split first.

"How come you're holding up so strong?" Curtis caught up with Adele but stayed behind her until they got through the lobby.

As Curtis pushed open the big glass door for her, Adele replied, "All I can figure is that we've seen this coming for so long."

Going down the sidewalk, Curtis kept his arm around Adele's shoulder. A strong wind was blowing from the east. Although the sky was clear over the hospital, it was obvious to anybody who was curious enough to glance up at the sky that a large storm was thrashing the ocean several miles offshore. If it hadn't been mid-December, Curtis would have worried about a hurricane.

Not usually fond of strong wind, today Adele found the gusts comforting. The palm trees lining the sidewalk rustled.

They reminded her of the voices she had been only half listening to for the last eleven months, people trying to give her hope. She had learned that nothing angered her more than people trying to give her false hope, people who had not seen what had become of her daughter.

The shivering palm trees assured Adele of just how meaningless all that sympathy had been. At least with the palm trees, Adele didn't have to pretend to be cheered up. What a relief, she was surprised to feel, to no longer pretend she felt comforted, to no longer have to work at hoping.

And Marleen was freed from the same responsibility to the people around her. How much weight had Marleen felt, having to convince all of her visitors that dying wasn't all that bad? And she had been so self-conscious about her odor. Smoking constantly to cover up the decay of her body.

"Curtis, you know she's better off now." Adele felt her words echoing inside her body, the way she had once made her voice echo in the gleaming hollowness of the milk cans that she and her brothers had to clean every morning. It was this hollowness that kept her from fainting, she realized. She was so empty at this moment that she had no place for grief.

"If I think about her body, I'm relieved for her." Curtis fumbled in his pocket for his keys. "But when I think about her voice, not hearing it anymore, not seeing her . . ." Curtis swallowed slowly and rubbed his nose.

Adele moved closer to her husband and rubbed his stomach. "From the first day each of them left home, I've missed them that way." Adele remembered that she would have to call Phyllis first. Then Dennis. She'd have to call him at work. He'd be able to keep on working until the store closed. Dennis could get comfort from the musical instruments he sold. Phyllis, on the other hand, would probably take a six-pack of beer and go sit beside her pool. Adele reminded herself to warn Phyllis about getting drunk around her pool.

As Curtis pulled out into the busy four-lane that would carry them toward the beach, Adele was aware that she was squeezing her hands together, one balled inside the other. She rubbed the knuckles of her left hand with her right thumb.

One trait that she and Marleen had shared was their ability to crack an apple in half with their bare hands. Adele could charge people at the factory ten cents to watch her crack open an apple with just a twist of her wrists. Or, as sometimes happened, she could win five or ten dollars when somebody would bet that she couldn't do it. Usually, Adele didn't like to bet, but occasionally, a salesman would wander into the factory or the canteen during lunch, and some foreman or supervisor would trick the stranger into betting against Adele. She didn't mind taking a salesman's money—or a truck driver's money. Marleen's second husband had been both a salesman and a truck driver.

In one part of her mind, Adele regretted that her hands had gotten so rough over the years. No matter how much Nivea or Oil of Olay she used, she still woke up every morning with the same calluses she went to bed with. But the grip of the stapling gun and the endless stacks of back panels she had to handle every day kept her hands rough and sinewy while the rest of her body grew rounder and softer. Adele wondered if her soul had gotten as knotty as her hands. Or did it take after the rest of her?

Although they usually got a motel room closer to the hospital, on this trip, Curtis had decided that they needed to room closer to the ocean. Adele knew her husband thought the ocean view might keep her mind off of the arrangements that would have to be made. Besides, in December, the oceanfront motels were even cheaper than the motels in downtown Wilmington. Adele was surprised to discover that she actually did like being at the ocean more in the winter than in the summer. At least in the winter, she didn't feel obligated to lie on the hot sand and get sunburned.

Then again, she and Curtis hadn't come down to the beach for vacation all that much since their three children had grown up. In fact, Adele couldn't count back with any assurance to the last summer that she and Curtis had spent their vacation at Carolina or Myrtle Beach. If they didn't visit Phyllis and Vernon in Florida, they usually went up into the mountains for vacation. It must have been at least fifteen years since they'd come to Carolina Beach with Dennis.

But the place hadn't changed from what Adele remembered. She had never paid that much attention to all the little tourist shops, which changed fronts and owners every year but always seemed the same. There was still the boardwalk, which started at one end of town where the carnival rides were located and stretched along the beach for fifteen or twenty blocks to the Rainbow Pier. Just one block down from the pier was the Sea Oats Motel.

Shortly after Curtis passed the Carolina Beach city limits sign, Adele realized that she needed to walk. Off to her right, between the beach houses and restaurants, Adele could see the ocean, steel blue, white caps heaving, waves breaking jaggedly, giving up part of their strength in spray and roar. The sky was more overcast here at the beach than in town, but sunlight still throbbed through the clouds in broad beams that made the spindrift and mist glitter all the way up to the very floor of the clouds.

"Pull over there by the roller coaster, Curtis." Adele gathered up her purse and began to button her coat. She noticed that Curtis had slowed down but seemed uncertain about her order. "Go on, right over there. I feel like walking back to the motel from here."

"Walk?" Curtis made the turn but stopped at the very edge of the parking lot. "This wind'll blow your eyebrows right off."

Adele pulled a scarf from her coat pocket. "I don't have to let it blow right in my face."

"But it's a mile down to the motel." Curtis started to maneuver the car around so he could get back on the road. "What if you decide to have your faint before you get back to the room?"

Adele took hold of the steering wheel, her other hand opening her door. "Don't make your wife jump out of a moving car, Curtis." She kept her hand on the wheel as Curtis steered up to the corner of the parking lot where the boardwalk began.

"You're being foolish." Curtis shook his head as he watched Adele climb out of the car.

"You've got your arrangements to make with Jessie. And I've got to let myself get settled." Adele leaned back inside the car and kissed Curtis on his rough cheek. Then remembering a Carter Family song that Curtis sometimes played on his accordion, Adele said, "I gotta walk that lonesome valley."

"The nearest valley, lonesome or otherwise, is probably three hundred miles away." Curtis frowned at Adele.

"Just be sure you get it definite when and where we can pick up our little girl's ashes next year." Adele tied a double knot in her scarf.

After watching Curtis disappear down the street, headed back to Hanover Memorial Hospital, Adele stepped onto the sandy wood of the boardwalk and walked down the nearly abandoned stretch of beach towel shops, novelty shops, arcades, restaurants, and bars. Most of them were shuttered for the off season. Occasionally, Adele would pass a store that was open for business. These places were usually run by retired couples who lived at the ocean year-round. They had nothing else to do in the winter but wait around in their empty shops for the stray visitors to the beach: fishermen who were looking for a place to eat, young couples who'd eloped, older couples who didn't want to take the chance of being seen together . . . Adele wondered if any of her children had ever come down to the ocean in the wintertime.

The light that came from the opened shops seemed weighed down by the overcast sky, bent down by the wind whipping off the ocean. It was the kind of light that Adele associated with nights of wondering how they were going to pay the bills. She knew that Marleen had stayed up many nights with that kind of worried light shining over her shoulder—back when she was married to that two-timing Walter Triplett. At least Jessie had kept her away from that kind of worry for the short marriage they had. Adele was grateful for that. But she couldn't understand why a man would talk his wife into giving her body to a medical school. Marleen never thought like that until she married Jessie. He just wanted people to think he was smart; that was all Adele could figure.

Squinting, Adele tried to see if anybody was out on the Rainbow Pier, but the wind kept making her eyes water. Surely, the wind was too strong for anybody to be fishing, but still, some people liked to go out on those creaking boards when the water was up, knocking against the pilings. Even in the quietest weather, Adele preferred to stay off the piers along the coast. Out on a pier, she was confronted with just how large the ocean was. Looking at it from the railing, Adele couldn't avoid thinking how solid the water looked and behaved. She had the sensation that if a person fell into the ocean from a pier, she wouldn't be able to break back through the surface—"swallowed up" was the phrase that came to mind.

By the time she was halfway to the pier, Adele knew she was too hungry to begin making those phone calls. For a moment, she felt guilty. A woman who'd just lost her daughter shouldn't be hungry. Her stomach should have been shriveled into a small knot of grief. Regardless of what her conscience told her, the craving was still there, a painful emptiness. For a moment, Adele thought she might be getting ready to faint after all. She hadn't had breakfast or lunch—and it was almost three-thirty. Come to think of it, she hadn't had supper the night before either. No. She didn't feel anything like fainting. This was a hunger that pulled her away from the heaviness of unconsciousness.

The faded primary colors of the shop fronts seemed to focus Adele's hunger. She wanted to eat something that made her think of those buildings, something dense but frivolous, something like life itself. It had to be a banana split. In this state of mind, Adele reached the heavy sun-bleached oak doors of the Coastal Ice Cream Emporium. Somewhat to Adele's disappointment, once she pushed her way through the heavy doors, the shop itself was like any other ice cream store, with a pink-and-white tile floor and uncomfortable metal chairs and tables. She had been hoping for something . . . something more like what Marleen had taken her to a long time ago when Marleen had learned that Adele had never tasted a banana split.

Marleen had just gotten her driver's license. Partly to show off and partly to bring her mother up to date, Marleen had insisted on taking Adele to the Scarlet Sow Drive-In Grill. Instead of using curb service as Adele had expected, Marleen had made her get out of the car and go into the dining room at the back of the grill. Back then, the Scarlet Sow had black wooden booths with red vinyl upholstery, and the air was a blend of cigarette smoke, french fries, onion rings, coffee, and brewing tea. And they thought they had invented banana splits.

Behind the long glass counter of the Coastal Ice Cream Emporium stood a girl, perhaps seventeen years old. Adele hesitated in the door. She wasn't sure if she was up to dealing with a seventeen-year-old. She had been expecting an older person to be running the store, someone who knew how banana splits were supposed to be made. And the song blaring from the radio, high nasal voices singing about dancing all night, caused Adele to further doubt the young girl's ability to make the right kind of banana split.

The wind coming through the door tossed the girl's hair into her eyes, but as she brushed it out of her face with her fingers, she smiled at Adele and said, "I was about to close up for lack of business. I thought all the tourists had been blowed away by this wind."

Ordinarily, such a declaration would have sent Adele back out the door, but she couldn't face her motel room just yet. "Are you too closed up to sell me a banana split? I know they're a mess to make, but I'll be glad to help you make it and clean up."

As Adele spoke, she realized that she would prefer making the banana split herself. It had to be put together correctly. Marleen had never outgrown her love of banana splits nor her superstitious conviction that there was only one way to make them.

"Oh, don't worry about how closed up I am." The

girl waved her hand in the air and shook her head.

Adele noticed how tanned the girl was—and it the middle of December. "I'd like a banana split. But I'd like to ask you to put it together in a particular way." Adele walked up to the counter and rested her fingertips on the glass.

The girl pushed up the sleeves of her pink sweatshirt—the outline of a flamingo decorated the front of the shirt—and nodded. "Do you want it in the regulation banana split boat bowl?" She held up a blue plastic bowl shaped like a rowboat.

"That'll do just fine." Adele dropped her attention down to the small barrels of ice cream on display inside the counter. "And I want a scoop of strawberry, vanilla, and chocolate. Strawberry in the front of the boat; vanilla in the middle. And chocolate in the back."

After lining the bowl with a sliced banana, and as she stooped over to dig the ice cream out of the barrels, the girl said, "Well, you are particular, ain't you." But the girl's tone was good-natured. She wasn't complaining.

While the girl leaned over the counter, balancing on her toes, Adele noticed that her neck and shoulders were more muscular than most girls she had seen. In fact, Adele became convinced that the girl was so good-natured because she was so healthy.

"How do you stay so brown this deep into winter?" Adele didn't usually trust people with year-round tans, but this girl didn't seem to be aware of how her skin gave off golden light even in the severe illumination of the fluorescent bulbs overhead.

"I surf." The girl straightened up and placed the blue boat on the stainless-steel work counter.

"Lord. I hope you don't go out on a day like this." Adele knew she sounded like a mother.

The girl walked back to the counter where Adele was standing and leaned across, gazing out the window toward the ocean. "The waves are good. But the wind is too much for me." She turned her eyes back toward Adele. "The best surfing on this part of the coast comes with storms, but when the wind is blowing this hard, it's just not any fun." Returning to the work counter, the girl said over her shoulder: "If the wind wasn't so strong, I'd have closed the store two or three hours ago."

"Don't your mama and daddy worry about you out there? Don't you worry about getting eaten by a shark?" Adele was glad to have raised her daughters in a time and a place where all she had to worry about was boys and driver's licenses.

"My mom's the only one who has to deal with the worry. My dad left when I was ten. He couldn't deal with me even before I started surfing." The girl lifted the steel lids off the vats of toppings. "You want the toppings arranged any particular way?"

Nodding, Adele remembered how serious Marleen was that first time they ate banana splits. Marleen had warned Adele that the pineapple topping had to be on the strawberry ice cream, the chocolate syrup on the vanilla ice cream, and the strawberry topping on the chocolate ice cream. "Otherwise, it'll make you sick," Marleen had declared.

Following Adele's instructions, the girl added the toppings, sprinkled on the nuts, spread the marshmallow sauce, sprayed on the whipped cream, centered the cherry, and slid the concoction across the counter to Adele. "I just might have to have one of these before I go home."

Adele took the banana split to a table in the corner of the shop where she could look out the window. The waves were breaking so loudly that their booming could be heard over the disco music coming from the radio. Adele bent over her ice cream. She didn't want to think about the waves or about the young girl wanting to be out there trying to ride them. Muscular or not, nobody had any business out in that heaving water.

Besides, according to Marleen's first instructions, a woman had to pace herself and concentrate while eating a banana split. At first, you wanted to move from front to back while eating the ice cream: a mouthful of strawberry, a mouthful of vanilla, a mouthful of chocolate. Eat a bite of banana. Then another mouthful of chocolate, a mouthful of vanilla, a mouthful of strawberry. The idea was to get the chocolate ice cream eaten first, before it melted too much and got the rest of the ice cream too chocolaty. Any straying from the set pattern, Marleen warned, "and you'll get sick."

Of course, eating the split too fast could also make a person sick. "On the other hand," Marleen said as she rolled her eyes around the dining room, appraising each man, "eating too slow leaves too much slop in your bowl."

Each bite Adele took produced a broad stroke of sensation in her mouth, across her brain. Each flash of pineapple-strawberry carried with it a memory of all the cheap perfumes that Marleen had ever worn; the chocolate-vanilla illuminated the memories of all the hairstyles Marleen had come home wearing, her permanents, her pageboys, her beehives; the strawberry-chocolate went straight to Adele's ears—her daughter's voice wrapped around her secrets, her complaints, her disappointments.

"You need some water to wash that down?" The girl, stooping now in front of the counter, paused in her cleaning of the glass.

"No. I want it to stay right where it is." Adele hadn't broken her rhythm even long enough to wipe the corners of her mouth. During the break in her eating, though, she now realized how uncomfortable the metal seat was becoming. And as far as she could tell, the girl would soon be ready to close. She pretended to study the beach for a few seconds. "Is it true what I hear about how storms make shells wash up on the beach?" Jessie, who pretended to be an expert on everything, had told Adele about the best kind of conditions for beach-combing.

The girl checked her watch. "You got to catch the tide as it's going out to get the best shells." She removed her hairnet. Honey-tinted hair dropped to her shoulders. "It's started coming in by now. But as windy as it's been, not many people have been out on the beach looking for shells."

As Adele stood up to put on her coat, she realized how much ice cream she had eaten. The chocolate was gone. Only two small lumps of vanilla and strawberry remained. She couldn't leave them, though. Marleen had cautioned her about always finishing her banana splits. It was bad luck to throw one away only partially eaten. A person had to earn the luxury of a banana split. "You ain't worthy of it if you can't finish it," Marleen had explained when Adele started to push the bowl away from her with even parts of the banana left over.

Pushing open the door, being careful not to dribble any of the melted ice cream and syrup on her coat or the floor, Adele said to the young girl, "Wait until the water calms down before you get out in the waves."

"If the water gets too calm, you aren't surfing. You're floating." The girl waved with one hand while pulling a ring of keys out from under the cash register. "But don't worry. I've made other plans for tonight."

Way back since Marleen had gotten old enough to make plans, Adele had been disturbed by where such plans sometimes led. Plans always seemed to create unhappiness. Even when you thought you were planning something that would give everybody a good time, you were most likely going to wind up sad. Marleen had planned on having a good third marriage. She had stopped smoking. She and Jessie had taken canoe lessons. She was reading books on ocean animals and seashells.

Even when she couldn't plan on living, Marleen had spent hour after hour rearranging her hospital bed tray. Her whole world shrank down to what she could fit onto that narrow surface: her pack of cigarettes, her lighter, her chewing gum, her glass of water, and her ashtray.

Adele took two big bites of the strawberry ice cream and scooped the juice out of the front of the boat. Because of her feet's tendency to swell, she never wore dress shoes anymore. Had she been wearing heels, instead of her pumps, she'd never have thought about crossing the sand and getting closer to where the water was roaring and ripping. It was like the noise she sometimes heard inside her head when she stood on a cliff up in the mountains and looked out across some gorge over the tops of tall maples and firs and she could see the ridges turning blue in the distance and curving toward the edge of the world.

She hoped maybe the thunder from the water could fill her up in a way the ice cream had failed to do. She wanted to split out of her skin. Get so full that she'd explode all at once and not ache herself through each coming night. She knew she'd be fine at work. But back at home, she'd have to watch herself. She'd have to put a sheet or a quilt over Marleen's red velvet love seat—the thing that had started all of her troubles.

Making sure that she was well beyond the water line on the beach, Adele finished her vanilla ice cream. Glancing around for a trash can, she caught a glimpse of a nearly transparent piece of marine flesh rolling onto the beach. It was about half the size of a human head, and as Adele approached it, she saw that the creature had bands of bright blue looped inside it like small ribbons. Shortly after Marleen and Jessie had moved back from Massachusetts, when Marleen could still walk, Adele had gone with them to another beach, and Jessie had given her a lecture on jellyfish. The same kind as the one now resting at her feet had washed up during that walk, and Jessie had told her that she was looking at a jellyfish referred to as sea blubber.

Back then, they had just walked on and left the jellyfish stranded on the beach, after Jessie pointed out the translucent gray tentacles hanging from underneath the jellyfish and warned Adele and Marleen about how painful the stings could be. Now Adele felt a deep urgency to get the thing back into the water. Today, she knew how alone it felt, lying on the strange sand, wondering what had happened to the world where it grew up. But she knew she had to be careful. A few short stingers were curled under the quavering jellyfish. Adele stooped down and with her plastic spoon gently prodded the jellyfish onto the banana split dish. Once she was sure she had it balanced, she eased her way calf-deep into the sweeping water. She hated the way the sand pulled out from under her feet when the water surged back toward the ocean. The coldness of the water added an edge to the current, pulling her breath out toward the spewing waves. For a moment, Adele thought she might drown just from the chill.

Waiting until the sand stopped rushing seaward, Adele carefully cocked her arm back and sideways and brought the dish over her head in a wide arc. She almost fell on her face. By the time she regained her balance, she looked up to see a huge wave rushing toward her. Clutching her pocketbook and the banana split boat, Adele splashed back up to higher ground.

Barely noticing the wind blowing against her wet and salty slacks or the sand gritting its way into her shoes, Adele stood watching the water rushing toward shore. She hadn't seen where the jellyfish landed, wasn't sure if she had thrown it out far enough. Then, after a few minutes, she saw the clear flesh rolling back up onto the beach.

Once again, Adele coaxed the jellyfish onto her banana split dish, noticing that the plastic was beginning to tear along the side close to the front where it curved. This time, waiting for a wide space between the waves, Adele waded out even farther, almost up to her waist. She felt seaweed brushing against her legs. Spray blew into her face. Her hair, no longer confined by the dissolving hairspray, clung to her forehead, ears, and neck. She couldn't remember being so sloppy since she was a child playing in the shallows of the Yadkin River. Despite the concussion of the waves and the steady pull of the back rush, Adele felt stronger at this moment than she had in two years.

She cocked her arm once more, even tilted her body slightly to the side, and flung the jellyfish with such a roll of her body that her face came within inches of the swaying water. By the time she straightened up, the jellyfish was out of sight. Crouching against the waves breaking against her back, Adele stumbled back to the shore. Her body thrummed from the pounding she had just taken.

Then, when she saw the sea blubber washing ashore a third time, Adele felt the strength leave her legs, her arms. As she sloshed to the jellyfish, she noticed that her banana split bowl had split even further. Flexing the side of the bowl,

Adele tore the boat almost in half. The rip angled from the front toward the back, promising to break all the way off with the next weight.

Adele went ahead and broke the boat in two, shoving the pieces into her coat pocket. Her eyes felt full of the angry ocean. Just before squatting down to perhaps apologize for her failure to save the jellyfish, Adele glanced around, hoping to find another container—even a wide piece of driftwood. As she looked around, Adele realized that she had slowly been drifting toward the Rainbow Pier. It stuck way out into the ocean. It was so long, in fact, that the last quarter of its length was obscured by the spray blowing up from the ocean, way out beyond where the waves were breaking.

That was where she needed to go, Adele realized. Drop the jellyfish off the end of the pier, and its chances of staying off the beach would be much better. But then, she had to carry it to the pier. She couldn't see anything to put it in or on.

Tiring of her own weakness, Adele cupped her hands under the jellyfish. She felt a flash of heat in her right palm, up the length of her middle finger, then a few sparks of burning in her left palm and along her thumb and little finger, but the pain couldn't compare to what her pneumatic staple gun could inflict.

As she hurried toward the pier, the burning changed to tingling, while a warmth moved up her wrists. The weight of the jellyfish seemed as transparent as its skin. At one moment, Adele thought her arms would cramp with the effort to support the creature. In the next moment, the thing seemed to weigh nothing at all, and she had to bob it in the air to reassure herself that it was still in her hands.

Adele shuffled through the pier entrance, a combination grill and game room, without glancing at the two or three people who sat in a far corner drinking beer and watching television. Even this close to shore, the pier shuddered from the waves slamming against the pilings.

Even on warm, sunny days, Adele had never cared much for piers. First of all, they took you too far out over the ocean—out there where the water was way over your head and the big fish swam. Of course, an ocean fish didn't have to be big to be frightening. It could be a puffer fish, or carry spines all over it, or have crazy eyes, or be some neon green color that made you think of poison gas.

Second, a pier didn't really take you anywhere for all of its scariness. It stuck you out just so far over the ocean and held you there. Walking out to the end of a pier was a lot like climbing a tree. Once you got to the top, where were you to go from there? And today, especially, walking out on the pier made Adele think back to those days when she did climb trees—only because her brothers expected her to. If she didn't glance over her shoulder, Adele couldn't really tell the roiling clouds and mist on all sides of her from the clouds that were stampeding along over her head. With the wide gaps between the boards, the pier could almost be a ladder. And for a moment, Adele felt a swirling in her stomach that always struck her when she'd ride the Ferris wheel, a dizziness in her stomach instead of her head.

And a third reason Adele preferred to stay off piers whatever the weather was because they sometimes fell down. Certainly, Curtis had told her over and over again that while less well constructed than, say, a bridge, piers didn't really have to support that much weight. Even the oldest piers came apart only during hurricanes. Bad as this wind was, Adele had to admit that she had felt stronger ones even as far inland as Hibriten—close to four hundred miles—during the few hurricanes that had made their way up to the Brushy Mountains.

Today, though, the pier seemed less substantial than Adele ever remembered it feeling because of the noise. Somehow, in blending its own creaks and groans with the roar of the running waves and the explosion of the breakers and the shuddering smacks of the water pounding the pilings, the weather-blackened planks of the pier felt as if they were about to turn as transparent as the jellyfish. Adele walked down the very middle of the pier and kept her eyes fixed on the boards in front of her.

At the end of the pier, the horizon had disappeared. Adele

had no line of sight to tell her how far she was from solid land. All she could see was a swirl of greenish gray clouds, silver mist, and greenish gray ocean. She stopped about five feet from the end rail. Warped and splintery, the rails had always struck Adele as ridiculously fragile, barely able to support the weight of fishermen's feet and elbows. Certainly not strong enough to hold back a rather heavy woman carrying a small jellyfish. And even on a good day, Adele couldn't bring herself to go to the very edge of the pier because she expected the end to tilt down suddenly and drop her into the water.

Overcoming her usual fear with careful side steps, Adele eased to the rail. She could feel the whole ocean surging against the pilings. This far out, the rhythm was more regular, deeper—almost calmer, despite the wind and the height of some of the waves that rushed by with the sound of a thick velvet curtain being slowly ripped apart.

With the rail pushing against her stomach, Adele leaned out, stretching out her arms, and offered the jellyfish back to the ocean.

Instead of dropping as Adele pulled her hands apart, the jellyfish hovered for a moment like a misshapen moon. Then for a second, Adele thought she was the one falling into the ocean because the jellyfish seemed to be rising above her hands. Adele grabbed the rail and found her feet firmly planted on the rough wood.

Once assured that she wasn't falling, wasn't fainting, Adele looked back at the jellyfish. It was now three feet above her head, steady in the wind, its stingers fluttering slightly. For just the few moments that Adele needed to reassure herself that it was there in the sky, the jellyfish trembled a bit and then, as if catching a gust of a world-long wind, it shot straight up, disappearing among the clouds.

Like a grateful soul, Adele told herself. She kept her hold on the rail but was in no hurry to return to solid ground.

FOR SENTIMENTAL
REASONS

IN THE BASEMENT HE HAD CARVED out underneath his house, standing on the cement floor he had poured himself, Curtis Holsclaw eased the edge of the oak scrap toward the humming blade of his band saw. It was a small saw, shaped something like a large milk shake mixer, painted a dull creamy green. He wanted to make sure that he got the blade to hit the wood just between two of the darker grain lines. Otherwise, the saw would be fighting him the entire time he worked to cut out the circle in this piece of wood.

Although he had been trimming a truckload of veneer all day, he didn't feel imposed upon by his wife for having to cut out the three circular pieces of wood that she, after he had nailed them together, would decorate for somebody's anniversary or birthday. Wooden cakes for special occasions had become Adele's trademark at the factory where she worked. They were valued by the factory workers as symbolic not only of significant events but also of their capacity to appreciate art for art's sake. Being completely nonutilitarian, wooden cakes represented the luxury of sentimentality. At the same time, a wooden cake also represented the workers' need for a good joke. Hardly a week went by that Adele didn't have at least one person asking her to make one of her trick cakes.

Five years she'd decorated cakes at the Stars and Bars Bakery. Five years of coming home with the powdered sugar crusted on the bottoms of her shoes until she was almost half an inch taller than she had been that morning when she left for work. Five years of working Saturdays and alternating Sundays and being on call for emergency decorating. Curtis had understood when she came home one night and as she scraped the powdered sugar off her shoe soles declared that she was gorged on the bakery business.

She had done factory work before, ten years in the factory cafeteria before working at the Stars and Bars, so she knew what she was getting into: better pay, better hours, and wood shavings on the floor instead of sugar. Then when she had landed the job in the cabinet room, she didn't even have to worry about the wood shavings because all they did in that place was put the pieces of the furniture together. It was a part of the factory that drew together the more ... the more refined workers. Curtis nodded to himself. Yes, people who worked with the nearly finished furniture seemed more finished themselves. But then again, in the factory, the women always seemed more finished than the men. They were more careful about the way they dressed, the way they smelled, the way they worked. Adele spent as much time getting ready for work as she did getting ready for church or for dinner at the fish camp. And she still could turn heads when she took time with herself, even though she was sixty-three.

Curtis pulled his attention back to his work as the saw nibbled the edge of the wood. His fingers told him that he had set the blade right between the grain. He shifted the pressure from his fingertips to his elbows and slid the pencil line smoothly against the blade, following the circle he had drawn, the heavy wood barely resisting the blurred teeth of the saw.

The slight pressure of the wood against the blade and the smooth rotation of his elbows translated into a pleasant warmth in Curtis's stomach. If a man could kiss a woman the way that saw split the wood, he would never have to worry about finding a parking place for his smooches.

He brushed the wood dust from the circle of oak. Its smell was mild and made Curtis think of autumn and mayonnaise. His favorite wood odor was cedar, but from what the govern-

ment said, too much red cedar dust was dangerous. Nevertheless, Curtis couldn't help but shut his eyes and long for a piece
of cedar to sniff. A good strong whiff of cedar might help him
keep his mind off the next couple of days.

Tomorrow, Adele would make the call to the hospital
down in Greenville. More than a year of waiting would be
over, and they could drive down and pick up Marleen's ashes.
What had been worrying Curtis for the entire year was:
where did a father carry his daughter's ashes when he brought
them home in the car? It didn't seem right to put them in the
trunk. They were more than luggage. But they were also less.
And it didn't seem quite right to carry them in the front seat
as if they were some kind of passenger.

What had been bothering Curtis more, much more,
though, years before the cancer had eaten his daughter away
was: what had he done as her father to make her love the men
that she had. Three husbands in the forty-three years she had
lived, and all three were so low-down they probably scraped
their elbow when they picked their nose. Curtis could, at
times, just about trace the reasons his other two children,
Phyllis and Dennis, had never wanted to stay at home. But
Marleen, his and Adele's firstborn, had always confused him,
even though she was more like him than the other two, who
took after their mother.

Maybe all Curtis had to do was drive down to Wilmington and tell Jessie, Marleen's third and final husband, that he
needed to have somebody explain his daughter to him. Curtis
would be willing to accept the blame for the life his daughter
had lived if whoever did the explaining didn't try to tell him
that Marleen had gone after such bastards for husbands
because her father had forced her to give up an illegitimate
baby.

No. That was one explanation Curtis wouldn't accept. He
was honest enough with himself to have long ago considered
what that adoption might have done to his relationship with
Marleen. But at the time, neither he nor Adele—not even
Marleen—had seen a way to keep the baby. For the rest of her
life, Marleen had never mentioned that decision the three of

them had made. But it had haunted her the last few days before she died.

She had been so insistent about seeing the son she gave away that Curtis stopped by the social services office and talked to a woman who went to his church. First, she'd told him that North Carolina was very strict about keeping its files closed. Second, she'd told him that she knew of a detective agency that specialized in finding such children as Marleen's, but the price per day was just about what Curtis made per week. And it got even more expensive if the detective had to go out of the United States.

Although Marleen had stayed clearheaded up until the second she died, she became convinced that her lost boy was going to come and visit her like all of the high school friends who came down to Wilmington, some of whom hadn't seen Marleen for twenty years.

Then again, Marleen had always been full of yearning. She had wanted to leave home long before she got into trouble. Long before she got pregnant the first time. Of course, if she hadn't been so man crazy and had just wanted to get out on her own, that would have been another matter. Right out of high school, she had wanted to join the U.S. Air Force, but Curtis had absolutely refused to sign the papers. The military was not the place for a woman like his daughter. From his own experience in the army, Curtis knew that every military moment was attached to a dozen or so powerful yearnings: for familiar food, for friendly voices, for a wife's soft skin. . . .

When he was actually shooting at the Germans and they were shooting back at him, that yearning opened up like a hole at the middle of his brain. It was fear and hunger and anger rolled up into one. Marleen had that look on her face during her last couple of days. Curtis had seen it on his own face several times in the last year. When it came, all you could do was go to the flea market or go look at fishing boats. Or pour a cement floor in your basement. Or dig you out a basement if you didn't have one. Or pour yourself a drink and talk to some friendly soul on your CB radio.

It would be like Adele to want to treat the ashes as if they were her daughter. Curtis shook his head as he dug through the pile of oak scraps on the floor beside his work table. The second layer of the wooden cake had to have a smaller diameter than the first. And since this particular cake had to be three layers, Curtis kept his eye open for a third, smaller, piece of wood. Ashes couldn't be his daughter any more than these slabs of wood could ever be a tree again.

Adele was sentimental. Curtis doubted if she'd stop her grieving even after they got Marleen's ashes back home. Adele still hadn't made up her mind. Part of her wanted to bury the remains, but another part of her wanted Curtis to help her find a special place in the house where they could keep the ashes in full view. That second idea scared Curtis. Because of her sentimentality, Adele tended to brood. And as much as Curtis missed his daughter, he was sure that he didn't want to come home every evening to find Adele staring at the ashes. You couldn't live with emptiness by looking down its throat twenty-four hours a day.

Knowing Adele, Curtis was certain that she'd want to buy a special container for the ashes, even if they eventually decided to bury them. Paul Wallace, the director of the cemetery where Curtis had bought plots for himself and Adele, had told Adele that she could order just about any size or shape urn that she wanted, but she had to allow three to six weeks for delivery. Those jugs came in aluminum, alabaster, marble, wood, steel, brass, ceramics. . . . Curtis wondered if anybody at the flea market sold urns. It didn't make any difference. Adele would insist that Marleen have a retail urn bought through the proper authorities. On this occasion, Curtis agreed with Adele's unreasonable distaste for flea market merchandise.

Of course, the real problem with Adele's desire to have Marleen's ashes prominently displayed somewhere in the house was that they had no spare display room anywhere in the house because of Adele's salt and pepper shaker collection, which filled up all of the wall space in the kitchen, the den, the living room, the spare bedroom, their bedroom, and one wall in the bathroom. And each salt and pepper set had its own sentimental value for Adele.

Despite how much space Adele's collection took up, Curtis thought she needed such a distraction. He wondered if women in general didn't somehow feel more threatened by their yearnings. So much of what they bought was decoration. Their clothes, their makeup, their knickknacks. Their salt and pepper collections. A lot of what they did was decoration, too. Adele's job, for example, required her to sometimes screw brass handles and porcelain knobs onto dressers and chests. Nobody really *needed* brass handles. But the brass *looked* pretty. Pretty things helped get people's minds off wars and dead children. Otherwise, everybody'd be mired up in depression and couldn't walk through an open field without being paralyzed by sentimentality.

All of Adele's family was sentimental, even the men. Curtis dreaded going down to Wilkes on Sunday to visit Adele's brother, Taft, because Taft and Cora, his wife, never failed to stir up Adele's sorrow. As soon as they'd finish eating lunch, either Taft or Cora was sure to make some remark about how much they missed Marleen. Maybe if Cora were a more precise cook, she and Taft wouldn't be so sloppy in their emotions. Curtis thought of Cora's watery creamed corn, her poorly strung green beans, the lumpy mashed potatoes, her powdery biscuits, the unevenly fried chicken—she wasn't in full control of her kitchen, and it showed in her response to people's tragedies. She and Taft always seemed squashed by some new worry.

Adele, by getting away from the Wilkes wilderness and learning how to distract herself, had developed some self-control over the years. Her cooking was precise but not artificial-tasting, like the food in the T&T Cafeteria. Whether she was feeding him gravy and biscuits or meat loaf and potatoes, all of Adele's food stayed in its place and kept the shape it was meant to have. To Curtis's way of thinking, that's how emotions should properly behave. You had to know what shape your sadness was if you didn't want it to catch you off guard.

World War II had taught Curtis that lesson. You had to keep control if you didn't want to lose your mind.

Rubbing his ear, Curtis had no trouble recalling the two winters he had spent chasing the Germans with his artillery battery. His son, Dennis, had gone through a Boy Scout phase, wanting Curtis to go camping with him. When Curtis had tried to explain to him that sleeping out on the ground had no appeal to him, his son had refused to understand. When Dennis had been a child, he had been fascinated by Curtis's war stories. He had been fascinated by the red veins that marked Curtis's brush with frostbitten ears and nose. But the boy had grown out of that fascination.

Curtis found a piece of wood he could use for the top layer of the cake. It was pine and didn't really match the two oak layers, but the frosting was what people really bought, after all. The decoration. Briefly, Curtis held the pine up beside the oak. The pine was paler, lighter than the hardwood. In the wood bin of his family, Curtis decided, his son was the pine; his daughters were the oak.

Dennis was more like his mother than either of his two sisters were. He was a joker like Adele. He also shared her deep mistrust of sex. This wasn't to say that Dennis was backward. He'd brought two or three of his girlfriends home at one time or another. He simply didn't trust his sexual instincts. Curtis had always suspected that Dennis took his Southern Baptist training too much to heart. The boy wasn't exactly a fanatic about his religion. He'd never get rich from it. And he wasn't a fanatic about his music business either. Maybe because he was religious, Dennis didn't have the frightening yearnings of everybody else in the family. Or maybe he was religious because he didn't have the yearnings to begin with. He had grown up much milder than either of his two sisters. Curtis wondered if being chased by that one-legged rooster had somehow damaged Dennis's self-esteem.

Thirty years later, Curtis's stomach still tightened when he thought about what the rooster might have done to Dennis if the bird had been working with two legs instead of one. Once out of the coop, Dennis was able to put a little distance between him and the rooster, but the cock continued to chase him, its beak snapping the air, and that one leg whipping out every other step trying to draw more blood from the child.

Curtis nailed the top layer to the second layer. He weighed the cake in his hands. Even with one layer made out of pine, the foundation was heavy enough to make someone think he was getting a real cake for his birthday.

When Adele had gone back to the factory, not too many days had passed before everyone knew that she had been a baker and a cake decorator. Pretty soon, the cake orders began coming in. Curtis understood that people in the furniture factories didn't like to drive up to the Stars and Bars Bakery to order their cakes. In the ten or twenty minutes it took them to drive to the bakery and fill out the order forms, they could be watching television or sleeping or cleaning house or playing with the kids or drinking. Adele, as a resident cake decorator, represented convenience. Not only could they simply saunter over to where she was stapling backs onto dressers or attaching the hardware and tell her what they wanted, they could also specify what color icing they wanted, and Adele would do her best to give them precisely what they'd asked for. Besides, her cakes were always a few dollars cheaper than the cakes at the Stars and Bars.

Then after nearly five years of increasing cake requests, Adele had come home and announced that she had to do something to discourage people from asking her to bake them cakes. That had been nearly ten years ago. That night Adele had wandered around the house in her curlers and her housecoat, puffing on a cigarette, trying to figure out what she could do to let people know she was tired of baking their cakes.

At the time, it hadn't occurred either to her or to Curtis to simply refuse to bake and decorate cakes for people. Even though Curtis had been raised in town and Adele had been raised in the country, Curtis by a preacher who was a carpenter, Adele by a farmer who was a moonshiner, both of them agreed that to say no to someone who asks a favor is the worst kind of presumption, the rawest form of selfishness. If someone, especially someone you worked with, asked you to do something that everyone knew you could do, and you refused, then you soon got the reputation for being stiff-necked.

Besides, being cooperative was another way to fill up a yearning.

Curtis leaned over the wooden cake and tried to gauge how well he had centered the two top layers. He had a pair of the best eyes in all of Hibriten if you needed a man to match the grain of two shipments of veneer, but he had certainly failed to match his expectations with his children's desires. Curtis laughed to himself and brushed sawdust from the edge of the cake layers. Maybe it was chickens that had caused him to lose contact with Phyllis as well. Maybe she had developed her rebellious streak after those hens had tried to eat her bones. All because Curtis hadn't given the hens their calcium supplement like his brother-in-law, Taft, had told him.

Such big problems could come out of such small moments of neglect. He knew he was a good provider, but he could see how he had been neglectful. He had let Marleen have her way, and she had gone wild. What was she looking for in Gaither, Walter, and Jessie? If he and Adele had punished her more, would she have acted more proper? Could parents beat the sex drive out of their children? Sex, after all, was just a raw form of yearning. It was like she was addicted to heavy men who used her until they couldn't keep up with her anymore. In some ways, each of her husbands picked up where the other one left off. Still, he had to admit that Jessie had stayed with Marleen until the very end. On the other hand, as Adele would point out, he had talked Marleen into giving her body to the medical school.

Curtis stood the wooden cake on its edge in the middle of his work table and tried to make it spin. All three of the children had their mother's blue eyes. But Marleen's had wanted to be brown. Even when she had been a baby, Curtis kept expecting her eyes to come after his. The wooden cake made one or two turns then wobbled to a fall. A collapse. Curtis flipped the cake right side up. He disliked instability. Whenever he had the chance to get the broad bottoms of things flat on the ground, he never failed to make the stack as straight as possible. That was what he yearned for.

He wished he had somehow learned to make his children more stable. He didn't know how a person could watch three separate human beings grow up and not figure out what each one needed to make his or her life fit flush with their expectations.

As far as expectations went, Curtis admitted to himself, it'd be nice if he could make his wife happy on a reliable schedule.

He wished that Adele could always stay as happy as she was that night when, drifting off to sleep, she had decided that she would go ahead and make a cake for the man who'd most recently put in his order. But she would give him a cake he couldn't eat. She knew that Curtis could cut the layers for her. When the man's wife tried to cut into her anniversary or birthday cake, she'd realize that all those relatives standing around with their cups of coffee would have to satisfy themselves with vanilla wafers.

From his forty-some years of being married to Adele, Curtis had learned that sentimental people all had a vindictive side to them.

According to Adele's late-night inspiration, when the rest of the factory learned that her cakes were being made of wood, she'd stop being bothered by people too lazy to drive up to the Stars and Bars Bakery. She'd been so relieved that night that she actually rolled over to Curtis and began stroking his stomach.

Curtis tried to remember how her fingers felt. Adele always had pretty hands. Muscular and smooth. She had a few brown spots, but they didn't detract from the white skin molded over the tendons. And she had just about stopped shooting herself in the hand with her pneumatic stapling gun.

Pausing as he cleaned up his saw, Curtis studied his hands. He'd squashed his fingers so many times under those cores of veneer that his fingernails had taken on a blue-yellow hue. They no longer followed the little grooves that made other people's fingers look so trim and civilized. Curtis's hands looked like something that belonged in a cave. And the skin on the back of his hands was beginning to get creased and saggy. Fat people aged better, men and women.

At least Marleen was saved from all of that sagging. All of that fading. Paul Wallace had told Curtis that after cremation a big part of the skeleton was left, but unless the family asked specifically for some of the bones, all they'd get was the ashes. That suited Curtis. He didn't want to deal with even the smallest part of his daughter's skeleton. Not that he was squeamish. Curtis remembered riding the truck convoy through the German countryside—a lot of it reminded him of the Blue Ridge Parkway—and seeing the bodies and body parts draped from the barbed-wire fences. Once he saw a perfectly preserved kidney frozen to a stone wall, only pieces of the body scattered around. First thing in the morning, Adele would call the medical school. Curtis wondered if they could pick the ashes up during the weekend. As much as he dreaded the trip, he wondered how Adele could stand the thought of driving down to Greenville, two hundred and seventy miles, knowing that all she'd be given at the end of the trip would be her little girl's ashes. Years back, when Marleen was still a small girl, they had gone through Greenville on their way to the Outer Banks. Dennis had been a baby because he slept stretched out in the front seat of their '51 Chevrolet. Adele was just barely recovered from her gall bladder operation. Marleen and Phyllis had decided to curl up on the floorboards of the backseat because it was warmer down there. Adele had already started collecting her salt and pepper shakers.

Adele's memory of Marleen's childhood had grown sharper with her grief. Curtis tapped his crooked fingers on the scarred surface of his work table. Where would Adele want to carry the ashes? In her lap. She'd hold them all the way back home. And when they stopped to eat or use the bathroom, she'd be worried sick that someone would steal them. If Curtis wouldn't let her take the ashes into the restaurant with them, then she'd insist that they take turns eating or peeing so that one of them could stay out in the car with the ashes.

Two hundred and seventy miles down and two hundred and seventy miles back—that'd be a funeral procession of five hundred and forty miles with nobody to talk to but Adele in one of her blue moods—her deepest blue mood. If she'd just let him talk on his CB radio on the drive, Curtis believed he'd be able to absorb all of Adele's sorrow and still be able to give her moral support. He'd get her to slide over right beside him, the way they used to ride thirty-five years ago. But she'd still cling to the ashes. She'd hold them in her lap until her feet went to sleep.

If Adele would just let herself listen to what all those people on the CB had to say, she wouldn't feel so alone. People's voices on the CB radio reminded Curtis of those old-timey singers he used to hear on the radio, back when the Carter Family was singing live out of Monterey. Of course, those live broadcasts didn't get as far as Hibriten, North Carolina, but when he listened to the records, Curtis could pretend that he was sitting out under a willow tree.

Even the fattest truck driver had a raw and lonesome voice when he talked on his CB. In the background, you could hear the road noises rushing by like time. But then again, whenever Adele heard a truck driver talking on the CB, she'd get angry because she couldn't listen to a truck driver without thinking about Marleen's second husband.

Before switching off the basement light, Curtis made a final quick check. The saw was turned off. He'd put his hammer back on its hook. The pile of wood scraps was as orderly as trash could be. Because Curtis had taken a nap before coming down to the basement, and because he worked more slowly these days, it was almost ten-thirty. Adele would be up until midnight decorating her wooden cake. Before Marleen died, he and Adele tried to get to bed before ten o'clock. Curtis had to get to the veneer plant and make sure that the glue had been properly mixed. Adele liked to get to work so she could gossip. However, Adele had trouble sleeping. That was a problem with sentimental people. Adele let her sadness interfere with her sleep. Curtis took one last look around the basement.

For a few seconds after the light was turned off, Curtis felt as if he were being funneled down into his shoes. On nights when he didn't think about it, the feeling was kind of pleasant, like the buzz from just the right number of beers. On nights when he stopped to try and figure out where he would wind up if he could be funneled into his shoes, the feeling was too much like what he felt when he'd had one too many swigs of hard liquor. Soon the starlight and the half-moon light from outside pumped Curtis back up to his normal height. He stepped out into his sloping backyard. Fifty yards to his left stood Leon Ballard's house. Perhaps a hundred yards behind Leon's house were four middle-sized trailers lined up side by side. Between them and Curtis's basement door stretched his small garden and his narrow backyard.

The March air was cool, but spring was definitely taking root. In another two weeks, Curtis predicted that he would have to tune up the lawn mower and cut the grass. Two weeks. All of this mess about the ashes would be behind him. It should have been over back in January, but some bookkeeper at the medical school had misdated Marleen's arrival, so Adele had actually waited a year and three months for her daughter's ashes. No wonder his wife had trouble sleeping. He moved slowly along the back of the house, the only light between him and the carport coming from the kitchen, where Adele would be mixing up the frosting and the decorating icing.

What a decision Adele had to face: which salt and pepper shakers would she have to get rid of to make room for Marleen's ashes. Curtis knew he would be of no help. When it came to her collection, Adele was sentimental to the point of superstition. And when she finally did cull the ones she felt she could live without, she'd have to go through all those hundreds left over and rearrange them. That job would surely shred Adele's heart, especially when she would have to dust and move all the shakers Marleen had given to her.

He took a deep breath. The air smelled moist and green. Its freshness made his shirt feel almost damp. Although the Catawba River was eleven miles away, Curtis thought he could smell the broad water, the curled odor of fish, the metallic glare of the sun, the astringent perfume of the pine trees that brought the taste of gin to one particular corner of his tongue.

Although Curtis always checked his car to make sure the doors were locked, the emergency brake was on, and it was in park, he always doubted if he really had checked. His car was a large blue Ford Galaxie that he'd bought used. One day, he planned to buy a brand-new car, but it'd have to be a small one because he wanted to wait until a year before he retired so he could have it paid for before he turned sixty-eight. He liked driving big cars. They were more comfortable and felt safer than the small ones, but he knew they weren't economical. Whatever that meant. Despite how many hours he and Adele put in, they always had to strain to pay the bills. Not too long ago, when Curtis played poker more seriously, he could blame himself for always being short of money.

Satisfied that his car was safe from the neighborhood vandals, Curtis wiped his feet on the doormat of plastic grass, bought especially to keep him from tracking sawdust into the kitchen, and after pausing for a second to glance at Hibriten Mountain's Easter lights, a huge cross that could be seen more than ten miles away, he opened the door and stepped into the kitchen.

On the table, a white oval with six matching straw-backed chairs, really too big for their kitchen but a gift from Phyllis, Adele had her bowl of white cake icing in addition to three bowls of pink, green, and red decorating icing.

Across from the icing, Adele sat at the table talking on the phone. From the way she propped herself on one elbow, resting her head on her hand, Curtis could tell that she had been talking for a long time. And she always complained when he spent an hour or two talking on his CB. Each time she started nagging him, he'd remind her of how long she talked on the phone, but by the next night, she'd be back again complaining about his CB. Curtis knew that she thought he was talking to some of those wild women up on Wiseman's Ridge, but that was just Adele being silly.

Adele didn't realize that, like her, Curtis just wanted to

keep in touch with what was happening to other people. People he knew were beginning to get sick and die at a pretty regular rate these days. And a man couldn't just call up another man and say, "Hey, what's the latest gossip?" A CB radio allowed a man to talk casually about what scared him. But if he were to call up one of his buddies on the phone and ask him how Dwight Marley was getting along after his operation, then all of a sudden, Dwight's condition seemed a lot more serious than it was before the telephone got involved. That kind of seriousness didn't come across when Dwight's operation was discussed over the CB.

After holding up the wooden cake for Adele to inspect, Curtis placed it on the table beside the decorating supplies and went to the refrigerator—which they were still paying on, another reason they couldn't ever get ahead of their bills, always some appliance needed to be fixed or replaced—and poured himself a glass of Sun-Drop Cola. He then stopped at the cupboard over the stove, pulled down a bottle of Jack Daniel's, and dropped a couple of dashes into his yellow soft drink. Curtis kept his back to Adele while he took a couple of swigs. He didn't want her scowl to sour the initial pleasure of his drink. She had her way of dealing with grief, and he had his. Grief and sex were connected by yearning. All adults, Curtis thought, needed to watch what they lusted after and what they grieved over. At least he didn't go out and play poker the way he used to. That had relieved some of their financial grief—at least that's what Adele maintained.

Still avoiding Adele's eyes, he walked over to the television, decided he didn't want to watch it, and sat down in his green vinyl recliner. It was a little loose in its joints and someday soon Curtis knew he'd have to try clamping and gluing the chair, but he hated working on cheap furniture. It never quite fit together the way it should. He couldn't remember why he'd wound up buying such a cheap chair. Probably because when he saw the price tags on really good recliners he had been demoralized. Four hundred and five hundred dollars for a chair. That was ridiculous. At least when you paid six hundred dollars for a refrigerator, you could get cold drinks and ice cubes from it. But what did a five-hundred-dollar chair give you that a hundred-and-fifty-dollar chair didn't? Monthly payments to a furniture store was all that Curtis saw.

Without the television yammering, Curtis could concentrate on Adele's salt and pepper shaker collection as he sipped his drink. She had gotten her brother, Walt, a plumber and a shelf builder, to put up the eighteen shelves that covered the four walls in their combined den and kitchen. To anyone coming into their kitchen for the first time, the shaker collection was overpowering. In fact, anyone walking through the house was likely to be overpowered by the salt and pepper shakers. Adele not only collected shakers from her and Curtis's trips; she also got other people to bring shakers back from their trips. Through his tired, squinted eyes, the four walls occupied by the shakers made Curtis think of some Mexican fiesta, all those bright colors and eccentric shapes.

Adele accepted any shaker set people would bring to her, but she secretly had very little patience with people who showed no originality in their taste for salt and pepper shakers. She felt compelled by that sentimentalism of hers to find a place for any shaker that came into her hands as a gift, but she'd complain for two or three days if the shakers were the sort that could be picked up in just any souvenir store: the miniature teapots, the miniature cowboy boots, the plastic Washington Monuments, the ordinary glass shakers with little stickers announcing the names of tourist attractions, the various shakers ornamented with thin, painted seashells, shakers made out of automobile doodads, those shakers shaped like the different states.

Slumping down more comfortably in his chair, Curtis concluded that Adele was fondest of salt shakers that looked like toys. One of her favorite shaker sets was supposed to be Adam and Eve. Both of them had flat heads and squat bodies. Adam had a fig leaf over his crotch, so did Eve, but she had these enormous breasts that Adele never failed to find funny, especially when she was showing her collection off to a new visitor. Now she could find that salt shaker's big breasts funny, but when the men at the factory had given Curtis a birthday cake in the shape of breasts, Adele had found it repulsive. Curtis had wanted to put the cake in the freezer, but Adele wouldn't let him. Instead, he'd wound up taking the cake to a poker game and sharing it with a bunch of men who won most of his money that night.

Adele was also fond of hillbilly salt and pepper shakers. She identified with hillbillies. Her family down in Wilkes still qualified as hillbillies. Adele's father had made moonshine most of his adult life. He might have become a rich man. Curtis paused and tried to remember the sensation of the moonshine as it wandered down his throat. Old Mr. Scott ran his stuff through about five times. It was better than anything that could be bought in a North Carolina ABC store. But he was too fond of his own liquor. Drank almost all of it himself. Curtis briefly tried to imagine what it would feel like being married to a rich woman, but his mind never cooperated.

Up on the shelves stood bearded hillbilly figures, hillbilly outhouses, hillbilly shacks, hillbilly hound dogs, hillbilly stills, hillbilly moonshine jugs, hillbilly mules, hillbilly Model T Fords, hillbilly tombstones, hillbilly banjos, hillbilly shoes. As much as Adele liked to visit her brother, Taft, who really was the only genuine hillbilly left, Curtis knew that she wouldn't be happy having to go back to that kind of life. He glanced over his shoulder at Adele. She wore her hair in a beehive, which she kept sprayed stiff. At night, she had to wear this little plastic fence around her hair so she wouldn't crack her styling. Even with the plastic and wire device riding on her head, Curtis found Adele fetching. She looked like a queen, maybe one of those queens from a Buck Rogers planet.

She had some older shakers that were Curtis's favorites. Back when she had first started collecting them, maybe 1953, thirty-one years ago, people had given her ceramic shakers, some shaped like fish, some like dogs, cats, bears, wolves, lions, tigers, lobsters, crabs, elephants. Other people had given her tropical fruit salt and pepper shakers. Curtis liked all of the tropical shakers because they reminded him of Hawaii, a place he always wanted to go. He'd grown up listening to WHIB's Saturday afternoon program, "Hawaii Calls."

Way back when Madison Rigsby owned the station, "Hawaii Calls" was a three-hour program. When his boy took over and tried to make it a modern business, the program had been shortened to thirty minutes. On one or two bad days, Curtis had selected his favorite shaker: two ceramic pineapples dressed up like hula girls on a plastic stand decorated with miniature palm trees—and sat in his recliner thinking about a warm island floating in clear blue water. But he had to get a new car before he took his trip to Hawaii.

Equally fascinating to Curtis were those salt shakers that actually performed some kind of little trick. He was especially fond of the piano salt and pepper shaker. It was an upright piano and the two shakers fitted down inside the piano. If you pressed the black keys, pepper popped up. If you pressed the white keys, salt popped up.

When Adele finished talking on the phone, she came over to the couch beside Curtis's chair and sat down. Under her apron, she wore a peach-colored turtleneck shirt and a pair of polyester slacks. She had to be the only woman Curtis knew who didn't own a pair of blue jeans. She was too round to fit into jeans. She looked good in her turtlenecks, but Curtis got tired of seeing her in them. Even before her neck started getting wrinkled, Adele had worn turtlenecks because she was so ashamed of her scar from her two goiter operations. Time and time again, Curtis had told her that no one noticed the scar. A rich woman would have gotten the scar fixed with plastic surgery.

"That was Virginia." Adele leaned back on the couch and rubbed her temples.

"Want a drink of this?" Curtis held up his nearly empty glass.

"Then there'd be two of us yelling into that CB radio." Adele didn't sound seriously disapproving tonight.

"What'd Virginia have to say?" Curtis liked Virginia. She reminded him of Adele in a lot of ways. She was a fetching woman too, built pretty much like Adele, but Virginia was more of a tomboy—at fifty. She had her hair cut in a short shag. She had gotten it cut short when she began bowling in the factory league. She and Adele had practiced together for a couple of years, but Adele had never picked the game up. As far as Curtis was concerned, Adele was too feminine to be a good bowler. Virginia, on the other hand, looked right at home with that big ball balanced in the palm of her left hand. She wore a glove on her right hand, which struck Curtis as a little kinky. Secretly he'd hoped that Adele might come home with a bowling glove, but she never did. Then Adele started having trouble with her joints getting soft or something. The doctors were never quite sure what happened.

"You know, Virginia lives beside Preacher Laxton." Adele sat up straight, a definite sign that her news was important.

Curtis knew the man. A few years ago, Preacher Laxton had worked in the veneer plant where Curtis worked. He remembered the man as being serious and proper, exactly what you'd want in a preacher but something of a strain on the people he worked with. He couldn't let people forget that he was an ordained minister. Then Curtis remembered that Preacher Laxton had a daughter. She wasn't really a wild girl, but she had developed a taste for short skirts and clingy blouses. Her outfits had grown so daring that Preacher Laxton had refused to let her attend the church where he preached. Lydia was her name, and she'd wound up coming to Curtis and Adele's church.

"Virginia was telling me that Preacher Laxton's daughter went out and got herself pregnant, probably by that little wormy boy that she comes to our church with." Adele spoke matter-of-factly. She loved gossip but more for its informational value than for its moral coloring. Adele actually sounded more concerned that Lydia had gotten pregnant by an ugly boy than that she had gotten pregnant. Of course, Curtis knew why Adele couldn't let herself sound judgmental when talking about illegitimate pregnacies.

Then Curtis thought of all the times he had admired those long legs of Lydia Laxton and felt guilty about staring at her. She didn't mind displaying her charms, but she had a modesty about her. She had been innocent. Curtis shook his head. "Pregnant. I wouldn't have thought she had it in her."

Adele took a moment to absorb Curtis's remark. Her blue eyes wavered. She smiled with a slight pursing of her lips. "Well, if she's pregnant, she had it in her."

"Why do you want to talk like that?" Curtis tried not to smile back at his wife. She had always been smarter than him in using her mouth.

"Like what?" Adele's face immediately became blank, her mouth compressed in an indignant line.

"Dirty." Curtis knew he was being pulled into a debate he couldn't win. Not only did Adele's brain work faster than his, but her face also shifted expressions more quickly. While he sat there with mock disapproval heavy on his cheeks and eyebrows, Adele was already opening her eyes wide in sarcastic curiosity.

"What dirty word did I say?"

"Oh, you know what you did. You hinted at it." Curtis didn't want to go any further with this discussion. But nothing gave Adele more pleasure than to fluster him.

"I've heard them old women on your CB talk dirtier than I do, and you don't get upset with them." Adele was good at changing subjects. Suddenly, they were no longer discussing her bawdy gossip but were discussing the faults of Curtis's CB buddies.

"They're just backward country people."

"Which country?" Adele leaned forward and squeezed Curtis's arm.

"Well, they could be from Wilkes." Just as Adele never missed a chance to criticize his CB, Curtis never missed a chance to laugh at Adele's hillbilly roots.

Adele pinched Curtis's arm and stood up. "Then you shouldn't be surprised that I talk the way I do."

She had trapped him again. Curtis flopped his head back and sighed. "You'd better be good to me." He almost went ahead and said, "Because I'm going to be doing a lot of driving for you in the next few days." But Curtis stopped himself. It was too late at night to get Adele thinking about the phone call to the medical school tomorrow.

Scooping up a pile of white icing, Adele smiled at Curtis

and said, "If I treated you any better, I'd have to start breast-feeding you."

To fill up the time while Adele iced the cake, Curtis volunteered to polish her gold loafers. He sat in the den and spread the neutral wax over the shoes. Before Adele had started spreading out, she had tiny feet, maybe a size five. Phyllis had taken after her mother in the feet department. Poor Marleen had taken after Curtis, with long narrow feet. It had been hard for Marleen when she was a teenager to go shopping with Adele and Phyllis. Either one of them could pick up any old shoe and have it look good on their feet. Then Marleen would try on the same kind of shoe in her size and suddenly it looked like a plumbing fixture or a piece of army equipment.

Now, after three children, a dozen operations, thirty or fifty extra pounds, and years of jobs that kept her standing eight or ten hours a day, Adele's feet were still pretty small. Curtis peered into one of her loafers to check the size: six and a half. He remembered a Sunday years and years ago, Adele climbing on the rail of a steel bridge—was it somewhere down in Wilkes or maybe up in the Gorge? She had on a flowered dress, mostly wine colored, with a wide white belt and white sandals, the kind that let just her big toe show. And she had wanted to stand on the rail while he took her picture. That must have been back before Marleen was born because once she started having babies, she didn't care much for climbing fences or bridge slats. But her feet fit right on the width of the steel rail. Curtis remembered measuring with his palms the width of the rail against the length of Adele's foot. She'd painted her toenails red.

By the time he got the shoes buffed, Adele had finished icing the cake and, in preparation for the decorating, had gone to the bathroom. After all these years, cake decorating still weighed heavily on Adele's bladder. Not wanting to lose a minute, Curtis slipped to the refrigerator, poured himself another drink, fortified it from the bottle in the cupboard, and stole into the living room where his CB radio waited in what Curtis liked to call the most technical corner of the house. The only corner of the house bare of salt and pepper shakers. He turned on the power knob, waiting a couple of seconds for the power booster to reach full capacity, adjusted the squelch knob, and slowly turned up the volume, hoping that the first flush of static wouldn't sour Adele's stomach, also hoping that the first voice to splash from the high-fidelity speaker wouldn't be some drunk who was still hoarse and strident from fighting with his wife.

When he talked on his CB, Curtis sat in the dark. All of the dials on the radio glowed with a diluted yellow light. It was the kind of light that used to come from the radio way back before television came into the house with its chilly blue flickering. It was the kind of light that used to come from kerosene lamps, back when the only yearning Curtis felt was to get out on his own. It was the kind of light given off by the single weak bulbs that had lit Curtis and Adele's first small house. Even the light in the factories was softer. Of course, you had to work harder in the factories back then.

He had started when he was sixteen. Pulling wood out of that planing machine. By the end of that first day, he hadn't been able to lift his arms past his hips, couldn't even get his hand in his pocket to pay for a Coke. His father had laughed long and hard at that temporary handicap. After a few years of the factory, Curtis was ready for World War II.

Maybe he loved the dials on his CB because he had yearned to go into the Army Signal Corps. The army had other plans for him. His brother, Daniel, though, had been a radio operator in the navy, and look at what had happened to him. Came back from the Pacific, got a job with Southern Bell as a lineman, and was now their chief technical adviser in Caldwell and Watauga counties.

Curtis scooted closer to the CB and took another drink of his Sun-Drop. As he twiddled with the frequency knob, he tried to squeeze the sound of the static into the sound of a heavy rain. Heavy rain could really interfere with his transmission and reception. And during thunderstorms, Curtis had to disconnect all of his radio equipment from the huge antenna on top of the house, his double-V quadrabeam antenna which looked like the rigging for a medium-sized sailboat. However, on clear March nights when Curtis wanted to pretend it was raining, the CB made him feel cozy. The lights from the dials glowed like the small mica windows on the front door of a wood stove his father had once owned.

When Curtis switched to band 19, he heard a throaty voice saying, ". . . was an ambulance here a little while ago."

Curtis pressed the microphone's call lever and said, "Breaker 1-9, breaker 1-9. This is Old Festus down in Hibriten Town. What's that you say about an ambulance?"

"Old Festus, this is Ridge Runner. I was just telling Hoss about my neighbor's boy. He broke into my house."

Curtis knew that Ridge Runner was the CB handle used by Clyde Monroe. He lived up on Wiseman's Ridge but worked in Hibriten in one of the textile mills. The boy he was talking about had to be Bill Saunders, a young man who had lost both of his kidneys and was living on a dialysis machine. Curtis's son had gone to school with the boy. People were just waiting around for Bill to die.

"You ought to have something to drink if you're going to listen to what that boy did." Ridge Runner sounded as if he'd already had several drinks. "Before it gets any later, I'm going to have to send my wife out to buy me a few more six-packs."

Curtis heard a blossom of static interrupt Ridge Runner's signal. He assumed the static came from Hoss. He hadn't heard that handle. Quite likely, Hoss was talking to Ridge Runner from the valley that ran adjacent to the valley where Hibriten was located.

"What about that ambulance, Ridge Runner?" Curtis knew it'd be easier talking to Adele later if he had some kind of gossip to share with her.

"It come to pick up Bill." Ridge Runner cleared his throat. Another flush of static told Curtis that Hoss was asking something.

"No. He didn't die. He was in shock or something. What's that other word when you're unconscious . . . ?"

"Coma?" Curtis had spent a lot of time around hospitals.

"Yeah. That's it. He was in a coma. Right down there in

the basement. My basement. Flat on his face in a big puddle of sauerkraut."

Before Curtis could ask about the sauerkraut, Hoss's static interrupted Ridge Runner's story.

"That sauerkraut that Melba spent all summer fixing when she got laid off. I don't know what we was going to do with all of it. Oh, Hoss, you saw all them jars that she put up, didn't you? That's what she's doing down there now, trying to figure out just how much of it Bill ate. One of the ambulance men said that's what put him in the coma."

This time, Curtis got to break in first. "That sauerkraut put Bill in a coma?"

"No, Festus. Not the sauerkraut but the salt. That's what the ambulance man said. See, Bill couldn't eat salt." Ridge Runner paused. "Wasn't too much of anything he could eat."

Another burst of static, which went on for several seconds.

"The reason I know is because I talked to him a lot these last weeks. I guess I got to be Bill's best friend."

Trying not to feel left out, as another paragraph of static came between him and Ridge Runner, Curtis just leaned back in his chair and took a long sip of his drink. However, he kept his hand on his microphone.

"Sure, I saw his machine. Didn't you ever get to see it? I saw it every day almost.

"Since I work at night, I got so I visited Bill. Helped keep up his spirits. He didn't have too much else to keep up." Ridge Runner stopped talking, but he'd left his microphone on because Curtis heard the pop of a can being opened. Then a longer pause followed.

Curtis heard Adele coming out of the bathroom. If she came through the living room on her way to the kitchen, Curtis knew she'd have to mouth off about his being on the CB at eleven-thirty at night. Instead, she went through the den on her way to the kitchen. Curtis relaxed. She was going to leave him alone tonight. Actually, since Marleen's death, Adele had been much less concerned with how much time Curtis spent on his CB. When he turned his attention back to the Ridge Runner, the man had resumed his dialogue with Hoss.

"I think the more you try to help people, the worse your luck gets. Look what happened to me today. I befriended that sick boy and he pulls this kind of stunt on me. The doctor—those guys in the ambulance doctors?—he said the police will come by later."

"Well, you'll be at work. Your wife can answer the police questions." Curtis checked his watch. If Ridge Runner worked the graveyard shift, he was already late for work.

"I'm not going to work tonight. I got Melba to call in for me."

"I'll tell you, Hoss, I'm not as sick as I was thirty minutes ago."

"When I went downstairs and saw Bill spread out face-down in all that sauerkraut."

"Yeah. I'll tell you how he got in. He had a key. Took it out of my pocket. He got to where he was doing little things like that."

"He learned to pick pockets from a book. That's all he could do was read."

"Yeah. He could get out a couple hours a day, but mostly he had to stay hooked up to that machine."

"That's when I liked to go over to visit. When he was hooked up to his machine.

"He looked terrible. For a long time, I didn't know what was wrong with him. He just come home all at once one day and stayed. Then his two other brothers come home, and they went to work in the mill with their mama and daddy."

"All of them are on the day shift. Easier to make production on the day shift, and God knows they need the money. Bill was always talking about how much that machine cost. I tell you, Hoss, it got on my nerves. I kept telling him over and over that he had to act like a man."

Curtis grabbed his microphone and in a high-pitched voice shouted, "Act like a man!?"

"Who's that?" Ridge Runner's voice took on an abrasive edge. "Hoss? Festus? You know who that is that just broke in?

Sounds like somebody who's been modified in his sexual parts."

"Never heard that voice before." Curtis regretted his outburst. "Could have been a mobile unit passing through."

"See, I got such bad luck that I can't even talk over the CB without getting defied by some smartass who could probably use a thimble for a jock strap."

"My luck is so bad, I could fall in a barrel of titties and come up sucking my own thumb."

"What do you mean I should have minded my own business, Hoss? The boy was in that house all day long by hisself. You just don't know. You think he liked to sit over there for at least eight or ten hours with no company except that machine gurgling away?"

"A tube come out his stomach."

"Because I got him to show me. That was another day I had to miss work. He was all shrunk and drawed up, like them cheap turkeys at the Winn-Dixie. The tube itself had a bandage around it so you couldn't see how it was fitted into his belly."

"Lots of times, I'd be over there when his girlfriend would come. Talk about a peacock. She wouldn't even sit on the couch where I liked to sit."

"It wasn't like Bill would get jealous. For one thing I was his best friend. And besides, he couldn't do anything with her. Not with his tube sticking out."

"Sure it would've got in the way."

Curtis remembered all of the tubes that had been attached to Marleen in the hospital. But then there had been that last night she spent at her and Jessie's apartment. It had been a Friday night because he and Adele had come down that Saturday morning not too long before the ambulance had come to take Marleen away. She had been in pain, even through the morphine cocktails that Jessie mixed for her.

Better than anybody, Marleen knew what going into the hospital meant. And Curtis had no doubt that she had asked Jessie to make love to her that one last time in spite of the damage it had to have done to her. At that point, what was her life compared to one last chance for . . . Curtis didn't have a word for it. None of the words used in the factory applied to the love that Marleen was asking for that last time. Neither did any of the words used on Adele's soap operas. Curtis remembered how the air would hum from the concussion of artillery being fired. Just before his skin vibrated, he had felt a moment of vacuum. That brief emptiness never failed to set his teeth on edge because in it he felt so open and fragile. How many moments in the eleven months it took Marleen to die had she felt that same kind of fragility? Curtis wondered if having her fat husband on top of her had made her feel protected despite the pain she must have felt.

Later, in their motel room in Wilmington, after Adele had been in the bathroom throwing up, she had stood at the foot of Curtis's bed and asked, "What kind of animal is that Jessie? Is it because he's from Massachusetts? Are they that different from us that the men can latch on to a girl who's already eat up inside with cancer?"

Before answering, Curtis had pulled himself up to a sitting position. "I don't know how he did it." But he wasn't even trying to answer Adele's question.

Curtis emptied his glass and scooted closer to his CB. At least he understood what motivated men like Ridge Runner and Hoss. Within the confines of Curtis's memory of Marleen, Ridge Runner's voice sounded peevish and irritating.

"It was bad, at first," Ridge Runner was saying, "trying to talk to him while he was hooked up to the machine, but I almost got used to it. It was a whole lot like them women you see on television who nurse their babies out in public. You know what I mean? You have to look, but you feel guilty at the same time."

"No. I never got a clear look at his machine. He'd always sit in the dark when I'd come."

"It was supposed to be blood. And once, he left a curtain half open, and I could see the machine in the light. It's just kind of a big filter."

"He was always saying nobody could afford to be too curious."

Curtis felt a wave of sympathy spread toward Bill Saunders. To his surprise, he felt ashamed that he was having to listen to Bill's story from a character like Ridge Runner. Somehow, the CB seemed to diminish the boy's suffering as well. Curtis blinked his eyes because never before had his CB sounded so much in cahoots with the voice whining from it.

"Well, of course it affected his mind. A boy can't be hooked up to a machine ten hours a day and not be a little touched in the head by it. Especially when he's all by hisself most of the time."

"No. His girlfriend works up at Asheville, and I don't think her coming to see him was such a good idea anyway."

"She's a peacock. She made the boy uncomfortable. I could tell. We'd all sit there in the dark with that machine gurgling. She'd put a record on the record player to try and cover up the sound. They never talked much. We'd just sit there."

"They couldn't have done nothing if I wasn't there. I keep telling you, Hoss, the tube was in the way. Not to mention the machine. When he was connected up to the machine, he couldn't even have played with hisself."

"No. His girlfriend didn't come every day. I was the only one who come every day. Most of the time, his family tried to work double shifts."

"They could've been rich working like that if they didn't have to pay for the machine—and the doctors. Can't forget the doctors."

"I don't trust them either."

"No. I think Bill liked doctors. He was always—always talking about how they was keeping him alive. That got on my nerves, too—like his talking about the expense."

"I did let him know how I felt. I told him there wasn't too much he could do about it. Why, he couldn't eat or drink anything except what the doctors said he could."

Curtis tried to remember just one face out of the line of doctors who came through to look at Marleen. All of them came, though, to observe. All of them felt compelled to tell him how remarkable her survival was. Remarkable but pointless, they should have said. Curtis couldn't remember one doctor actually touching Marleen. They didn't even bother to take her pulse. That was what disturbed him about all those high technology and expensive machines in her room. The doctors could take her vital signs and not have to touch his daughter. Curtis squinted, trying to squeeze out of his mind the thought of how Marleen's story would sound coming out of Ridge Runner's mouth over the CB. He had a vision of all the men in the surrounding counties, half drunk, half dressed, half amused by the time when Marleen, having to wait for a bed on the terminal ward, was put on the maternity floor. After three days of listening to the babies cry she had demanded to be put where she could get some sleep. Otherwise, she was going to start tossing infants out the window.

From the self-pitying tone of Ridge Runner's voice, Curtis could tell that the story of Bill and the sauerkraut might, mercifully, never get finished, not in this transmission anyway. He switched off his CB. Already past midnight, and he had to be at work in the morning. A shipment of veneer was coming in. The truck would get in around nine. Take a couple of hours to get it unloaded and the different cores sorted. Then he'd have to start opening the crates and begin matching the grain. He could take his time doing that. So tomorrow would be pretty relaxed—up until Adele made her phone call.

Curtis shifted around in his chair and wondered if he was steady enough to walk to the kitchen. It was time for him to ask Adele how she planned to carry Marleen's ashes back. He admitted to himself that he wanted the ashes, too. He yearned for his daughter. Wanted her back home—since the day she had moved out as the wife of Gaither Drum. Or had she moved out before then? Tonight, Curtis had trouble pinning down when this emptiness began. But he could make room for *where* the yearning might stop or at least be placed.

Draining the last of his Sun-Drop, Curtis pushed away from the CB, then reached under its table and pulled the plugs on the receiver, the power pack, and the antenna. After disconnecting all of the cables, Curtis picked up the transmitter and swayed into the kitchen, on his way to the basement.

Adele looked up from the rosebud trim she was putting on the wooden cake. "You think you'll get better reception if you go outside?"

Curtis motioned with his chin for Adele to come and open the kitchen door for him. "I'm opening up some space in the living room. We don't need to disturb your collection, after all."

Wiping her hands as she stood up, Adele said, "But, Curtis, that's your radio. You don't need to move it."

"Don't argue with me." Curtis jerked his head emphatically in Adele's direction, then frowned at the door. "I'm not as sentimental about such things as you are."

"And a cat's butt ain't puckered either," Adele replied, feeding Curtis a rosebud of icing.